Books by *April Alisa Marquette*:

Fiction

~The Cohort Trilogy
Absolution
Progression
Iniquities

~The Cohorts, Generation Next
Improbable

~The Sea Isles Series - A Trilogy
Exodus
Affinity
To Be Announced

Turnabout

~A Tranquility Tale
Rebuke

*

Non-Fiction
Co-Authored with Jessica Janna

~The Relinquish & Reap Series
Seedling
Sowing
Yielding

**Ask for them … at your local Barnes & Noble,
or Books-A-Million bookstore!**

For my late father, a brilliant man who never missed the chance to read anything I wrote...

To My Creator,
and the Ancestors,
Sometimes you allow me to be the first to read what you impart.

Briceno– thank you for helping me get Noel's accent right.

Exodus

The Departure…

The Sea Isles Series

Book I

by

April Alisa Marquette

Books that captivate

Exodus
© Copyright 2010 by A. A. Marquette
Cover Design by April A. Marquette
Photograph: A. A. Marquette

ISBN 978-1-61539-571-2
Printed in the United States of America

Visit the author at www.aprilalisamarquette.net
Library of Congress Catalog Card No.: On File

Publisher's note:
The novel *Exodus* is a work of fiction – for adults, only.

... I will bring you out from under the burdens...

And I will rid you of bondage . . .

Exodus 6:6

Chapter 1

AQUA Mira loved Dyson Eamon, couldn't see herself *not* loving him, although he was a monstrous storm of a man, one whom some feared. However, she felt quite safe with him when she was wrapped up in his immense arms.

Dyson, an Atlanta supper club owner, was an entrepreneur. He managed a few businesses. Yet, the truth was…he had dealt drugs and thereby, set himself up. He had not been the little guy on the corner, hoping to move into the big time. He had been the man from whom orders came when those same commands came from 'the organization.' Thus, the power he wielded was no secret.

Therefore, despite her morality, Aqua never forgot that Dyson's business had initially been iniquity. However, she pushed the knowledge aside to do what she had, for nearly a decade; love Dyson Eamon.

Never would Aqua forget that early spring morning in the late 1990s. A man had driven slowly behind her. The sun had been shining, and new buds were on the trees. Tulips had had their pretty heads up, and Aqua had walked through the Donut Makery's busy parking lot. She'd thought the man was nosing around for a parking space.

As Aqua neared her car, the man called out, "Hey lovely." Slowly, he'd driven alongside her.

Aqua heard cars passing on the other side of the thigh-high hedge. In the colorfully bustling commercial district, she heard SUV doors slam. She saw a girl dash by, her braids flying. With a smile, Aqua balanced the treat box that she would take to her co-workers. *Lord* was the man fine. As a matter of fact, she had thought the same thing on all the other mornings that she had seen the man with the smooth brown skin and luscious lips.

Not one to waste time, the man in the nearly idling car got to the point. "I'd like to see you again, lady. You think that's possible?"

Aqua stopped walking. Sure, men approached her because she was sexy, with her amber-colored eyes, healthy mane, and five-foot-nine lush frame. Still, not many came correct. They had game, of which she had grown fatigued. She often felt as though some men insulted her intelligence because she was more than just a curvy body and a cute face. However, *this man... he* hadn't spit game.

Therefore, although she might wind up a little late, she turned. With the sun breathing warmly on her, Aqua forgot about work for a few seconds. Heck, in four years, she had only been late once. That time, circumstances had been beyond her control. Eyeing the man who had not yet introduced himself, she inquired. "You got a name?"

That was when he got out of his car, and Aqua's breath caught because he was tall, massive, and wide, like a linebacker.

"Come on now," he cajoled. "I frighten a big pretty sista like you?"

Aqua could barely breathe. "No," she lied, then told the truth. "It's just that I didn't expect—all *that*."

The man chuckled. As a couple passed, he said he liked a woman who spoke her mind. "I'd like to hear more of your thoughts," he suggested. "When you let me see you again."

Aqua licked glossy lips and forgot her co-workers. Sure, they'd expect breakfast before their departmental meeting. Well, sorry. It was why she asked, again, "So, you got a name?"

The man smiled because he definitely liked her style. He also liked her bronze skin and burnished brown hair. With honey-gold highlights, it blew in the breeze.

"I've got a name," he replied. "Got numbers, a home —actually a couple of homes— but I'm just missing *you*." The man took Aqua's free hand. "The name's Eamon. Dyson Eamon."

"Nice name Dyson Eamon. Mine's Aqua Mira [Mee-ra], last name Moine." No, she thought. Dang, her hand had begun to sweat.

Dyson didn't seem to notice as he spoke. "So, Aqua Mira, about those digits..."

She gave him her cell number. Then when he had helped her—donuts and all into her car—he promised to call.

Just as Aqua pulled out of the busy parking lot, her phone jangled. Fumbling, she answered it. She laughed too because Dyson Eamon said he wanted her to know, "I keep my promises."

Seated in the doctor's office with her friend Phédra, Aqua further thought about Dyson, the man who sometimes seemed to be just what her body and soul needed. He was firm where she was occasionally weak. Often, he advised her not to be a jellyfish. Then she would use his nickname that sounded like 'dice' as invariably she would retort.

"Dys, even jellyfish pack a mean sting, on occasion."

Seated beside her friend Phédra, Aqua dismissed the fact that Dyson had called her a jellyfish just that morning. He had asked why she needed to accompany Phédra to the doctor.

Dyson had quipped, "Fay is a big girl."

Aqua knew Dyson didn't understand. Phé needed her, for moral support. Men. Sheesh, there really were things about women that they would never understand.

Forgetting that, Aqua thought about the man who had no problem expressing his feelings. Well, mostly his sexual feelings. He been her lover on times too numerous to count.

In the doctor's pastel waiting room, seated beside nervous Phédra, Aqua re-lived the way it felt to have Dyson's large arms around her. Sometimes she would be planted on his lap. She'd feel his man-man beneath her ample thighs and booty. Other times they stood or lay facing each other. What she loved most was the way he scintillatingly assaulted her senses. He often started by taking his lips on a slow, sensual hike over every inch of her body.

Ohhh, Aqua recalled, that relaxed her like nothing else could.

Actually, Aqua thought, as Phédra glanced nervously about, Phé's man could become a bit more sensitive. Yep, since Phédra was carrying his baby. Then the tall, dark publicist could relax Phédra too. Lord knew Phédra needed to relax these days. Ever since the gray-eyed one with the near-white skin had peed on that little stick, and wet her hand in the process, she had been a wreck.

"Phédra," a nurse called out, "FAY-dra Wooten?"

Aqua squeezed Phédra's arm. She watched as her willowy friend disappeared. Then curvy Aqua's mind journeyed from the magazine page before her, back to Dyson.

Chapter 2

FROM the start, she believed he could love her right because of his love for his mother. Although Lena Eamon was deceased, Dyson spoke of her with such reverence until Aqua was touched.

Dyson divulged that never far in spirit, Lena Eamon was the reason he had initially begun dealing 'iniquity,' as Aqua called it.

One rainy night in his cosmopolitan Perimeter, Georgia penthouse, Dyson and Aqua lay sated. After making love, they spoke, and with his eyes on flickering flames, Dyson revealed things. One was that his mom had worked very hard. Gazing into the fireplace with its marble surround, he said Lena had done so to keep her three sons from the streets of an area called Duck.

Dyson explained the area was called that for one reason. The only way to survive was to do as the name suggested. Therefore, he and his brothers, who were twins, had learned to avoid those who meted out destruction. However, the Eamon boys were no cowards. Wherever they went their presence was felt. The latter, Dyson claimed, was necessary for respect, or the three brothers would have been better off dead.

Aqua didn't like that kind of talk, but she understood why swaggering Dyson and the twins blustered. Now, they had done it for so long, until their gruffness seemed inherent.

Dyson also admitted that Lena Eamon's boys had worked at their studies, too. It had been Lena's rule. As a result, all three received full academic scholarships. But, Dyson told Aqua, back then, he had known one thing. Academia, nor athletics—for which he had prowess—would get his mom or siblings out of continual danger.

"So I went into business," Dyson truthfully stated, his eyes on the dancing flames. "It broke Ma's heart." He revealed that Lena Eamon had wailed, "I don't want 'blood money' in my house."

"Dyson," Lena spat, "I won't allow you to destroy all I've worked for just so you can impress people!" Lena had also hissed, "This ain't how I raised you! None of y'all!"

Dyson sounded far away when he revealed trying to reason with his mother. He'd cited back to her, numerous above 'n beyond the call of motherhood things she had done for her sons. "It's the reason I want to help, Ma. I just want to move us all to a nice neighborhood," one where she could walk, alone, to the market, if she chose.

Dyson had wanted his mother to work less. He'd suggested she get a part-time position, perhaps at a department store. "You'll still have a daily destination," he pointed out. "You could even work your way up again, to supervisor, if you want. You'd meet new people *and* get discounts," on the pretty things she loved. He'd thought that would appeal to Lena.

The woman would not hear of it.

Then Dyson begged his small, wiry mother to see that it was only a matter of time before she lost either him or one of the twins to Duck.

When Lena remained resolute, Dyson made her cry. "I had to," he told Aqua with his heart in his words.

Dyson divulged that he'd hated himself afterward, but his statement had galvanized Lena.

She'd started packing, with ominous sentiments ringing in her ears...

"Ma, you know that dress," Dyson conversationally began, "the bright colored one you put on lay-a-way, for graduation? Well, you might need to exchange it...for something more suitable...for a *funeral*, because one of us *will be* dead soon. After all, you vacillate."

Lena's eyes had widened as her heart stuttered. "Don't you dare say those things, young man. I don't receive that. I've prayed, and you boys have been safe this long. Y'all just need to stay out of trouble."

"You believe that, Ma?" Dyson asked feeling incredulity. "You think we can go back 'n forth—to some college, without people hating?"

Dyson knew he'd raised his voice, but he couldn't lower it. "Ma, these people *can't* get out! Soon they'll know *we* can. Then they'll hate on us even more...and shatter your pretend world." He whispered then, to give his words emphasis. "After bullets have rained in on us Ma, remember...I tried, to save you—from heartache. I tried to save *us*."

Dyson touched his face where Lena had slapped him, with a ferocity he had not expected.

Despite the sting, he'd still informed her. He wasn't not doing any different than what people throughout American history had done. Dyson said people had long pursued life, liberty, and happiness. People wanted to make better lives for themselves and their families.

Lena had had enough, and so she said.

But, Dyson told Aqua, his mother allowed him to move the family.

"Was she happy?" Aqua wanted to know, "after moving?"

"She was happy enough," Dyson solemnly stated, "until cancer started eating her up. *That* I couldn't save her from."

Aqua sniffled.

Not wanting her to cry, Dyson pulled her closer. "I didn't tell you that to make you sad, A. I just wanted you to know what type of man I am. I take care of my own. I gave my mother a few years of peace before she left here—even though I had to scare her, to make her accept my offering."

"Aqua…" A woman's voice pulled the sultry bronze woman from memories. "Aqua honey, we can go now."

Aqua looked up and into her friend's clear gray eyes. Oh, Phédra. Realizing they were at the doctor, Aqua spoke while gathering her things. "So Phé, how'd it go?" She followed the willowy woman from the quiet pastel office.

"Fine, I guess." Phédra smiled. "I'm five months! How did I not realize?"

As she held the door for her photographer friend, Aqua said it was exciting. "And things like this happen, Phé. Look at it like this, now you don't have all that long to go…."

Phédra turned, her gray eyes wide. "Now that it's real, A, I'm scared. I'm literally shaking." She held out trembling hands. "See?"

Aqua hugged her friend. "That's normal. I think."

Chapter 3

SHE put her thigh over his, as nude, they lay facing each other. He drew circles on her hip while a gold chain nestled in the tangled hair on his chest. Suddenly Dyson slapped Aqua. The noisy spank on her shank startled her. "Time to get up." Kissing her nose, he attempted to rise.

"No..." Aqua said and held onto him. "We don't want to."

"I know." He pulled away, "but there's a party to attend."

Aqua sighed, and Dyson told her, "Don't sound so glum." Towering over her, he advised, "If you pull a no-show, your fam will give you fever, so let's go, and bounce before they notice."

Languidly Aqua stretched and faced the large window. Outside, evening approached. Turning back, she intended to speak, but the sight of Dyson's erection jumbled her thoughts.

"See?" she managed, feeling the need to ride him. "You really don't want to go either." Spreading her legs, Aqua ran her hands from her torso, up and over ample breasts. "Let's stay," she whispered, her nipples pearling, "and play..."

"I never said I *wanted* to go," Dyson chuckled as he dropped to his knees. Further spreading Aqua's thighs, he kissed her belly, and her lower lips. "I only said I would." Using his tongue, he teased her, savoring her taste. Rising, hungrily, he used his mouth to slather her nipples. Then unable to help himself, he thought 'witch,' as he pushed his mighty erection into her.

Aqua sank her fingernails into Dyson's flesh and her teeth into his neck.

He pulled out but drove back in, loving the feel of her clasped around him, her heels pressed to his buttocks.

Aqua gasped because, mustering every ounce of willpower he had, Dyson tried to pull away. Gritting his teeth, he said they needed to get going.

Greedily wanting, Aqua attempted to leg-lock him. "Don't do me like this," she moaned. "Gimme some—just a little more. Then I'll gladly go."

"You'll never gladly go, but promise, I'll hook you up later."

As he walked away, Dyson knew Aqua had no idea. He was so ready to give in. Entering the spa bath, he called, "A, I'm doing this for *you*."

With a groan, Aqua rose and followed Dyson into the travertine-tiled room. Bracing one hand on the sink, she slipped the fingers of her other between her silken fold. Knowing Dyson watched, she stroked herself and whispered that she wouldn't be left unfulfilled.

Licking her lips, she also squeezed a pretty, plump breast.

Unable to take any more, quickly Dyson turned her. Forcing her onto the sink top, smoothly, he entered her, and she laughed in welcome.

Sated afterward, Aqua slipped into a satin robe. She reached for her car keys. With her long trench coat belted, Aqua poked her head back into the oversized master bath. "Pick me up after eight?"

Dyson cut his eyes and turned on multiple sprayer heads. Wanting Aqua again, he wondered why she kept going back to that little apartment in Alpharetta. Her things were at his place. She very nearly lived with him. She would if he could have his way. Heaven knew he had the room. His penthouse was panoramic, spanning a whole floor of the gorgeous high-rise in which he lived. It was stupid for her to keep paying for a place. His was paid for, and her flimsy argument about them needing to be married she could chuck.

Forgetting meaningless words, Dyson sighed. He knew Aqua was most likely in the brass and mirrored elevator, descending, and didn't hear. Lathering up, he called out anyway. "You just be ready!"

Getting in her car, Aqua—who hadn't heard—pondered how much she hated going to her father's home. He said he'd inherited it. However, her aunt and uncle, her father's siblings, said the same thing. Well, usually, they hollered it, amid a family fistfight.

Later, Aqua would see them all. The fam would gather for her father's birthday. It was just another excuse to get all up in each other's affairs. Behind her steering wheel, Aqua sighed. She recalled something else. Her father had never been a real dad to her or Ava. Their mother, just as irresponsible, had never been a real mother. Both had been too self-centered to care for children.

Rayfa, Aqua's mother, said Silas's people had never liked her. –But, Aqua's mother would show up later in at the evening. Go figure. Rayfa claimed Silas's family had been jealous of her because she'd been young and cute. Aqua didn't know about any of that. She only knew that her mother drank too much. Word was Rayfa had started chugging liquor long before she'd met Silas, the con artist.

However, Silas had laid his tired rap on Rayfa. Eager to become part of the dream Silas wove, Rayfa got sucked in. Aqua knew Silas must have mentioned money. Money was all Rayfa cared about—that and talking about the feel of Silas' hands on her light brown skin.

Aqua had been six when she'd first become cognizant of hearing that tale. Her mother had been tipsy, as usual. Aqua let herself into her apartment while wondering, what six-year-old needed to hear that?

Since she would see them soon enough, Aqua forgot her family. She thought about her home while walking through it. Compared to Dyson's, it was relatively small, but it was neat, cute, and hers.

Uh-oh, thoughts of the fam again intruded. Aqua remembered that at six, *she* had been more of a mother to hazel-eyed Rayfa than Rayfa had ever been to her. Aqua had also been a little mama for her younger sister.

As Aqua showered, she recalled that she and Ava had been taken from Rayfa and Silas. The small girls had been moved to a little house. There, life had begun with the old people, their grandmother, grandfather, and great grandmother.

Aqua's short, bright, nearly white-skinned hazel-eyed Grandma, Gloria Bayliss had often tsk-ed while rearing her daughter's two girls. With no malice, GB told them that their mother suffered a 'curse.'

Patting herself dry, Aqua smiled because Grandma Bayliss still believed her daughter's drinking was a *curse* come down through the family, like the color of their eyes…

Aqua applied scented lotion, knowing it would drive Dyson wild. She wondered what to wear. Then Aqua asked why? *Why* would she spend a disquieted evening in a small smoke-filled house. It would be teeming with cheaply perfumed people, some of whom would get offensively drunk. She and Dyson would leave smelling like smoke and greasy fried chicken. All for what? To please parents who had never given a fig about her or her sister.

Why Aqua wondered, did she put herself through this?

Ava didn't. Younger, Aqua's sister, also a buxom bronze beauty, had a different temperament. Ava, who had naturally pouty lips and tousled hair—that she pinned up for her job as a bank manager—would never appear or smile. Ava would never nod when someone hooted, 'Ain't this fun?' She wouldn't flee into the chilly night either, while some busybody called after her, 'Let's do this again!'

Ava, too, despised family farces, so she did not attend. Ava would never pretend all was well. Ava also hated their mother's begging. And she never gave Rayfa money. Ava refused to feed the drunken monkey on Rayfa's back.

But Ava was amused because their mother always asked Aqua for a light, when Aqua had never ever smoked.

While pulling on an ivory top with black beads at the hem, Aqua knew one thing. Soon she would never again attend another family event. Heck, her life was so different from that of her parents. It had been, ever since they'd given up all parental rights. That had been over three decades ago.

Stepping into silky black pants, Aqua realized. She could no longer stomach Silas acting like he was a baller. She was tired of Rayfa girlishly flitting about, when she was simply a rip-roaring drunk.

Spritzing herself with what her grandmother would deem outrageously expensive fragrance, Aqua knew realized her mother would likely push up on Dyson. During the evening ahead, Rayfa might even pull up her dress; panty-less, she would not be ashamed of her chicken legs. Rayfa might even offer Aqua's man 'some,' as she staggered about. Then Aqua's mother would most assuredly beg Dyson for money. She would also hiss, "Shet yo' mouf Aqua. He can afford it."

Then Rayfa would demand more money from Aqua, her firstborn.

Stepping into high-heeled ankle boots, Aqua spoke aloud. "After tonight, I won't do this anymore."

Viewing herself in her full-length cheval mirror, Aqua thought, *wow*. She looked too good to go slumming among her parent's people.

Grabbing a three-quarter-length leather jacket, Aqua shrugged because it couldn't be helped now. Sure, she would much rather go somewhere trendy with Dyson. She would even love to hang out with her girlfriends or her sultry sister.

Aqua knew that each other woman would have chosen to go to Dyson's supper club, aptly named *Apropos*. There, they would have been treated like queens. At the elegant club, with its cocoa-colored velvet sofas, cozy lighting, and laid-back atmosphere, they'd get great food. For them, drinks would be unlimited. Showcased would be unparalleled live bands and song-stylists. In the ATL, it just didn't get any better.

Oh, forget all that, Aqua told herself as her buzzer sounded. Glancing at her watch, she figured it was Dyson. She headed for the door.

Time to smile, time to have fun, this Aqua wryly told herself. Still, she could only feel anxious and sweaty-palmed. Aqua abhorred the feeling. It reminded her of how she felt just when she was about to board a roller coaster.

Chapter 4

"SO girl," Cadence lounged on her chaise, "how was it?"

In Cadence's luxury townhome, Aqua sat on the loveseat next to her friend who'd recently found out she was pregnant.

That friend, gray-eyed Phédra, spoke. "Cae, you *know* how it was."

Petite and brown, Cadence Dance quipped, "I didn't ask *you*, Faydra." Cadence with the corkscrew curls often spoke her mind.

The expectant one remained undaunted, "But we all know how Aqua's family affairs go."

Ignoring gray-eyed Phédra, curly-haired Cadence leaned closer to Aqua. "A, tell me what happened."

Seated in the home designed for romantic rendezvous, Aqua shrugged. "Like Phé said, it was the same old thing."

Aqua noted the sage green walls and the blown glass vase filled with creamy hydrangeas. Eyeing the hassock on which her feet rested, Aqua felt her coils of unease begin to unfurl. Curly-haired Cadence's home always had that effect on her.

But oh—Aqua remembered, her friends wanted a description of last night's events. She told the truth. "I put up with the same old stuff." Not proud of it, Aqua stated, "Again."

Curly-haired Cadence pointed. "You didn't have to."

"I know, but I went because Dys said if I didn't, I'd never hear the end of it, from my mother."

Cadence appeared pensive. "Dyson said, huh? Aqua, when are you going to think about what *you* want and stick with that?"

Aqua knew it sounded harsh. Yet, Cadence, the makeup artist who worked for a daytime television show, was right. Aqua needed to ditch the irritating habit of doing what others wanted. She did it to keep the peace. Lately, however, Aqua had grown tired of being peaceful and putting her desires on hold. She just didn't know how to stop.

Aqua also knew that 'keeping the peace' was why Dyson called her a jellyfish. He said she needed to get a spine. Aqua also wanted to do what her sister said. One day Aqua was going to stop letting others pimp her.

Then, perhaps she would become more like her petite friend. Aqua glanced at curly-haired Cadence, whom she really admired.

Seated on her oversized chaise, Cadence called out, "Details A, I need them."

"Well, we went over there," Aqua began, "and everybody was there."

"As usual," gray-eyed Phédra interjected.

"I know your sister wasn't, but was your mom?" Cadence asked.

Aqua nodded.

"Was she falling-down drunk?"

Gray-eyed Phédra put her head down, thinking Cadence was crass.

"Yes, as usual," Aqua acknowledged, eyeing both of her friends. Aqua smirked. "Oh, you two."

Expecting, Phédra attempted not to laugh. "I'm sorry," she chuckled, "but I can't forget the time Cae and your mother got into it. While we took wedding photos, remember?"

"Yeah, at Ava's wedding." Cadence added.

Aqua recalled her younger sister's nuptials. Curly-haired Cadence had made the occasion memorable by tongue-lashing Rayfa.

"I'd have kept quiet," Cadence pointed out, "had your mom not tried me; I had to tell the truth. She needs to quit drinking—just like my mother-in-law."

"You also said Ms. Rayfa should stop hating on you," Phédra chuckled, her hands splayed over her rounding tummy.

"What I *said* was…just because I'm young, educated 'n paid doesn't mean I give people hand-outs." Curly-haired Cadence waved. "Hell, Aqua's mama didn't need my money. Everybody knew Ava's reception would host an open bar—with all the liquor anyone could want." The petite one eyed the mom-to-be. "Ain't likka what they mama uses all her money for?"

Gray-eyed Phédra was shocked at Cadence's candor. "Cae!"

"Well, Rayfa cut up this time too," Aqua dryly announced.

"No…" Cadence gasped. "What'd she do?"

Aqua felt annoyance as she said, "Rayfa begged me for a light, as usual. Then with a cigarette dangling from her mouth, she pushed up on Dyson. Later, she whined that she did it to make Silas jealous. His girlfriend was there," Aqua explained. "She has huge new boobs."

Forget the fake ta-ta's, Cadence marveled that Aqua never called her parents mom and dad. She always called them by their given names.

"So your mother tried to make your father jealous," gray-eyed Phédra deduced, "by flirting with *your* big fine Dyson." What a mess.

Aqua nodded. "That's it, in a nutshell."

Phédra was curious. "How did Dyson react?

"Like it was nothing, and Rayfa was crash-banging drunk by then."

Cadence howled with laughter as Aqua continued.

"Rayfa wound up slapping the girlfriend. Then Rayfa threw up, all over Dyson's shoes, just minutes after the hair-pulling melee."

Cadence's corkscrew curls bounced. "Dyson is good because my husband would have had a fit. The way he babies his clothes and shoes, you'd think they were made of gold."

"Well," Aqua closed her eyes. "Dyson shrugged it all off, but *I* was mortified. Especially when with puke on her breath, Rayfa hit him up for cash. I mean, why does *my* family always have to act out?"

"Every family has its moments," Phédra soothingly stated.

"Yeah, but how many people's mothers are so childish and such drunks that they have to live with their own mothers? And the worst part," Aqua revealed, recalling the party, "was that Dyson and I had to fold Rayfa into his car. We took her back to my grandmother's house because Silas," Aqua's father, "and his girlfriend wanted Rayfa out."

Phédra's gray eyes lit at the mention of the older woman whose pale skin was almost the color of her own. "You saw Grandma Bayliss?"

Aware that her friend adored the older woman, Aqua said, "I did. GB even offered to clean and disinfect Dyson's car and shoes."

Curly-haired Cadence shook her head. "Your evening really was a mess, A. Still, think about it like this. With your unpredictable family, you'll never be bored."

Aqua cut her eyes because that was just what she *wanted*, a family, a real one, of her own. That she prayed for, and a little predictability, for once in her life.

Chapter 5

WHY the ringing? Aqua wondered *again* as the phone in her small purse vibrated. It had done so, non-stop, for ten minutes. All while she attended a most prestigious awards presentation. Some of the judges were editors and even auctioneers of black and white photography.

Aqua was starting to feel annoyed. Ten minutes could seem like a long time, if a phone vibrated, in the quiet, *and* when Aqua's friend, a professional, would soon receive the photographer of the year award.

Attempting not to disturb those around her, Aqua reached into her purse and angled her phone so that she could ogle the number. Just like before, unrecognizable. Ooh! Wait, she thought. If this were a wrong number—or some silly girl pestering a boy—she would go *off*.

When her phone buzzed again, Aqua squeezed Phédra's hand. Aqua whispered she'd be right back. Rising, Aqua recalled wanting petite Cadence present. Now Aqua was glad Cae had not appeared.

With a soft cloud of fragrance about her, Aqua awkwardly stepped past seated people. She whispered, "Excuse me." She knew that had Cadence been present, Cae would have had questions.

The same ones that surfaced on Phédra's face just moments ago.

Unable to forget the semi-shock in Phédra's clear gray eyes, Aqua knew. Phédra believed Aqua would miss her moment. However, Aqua figured, wending her way through linen-covered tables, if she hurried, she could return before Phédra's name was called.

In the carpeted hotel hallway with warmly glowing wall sconces, potted trees, and gilded artwork, Aqua dialed the unknown number.

She swore when she could not connect. No doubt, the caller had used a prepaid card. Oh well. Aqua thought it as she hurried, on rhinestone-tasseled high heels, back toward the reception room.

En route, she distractedly waved at a silver-haired virile male admirer. She did not notice. He stood mesmerized, struck initially by her amber-colored eyes. Then he turned to watch the graceful sway of her hips and the swell of her bottom in her elegant, near-backless attire.

Again, Aqua threaded through, and past people, one of whom groaned at the intrusion. Ignoring the disgruntlement, Aqua sat; and *vibrate*—again! She shut her phone off, just as Phédra was introduced.

Then although she tried, Aqua could barely focus on her friend's acceptance speech. With eyes on Phédra, Aqua vaguely acknowledged that the willowy woman looked lovely. A shade darker than Phédra's eyes, her garment was beautiful. It also camouflaged the rounding tummy of the mom-to-be, but Aqua's mind drifted to her phone.

Someone desperately tried to reach her. Therefore, she whispered a prayer. *God, please let nothing be wrong with Grandma Bayliss.*

Aqua applauded, along with others. She vowed to call her sister the moment she could. Sultry bronze Ava would know if GB was not okay—God forbid.

Feeling all wrong because she worried, Aqua only wanted this part of Phédra's ceremony to end. That had to mean Aqua was a no-good friend. This was Phédra's big night. Phédra had worked tirelessly toward the receipt of this award. Now Aqua couldn't muster happiness for her because of gnawing anxiety.

After sincerely congratulating and hugging Phédra, Aqua nervously picked at red snapper. She pushed crisp vegetables around on her plate. Every so often, she glanced at the door. Dreaming of her exit, she sipped champagne that she didn't taste. She glanced at her watch. Aqua crumpled her linen napkin. Then unable to stand it, she escaped.

In the night, briskly, Aqua teetered away. Beyond the brightly lit hub of activity, she left bellhops and valets. On high heels, she left those exiting or entering the stately building. Hurriedly, she opened her purse.

Within moments, her phone began to vibrate.

"Hello?" Aqua was breathless, longing to hear that GB was okay.

"Hey, baby. I need you."

Rayfa! Aqua's shoulders sagged, and her eyes narrowed. She sighed because there was nothing wrong with Grandma Bayliss. Rayfa would have said so, first thing. Therefore, Aqua thanked God. Then she felt erupting anger. "Rayfa, have *you* been calling me *non-stop* for the last hour? And is GB okay?"

"I ain't seen her, I guess she alright. You wouldn't pick up," Rayfa whined, her elderly mother forgotten. "How come?"

Aqua turned in a semi-circle. She could have screamed. She couldn't go *anywhere* without Rayfa tracking her, to get on her nerves. She was sick of it! "Rayfa, where are you calling from?"

"Got me a cell phone, now." The older immature woman proudly stated. "I bought it from Ju-Ju Bean. You didn't answer, A. I need you."

Aqua rolled her eyes. That phone from the hood hustler meant Rayfa was using a calling card. Stolen—no doubt, like Rayfa's 'new' phone. The woman had probably paid Ju-Ju for both too, with money pinched off Aqua. "Rayfa, what do you want," now.

"I need cash. Oh, and brang me a lighter."

Aqua exhaled because it was always the same thing. Rayfa had some new thug she was indebted to, or she wanted to buy liquor.

"You ain't said nothing," Rayfa moaned. "When you gon meet me?"

"Not tonight," Aqua hissed as a kissing couple made it past.

"But I'm in a hurry," Rayfa whined.

Not enough to *get* a *job*, Aqua thought. However, she calmly informed her mother, "Rayfa, I cannot drive out there tonight."

"Why? Your car is good; where you at?"

Aqua was in downtown Atlanta at a gorgeous gala, but Rayfa need not know. "I'm not close."

"Shit." Rayfa sounded angry. "Well…" Aqua could hear her thinking. "Can you get here 'fore you go to work in the morning?"

"No." Aqua really felt upset then. To do so would be the biggest imposition. For Rayfa to even ask was unfair. "I'd have to get to you at five. That means I'd have to get up at three-thirty."

"Well, why you working a job that makes you work on Sundies?"

"I don't work every Sunday," Aqua retorted. Oh hell, why explain? It was her life, "And without my job," she quipped, "I wouldn't have the money you're always begging me for."

"Hey, you watch your mouf," Rayfa snapped. "You may be grown and—all that shit, but I'm still your mama."

No, you're not. You have never been, the nearly forty-year-old Aqua wanted to yell. If anybody was the mama in their twisted relationship, it was she, the daughter. She had been, for as far back as Aqua could remember. Now she was *sick* of it. Aqua was too old for the shenanigans.

"When I'm gon see you?!" Rayfa hollered. "And you can't just sit on my phone saying nothing! When you thinkin' it uses up my minutes!"

Forgetting all that she could have snarled, Aqua sighed. She knew that by not setting Rayfa straight, she was again mirroring Dyson's jellyfish; but Rayfa was the mother. How could Aqua disrespect her?

Although it seemed Rayfa was always disrespecting Aqua...

Still, Aqua thought, how could she—in good conscience—turn Rayfa down?

"I may see you after work," Aqua managed. Then as was often the case whenever she dealt with Rayfa, Aqua's head began to ache.

"You'd better," Rayfa groused before issuing an order. "Meet me on the corner, near the club."

Aqua stared at her phone. That near-the-strip-club mess meant Rayfa didn't want *her* mother, Grandma Bayliss, to know she was bumming money off her daughter again.

Aqua thought about going back into the hotel to bid Phédra and others adieu. As she about-faced, she nearly wished one thing.

She would love to get shed of her mother...for good.

Chapter 6

IN his quarters at the club, Dyson walked into his office. In his personal space, surrounded by modern art, he eyed a silver sculpture. Dyson passed a hickory leather sofa and seated himself at his glass and steel desk, kept meticulously neat.

Dyson lifted a paperweight. He really hated that now he had to look for a hostess because his had been swindled away.

He stared out of the window at the small courtyard. There a fountain nestled on brown grass. It was late fall, but in the summertime, that grass would turn verdant green. Dyson's eyes caressed a weathered black scrolled iron bench. It was now apparent. Judy had been wooed by spies. They'd come from *that* supper club, the one owned by a *celebrity*.

Dyson recalled the spies visiting *Apropos*. They'd worn hip-hop gear. Their eyes had tracked Judy. They'd seen how good she was, how people took to her. And because *he* had taught her, because this little gig of his ran like a well-oiled machine, the spies thought Judy was the magic. So they propositioned her ass. The little turncoat had high-tailed it away, betraying him. However, what the interlopers didn't know was: *he* was the magic. Dyson was the effin' glue—*not* that Judas, Judy.

Now, however, Mr. Magic had another problem. He had asked Aqua to quit her job to help him out. If she took the hostess position, he'd said, they could both be happy. It called for far fewer hours than her day job. She would be on her feet a lot—he hadn't failed to state. Dyson had reminded Aqua that weekends would no longer be her own. However, he'd said, he could pay, beyond what her day job paid.

Ms. Sunshine had said, "Nope."

Dyson had asked, "Why not?"

Then sexy had gotten cute. She'd said, "I'd *think* about it—if we were *married*."

That Dyson didn't understand, because what the devil did marriage have to do with business?

Didn't Aqua see? He needed help. Didn't she care? So what? He couldn't offer her a 401K or health care. With the extra money he was offering, she could get those things, and so he had said.

That was when Aqua nodded. "You've just proved my point. If we were *married*, I could take the job because I'd have a stake in what we'd be building, together." She said if they were married, she wouldn't mind not having those other things, for a minute, because they could be worked up to.

Dyson wondered what that meant because *he* had plans in effect, and Aqua knew it. He would never be without. She knew that he, and the twins, his brothers, had decided their kids would be seen to.

Dyson passed his paperweight from hand to hand. Aqua was being facetious. However, what Dyson did not understand was why she was marching to this beat. Lately. Since she now sounded like Edna, his daughter's mother, he wondered.

Did women have a timetable? Did it say that when they'd been involved for X amount of time, they had to get married? They always pushed for the 'next level' and permanency. Why couldn't a sexy sista be happy when she was getting it good, and on the regular? Why'd shit have to be written in stone?

And why had Aqua said, "Dys, you're too secretive." So what, all his cards weren't on the table? Like most women, Aqua wanted in on every little detail of his life. Frankly, Dyson thought that was going too far.

Sure, Edna had been the same way, but *she* had Isis, his kid.

Although he didn't want to, Dyson thought about his daughter's mother. She was a giving, loving woman. When she allowed one a glimpse past her perfectionism.

And to think, he had been enamored with Edna. Back then, she had worn her wavy hair just like now, pulled back in a sleek chignon. She'd worn long dangling gemstone earrings, her only jewelry. Dyson didn't think she wore anything other than dance clothes—leotards, and leggings; but then again, anyone with a compact body like hers, with toned abs, curvy hips and great legs, would need to flaunt it.

Dyson recalled that he'd *had* to let Edna in because what if he'd gotten offed? His kid had to be taken care of. So he had explained a few things.

Even though Edna also sang the marry-me song. Dyson hated to think about how Edna, who wore pashminas and jackets to add color to her typically black attire, had cried when she'd found out she was pregnant. Edna had been on the pill, and finding out, she'd wanted a loophole. But Edna had not believed in abortion. Yet she'd wanted her dream.

Day and night, to Dyson, Edna had moaned that she had been well on her way, right at the threshold of becoming a prima ballerina.

Edna had yelled and asked if Dyson even knew how many African-American prima ballerina *absolutas* there were in major ballet companies.

Dyson had not known, nor had he cared. He just hadn't wanted Edna killing his kid or putting it up for adoption. So he'd talked incessantly. He'd tried to say stuff that would make her keep his baby.

He had attempted to make her forget that extremely rare accolade, that 'absolute' stuff, associated with her dancing. He had tried to make Edna forget her recent promotion to the rank of soloist.

Then with hope in her brown eyes, Edna asked if Dyson was going to marry her.

Horrified, he'd felt like some man had punched him in the gut. Softly he'd said he wasn't the marrying kind. Of course, Edna had asked why, and Dyson explained. He had never seen a marriage that worked. He had also mentioned his mother. She hadn't needed to tie a man to her.

Then Edna had spit fire! She wasn't trying to tie him down. And, she was *not* his mama! Evidenced by her belly being hard with *his* baby.

Dyson had shrugged again, saying he hadn't seen a marriage that worked.

Edna countered by saying her parents' marriage had been working for well over thirty years.

Dyson dismissed that because he only knew one thing. He could not let Edna destroy his seed. Dyson had thought of his deceased mother. She would have been bursting with joy at becoming a grandmother. But then again, Lena Eamon would have asked when was he going to marry that girl. So Dyson forgot his mother, who had briefly been married.

He ignored the trouble he'd had with Edna, who'd finally decided to have his baby. He forgot that since he hadn't wanted to marry her, she'd kept him from seeing his baby for nearly six months.

Then realizing she was wrong, Edna brought bundled Isis to him. Edna said she couldn't be like Dyson, big, selfish, and self-centered. Placing his tiny daughter in his arms and her bag of formula/diapers at his feet, Edna threatened Dyson. "Take care of my baby. If I see one scratch on her... I will *kill* you." In her little coupe, Edna drove away.

Dyson had been scared that whole weekend. Tough little Edna was a monster. He'd had to get his brothers wives involved, because he hadn't known the first thing to do.

Now, sometimes, Dyson felt like he had lost something during that months-long stretch when he'd been unable to see his daughter. When he was with his kid, who was a bright, sunny, thirteen-year-old, now he felt like Isis had a bond with *females*.

There was the one with Edna and Edna's mother. Isis had a bond with her aunts, his brothers' wives. And his kid had a tremendous bond with Aqua. Dyson felt he didn't stand a chance.

Although without knowing it, Aqua had said the same thing that Edna had. Isis knew who cared for her. She knew who was actually interested in *her*, and not just the *idea* of her.

Dyson hated women-speak, the riddles that no man wanted to figure out. All he knew was that when he and Aqua had gotten together, his kid had been little. The first morning that his kid realized Aqua had slept over, his kid hadn't wanted him anymore.

The kid had wanted Aqua. She'd climbed all over Aqua, playing, singing, and hugging her. Baby had wanted Aqua to comb her hair. Combing had been his job, but Dyson's baby had insisted that Aqua 'fix her.' Promptly baby had placed her comb and brush on Aqua's lap. Then the kid had plunked her small chubby butt down on the floor between Aqua's knees. Pretty baby hadn't wanted him to bathe her anymore either. Now she was thirteen.

Tall, slender Isis, with the sunny face, the unprocessed mane of wavy hair, and the button nose, still wanted Aqua. The girl who had been named for an Egyptian goddess proved it every weekend that she visited. She did so mostly to see Aqua.

Seated in his office, holding the paperweight, Dyson recalled his baby sliding onto his leather car seat. She always asked where Aqua was. Isis had done so last week.

Dyson had said, "What? No kiss for your old man?"

As an *afterthought*, Isis pecked him on the cheek; but she asked about her 'buddy.'

Even when she went to the club with him, Isis looked for Aqua.

Actually, the thirteen-year-old had given Dyson the hostess idea. The kid mentioned how club patrons took to Aqua. The kid pointed out the way patrons thought Aqua was the lady of the house.

April Alisa Marquette
27

With her gentle mannerisms, Dyson had to admit, Aqua was hostess material. His kid was right. Wonder why he hadn't seen it before? Probably, because he usually saw Aqua tousled, naked, bronze, and curvaceous in his bed.

Oh, forget Aqua like that, right now.

Dyson couldn't think about her big pretty tits, her rounded hips, her juicy ass, or her warm, moist—

For - get it! Dyson hollered inside. He didn't need a woody, not when the inspector was coming.

Therefore, Dyson would give Aqua a few days. Then he'd call her stubborn behind. Perhaps by then, she would be ready to help him out, without sarcasm, stupid suggestions, or tiresome marriage inquiries.

Chapter 7

HE wants everything *his* way. This Aqua told herself before again deciding she could deal with it. In her cheerful one-bedroom apartment, She sat. She liked the white trim. The honey-hued walls reminded her of sunshine, as did the satiny-finished pine wood floors.

With her feet propped on an ottoman, Aqua pulled her fleece throw tighter. Staring into the flames, she glanced at her small fireplace with the red vase on the mantel. While doing so, she acknowledged something.

She really didn't know if she *wanted* to deal with all of it anymore. Shoot, there were things *she* wanted, like to live in a house. Although her taste ran to the eclectic, she would not want her house filled with a decorator's stuff. Each piece would need to mean something, to her.

Sure, Dyson's penthouse was fine, for *him*, a bachelor. However, a *house* was more her style, now. With two kids, perhaps, and a cat, or a dog. Yes, Dyson said she would get used to the penthouse if she took the plunge. Dyson didn't want pets. He said they were messy.

Why, Aqua wondered, couldn't his big self lunge and marry her?

They'd been together so long. However, maybe Aqua was now the cow that had given away the milk for free. Whatever. It just seemed as though every chance Dyson got, he told her, in not so many words.

He didn't feel the need to commit to her.

Aqua wanted a *husband*. She was thirty-nine. She wanted to walk with her husband while holding hands. She wanted him to have *time* for her, instead of always having an earpiece affixed to his ear.

She wanted someone who desired to see her in sunlight as well as the moonlight.

Aqua wanted to take trips.

Dyson said they could go on one, but he was placating her, again. And she had grown tired of it. Aqua was tired of being quiet, and keeping the peace, and lurking in the background.

She wanted to be in the foreground, for once.

Aqua suspected Dyson mentioned a trip because she had been at her own home lately. She hadn't accepted that silly position at *Apropos*, either. Sure, she had outgrown her job at the publications company. Aqua was tired of the conglomerate that mass-produced magazines. She no longer felt challenged, and Dyson knew it; his reason for offering the vacated hostess position. It was another form of manipulation. Aqua was tired of it.

Although, when she capitulated, Dyson's 'manipulations' did work wonders on her body...

If Aqua let herself think about it, she could nearly feel the cylindrical circumference of Dyson's male member as he sensually pushed it into her. She could almost 'feel' herself expand around him, as holding her close he would put those magic hands on her. Closing her amber eyes, Aqua imagined herself beneath Dyson. She imagined his mouth on her breasts, her nipples, and—wait.

She could also feel...what?

The *island* breeze that would blow through her hair.

Forget getting wet and woozy for Dyson, Aqua decided. She would go alone. She'd go online and reserve a yoga spa retreat because *that* she wanted more than she wanted to be touched and luuved into submission. She wanted to go to the beach. She wanted to be touristy.

No longer willing to allow life to pass her by, Aqua swiped at a tear. She felt angry because everything that man had asked of her, she had done. She had even anticipated and had done things he hadn't requested, for nearly ten years! What had it gotten her?

Most of the time, she was alone, and she still didn't share the bond with her man that she really desired. Then again, she *had* a man. She reminded herself; a lot of women didn't. So she needed to be grateful. Right?

Aqua needed to be thankful that her man wasn't like Phédra's. Mycah was so into his career until the mommy-to-be might wind up parenting alone. However, Mycah was more sincere than Dyson. Mycah said he wouldn't always work as he did now. He planned to retire young and world hop with Phédra.

Aqua hoped her friends would do all they planned.

Again Aqua thought about herself. At this rate, *she* might never wind up a parent. The thought was sobering. Aqua wondered, pulling the throw tighter, when had these feelings begun?

Sure, she had been having erotic dreams and niggling thoughts of *more*; but maybe she was just PMS-ing...

No, something was amiss, Aqua realized, because here she was, a stone's throw from forty, and her only claim to fame was running around after Rayfa, her drunken mother. Lord! One day, maybe even soon, she would begin menopause, after a life on *self-imposed* pause. Wow.

Aqua tossed her cozy throw aside because she would go out, but where? En route to her room, she decided. She would go where she always went when she needed answers. Aqua didn't even have to call.

At her armoire, she opened a drawer and removed soft velour pull-on pants. The matching top, she also donned. Grabbing her purse and stepping into jogging shoes, she snatched up her jacket and left.

While driving, she noticed trees, nearly nude now. She saw the late autumn sky. Months ago it had not appeared so dour. It had been blue and sunny, with clouds scudding across. Back then, it had mirrored the way she'd felt. Now, she simply felt grim and gray, like the day.

Maybe she should turn her car around and go see Dyson. He *had* called, again, about his hostess mess.

Nope, she had given him her answer. Perhaps she needed to tell him to forget everything but sexing her up. Maybe in his arms, Aqua would find release for all her pent up emotions.

The sultry bronze woman drove on. She realized; no. This was one time when sex would not fix what ailed.

Chapter 8

DYSON figured he had better try out a *few* girls instead of one since Aqua was acting up. This way, if one didn't work out, or if a girl ran off, like turncoat Judy, he wouldn't be left in the lurch.

What was that old saying? A poor fox only had one hole.

So he called a woman he had known, in the biblical sense. After sweet-talking her, she, a recruiter, sent over a bevy of fine young things.

During their separate interviews, Dyson found the nubile young women eager to please. Therefore, he selected the ones he was keen to teach. He suggested the top three come Tuesday, daytime, when the club was closed.

They did, and Dyson walked them around *Apropos*, apprising them that each would get a trial run.

"What does that mean?" One young woman asked.

Dyson explained. He would pay them to work one upcoming evening. He revealed that only two would be hired. He explained duties, answered questions, and made a schedule.

The young woman scheduled to start within days did not show up. She did not call, and she would not take Dyson's call. Boiling, he scratched her off his list and made do without her monkey ass.

On Thursday evening, the blond, Amanda, did call. Claiming car woes, she said she would be late.

She arrived an hour and a half later.

Dyson met her at the door. Standing just beyond the gold shaft of light from inside his club, he bluntly said, "This won't work."

"I had problems," Amanda sneered. "I'm here now."

Dyson shook his head. He said problems he did not need.

Amanda attempted to rush by him. "I gotta get inside."

Unyielding, Dyson quipped, "Should'a thought about that—before."

As a dog-walker passed, Amanda demanded, "What about my pay?"

"What pay?" Dyson snorted as the club's door was opened. A snatch of music, as well as the sound of voices, wafted out.

Absently pushing blowing frosted hair from green eyes, Amanda replied. "The money I am owed for showing up here."

With the wind whipping, and a few cars nosing around for parking, Dyson explained. "You work, you get paid. Here, no work, no pay."

Wildly, Amanda waved slender arms. Raising her voice, she rivaled Tupac loudly streaming from a car on the cross street. "You won't *let* me work! I'm here," Amanda jabbed with polish-peeling nails, "but you're blocking the door, playing some stupid game."

"You're *two hours* late." Dyson nonchalantly lit a cigarette. He nodded and stepped aside to allow a multi-ethnic posse to enter.

Watching, Amanda pointed, indignantly inquiring. "Who is *she*?"

Dyson didn't look. As was his way, since he'd had to brave the mean streets of Duck, his eyes instead darted over every person and car, moving or not. He scanned every window and doorway on the street.

"You gave *her* my job," Amanda surmised, freezing in her sateen blouse and short skirt. "You did it because I was late?" Amanda angrily demanded, "Or because she's black?" Amanda slung her purse strap over a shoulder. "You don't think a white girl can do this stupid job of yours, do you?" She sneered. "You reverse racist."

Dyson was through. If the irate young woman before him couldn't see that some of his staff and a great many of his patrons were white, and otherwise, there was nothing to say. "Mandy, there's no job for you here, but you've got balls, pulling the *race* card." He became sarcastic. "Go get a law degree, lil girl, become *Jenny* Cochran. Then sue me."

Amanda had seen him hungrily eyeing her. Since it was now apparent that the big man was an ass, he would never get any of hers. She gave Dyson the finger. "Go get laid, you fat pig. And it's Ah-MAN-da—to you!"

Looking at the young male server who'd just stepped into the chilly evening, Dyson said, "Fat? Pig? Is that what she just called me?"

Over the roar of Amanda's sports coupe, the server forgot why he'd approached the boss. Oh, a call. The youngster tried not to laugh. He appeared sheepish when he said, "I think she did, sir."

Turning then, as he flicked his cigarette away, Dyson realized something. Despite his best efforts, he had one chick left.

She had better be an improvement over the first two, or else.

Chapter 9

AQUA exited her car in the quiet, manicured little enclave. In the dark, she hurried, noticing chrysanthemums. As the wind whipped, she heard music, seemingly carried on the wind. Soaring, it was melancholy, but there, it was also unerringly triumphant.

The song *Precious Memories*, sung by Bishop Carlton Pearson, wafted from the CD player that Ava had purchased for GB.

Knocking once on the lovely red door, Aqua turned the knob. The music was lowered as she stepped into a small arched hallway.

Not startled, Aqua's small, fair-skinned, white-haired grandmother stood in her warm, quaint living room. Holding the audio system remote, Gloria Bayliss delightedly spoke. "Well, hello, Baybeh."

Turning from the coat tree, Aqua smiled and toed off running shoes. Grandma Bayliss dropped the remote onto the large plush couch. It was so comfy now until Aqua couldn't sit on it without falling asleep.

"Sweet girl, looks like you could use a cup of spice tea."

Aqua could, after that chilly little walk. She followed her grandmother through rooms that hadn't changed in decades. The sight nearly transported Aqua back to when she had not known real anguish.

Back in the day, Gloria Bayliss had looked almost as she did now. The only difference was that at a spry eighty-two, the older woman's fine hair was now white. In the past, it had been sandy brown. It was remarkable, Aqua thought because, with minimally lined skin and laughing hazel eyes, Grandma Bayliss looked sixty.

Passing the living room, Aqua noted the crocheted throw on the overstuffed couch. She saw a Tiffany lamp hanging from the ceiling by a brass chain. A giant bible sat in the place of honor on the coffee table. Aqua remembered pictures from that bible: David slaying Goliath, Moses parting the Red Sea...

Aqua recalled other stories. Grandma Bayliss had told her and Ava aplenty. She'd told them about growing up Gullah, on a small isle off the coast of Georgia.

GB said the *Gullah,* African-Americans, resided in the Lowcountry. It was the region between South Carolina and Georgia. It included the Sea Islands.

Grandma Bayliss said the Gullah, from which she'd descended, were people who had preserved their linguistic and cultural African heritage. Even today, their language was related to the Krio dialect of Sierra Leone in West Africa and Jamaican Creole.

Speaking the hauntingly beautiful, lilting language, Grandma Bayliss told her girls that she'd had brothers but no sisters. However, GB had a female first cousin, Hy.

Hy was two years younger than Gloria. Hy only had brothers too. It was the reason Gloria and Hy had grown as close as sisters.

Therefore, Hy's heart broke when newly married Gloria Bayliss left their beloved Gullah Island with her new husband. Gloria and her groom had gone, GB explained, to find opportunities on the mainland.

GB often choked up when she mentioned having lost touch with Hy, back a few years.

Aqua smiled. It had actually been about forty years. Aqua knew GB often wondered if her cousin Hy was yet alive, or if Hy had departed for the great beyond.

Grandma Bayliss had told Aqua and her sister Hy's full name. Aqua couldn't remember it.

In the kitchen where the clean calico tablecloth matched the curtains, Aqua realized. There was always something simmering on the polished white stove. This evening was no exception, and Aqua took a seat at the old metal-sided table. In a matching chair, she thought, funny how the dinette set looked like those in décor catalogs. The ones that touted 'retro' furniture.

Grandma Bayliss fired up her kettle. "So how yuh been, baybeh?"

Aqua had never been less than truthful with the short, now slightly stooped woman. The one who placed a pan of risen yeast rolls in the oven. Not even when that woman had had a switch ready, to sting Aqua's legs when she'd been naughty. Therefore, Aqua opened up, in the kitchen where all food was homemade and savory.

"GB," Aqua watched as a pot of beans and tender beef was stirred. "I've been feeling out of sorts, for a while now."

"Like something ain't right?"

"Yes." Aqua watched the older woman whom she thought of as love personified. GB reached for two dainty cups and saucers. Aqua continued. "I don't know exactly what I feel, but my energy is off."

Gloria Bayliss smiled because young people sure loved to speak of 'energy.' They did it, she knew, to reduce the *spiritual* to something to which they could relate. Yet GB also knew, *this* child of hers was born for more than that energy mess.

But before Aqua got that more, she would have to *acknowledge* the spiritual.

"I've been thinking of taking a trip," Aqua announced. She received spoons, the sugar bowl, and the cream pour, "To re-center myself."

"Oh, to do your yoga." Grandma Bayliss handled the whistling kettle.

"Yes." Feisty wind rattled windowpanes as Aqua continued. "I need to figure out why I'm not doing the things I really want to."

"In general or on your job?"

"In life, work is just work." Aqua sighed. "Really, GB, I feel like I'm always doing what other people want."

...Like earlier in the week when Rayfa had called again.

"Oh. Yo' mama called the other night, begging again, didn't she?"

Aqua looked up. "How'd you know?"

"I know my chile." Grandma Bayliss smirked, "Where else she gon' get money enough for a new dress—*and* likka? Mens nowadays don't pay for both. Well, not the ones that *Rayfa* fools with, anyway."

Aqua smiled. "GB, I just don't want her bothering you."

"I know, but when you're my age, baybeh, nothing slips past yuh. Howsonever, I know you're doing yuh mama a disservice. She got that curse in huh, and you ain't helping by supplying huh wit' drink."

"Oh GB," Aqua put her head in her hands. "I didn't come to talk about Rayfa. I wanna discuss me," now.

"Then we shall, and I'll tell you, Ms. Aqua. Unlike our Ava, *you* have always accepted your mama, instead of trying to change her. You accept huh limitations, as well as her good. Now, why not do that fo' *you*..."

It was as if the molecules in the room changed. The kitchen became brighter, somehow, because that was *it!*

"GB!" Aqua stopped stirring her tea. "Wow. There *are* things I need to accept. Right?"

Gloria Bayliss gingerly sat. "You would know better than I."

Aqua reached for her grandmother's soft bony hand. Aqua loved the woman who'd reared her and her sister. Grandma Bayliss never jumped to conclusions. Gracefully, she only allowed a woman to feel her way, while she, the elder, played the role of sounding board.

"I've got restless energy," Aqua stated over her cup.

GB knew Aqua was still trying to relegate the spiritual to her 'energy' mess. Despite the knowledge, GB spoke kindly. "Perhaps, sweet girl, you're trying to do things *your* way, when Spirit is saying do things diff'ently. Perhaps you're not ready to hear, *or* heed, yet.

"You *have* always had 'the gift' baybeh. So if you ain't *seeing*, mayhap yuh ain't yet ready..."

Aqua held her breath because she had known her grandmother would say that. Not because GB had in the past, but because from the moment she'd stepped inside, the evening had been steeped in déjà vu.

Sipping steaming spicy tea, Aqua knew she should go. Yet she sat, remembering GB's mother. The woman's name had been Ursa. Since Ursa had been the great grandmother, Aqua and Ava had called her Great Ur.

Great Ur had looked like a white woman. She'd had the same hazel or amber eyes as GB. Ursa's skin had been pale. Ursa's hair had been as white back then as her daughter, GB's hair was now.

Come to think of it, Ursa's father had been a Spaniard.

Aqua wondered why she remembered such things. She hadn't pondered Great Ur in years. God rest her great-grandmother's soul.

Sighing, Aqua rose and bent to hug her grandmother's neck. Pressing her face into the soft folds, Aqua breathed in lavender. "Thank you," she murmured.

Feeling unshed tears that caused her throat to ache, Aqua placed her cup, saucer, and spoon in the sink. Knowing her grandmother would never allow her to wash the fine china, Aqua croaked, "I love you, GB."

Grandma Bayliss nodded, "And I you, Baybeh. Why not take a plate to go? Yuh always need to eat."

Aqua said, "No GB, not this time. Don't get up, love. I'll lock the door when I go."

In the small front hallway, Aqua stepped into footgear, as her grandmother called after her.

"Let the Lord lead, honey."

Chapter 10

AS she drove, Aqua's throat burned with unshed tears.

Since she had been out to see Grandma Bayliss, Aqua felt something coming up.

In her apartment, Aqua sat in the dark. In her living room, she felt empty and hollowed out. Aqua wanted to cry, but she couldn't. *Lord*, she just wanted to fall onto the floor.

Down on her knees she wanted to pray, but no words would come. It had been that way for days. Therefore, Aqua sat on the pine, with folded hands. She wondered, what was the use?

She placed her arms around herself, in a makeshift hug. "Oh God," she murmured, summoning the tears that remained just beyond reach.

Lord! All Aqua felt was wrong.

Maybe she needed a laxative.

Or maybe GB had been right, Aqua suddenly cogitated. Perhaps she had been trying too hard, to do things her way. Aqua had prayed, but she'd received no answer. Then again, she had only told Spirit what *she* wanted. She hadn't listened for what was wanted *of her*. Maybe that was why no response, and why nothing was going smoothly. Perhaps she really did have to give up, but *how*?

In the dark and the quiet, Aqua made herself speak. Her voice sounded foreign, devoid of emotion. Perhaps it was because she had given all of herself away, trying to make other people happy.

Aqua forgot the sound of her voice, to simply speak out loud.

She said, "You know I've tried. You also know I'd have fixed whatever's wrong, if I could have. But now...I need your help, please..."

Then the tears that had been damned up began to flow. Like rain from the skies, they dropped. Aqua felt a bubble, one that rose from her solar plexus. It moved from the soul of her, to her mouth. Hurriedly, she clutched her lips to arrest the eruption, but such was not to be.

Wailing poured from her lips. As she rocked back and forth, Aqua allowed the storm to take her. Many things plagued her. Some were things she'd thought she wanted. Others she now knew she had to let go. Although *before* it had seemed as though those things had a hold on her.

Rocking, Aqua wept, for what she'd once believed could be, because maybe now it could not. She cried for all the years passed and for those encased in an unknown future. But mostly, she wept to cleanse and purge herself, so she could begin again, anew, afresh.

When she no longer cried, Aqua felt spent. Therefore, she let herself slide down, in the dark...to rest, in the arms of her Savior.

IN the days that followed, Aqua felt exhausted. She very nearly looked it too.

Dyson didn't even notice.

Guess that was how much attention he paid. Aqua didn't care, because slowly, she was emerging, like a butterfly.

Aqua began to feel buoyant, and like she'd left the darkness, and was headed for the light. She again felt beautiful, energetic, and magnetic.

Aqua kept having dreams, though. Well, truthfully, it was one dream, with a few variations. Always, she found herself in a large old house. In that house, she would enter a bedroom, presumably hers. On her bed, a snowy white garment would be laid out, seemingly for her.

Then Aqua would see herself wearing the flowing garment as she walked down a moonlit hall –to meet her lover.

The thing that bothered her was that her lover was always faceless, or in shadow. Aqua didn't think it was Dyson. Still, she could not shake the sense that she knew the indescribably familiar man...

As the days progressed, Aqua forgot the slightly puzzling dream. Instead, she thought about her life. Without fear, she realized it would now most likely take turns she hadn't planned for. That was okay, now.

Aqua even prayed the simplest prayer.

"Father, please don't allow me to miss the right path."

Aqua had no idea where she would wind up, but she realized one thing. Grandma Bayliss had been right. In the past, she had not wanted to see or to know; but now...Aqua felt it was time. She desired clarity. It would get her off the dizzying carousel that had been taking her nowhere, fast.

Now Aqua wanted to be led...but not by *man*.

Chapter 11

Isis was bored. At Dyson's house, she usually was, unless Aqua was there. Then Isis had fun because Aqua wasn't like Dad. Aqua had ideas. She enjoyed going places. Aqua played *Uno*, too, making up rules as she went along. It was ghetto, Aqua admitted, but fun.

Sure, Isis knew Aqua probably cheated, but Aqua made things exciting. Like once when they played *Monopoly*. Aqua knew she was losing, so she asked Isis, "Want a veggie burger?" Aqua had said they'd go *out* for it. That had been slick, but Isis's move had been smoother. Isis said she'd go *if* Aqua took her to the *mall* food court. Aqua agreed because she liked to shop, just like the thirteen-year-old Isis.

The two had thrown their 'money' down and scrambled to get their purses. Isis carried one because Aqua said it was time. Isis now kept her stuff in the small designer purse that Aqua had bought for her.

Isis, who had been named for a mythical Egyptian goddess, hoped she'd one day be fashionable like Aqua. That was probably why Dad liked Aqua. Isis wasn't sure if he loved Aqua because when a man loved a woman, he married her. At least that's what Isis' BFF, slightly freckled, strawberry blond Sherry said.

Still, Isis knew Dad *liked* Aqua because he and Aqua did 'it.' They thought she didn't know, but she'd heard them. Early one Saturday morning, Dad and Aqua had been murmuring. Then Aqua sighed and made meowing-like noises. Dad had sounded growly. Then Isis reached for the remote. She'd turned up *The Proud Family* because, *ick*, she didn't want to listen to *that*.

Isis liked that her father and Aqua did it. That meant Aqua would be around a long time. Ladies liked doing it, Sherry said. She and Isis giggled about doing it when they were old, like seventeen.

Isis wondered if she would do 'it' with Dylan. Not now, though, because she didn't want to be like a few girls at school, with big bellies and partway open jeans. Cute brown Dylan wouldn't like her like that.

Isis recalled Aqua. Why wasn't she at Dad's? Aqua usually was, on Saturdays, sometimes even on Friday nights when Dad picked up Isis.

The funny thing was, Isis's *mom* liked Aqua. Isis knew it was strange because Sherry had called her nickname, icy. Blond Sherry said, "Isi, grown-ups don't get along, especially if they're parents who broke up."

But Isis's grown-ups were different. She didn't really remember being little. Still, there couldn't have been much meanness because her mother, Edna, had said to Dad once that she hoped he'd do better. Edna said she prayed Dad wouldn't screw with Aqua's head, like he had with hers. Edna had said if things headed 'that way,' and Dyson still felt, 'you know,' he should tell Aqua and give her the option.

Isis guessed that was about marriage because her parents had never married. When Isis asked why, Edna said, "Your father didn't want to." Edna also said—so many times—that she, Edna Jean Beck, had been well on her way to becoming one of the highest types of ballerinas. Isis forgot the name, but Edna had gone to Germany, France, and everywhere with her dance troupe. She'd garnered lots of praise. Accolades, Isis recalled. *That* easy word had been in the spelling bee.

Isis flopped on her father's sofa, a sectional, really. It was big, comfy, and pretty, with matching pillows. It had ottomans, so she put her feet up. Her father's penthouse was *extra*, so Sherry said. To Isis, *without Aqua*, it was nothing. Yeah, Sherry thought it was neat that windows took the place of walls, and the whole glittery city of Atlanta was showcased. Isis forgot that, because she couldn't just sit around *thinking*! She hated wasted Saturdays. This Isis thought as her poufy ponytail bobbed on the back of her head. Shoot, if Aqua didn't show, Isis would be stuck doing nothing until time to go to the club.

Isis liked her father's supper club. It was a nice, almost-dark, comfortable place with cute tables with snow-white linens. There were comfy, hot-chocolate-with-milk-colored sofas. There were pussy willows in metallic vases, and a big shoji screen. It wasn't like the one at mom's with the wood cutout squares and the rice paper. Dad's screen covered a whole wall. It was made of black lacquer and had a city that lit up painted on it. The screen made the club's dining area impressive. People remarked, in low voices. Isis could tell they thought the place was— what's that word Sherry used? Posh. People thought Dad's club was posh. That meant elegant.

Isis knew everybody at *Apropos*, too. That was the club's name. It meant appropriate or opportune. Isis knew because she loved words, almost as much as she loved to dance. At the club, she could have all the Shirley Temples and bottled fizzy waters she wanted. Gary, the cute blond bartender, poured her water into the crystal goblets used for patrons. He always asked if Isis wanted a twist. She said yes, thank you. Isis liked the way her mom and Aqua drank their water.

Isis also liked that Aqua had asked Gary to keep some of the yogurts she bought in the bar fridge, just for Isis. Edna, Isis' mom ate lots of yogurt. Sherry said that was why Ms. Edna and Isis could almost wear the same size. Even though Isis still needed to 'fill out." Then, Aqua had said, Isis would be a knockout. Isis couldn't wait.

Aqua didn't eat yogurt; Isis remembered. Aqua said it reminded her of sour milk or the smelly buttermilk her grandmother loved. Aqua said it all stank, and Isis cracked up. Isis loved Aqua. Isis had even gone to Aqua's grandmother's house. It was when they'd all gone to Six Flags.

Isis loved Grandma Bayliss. GB wasn't Isis's real gran, but for Isis's birthday, the white-haired lady had sent a sterling charm bracelet.

GB's house was nice too, and old fashioned. It was where Aqua and her pretty sister, Ava, had grown up. Ava had a smiley baby. Ava was was married too, to super cool, big black Melvin. He was dreamy.

Isis would not have minded growing up with GB. She just would not have wanted that woman Rayfa. *She* wasn't like a real mother— Hey, maybe that's why Aqua never called the woman 'Mom.' Ms. Rayfa was like a trampy girl, but in a skinny, old-ish body. Her breath smelled sort of vomit-y, and she drank and smoked too much.

"Dad!" Isis yelled, tired of *thinking*, "Where is Aqua?" Isis had asked before. Like last time, Dad put up a finger, on his cell. Isis rolled her eyes. He was always on the phone, maybe with the club manager, his supplier, or his brothers.

Isis liked her twin uncles, Stanton and Zion. Isis liked their sons, her cousins, too. Older, like eighteen, her cuzzos were nice. Isis suddenly wondered, were *they* were doing 'it?'

That brought her back to Aqua. Isis saw her Dad walk into the kitchen. Isis followed. "When you gonna marry Aqua?" If Dad did, then Aqua would live there.

Dyson looked at his kid. She'd been asking that question for years. What was it with females? They were obsessed with marriage.

"I know you heard me, Dad." Isis opened the stainless steel refrigerator. She took out fizzy water. Dang, no lemon wedges. See? If

Aqua were around, she'd have cut up some and placed them in a small, pretty bowl with plastic wrap. "Dad, don't you *want* to marry A?"

Dyson and Aqua had had the same conversation. But he couldn't tell his kid what he'd told his woman. "Aqua and I like our relationship," Dyson lied as his daughter rolled a lemon. "Okay, nosey-posey?"

Isis didn't answer. She simply pulled the knife she'd seen Aqua use.

"Hey," Dyson called, leaning against the granite-topped island. He hated when Isis ignored him. She'd started at three-years-old. If Isis felt something was unsatisfactory, she withheld words. Although Isis looked like a slender, pretty, girl-version of Dyson, the kid was much like her mother. Dyson loved Isis's sunny face and mane of unprocessed hair, pulled back into a huge puff, like a cloud bobbing along behind his baby.

Isis cut her lemon. "I don't see why you have to string A along."

"Look at me," Dyson told his sometimes too-grown kid. "What do you mean?" Where had she heard that—her mother? Or had Aqua said something? She and his kid spent enough time together. Dyson would bet his kid preferred Aqua to him. Maybe that was her problem.

Isis hadn't been her sparkly self when he'd picked her up last night. She'd gotten in the car and hadn't seen Aqua. At home, he'd ordered pizza, and Isis had become sullen, not wanting to eat. She'd mumbled about not wanting additives in her body. She'd griped that Aqua would have cooked, or had yogurt in the fridge, "Just for me, even though she doesn't like it," Isis had yelled, thrown across her bed. "Still, A would have bought some, for me!"

Then the kid refused to speak, even when Dyson said, "Get your grown butt down to the car." As he drove aimlessly to find something Isis would eat, she kept her arms folded and stared outside. When they'd returned, with yogurt, among other things, the kid hadn't behaved any better. She'd texted her friend with the braces, Shelley or Cheryl.

Isis spoke, getting the bowl that Aqua used for the lemon. "Why do boys play games? Why don't they say how they feel and mean it?"

Dyson's eyes widened because his kid sounded like the *women* in his life. If Isis was having boy trouble, Edna needed to do something. Or he would beat the boy down, don't care what age the little dick was.

"What should a boy say," Dyson asked, not knowing whether he and his kid were speaking of him and Aqua, or of her and the boy he'd kill.

Isis opened the pantry door. "If he likes her, he should ask what she wants." Tearing plastic wrap, Isis said, "Then he should try to do it."

Dyson nodded. "If the girl wants to go steady, the boy should?"

Isis wrinkled her nose. "That sounds dumb, Daddy, but yes."

"Shouldn't the girl do what the boy wants, too?"

Adding lemon to her effervescent water, Isis nodded, her cloud of hair bobbing. "The girl already does. Girls try to please." Isis hid beneath long lashes. "So since Aqua does 'it' with you, you'll marry her?"

Dyson was taken aback. First, because how did his grown-behind kid know *what* he and his woman did? Secondly, little Miss Grown-Ass had asked that same thing about her own mother, Edna. Moreover, his kid would never understand. Heck, how would she, when even *he* didn't? So he said he'd be in his office. He called out, "Yo, get your homework."

Isis rolled her eyes. "I did it last night when I couldn't sleep."

Dyson about-faced. Was his smart-mouthed kid sick? He put his big fingers under her chin and tipped her face up. "You feeling okay?"

Isis narrowed her eyes. "Why?"

"You said you couldn't sleep. I don't want you sick."

"I had stuff on my mind."

Dyson nearly laughed. "Stuff like what?"

"Stuff like that gross food. And people."

"What food and what people?"

Isis lowered her eyes. "The food last night, and Aqua..."

Dyson's heart lurched, as slowly he asked, "What about Aqua?"

Isis raised her chin. "She wasn't here. What did you do?"

Dyson dropped his hand. Now he understood why women had often said he couldn't meet their kids, not until the woman felt the relationship was going somewhere. The big man guessed that was why he hadn't met many kids. Maybe he should have kept his kid out of his relationship. Yeah, like that would have worked. Aqua was his pinch-hit babysitter.

"Yo, go get your homework. Put it where I can see it," Dyson suddenly ordered, for lack of anything better to say. "You hear?"

Isis had something akin to contempt in her eyes. "You'll get it."

Was the kid trying him? She would never have done that with Edna, or Aqua. "No." Dyson became firm, when often he was not. "Get your books, now. Put them on the table, and no back talk."

Isis sucked her teeth.

"Watch yourself, little girl..." Dyson warned as he turned.

Isis raised an eyebrow and picked up her cell phone. Putting books on the table, she forgot her Dad. She texted Sherry about the cute boy.

THE house phone rang. The loudness startled Isis. "Dad," she called. It kept ringing, and Sherry needed an answer.

"Dad!" Isis yelled. Heaving up, she picked up the landline. "Hello?" She listened as her thumbs hovered over her own phone. "He's here, maybe on his office phone." Isis didn't really know or care. "Dad stays on as long as he wants. Who is this?"

Zenda? What a stupid name. "Where you know my Daddy from?" Isis inquired, feeling anger. "I ask," she said, sounding older, "because he's *my father.*"

Isis listened. "Oh. You can't answer *my* questions, but now you trying to tell me what to do?" Isis wanted to hang up. "You tried his cell and didn't get him?" Well good. Isis had to be loyal to Aqua, not to this unknown Zenda person.

Aqua was the only one, other than her mother Edna, Uncle Stan, and Uncle Zion, who called on the house phone. Isis didn't like that this Zenda was horning in on what was only for family.

Isis projected all the malevolence she could into her words. "I'll tell my Dad." Isis raised her sophomoric voice. "Don't yell. Brenda. You're being stank. Whatever. My *mother will* call you—we have caller ID! She'll get you straight. She'll tell you how to talk to me. She may even shoot you."

Isis slammed the phone into its cradle. She wrinkled her pug nose and couldn't wait to text Sherry. She'd say forget Dylan, and get this; there's some woman around ...sounding all desperate.

Chapter 12

AQUA met her friends at the club. She needed to look around. Not from the standpoint that she had in the past, but as a worker. She wanted to envision what it would be like to work at *Apropos* since Dyson had asked, again.

Aqua didn't really want to be a hostess, but perhaps she could give it a go, while she decided on her next move. She really wanted her own business. Toward that end, she'd applied a federal ID number and other things. Now here she sat, with her girls, weighing a temporary option.

Aqua intended to observe Dyson's club as she never had before. She'd use the patron's point of view. Ever since her first arrival, Aqua had been treated royally because she was involved with the boss. However, on this evening, she wanted to see the place through someone's eyes with no such connection. Thus, she'd invited her girlfriends. She needed Phédra and Cadence's company so she wouldn't look so conspicuous.

To Aqua, on the phone, curly-haired Cadence had sounded distracted, but Phé the photographer had readily agreed. Phédra said she had something she wanted to run by the others.

AT *Apropos*, Cadence did not remove her jacket or silk scarf. She didn't care to listen, because Phédra spoke of some photo journal she was thinking about doing. Cadence wound her curls around a finger. Was Phé blathering about the color of her skin again, and how being bi-racial, she felt as though she didn't really fit in anywhere?

PHÉDRA said she had been thumbing through *Newsweek* when an article caught her eye. It was about a phenomenon taking place in the coastal American isles. There was a woman, a High Priestess, actually, who had stirred up quite a commotion.

From what Phédra read, people flocked from the states and from Europe, to a little island called Karina Cay. The article said people believed something spiritual took place, with this woman at the fore.

Phédra said she pictured what was happening as a movement. Sort of like that of the 1960s when civil rights activists spearheaded the quest for change. This new movement, Phédra wanted to be part of, especially after what she'd read. The Priestess was a direct descendant of African slaves. They had long ago been dragged to American shores. Phédra said she could take her equipment and create a photo journal.

Gray-eyed Phédra the photographer did not say so, but maybe…the Priestess could help her with whatever she was searching for.

CADENCE vaguely heard Phédra mention someone named Odyssey, a Priestess. Steeped in her feelings, Cadence twined a corkscrew curl around a finger. Suddenly, Cadence tuned back in.

Was Phédra interested in some *Voodoo* Madam? Cadence sure hoped not. She prayed Phé wasn't 'bout to act like the girls with whom she had gone to college. They had been into some knockoff voodoo shit. Unaware, Cadence took a trip with them to New Orleans. Then those kids had her skulking around St. Louis Cemetery #1, at night. When the girls knocked three times on Priestess Marie Laveau's crypt, Cadence could have strangled them all, right there in the dark.

Wait, had Cadence heard correctly? Did Phé think this new Priestess from some island could heal her, or make her mixed-chick self *feel* more black? Cadence sighed, because it was all balderdash.

The truth was *she* was the one with *real* problems. Here, Phé was, moaning about fitting in, when she had a real man. Mycah had not misled Phédra. Now Yael? Cadence's husband had not been up-front. Mycah, on the other hand, had told Phé he traveled, often. He catered to his really rich, spoiled, and sometimes famous clients. Gray-eyes had known. Unlike Cadence, who hadn't known a thing until after she'd married.

Yeah, Cadence had *thought* she'd known her husband. Now she knew she had not. The curly-haired one covered her face with both hands because oh, Lord! What if Yael really was *gay*?

Cadence felt sick to her stomach. But she should have known. Now looking back, so many things had given her husband away. Curly hair guessed she hadn't seen because she hadn't wanted to.

She felt like throwing up.

She was a *cover girl*! Yael had used her to mask his gayness!

Curly-haired Cadence realized, she'd thought her husband was perfect. She'd thought she'd lucked out, landing him, but now it was apparent, she'd struck out. The man had duped her.

Seated in the semi-circular booth across the table, Aqua noticed her friend. There was an angry set to Cadence's mouth, and curly-girl stared out into the chilly, late-autumn night. "Cae," Aqua called, "you alright?"

Cadence blinked. "Yeah. Sure," she lied because she couldn't share *this*. Not even with the women with whom she shared nearly all.

Phédra mentioned Mycah, and Cadence lost it. Curly-hair yelled before she knew she would. "At least he's not *gay!*"

A few of those at the nearby bar glanced over.

In the booth with her, Cadence's friends stared. Then with a frown, Aqua spoke, slowly and softly. "Cae, are you telling us something?"

Cadence shrugged. "Can't tell what I don't even know myself."

Gray-eyed Phédra appeared mortified. Her cheeks pinked up and the color became mottled. "Cadence, don't say you're having trouble with *Yael*." Phédra hugged her baby bump. "Cae, your husband is perfect—or darn near it."

Curly-haired Cadence sipped from the glass she'd barely touched since Gary, the bartender, had sent it over. "Then I won't say."

Aqua leaned forward, knowing how much her friend loved her husband. Aqua forgot perusing Dyson's club from an altogether different perspective. She knew she had to give her girlfriend her undivided attention.

Aqua knew too that later that night, when she prayed for herself and her 'dicey' situation, she would pray for her friend. It appeared that both she *and* Cadence sure could use the Savior's help right about now.

Chapter 13

DYSON was angry. Didn't people know he saw everything? It was *his* club, so nothing happened that he didn't know about. *That* was why the happy birthday man, the one who'd splurged for the big Sunday Brunch for his loud-assed family, should have known he was watching.

But then again, Dyson thought, the family man didn't know him. *But,* Dyson thought, the man should have figured that a fine, curvy sista like Aqua *had* to be taken. Mister should have known that!

Although Aqua *had* given family man a look that Dyson had never seen. Seeing that look, Dyson had felt like an outsider looking in. He had noticed when he'd glanced up from his accounting logs. There on one of six monitors affixed to the wall, Dyson saw Aqua, standing beside the huge-party table.

A woman with a baby in her arms spoke, and Aqua bent to give her full attention. She had thereby also given 'family man' a generous view of her cleavage. Watching from his vantage point, Dyson saw that when Aqua stood back up, signaling to one of the wait staff, the man's appreciative gaze never left her.

Actually, once or twice, when Aqua had glanced at family man, her eyes appeared as they had when she'd first met *him*... She had even laughed a few times with 'family man.' Damn! Dyson felt tight again, just thinking about it.

Prowling the length of the panoramic wall of windows in his home, Dyson felt akin to a caged panther. Man, did Dyson itch to tear the head off something! Why did he feel this way?

He paced back, with his hands jammed deep in his pockets. He knew Aqua loved him. Wasn't all her 'marriage' talk proof? She would never leave; she would just forever nag him about walking down the aisle. If he held off long enough, she'd realize she needed to be happy with what they had.

It was good, right? Oh, please. Dyson had to admit if it was all good, why wasn't he getting any? Hey, when had this *not* getting his dick slicked begun? He couldn't remember. Had it had been *that* long? It was late fall. So maybe about a month ago, Aqua had cut him off.

Suddenly Dyson stopped. Before floor-to-ceiling glass, he gazed out over the lights of the ATL. With his sumptuous darkened Perimeter penthouse at his back, he thought. Since Aqua hadn't laid spread-eagle, nude, and tussled for him, sexy as sin—in Heaven only knew how long—was it possible? Was she giving *his* honey to family man?

Sure, Dyson let other women lick the lollipop, occasionally, but that was just how he rolled. He liked a bit of variety every now and again. But Aqua? Naaah. Dyson prowled again. He couldn't see A doing that, although men were always checking for her. Dyson often saw them.

But Aqua wanted *him*. Yep, so much, until she wanted his name and his baby. But *Edna* had his baby, that thirteen-year-old too grown Isis.

Oh, forget Edna. Dyson's thoughts returned to Big Spender. Why had he chosen to have his family get-together at *Apropos*? Yeah, the club had made a mint off the gathering, but the man's eyes had lingered on Aqua's ample ass and round hips one time too many. Big Spender's eyes had dipped repeatedly to Aqua's tits, their outline visible through her lacey top. The titties that Dyson hadn't had his mouth on in how long?

Dyson slammed a fist into its opposite palm. He would have to do something about getting Aqua back over and into his bed. They could start with a steamy shower. Dyson would hold Aqua's glistening, lush, bronze body against the wet tiled wall. Drops of water would fall from her peaked nipples, while his missile would seek her heat.

Dyson could see himself driving into Aqua as she braced her legs around him. She would urge him on with parted wet lips emitting greedy, low-spoken words. He would draw back and drive into her again. The club owner would give it to her until neither of them could stand. Then he'd carry her to his massive bed and begin all over again, slowly. He'd kiss, caress, and probe heated wet orifices— wait.

Why was 'family man' intruding on Dyson's fantasy? Was it because 'family man' had celebrated *his* mother's birthday? Shit, Dyson could only celebrate Lena Eamon's birthday by taking flowers to her grave.

Again Dyson smashed a fist into a palm, because heck, if he could even picture what his mother would have looked like, had she lived to just fifty. Perhaps *that* was what really bothered him.

Family man had a mother.

Soon—it seemed—that man would have Aqua. *If* he hadn't already had her...

Chapter 14

SHE had agreed to host. Therefore, while at home, Aqua beat her face and did her hair. She pulled on forest green velvet pants and a cream-colored lace v-neck. She sprayed on scent and adjusted freshwater pearl accessories. She also wore snazzy leather boots.

Aqua remembered walking the club. She made sure patrons' drinks and meals were artfully supplied. Catering to them had been fun. She recalled thinking, shoot, if Dyson wanted to pay for *this*, then, gladly.

Uh-oh, the memory of a man she'd met while doing her 'duties' surfaced, and Aqua's heart began to pound. She couldn't remember his first name, but his last was Ocaña.

O-CON-ya had stuck in her head, as did the chemistry between them. Although Aqua was loath to admit it, her involuntary reaction to the man's overwhelming virility had been instant. With his reaction to her, what was between them had been combustible.

Aqua recalled that she'd had to consciously tamp down her reaction to the man who'd smelled decadent. Rampantly attracted, she'd had a job to do, while her boss, the man she had refused to continue sleeping with, had been nearby, watching, no doubt.

Aqua thought back to the other man, the gold-skinned Noel or Noah; she couldn't remember his first name. He had appeared for the club's Sunday Brunch, so had his extended and lively family. Filled with babies and children, the Ocaña clan had celebrated their matriarch's seventy-sixth birthday.

Beautifully white-haired, the birthday 'girl' Mrs. Elaine Ocaña had smooth brown skin, which was nearly unlined. Jovial and spry, she'd clearly been the queen presiding over her African-American/Latinx clan.

Aqua recalled chuckling along with Mrs. Ocaña's family. While the house band played *Sister Sledge's* 'We Are Family,' queen bee went for a gentle whirl on the dance floor. She did so with each of her grandsons. Ranging in age from mere-months to twenty-something, each young male obviously adored his granny, as did the girls who anxiously awaited their turn.

In her maize yellow bedroom, as she remembered all, Aqua felt like the sun was shining, even though it was misty outside. Seated on her bed, she hugged her knees. She also remembered the way the impeccably dressed Mr. Ocaña's eyes had traveled admiringly over her. Then, like now, Aqua had been suffused with the most delicious heat. She'd wanted to squeal with delight, like young Isis.

Oh. *That* squealing was Aqua's whistling kettle. In her small cooking space, Aqua prepared fragrant tea and remembered close... She'd stood at the door of *Apropos*, bidding the stream of Ocaña family members and others *adieu*.

Finally, only a trickle remained; Aqua distinctly remembered three. There was the white-haired African-American matriarch, Mrs. Ocaña. She'd been on the arm of her salt-n-pepper-haired Latino husband. Escorting them had been the couple's son, tall, thickset, Noah, or Noel.

Approaching, in a beautifully tailored camel coat, the forty-something gold-skinned man took Aqua's hand. Gallantly, he bowed as softly he informed Aqua that the pleasure had indeed been his. Then turning slightly, as a hint of snow flurried beyond *Apropos'* entryway, the tall, broad-shouldered man took his mother under a protective arm. Tenderly he kissed her white hair, but his eyes remained on Aqua as he spoke.

"*Mami*, I do believe I've found the woman I am going to marry."

For Aqua, the memory raised gooseflesh, but for Lord's sake, she thought while sipping tea, she was being silly. The man didn't really *know* her, or she him.

Sure, she had seen and spoken to him in the past. Several times, he'd visited the publishing house where she worked. The thickset man had done so, ferrying specs for a project. And the ladies had been all agog.

Forgetting that, Aqua could not help but recall that Mrs. Elaine Ocaña had accepted her son's declaration with alacrity; *I do believe I've found the woman I am going to marry*. Mrs. Ocaña had opened her arms. With birdlike little hands, she'd pulled Aqua down for a hug.

"My son is a *good* man, a gem," Mrs. Ocaña had simply stated.

Then when the older woman had tottered out into the flurrying cold, escorted by both her virile handsome son and her husband, she'd left Aqua thinking. All while the matriarch's preciously old-time spice perfume clung to Aqua's clothing.

Chapter 15

HE walked his fingers up her arm, attempting to tickle her. However, Isis wasn't in the mood. She only wanted to know what twelve-year-old strawberry blond Sherry had to say about Tonna McCarthy. That girl was pushing up on Dylan. Tonna didn't realize that Dylan didn't like braces, and Isis didn't have braces anymore.

Realizing he was being ignored, Dyson attempted to bother Aqua, until the house phone rang. He hurriedly got up. Aqua recalled that Dyson usually took his time about answering his home phone. Sometimes if they were eating, he would even let it go to voicemail.

In the kitchen, he snatched up the receiver. Realizing who the caller was, he spoke in a barely audible voice. Then Dyson hurried away.

Aqua noticed, and that on the phone, the hold light blinked. So Dyson was going to take the call in another room, huh?

When he returned, he thought he appeared nonchalant. Nevertheless, a muscle in his jaw ticked, and Aqua knew. Dyson was angry. Yet he tried to fool her. He took a seat on the floor beside Isis, who was busy with her phone. Between Aqua's knees, Dyson rested his head against the sofa cushion. He sniffed and whispered, "You smell good, babe."

Seated down before Aqua, Dyson realized. He had forgotten how nice it was just to sit with her and watch TV. Aqua was a peaceful woman. She didn't keep drama going. Back in the day, soon after meeting her, Dyson had known it.

As he closed his eyes, he recalled other times when he'd sat the same way, with her legs on either side of him. She'd oiled his scalp. She really had magic hands. Now though, Dyson thought and ran a nervous hand over his head, his hair lay smooth. Nevertheless, maybe Aqua could brush it because he was all about the feel good.

Dyson forgot feeling good. That could get a man in trouble. He well knew. Scrubbing hands across his face, he didn't want to think about trouble right now, so he again mentioned Aqua's fragrance.

With the TV's flicker creating blue light, along with the glittering city beyond the windows, she tartly replied. "It's what I always wear."

Dyson turned and allowed his eyes to travel over her. Why did Aqua seem so tense these days—with him? She was okay with Isis. Had somebody said something? Or, all-seeing woman that she was, had Aqua noticed something? Dyson told himself to quit being pessimistic. Things were as they always had been and as they would be, forever. Right?

Dyson did not know, but he did know that Aqua's fragrance was her usual, as she'd said. Therefore, he absently replied, "I know."

Aqua cut her eyes because Dyson was getting on her nerves. "Then why ask?" she quipped. When he got up to sit beside her, she wondered, what she was doing there, at his house.

Dyson's lips met Aqua's ear. "I meant I love the smell of *her*."

"*Who*?!" Aqua felt anger as Dyson attempted to whisper again, but roughly, she pushed him. Aqua also advised, "Don't make me slap you."

Preoccupied, while texting Sherry, Isis said, "No fighting, you two."

Dyson whispered again, and with knotted lips, Aqua rose, thinking he had gone too far—talking to her about some other woman! Heck, if his daughter was elsewhere, Aqua would have whacked the crap out of him. Disrespectful sod. Attempting to get her leg over his, Aqua ordered, "Stop playing." When Dyson held her arm, she hissed. "I'll act out..."

He released Aqua, because like a jellyfish, she *could* sting. However, Dyson followed her into the hallway and flicked on overhead lights. Cornering Aqua, he knew he'd better explain because she was prickly lately, or maybe he just felt that way since *other* shit was going wrong. Stuff of which she had no knowledge—or did she? Forgetting worrisome inquiries, Dyson spoke softly, trying to get them back on track.

"Aqua, I was talking about *you*, your natural scent. I could barely smell it." Dyson licked his lips. He thought he appeared suave. "I love it. It calls to me—"

"I don't wanna hear this," Aqua cautioned, an eyebrow raised. Her neck hurt and she was tense. She sensed something was wrong. Aqua felt it in the pit of her stomach. Therefore, she decided. She would go home. There, she would pray and try to shake off the feeling that said there were things she needed to know and do, to make her life the life that it was supposed to be.

"Listen, smelling you made me want you," Dyson said. He tried to nudge Aqua into the half bath. "Go," he whispered. "Don't turn on the light."

Standing her ground, Aqua stared at the man who made her so angry lately. Why would she want to bend over for him? When she spoke, it was with incredulity. "You think I'm some kind of sex toy, don't you?"

Dyson winked. "You're my woman. That encompasses sex toy."

Aqua's voice became gruff in imitation. "You're my woman." Then her voice became her own, dripping with disdain. "You're a caveman."

Dyson shrugged because in some ways it was true. Therefore he said, "This 'caveman's' got a 'club' that he's aching to use."

Aqua would have retorted, but young Isis sauntered up.

Extremely intelligent, she leaned on Aqua. "A, you and my Daddy fighting, again?"

Dyson attempted to respond, but the slender girl ignored him. "You can tell me, A." Isis also pulled up the low rider jeans that both her mother and Aqua had spoken to her about. The women had advised that the jeans should not hang too low, thereby exposing her pelvic area. Both women had said that men, and boys especially, got wrong ideas.

Aqua had advised that Isis should leave something to the imagination, and Isis listened to her. Isis wanted to be in her classmate Dylan's imagination. So again Isis pulled at her jeans. They weren't as tight as those worn by skanky Tonna with the braces.

Looking at the woman who'd become another parent, Isis knowingly asked, "A, what did my Dad do, now?"

"Yo, why's it gotta be me?" Dyson queried, turning his daughter to face him. "You're *my* baby," he reminded her. "Therefore, Isi, you're supposed to be on *my* side," no matter what.

Chapter 16

NOEL C. Ocaña could not get the unforgettable bronze woman off his mind. He kept seeing her lush curves, so like those that the artist Annie Lee painted. He recalled Aqua's smile and her gentleness. Just being near her, Noel remembered, caused him to feel calm, like the proximity of the ocean. Therefore, Noel mused, 'Aqua' was the perfect name for her.

Hadn't he been surprised too when she'd called? In his office, he had answered his cell without checking. He'd had no time to still his heart. However, *she'd* had months, and yet she had been nervous.

"Oh God," she'd half-whispered. "I feel so shaky." Then her voice had become a tad louder. "Hi No— what *is* your name?" She'd asked, tired of wondering, "Noah or Noel?"

"*Me llamo Noel* Cristián Ocaña," the r's rolled off his tongue, "but you must call me Noel." The broad-shouldered man with silver strands threaded through the darker hair at his temples also stated, "I can't believe you're the lovely lady I used to know."

"You used to *see* me," Aqua corrected, her own smile audible, "when you visited our offices."

"Okay. I used to see you at the publishing house," Noel acknowledged, his slight Latin accent apparent. "I'll tell you, I thought you were beautiful then, and sweet; you always had a kind word."

"And now," Aqua dared to ask, very nearly holding her breath.

"Well, now," Noel stated, "you have been elevated to goddess."

Aqua chuckled. "You've certainly got a way with words."

Noel felt he'd waited long enough, from late fall to the winter. Therefore, he inquired without preamble, "When may I see you again, *lirio*?"

"What did you just call me?" Aqua asked.

"Lily, in Spanish."

"Why?"

"Well, at my mother's party, you smelled like a flower. So standing beside you, I thought of lilies. Therefore, to me, you are *lirio*."

Wow. Aqua swallowed. "So, do you..." she knew she was fishing, "do you think of me...often?"

Noel's voice was soft. "I do, *lirio*. It is why I need to know when I can see you. So *mi corazón*, my heart can beat normal again."

The man was too smooth, Aqua thought, unable to form a suitable reply. "Uh, what if I'm involved?"

"Cut him—or her—loose, so you and I can become involved."

"What if I don't want to?"

"Become involved?"

"With you..."

Noel chuckled. "Ahhh, but you do, *lirio*."

"I do—what?"

"*Desear*, wish, or want involvement, *conmigo*, with me."

"Did I say that?"

"Not in as many words, but you will, love," Noel chuckled, enjoying the game. "I only need you to tell me when."

"When what?"

"I can see you and become seriously involved with you."

Aqua thought, long and hard, even as she tried to shake the delicious shivery feeling that Noel's words prompted within her.

In the silence, he imagined being wherever she was. He would gently aid Aqua to do what she had all but resolved within her heart to do. "You want this," he told her. "You want *me*. Therefore, if I were with you, I would further persuade you, with my lips, on yours, on your face, your neck, your hands, and your beautiful breasts."

"You noticed..." Aqua said without thinking.

"I did. How could I not? Splendid, every part of you begs for notice."

Aqua fanned herself because she had met candid men, but not one more so. "Are you a poet, No— Noel?"

"I am not," he said and consciously attempted to forget things that made what he'd been thinking of doing to her ostentatiously obvious. He did so because, within minutes, he had a client meeting over drinks.

Aqua had to ask. "Noel, are you married?"

"If I were, I'd *not* have approached you. It is old fashioned, I know, but I do believe in marital *fidelidad*, fidelity." Sensing that he and Aqua shared a connection and knowing that she was also aware of it, Noel pointed out, "You and I have chemistry." And a lot of it!

From the brief conversations they'd had in the past, he knew she was a spiritual woman, so he knew the force of their feelings, crackling like electricity between them, she would not dismiss. She'd not have called otherwise. Therefore, he said, "I wait to hear when we will be together."

Aqua inquired of Mr. Successful, who had said, in the past, that he had hands in a few building companies. "Why would we get that far?"

Noel sounded amused. "Well, because like you, *I* happen to be irresistible—to *you*, beautiful flora."

With a sigh, Aqua spoke the truth. "Noel, I really shouldn't see you. I've been involved. For nine years, and...I'm afraid—"

"You fear *me*? You feel I'd abuse or abscond with your heart?"

"No. But since we're on the subject..."

"*Lirio*, listen, abusive and thieving men need their asses kicked, perhaps more, pardon the expression. Now, back to me; you fear me?"

Aqua sighed again. "I'm more afraid of *us*—together, of what I could feel. I also don't want to risk losing years of involvement."

Noel didn't want to sound derisive. However, he knew Aqua's answer, if truthful, would benefit them both. Therefore, he asked, "*Lirio*, is this 'involvement' going anywhere?"

Something about Noel, his slight Latin-accent, and his old-world mannerisms, forced Aqua to speak the truth. "Not where I wanted."

Noel's voice was soft. "Where do you want to go?"

He seemed so concerned and genuinely interested until Aqua had no choice but to level. "Like many women, I want the altar."

"What keeps you from it?"

Aqua sounded slightly peeved. "I can't go it alone."

"Surely *someone* would meet you there."

"He doesn't—"

"For – get – him," Noel interrupted with an impatient flick of elegant fingers. Noel didn't need the other man, whoever he was, coming between them, not any longer. As far as Noel was concerned, and he said so, "The other man's time is up."

Aqua sputtered, and Noel smoothly continued. "Whoever you *were* with had *long enough*. If you truly want the altar, I can offer it."

Aqua was stunned and said Noel Ocaña spoke like getting married, to the right person was just a matter of making up one's mind. "What about my *heart*?" Aqua asked, feeling something akin to anger. "What about my *dreams*—and my future? What about love, and compatibility?"

"Your heart, *niña*," [neen-ya] little girl, "is capable of encompassing another. And your dreams, of love and compatibility, can become a reality."

"With you, huh?" Aqua near-cynically quipped.

Nevertheless, Noel remained undaunted because he knew Aqua had been hurt and disillusioned. Her amber eyes that should have sparkled with verve and a lust for life said so. "The decision is yours, lovely lady. Therefore, it is for *you* to decide."

Noticing the blinking light on his business line, Noel murmured. "I will call you again, *lirio*. Share with me then what you have decided."

Aqua asked, "What am I deciding?"

Noel Ocaña's voice smiled, as patiently he spoke. "That is what you will tell me. Perhaps you will even allow me to see you. Maybe you will allow us to go for walks, and dips in the moonlit ocean. Then *maybe* on another occasion, you and I will meet, at your altar..."

Noel's voice dropped to a whisper as the light on his business phone pulsed. "I must go, *lirio*. However, I can call you at this number, yes?"

Aqua hesitated before she agreed, "Yes."

Noel chuckled. "I have to admit, *Aqua Mira*, I am now anxious to hear what decision I shall have to live with. We will talk soon, *niña*."

Noel disconnected.

Aqua stared at her phone and realized her palms had gone damp. Well, who could make the kind of decisions that man requested? She wondered, and all seemingly on the spur of the moment.

However, Aqua already had answers. They had been delicately etched on the tables of her heart...way back, when the stars had been flung out into space.

Chapter 17

DYSON passed the marble kitchen countertop at which Aqua sat. Running a large hand over her riot of burnished brown curls, he said, "Move in with me, A."

Sipping hot tea, Aqua spoke. "I'm not your wife."

Dyson closed the stainless steel fridge, an orange juice carton in his hand. "You know how I feel." They had been over it numerous times.

Wearing a leopard-print silk robe with nothing beneath, Aqua nodded. "So you've said. You've never seen a marriage that works."

"So since you know..." Dyson drank and set the carton aside. "Why we gotta keep going over it?"

"Dys, just because *you* have never seen a marriage that works doesn't mean they don't exist." Aqua crossed one bronze leg over the other and unwittingly caused the man's heart to race. "You've never seen the wind, but it exists, and it works." Aqua shrugged. "You know this."

"Be philosophical," Dyson stated. "You still know how I feel."

Aqua slid down from the black marble countertop. Dyson knew how *she* felt too. With her robe billowing out behind, she quickly left the kitchen. Why had she bothered to visit? Why had she let him talk her into doing so? Why had she stayed the night? At least she hadn't given him any. Mr. Self-Centered only wanted what he wanted. He didn't care about her wishes and desires; that fact was glaringly obvious, now.

Dyson saw Aqua's unconcealed body as she went, and felt his loins tighten. Moments later, in his huge bedroom, he turned Aqua to face him. He needed her to relent, let her guard down. If she did, he could make things better between them.

Suddenly talking sweet, Dyson felt he could beguile any woman.

"Where you going," he asked, his voice husky with desire, "that you need to get dressed, on a rainy spring Saturday?" He'd had hopes of getting her into his bed, or in a hot sultry shower, before his kid rose.

Now it was imperative that he do so, because things between them were unraveling. Why? He did not know. He didn't really care, either.

Attempting to hurriedly pull on a top, Aqua felt drained. Lord, was she *tired* of wasting time! She had been at this hit-n-miss mess with Dyson for nearly *ten years*! Now she seriously pondered moving on.

Extracting herself from the man's arms, she went to her drawer, in his enormous cedar-outfitted walk-in closet. She removed all that belonged to her. Back in the bedroom decorated in sleek silver and ebony, she stuffed things in her satchel. She would leave nothing for later, because, Aqua realized, she would go for good when she went.

As she zippered her bag, Aqua tried not to cry. She simply could not do this any longer, and her throat ached with unshed tears.

Believing she was upset about that stupid marry-me mess they'd narrowly avoided, at his bedroom door, Dyson caught Aqua around the waist. Pressing his nude torso to her back, he ground his lower body against hers. At the same time, he whispered. "So you gon leave me, like this?" He eased a hand down, starting at her breast. Pressing his elongated hardness to her, he relieved her of her satchel.

Aqua inhaled. She tried to clear her head while her body responded to Dyson's ministrations, and betrayed her. She felt naked need. Folding her arms over her peaked nipples, Aqua attempted to hide it.

Dyson felt she was powerless to withstand. And placing his lips on hers, he smiled. Gently he lifted her top, and with a sigh, Aqua let him.

When he placed both big hands on her back, drawing her to him, Aqua knew he fought dirty. He pulled her close, and she glowered as he opened his wanting mouth on her. Aqua knew she was stupid to get sucked in, but *oh*, how he was making her want right then.

Sullenly, she allowed Dyson to remove her bottoms. Then she let him carry her into the spa bath. With his lips racing over her like molten heat, Aqua could only murmur, "Not fair."

"All is fair in love and war," Dyson told her, stretching her arms wide along the shower wall, after he'd turned on the water.

But did he love her? Aqua wondered as multiple sprayers pelted her. She also acknowledged, Dyson used sex to emotionally bind her to him.

"You know this is what you need," he said, as his mouth trailed from her wet bountiful breasts to her navel.

Suddenly she saw a blinding light, so like sunlight, but brighter, even though her eyes were closed. Aqua heard another man's voice, which said in unison with Dyson the same thing that Dyson had just said.

Aqua felt both men's knee, as Dyson used his to push hers apart.

Then it was Dyson alone pressing his face to her core as she throbbed with anticipation while water sluiced over her and him. Aqua's heart raced, not so much from the thrill of the act that she was caught up in, but more so from what she had just experienced.

Lately, it seemed whenever she was asleep and dreaming, another man's face appeared. Sometimes, this other man attempted to ride her. However, the other man's face was never clear. She could never make out his features, although something about the man was familiar.

This time, though, she had been *awake*...

Dyson had his face between her legs, and just when Aqua thought she couldn't take any more of his tongue-teasing, he rose. He lifted her.

Like a soldier of old, wielding his sword, Dyson drove into her.

Aqua moaned because, after a few sensual strokes, Dyson allowed her to slide to the floor. As she stood before him, anticipating what he would do next, his weight hit her, his bare chest slammed into her breasts, and he kissed her until she was breathless. Then he took her up. Against the shower wall, pelted by the water, skin slapped slick skin.

Suddenly Aqua wanted to stop because it seemed like someone unseen watched. Turning her head, Aqua sputtered against pelting water. It hit her from too many angles as Dyson continued his thing.

He bit at her nipples, but she refused to nibble his neck. He fingered her anus, but she did not grope him. Instead of her body straining toward his, to receive more of him, as she had in the past, now Aqua felt different. Dyson's mouth covering hers felt wrong. Aqua gagged.

With him quickly thrusting, she nearly felt violated. She screamed suddenly—and not because it was good—then she remembered Isis.

Dyson had known Aqua would scream. It was one of the things that always further aroused him. He covered her mouth with a hand. He kissed Aqua between splayed fingers. Dyson did so because he didn't want his kid poking around while he was poking his woman, even though it seemed, like somehow, Aqua fought him... until he was spent.

SHE watched the rain as feeling wooden, she pulled on her clothes. One raindrop caught her attention. Slowly, it slid down the windowpane.

Then Dyson touched her from behind, and Aqua became cognizant of the heat. Heck, if he thought she was going to lie down for him again. She had been a doormat for far too long.

Aqua looked at Dyson as he stretched out on his huge bed. He smiled, but it did not quite reach his eyes. Why had she never before noticed?

As she picked up her satchel, Aqua felt a teardrop.

The man that she'd once believed was hers watched.

Aqua's tear slid downward, just like the raindrop on the windowpane. Unhurriedly and *unnoticed* it descended, to caress her cheek.

Chapter 18

MORE than a month later, Aqua reached to pick up her ringing phone. "Hello?"

"*Lirio.* What're you doing?"

Recognizing Noel's sexy voice, Aqua felt deliciously naughty. "I happen to be resting, Mr. Ocaña. What about you?"

"The same," he replied, keeping up the routine they'd started a few months prior. He would call, nearly every evening. He and Aqua would begin with the same questions before the conversation took whatever turn it would for that night. Like Aqua, Noel found their chats informative and exciting. "*Lirio,* you're resting from?"

"A long day at work; then errands. Those things were *before* I ran around for Rayfa—who smokes but never carries a lighter. She always asks me, a non-smoker, for that. So, ask me what have I *not* done today?"

Noel chuckled because he had heard a little about Rayfa. Aqua once gave him the abbreviated version when he and she had gone to dinner. Another time, the older woman disturbed a lunch. Noel now knew that Rayfa, like the family members of others, was Aqua's cross to bear.

"Okay, *lirio,* I assume you're lying down—but where? And what are you wearing?" This Noel inquired, as consciously he forgot everything but the buxom bronze beauty with whom he spoke.

"I'm on my bedroom floor—"

"*Por qué,*" Noel interrupted. "Why?"

"I was stretching, getting the kinks out of my back."

"I could be there in half an hour to work you out..."

"You mean you'd work me *over,*" Aqua knowingly stated.

Noel chuckled. "Well, I do have great workout 'equipment.'"

"Oh, don't use that tone on me, Ocaña," Aqua pled. "Not now, not when you're there, and I'm here. It's not fair."

"What do you mean? What does my tone of voice do to you?"

Aqua slid a foot up, then down, a shapely leg. "It makes me *want.*"

"You want me?"

"Yes, *all* of you..."

Noel's accented voice became husky. "You still didn't tell me what you're wearing. I need to see you, in my mind, *lirio*, since we're apart."

Aqua informed Noel as though it were all blasé, "Oh, I'm wearing a nightgown. What are you wearing?"

"Sweat pants."

"With what else, O?"

"My birthday suit. Now about this gown: sleeves, no sleeves? Long, short, tight, loose, what?"

Boy, was he curious, Aqua thought with a smirk. "Sleeveless, spaghetti straps, short, sexy, and shimmery."

Noel bit his lip, picturing all as described. "Your *tetas* visible?"

"Yep," Aqua sounded amused, "cleavage, nipples, and all."

"Ow, you're killing me, girl. Panties?"

"Nope. Not wearing any."

"And you were stretching, you say?"

"With my legs in the air and my naked booty up for all to see."

"Damn, *lirio*! Why must you torture me? Now my cock is rock hard. Hang on, I've got to lose these pants."

When Noel returned, Aqua whispered, "Ocaña, I'm wet, and my titties are tingling, for you. So guess I need you to do me, now."

Noel spoke softly, "Do me a favor since you won't let me come over."

Breathily, Aqua whispered, "Anything."

"Touch yourself. For me."

"Where?"

"There. Just open yourself, and press your fingers to the heat."

Aqua moaned as she did. "Mmm. That feels good."

Noel handled his thick male member. "Open your legs wide, *lirio*."

"Doing it..." Aqua revealed.

"Now use a finger or two," Noel suggested. "Push them slowly inside yourself. Get them good and wet. Now spread that wet to your clit. Do it until you feel mellow. Then get more wet, and spread it backward, to your bottom. Ooh, baby, do it again, and again..."

Forgetting Noel was not physically there with her, Aqua moaned. "I'm doing it, but I need to know. What part of you is this, inside me?"

"My tongue. Now move my big greedy tongue slowly back and forth across your clit. Lick your 'walls' and keep everything *mojado,* wet."

Noel spoke while looking at the head of his shaft, at the glistening mini bubble of fluid. "My cock wants you so, he is crying over here."

"Well…" Aqua's breathing became audible. "Use your finger to smear his tears all over his head."

"Doing it," Noel murmured, concentrating on the act.

"That's *my* wet you feel. Oh!" Aqua breathed harder. "I'm pinching my nipple. That's you biting me."

"Do it again," Noel told her. "Get some of your juices on your fingers and squeeze your whole round tit. Then pinch the nipple again."

"Ooh, that's nice…"

"I know. I'm sucking it. Okay, *espera un minuto* —wait a minute."

"I don't want to," Aqua near-whined.

"I know, *lirio*, but you need to get something the size of my cock."

"What size is your—"

"Big. Now get it and ease it in you…"

"Wait." Aqua fumbled for her dildo. "Okay, back, got you."

"I'm not inside you yet, babe," Noel breathed, "because I work best when you're fully nude; gotta see it all. So drop that dress."

"It's a gown," Aqua corrected.

"Gown-schmown," Noel scoffed, "like it matters. Lose it, now."

"Hang on." Aqua grasped the hem and pulled the whole garment up and over her head. She dropped it aside. Boy, was she excited. On speakerphone, she said, "I did, and gave you a little lap dance."

"Girrrl," Noel growled. "I'm gon tear that mmph *up* if you don't stop. Now," Noel caught his breath. "You're naked and ready, so stick my cock up in you, as far as it will go."

"Oh, Jeee—" Aqua moaned because she had never before had phone sex so erotic. Also, since she and Noel had never gotten past the second base, she would consider this their first time.

"Feels good, right, bae?"

"Oh…yes."

"Now pull me out. And push my rock hard cock back in."

"Oooh, yes. I'm looking as I do it O. You're big, shiny, and wet."

"I am, *lirio*. Do it again. Push me all the way in and up. Now stir my big cock around inside you. Touch every place you can. Yeah, that's it," Noel panted, also 'doing' Aqua on his end of the phone. "Take every inch of me, *chica*. Feel my lips on yours, on your *tetas*. Feel my fingers probing your ass. Feel me fill you."

"Ocaña, you'll make me cum," Aqua groaned in ecstasy.

"That's the whole point, sweet baby," Noel grunted as vehemently he pumped himself. "I give you *todo lo que*—everything I've got."

"I'm pushing it fast now," Aqua moaned, "in and out. Ocaña, I'm wanting you more and—Oh! Ooh! I'm squeezing you with my va-j-j."

"No. Squeeze me with your *pussy*. This is a fast hard screw. No time for clinical," Noel informed Aqua between avaricious pumps. "I'm hitting you hard, girl. Can you feel how I've tilted you up so I can reach your core? My thighs are slapping against you. My balls are getting wet hitting your juicy ass over and over."

Aqua mewled, sensing she would soon climax.

Biting his lip, Noel allowed himself release, too.

"Now, *lirio*..." He spoke, softly, calmly, after a few moments. "I'm holding you and kissing you. Give me your tongue."

Aqua stretched like a contented cat. Aloud, she wondered, "Was it as good for you, O, as it was for me?"

"One thing only would be better."

Aqua longed to know, as languidly she allowed her fingertips to drift over her naked body. "What would that be?"

"Doing it again, e*n personado*..."

"Ooh, that would be extra." Aqua smiled. "We should set a date."

"Name the day and time, and I'm there," Noel promised, "equipment and all."

Chapter 19

AT noon, she stood in the restaurant parking lot. Wildly, spring winds whipped her hair and sienna-hued skirt ensemble about her.

He appeared, seemingly out of nowhere. Touching his lips to hers, he let them linger. Then he quickly turned while catching her hand.

Aqua looked around. Trotting after him, she wondered if someone would notice. There were chic eateries, a collage of stores, including a bookseller, a high-end furniture maker, and a designer boutique. There were scores of cars. too, Aqua thought as she trod double-time to keep up. In the upscale shopping district, anyone might see her...with Noel.

With his long black trench coat billowing out behind him, he turned. Looking much like a mythical warrior god, Noel strode away from the structure that Aqua had assumed they would enter.

They stood at Noel Ocaña's car. The sleek ballsy vehicle induced phallic images. Those Aqua pushed from mind as chivalrously her door was opened. It closed with a muted thud. The owner slid in beside her. Laying his coat in the back, the machine was put in gear. Surrounding Aqua, Smoky Robinson crooned about *cruising, away, from there.*

Aqua did not speak, only braced herself as the V8 engine and 6-speed transmission seemingly launched the ergonomic über car. What was she *doing*? Aqua wondered, jetting off with a man she barely knew, one who had all the potent sex appeal of Cristián De La Fuente, the Chilean actor. What would *Dyson* think?

Suddenly Aqua did what corkscrew curl Cadence often suggested. Aqua pushed others from her mind. Instead, she pondered what *she* wanted.

She noticed Noel's hand on the steering wheel while his other rested on the gear shift. Both were beautiful, with long fingers and neatly tapered, clean nails. On the ring finger of his left hand, Noel wore a large sapphire ensconced in silver. Aqua made a mental note. The man's fingers, although sexy, were not slender. That thought was chased by another. Perhaps Noel had some *other* non-slender member as well.

Aqua blinked. Attempting to override erotic thoughts, she spoke.

"You like that?" Noel replied a moment later, steering with his right hand as he raised his left. Placing his bejeweled hand back on the wheel, a mischievous look crossed his face. "Maybe soon, *lirio*, you'll give me another, more significant ring...one that says lady fantastic loves me."

Aqua stared as her pulse raced. "Now why would I do that?" she teased, running her tongue seductively across her lips.

"Uh..." Noel winked, showing her the gesture hadn't been lost on him. "Because as my *wife*, you might love me. You might even want the world to know I'm all yours. So why not say it with an exquisite ring?"

Aqua told Noel he sounded like a corny commercial.

He told her she was funny. "Really."

The jewelry he currently wore looked like it had descended from nobility down through generations. Thus, Aqua didn't quite know how to respond. Yet she realized that if the little she knew of Noel Ocaña held true, she would be proud to call him her husband. One day, if they made it that far. Reining in wayward thoughts, Aqua decided to simply deal with today. Watching as familiar surroundings disappeared, she tried to relax. She also voiced her curiosity. "Where are we going?"

"I want to show you something." Actually, Noel wanted to show Aqua a great many things, now that he thought about it. He couldn't remember feeling the same way about another woman. Sure, there were plenty of them, models, socialites, and actors. There were tigresses too, who masqueraded as lawyers and unassuming accountants. However, not one captured his attention like the bronze goddess beside him.

Although she felt somewhat nervous and tingly inside, Aqua smiled. She could never have explained why, but she became excited each time she was near or spoke with Noel Ocaña. However, guilt tried to choke her excitement. Maybe she should have been somewhere trying to work things out with Dyson, despite their having been all but off for the last couple of months. The truth was they had been together one year less than a decade. Didn't she owe them that much?

"You want to show me something." Aqua repeated, needing to forget other things, if only for a while. "*That* I've heard before." She wished her heart didn't race and that she was her usual calmer self.

Noel smiled, not taking his eyes from the road. "You've heard that and more, love. However, you will learn to trust me, a little at a time."

Hearing Noel's sensually lyrical voice that conjured up images of warm days and swelteringly sexy nights, Aqua felt her nipples peak. In the effort to ignore the sensation and the gentle clenching of her nether region—a sure sign of desire—she studied the man's profile.

Noel's naturally gold skin was smooth and unblemished, even where he shaved daily. His forehead was flat, and naturally-arching brows gave him a proud look. With his broad shoulders and upright carriage, he appeared regal. Even the silver threaded through the hair at his temples did nothing to diminish his virility. It only heightened the distinguished air about him –and his cologne!

Aqua realized she was staring. She turned to gaze out of the passenger window. As she cogitated on opening it, she also wondered if a bit of air would aid her to diffuse Noel's dark and sultry inviting scent.

Immediately the sunshine became too bright. Through it, Aqua 'saw' the flowing layered chemise she'd have worn, if her recurring daydream were to come true. In the vision, again, she darted aimlessly through the bayou, while on horseback, some man intently pursued her. Abruptly stopping at a clearing, she watched a heron soar upwards, its white body piercing the sky blue, and she wondered if she could outrun her pursuer.

Aqua heard an amused male chuckle, and looking over, she was transported back. Again, she was cradled in the gray leather interior of Noel's car. She saw a polo-necked long-sleeved shirt. Not the white cotton that hadn't concealed her pursuer's broad chest as the sun peered through tree leaves at him. In Noel's car, and not in her dream's copse of trees, Aqua could no longer see the skein of dark hair that started beneath the man's navel. It meandered down golden flesh, to his...

When Noel chuckled again, Aqua asked what was funny.

Driving, Noel glanced over. "I find it good to know that you have the same reaction to me that I have to you," he admitted.

Tearing her eyes from the perfection of his teeth, Aqua noticed her hand. Be-ringed, it fluttered before her, creating a breeze. The sight embarrassed her because Noel guessed where her thoughts had veered.

"Perhaps," he grinned, winsome, "I should up the a/c." He whispered as his eyes flickered over her breasts, "Seeing that we generate heat."

Aqua knew he had seen her nipples through the thin fabric of her crossover top. Therefore, unable to say anything, she traced the outline of her lips with her tongue.

How she *wished* her bayou dream would come true, she thought. Come to think of it, she'd had the dream ever since she'd again met Noel at *Apropos*. Initially, she'd started having the real-seeming erotic dream years back, when on business, Noel had visited the publishing house where she worked. There had always been something about him, something that seemingly transported her to another time and place.

Hastily pulling over and bumping onto the road's gravel shoulder, Noel felt Aqua's reaction to him had been all too enticing. Abruptly stopping, he put his vehicle in park. Heedless of cars whizzing by, Noel reached for the woman who had no inkling how much he *wanted*. She had no idea how much he would give, to have *her*, although there were dozens of women who'd kill to have *him*. With a sigh, Noel forgot others. A confirmed bachelor, Noel forgot that he had been begged, cajoled, and proposed to on numerous occasions. Noel forgot everything but the woman whose perfume lingered, even in his dreams. Gathering her close, he lustfully commanded, "Come here."

Within seconds, Noel's arms surrounded, his sultry scent enveloped, and his lips met Aqua's. His mouth opened on hers, but as hungry as he was for her, he gentled the probing. He didn't want to scare Aqua. However, when her tongue pirouetted with his, the need in him rose, as did his manhood. Then Noel allowed desire to demonstrate.

Aqua moaned, and the utterance caused Noel's heart to stutter. In his arms, engaged in kiss, Aqua tried to fit herself to Noel, and with his hand at her nape and his fingers splayed in her hair, he sighed. Noel rested his forehead on Aqua's and softly he spoke.

"*Lirio,* that was not what I intended to show you—*if* you were wondering."

Aching with desire, Aqua was speechless. While unbeknownst, her doe eyes nearly became Noel's undoing. He released pent breaths as she spoke, mostly to herself. "Lord…have we got to get going!"

Laughter barreled out of him. "Which way?" Noel pointed between them, "This way?" He saw the road, "Or *de esa manera,* that way?"

"Doesn't matter," Aqua waved, "because either way, I think I'm going to be shown more than you *say* you had in mind."

Noel attempted to sound offended. "It seems you don't believe me." He wanted her complete trust, he realized with a jolt.

"I believe…" Aqua lowered her lashes. "There are a few things, now, that *I* just might show *you*."

"Then bring it," Noel challenged, his pearly whites gleaming.

Slowly Aqua reached up to grasp his fingers. "I wish these were *in me*," she whispered, placing his hand on her lap. "Not in my hair."

"Well not your *top* hair anyway," Noel teased, the skin around his eyes crinkling with amusement. Gently, through her clothing, he rubbed Aqua's stomach and told himself not to move his hand anymore, not to feel for what he couldn't have, at the moment. But how Noel wanted!

He somehow wanted to even possess Aqua's soul. That, Noel thought, was strange, for him.

With his lips not on hers, but close enough to feel her warm breath, he spoke. "*Aqua Mira*, you are driving me mad."

She loved the way he called her name. He made it sound musical and thereby conjure images of a turquoise sea. When she spoke, she sounded the total innocent. "Noel I'd stop driving you mad, if I could."

The man's clap of laughter filled the car. "I wouldn't *want* you to stop." His Latin accent again became apparent. "I like feeling insane for you."

Noel dropped his eyes to Aqua's rising and falling breasts, cleavage visible in the v of her blouse. "Push me away, love. Tell me to move it," he whispered, riveted. "Just stop looking like you need me."

Aqua sighed, and Noel's eyes again dipped to her ample breasts, nearly heaving as each breath came quicker than the last.

Suddenly, Aqua couldn't tell Noel Ocaña any of what he'd just suggested, because finally! She had stopped thinking of others. Aqua forgot begging Rayfa and self-centered Dyson. Aqua no longer cared what Cae and Phé might say. Now, she only thought of herself, of what *she* wanted, and of what she knew Noel wanted.

Aqua desired Noel like he claimed he desired her. She didn't know if she'd want the thick, sexy, golden man the same way the next day, but she knew she couldn't want any more than she did right then. So she forgot doubt and self-loathing. "You know what, O?"

"What? *Aqua Mira*, who seldom uses my first name."

She very nearly blushed as she stated, "I look like I need to have you—as you said—because I do." Again, Aqua licked her lips, this time for courage. "So I pray that some of what you want to show me," she said, guiding his large hand down, past her skirt's waistband. "—Is you."

In reply, Noel's mouth quickly and hungrily covered Aqua's. His tongue simulated sex, as beneath her skirt and her thong's triangle of lace, his warm hand expertly opened her. Noel stroked moist flesh, frenzying Aqua, while his other hand fondled a plump breast.

"*Lirio, ascender,* scoot up, *levantate,*" he suddenly urged. His need to be inside her caused him to work the hand he'd had on her breast, around and behind her. Beneath her clothing, he slid that large hand under her bottom. Ravenously, Noel kissed Aqua as his hands worked her, back and front. How, he wondered, had he gotten his mouth on her breast?

Ecstatically, Aqua gasped, knowing the man performed pure lustful magic on her. And she gave herself up to the decadent pleasure.

When finally Noel allowed her up for air, his eyes, like hers, were wantonly glazed. Licking his lips, Noel forced himself to relent, for the time being. But he did intend to touch Aqua so much more. He intended to feel the wonderful weight of her twin orbs in his hands. His rod would ignite places inside her, areas of which she had not been aware.

He spoke with merry eyes. "I gather, *lirio*, that you like appetizers."

Aqua was breathless. "That's what you call what you just did to me?"

Boyishly, Noel winked and put his car in gear.

"Don't you want a tissue?" Aqua asked, wishing he yet ravished her.

"Not a chance," Noel replied, looking for his traffic entry.

"But you'll smell...*me*, every time you move."

"That's the purpose, to stay *enfocado*, focused."

"Oh, so we won't stop again, to finger fuck beside the road."

Noel's laughter thundered out. He expertly zoomed into traffic as he asked a question. "*No lo disfrutarás*—did you not enjoy it?"

Closing her eyes, Aqua placed her palms beneath her breasts. She scintillatingly cupped the fullness, the way Noel longed to, as she said, "I did. I only thought appetizers were usually followed by...a meal."

Within his clothes, Noel's rod jumped. "Well, I guess I'll have to 'feed' you. However, when I take you, *lirio*," Noel pledged, "it will not only be effing that we'll do. We will make the pure sweet *musica* of love."

Aqua's heart somersaulted. Okay, a little at a time, she thought. Then she became aware of Ms. Cole, singing in Spanish. "What a pretty song."

"Yes, *lirio*, this is lovely Natalie."

"What is she saying?"

As he drove, Noel repeated the refrain, "*El dia que me quieras.* I will tell you what this means when it happens –to us."

"Deal." Aqua nodded. "Just don't forget."

"I will not."

Exodus

Beside Aqua, while driving, Noel thought, Man! This woman was so effervescent and sensual when she let herself go, until she caused him to feel electric and alive.

Therefore, he simply had to ask, "*Aqua Mira*, was I really living, before you?"

Chapter 20

IN her room, Isis played *The Poetry Man*, again. In the kitchen, Edna sighed. Ever since Aqua presented that CD, Isis had played it non-stop. When asked why, Isis replied, "Because there's nobody like the Queen."

The short, nearly flat-chested Edna smiled. *That* was pure Aqua; the woman was Queen Latifah's most dedicated fan. Apparently, Isis was too, as glumly she sang, "*Oh-oh, talk to me some more...*"

Edna knew a little sit-down was in order because her youngster was in a blue funk. Talking about it might help. Suddenly, Edna, with the toned, tight body, felt she could kill Dyson. Her baby was blue because he was so pot-stupid and losing Aqua.

Now *Isis* felt she too was losing Aqua, and the child was heartsick. It had been months since Dyson and Aqua had been on. And, Edna dispassionately mused, Dyson was too cock-sure to see the nearing curtain call; yet Isis knew, primarily since she hadn't heard from Aqua in tantamount to a week.

Isis didn't want to lose Aqua, and Edna felt the same way. Striding up and down in her kitchen, with curvy little hips swaying, Edna thought of the Amazon Goddess who loved young Isis. Doing *chaînés*—a series of quick turns on alternating feet on pointes—Edna knew it had been fated for her and Aqua to become friends. How could she *not* become friends with someone as good to her baby as Aqua was?

Edna sighed because all this stupidity had picked up steam when someone named Zenda called Dyson's home while Isis was there. Baby girl said she'd answered, "Because Dad wouldn't get the phone." Then Isis wound up giving the Zenda woman a few choice words.

Hearing this, Edna, a disciplinarian, reminded Isis that she did not condone mouthing off at adults. Afterward, Edna confronted Dyson via phone. Of course, Mr. Self-Important knew nothing, or so he said. Therefore, Edna instructed big daddy to get her Zenda's number. He'd blustered, Edna remembered until she'd cut to the chase. "I've not been happy with your parenting skills for a while. So let's not push this."

Dyson had been furious. He had also wondered aloud if Edna was threatening him with the court system.

"For a relatively smart man Eamon," Edna rejoined, "you can be stupid. Why would I involve them? You think I want some court-appointed clown monitoring *me* and mandating *my* shit because of you? No, honey. You are not that important, not to anyone other than your bimbos, hos, and employees. I'd simply do your big ass much worse."

Dyson didn't know what the vindictive little woman would do, but she knew how to get what she wanted. So he'd recited the number and felt smug. That trollop Zenda was about to meet her match.

Edna grumbled that she was tired of fighting Dyson's battles. However, he didn't care because the younger Zenda thought she was smart. Zenda was manipulative too, but that crafty little witch had never run up on anyone like Edna. Thinking about it, Dyson could hardly wait to hear what would take place. He'd have liked to see a good catfight, too.

Short, hippy Edna did call Zenda. Edna removed a signature, long dangling gem earring, her only adornment ever. Edna informed Zenda that she was Isis's mom. "Dyson's daughter, remember?" Running a hand over pulled back wavy hair, Edna said, "Zenda, you recently called Dyson's home. Oh. Now it comes back to you, unh-huh." Edna advised if Zenda had a problem with Isis, Zenda should have informed Dyson. "But seeing you didn't, *I'm* now in the picture. I gotta tell you, problems with my daughter's *father*, you don't get to take out on my child."

"Or what?" Zenda scoffed and issued a threat. Edna silenced Zenda by briskly saying, "Well, why not meet me? At Dyson's club. Friday, eight sharp. You hosted there, briefly, so you know the address."

Zenda blinked. She couldn't go there! Dyson hated her now; he'd have her thrown out. Anyway, Zenda thought, phone woman was crazy, one of those over-protective mothers. She probably kept Smith & Wesson in her purse, too, right next to her lipstick.

Edna waited, rising *on pointe*. On Friday, she could drop off Isi instead of waiting for Dyson, who was always late. Then Edna could kick the crap out of Dyson's current, simple-minded girl-woman. Then Edna would meet her lover for their weekend tete-à-tete.

"My problem is not with you or your kid," Zenda finally huffed.

"I didn't think it was," Edna revealed, her voice a study in rationale. She further gentled it. "Young lady, I think where my daughter's father is concerned, you will always find yourself unhappy. He has that effect on women, you know."

"Why would you tell me this?" Zenda asked, amazed at the woman's candor. She could feel it; the Edna-woman wasn't being a bitch, but instead trying to help. In her short life, Zenda had learned the difference.

"I tell you," Edna sighed, "because had someone told *me*, warned me, when I was your age, I'd have been saved a world of heartache."

Zenda was flummoxed. She'd thought she had a plan. Now it seemed she might need to alter or abandon it. "Oh…okay," Zenda said hesitantly. Confused, she added, "Thanks. I think."

"You're welcome," Edna replied and hung up. Then she noticed Isis.

Taller, the slender youngster bent to rest her head on her mother's shoulder. Edna embraced the girl whose face often reminded her of an upturned sunflower. Today, however, the sun hid. "It'll be alright, Isi."

Suddenly Isis turned her face into Edna's neck. Crying, the youngster didn't want her mother to know, but the tears wouldn't stop.

Feeling the wet, Edna murmured, "It's okay, baby."

Isis' voice was muffled, "It's not." Forgetting the attempt to be strong, Isis cried, in earnest. "I'm losing her," the girl sobbed. "I am."

"Talk to me." Edna raised her daughter's head. Looking into brown eyes, Edna coaxed Isis to admit how she felt.

"I don't want Aqua and dad to be finished. I don't want her to leave, but she will. Dad won't marry her, and he gets on her nerves, even though she lets him do 'it' to her. And at the club, one of the girls told Gary about that man who wants Aqua."

"I see." Wow, Edna thought, *that* was a lot, but she'd brought Isis up knowing Isis could tell her anything, provided Isis was respectful. "Answer this though, Isi," Edna began, "doesn't Aqua deserve joy?"

"No," Isis replied, then recanted. "Um…yes?" Dejected, she finally said, "I guess so, but what about me? I want to be happy, too."

Edna nearly chuckled because in thinking mostly of herself, Isis was a lot like her father. It was something that Edna and Isis worked on. Edna didn't want missy self-absorbed and dismissive of the feelings of others.

Unaware of her mother's thoughts, Isis spoke on. "Now, Aqua will be gone…just like Auntie Mia."

Oh. So *that* was it. It was worse than Edna thought. She wanted to drop kick Dyson for re-opening that wound. Enfolding her daughter, Edna spoke of her only sister. "Remember the tsunami that caused Mia to drown while on vacation?" Again feeling the ache and the longing for the sister who had also been her best friend, Edna explained how Auntie

Mia had not had a choice. She'd had to go, "But Aqua has a choice. She might choose to go, but she'll be alive, so maybe you'll still see her. Aqua does love you, Isi."

Edna realized her daughter held tightly to her as she continued. "Aqua's loved you a long time, baby. Tell you what. We'll give her time. Then we'll call. How about that? We'll say we want her to be happy—"

Isis lifted her face. "Can we say we want happiness too?"

Edna smiled. "Sure we can. We can say we'd be happy to all remain friends, even if Aqua can no longer be with your father. Okay?"

Isis smiled, and the sunshine reappeared. "Okay. Um…Mommy? Can we buy Aqua a present, too? You know, to help her decide."

Edna heartily laughed while hugging her daughter. "Yes, baby." Edna then recalled something. Although Dyson would scowl at the very notion, Isis actually considered herself more Aqua's child than his.

Chapter 21

NOEL Ocaña pulled back onto the road. He'd intended to take Aqua to his Georgia home. However, they had been waylaid...by desire, the beast that still fiercely rode him.

Noel sighed because he only wanted to bury himself in Aqua. He wanted to sit or lie beneath her as he pushed higher inside her. Noel wanted to hold her hips. Then with fingertips between her shoulder blades, he wanted to press her close, as her naked *tetas*—bazooms would lie flush against his bare chest. He wanted to kiss her and thoroughly immerse himself in her, and he didn't want to come up for air, ever.

Mentally, Noel shook himself. *What* was he thinking, and doing? As he drove, he recalled. He *never* took women to his home. He met them at nice hotels or elsewhere at neutral sites. That way, he could quickly extricate when the fun was done.

Nevertheless, with Aqua, his home was something that Noel *wanted* to show her. The desire puzzled him, yet soon enough, he was pulling up, past the manned gatehouse. He nosed his vehicle through massive stone and iron gateposts.

Aqua read the sign aloud, *"Mislaid Mountain."* Looking around, all she could say was, *"Wow."*

Noel admitted he'd had the same reaction on his initial visit.

At what she guessed was his home, Noel opened Aqua's door. He also wondered, why did he tell *her* things he'd never have told another?

Then he smiled because she sat, in his car, merely gazing about.

Aqua took in Noel's vast, sun-drenched manicured lawn. She also peered past him as he held out a hand. She eyed red ruffle azaleas; their rich color was striking against that of the house. *It* sat up and back on a grassy knoll. Nearer to where Noel stood, a low stone wall was crafted of the same beige stone as the opulent house. There were clusters of gardenia bushes, too, their subtle scent wafting on the crisp spring breeze. In a berm on the front lawn, a profusion of ornamental grasses rose, with tall, feathery, off-white plumage majestically waving in the wind. Aqua looked up at double ornately-carved wood and glass entry doors. Absently, she reached for Noel's hand.

Noting where her eyes landed, he spoke. "Those are Honduras mahogany."

"From one of your companies. Magnificent," Aqua breathed. She then finally allowed Noel to assist her from his vehicle.

Closing her door, he said, "This mountaintop happens to be one of ATL's uppermost that's developed."

Together, Noel and Aqua mounted three stone steps that ran alongside the low stone wall. They mounted others, and others, before they trod a stone path, shadowed by the great house. With lush green grass all around, a profusion of brilliant flowers, and tree leaves shimmering in the breeze, Aqua followed Noel. While scanning the surroundings, aloud, she surmised, "There can't be more than twenty homes up here."

Noel nodded, impressed at her accuracy. "How'd you know?"

"I didn't," Aqua admitted as the wind carried her voice and flurried her beautiful hair. "But to me, it wouldn't be feasible to have more. Then it would no longer feel exclusive or nearly unpopulated."

Moving quicker, Noel grasped her hand. "The vista from up here spans a few states." He pointed. "You can see all sorts of animals, too."

"Ohhh...and is that downtown?" Aqua inquired, awed. It seemed they had walked at least a quarter of a mile.

"It is." Noel nodded, "and those are the Appalachians."

The view, as Aqua and Noel walked around his massive multi-million dollar home, was stupendous. It seemed that even the clouds in the cerulean sky were so close they were attainable. Walking beneath them, Aqua nearly felt dizzy, and so like she was on top of the world. As Noel unlatched a gate, he informed Aqua. Off in the distance, spearing up and into the heavens, were the Blue Ridge Mountains. As Aqua peeked downward, she saw the valley. She had to remind herself to breathe. On a plateau, she stepped backward. Her heart beat fast too because, beneath them, she'd seen a tiny town. Again she peeked from the mountainside on which she and Noel stood. Lord, what a straight perilous drop.

With shining eyes and the sun burnishing her blowing brown-gold hair, Aqua just had to admit, "Ocaña, this is breathtaking."

As are *you*, he thought. With a strong arm wrapped suddenly around her, Noel caught Aqua to him. He loved the feel of her warm body against his as he turned her. They faced the house back. Made of mostly glass, to maximize the glorious view, its windows sparkled in the sun.

Gazing up, Aqua simply said, "She – is – beautiful."

With eyes on the woman, not the glass and stone, Noel agreed. "She is, most assuredly." He extended a hand. "*Venir*, come," he said as they climbed the embankment that led up to the house. When there, Noel steered Aqua to treated wood stairs, and behind her, he too climbed.

Aqua became cognizant of Noel's searing gaze. Without turning, she felt his eyes roam her entire body before they caressed her derriere.

Behind Aqua, Noel thought about stopping and just watching. Heck, the gentle sway of her hips, as she ascended, mesmerized him. Aqua's shapely legs, too, in that half skirt, and those killer heels, the backs of which were only a singular sexy strap... Wow! For a moment, Noel had to force himself to look elsewhere.

Regaining himself, the homeowner ascended. He also thought Aqua smelled lovely and soft. With her scent drifting back to him on the breeze, he realized. It wasn't floral today, but more like…a ripe peach. That was it, with a hint of something heady, for a sensual jolt.

Aqua smelled like Noel's idea of a woman. He thought it, although he hadn't been aware he'd had such, but Aqua was it, fresh and intoxicating.

She stood on the carved teak wood deck that wrapped around three sides of the house. Aqua saw beautiful resort furniture. Its plush ombré cushions bled new grass green, into turquoise and pavonian blue. Each color flowed into the other, like the meeting of earth, ocean, and sky.

Soundlessly, Noel slid back glass doors. Then he ushered Aqua into a large modern kitchen, afire with the splendiferous afternoon sun.

Aqua noticed the sand-hued floor and immediately longed to feel the cool of the large tiles beneath her feet. Therefore, she bent. "I'll just remove these," she said and flicked a sexy slingback from a foot.

Standing behind her, Noel sucked in a breath, because great *goddess* was she a sexy thing! He had been about to suggest the shoe removal, but easy-going and earthy, she'd beat him to it. And Aqua looked sexy as all get-out, extricating her pretty feet from the heeled sandals that fell over.

Willing himself to breathe, Noel slid the doors closed. "I'd like to give you the tour." He warmed to the sudden idea, although he had never done it for anyone other than his mother. "But first—"

They nearly said it in unison. "Let's have something to drink."

Both people's eyes twinkled as Noel gestured to the table, bar height. Surrounding it were high stools with carved backs. "Want a seat?"

Aqua glanced from the table's centerpiece, a clear glass bowl of fleshy unblemished lemons. "Only if I can watch you..."

April Alisa Marquette
81

Noel grinned; because of all things, was this woman about to make him nervous? That would be a first when usually, he rattled women.

"You can do better than watch," Noel advised. "You can help."

Aqua joined him at the little island sink, laughing when Noel slid his soap-slippery hands over hers. She tried not to think of his body that way, glistening and slip-sliding over hers. "So, what are we making?"

"Grand Marnier lemonade," Noel replied. He produced an old citrus juicer. "Grab some of those lemons, and I'll get the kick, *la botella*." He retrieved a liquor bottle, and Aqua murmured because she needed one, "Knife..."

Noel offered a gleaming chef's issue.

"Nice," she nodded. "Pitcher..."

Noel handed it over.

"Pretty," Aqua stated said, eyeing the hand-painted floral on glass.

"I thought so," Noel admitted. He produced sugar and a long spoon. "Looks like it's all you, lady." He watched her work, and it hit him.

She *belonged* there, in his kitchen, in his home, in his *life*!

Noel set stemware on the countertop as his heart crazily danced.

Unaware, Aqua smiled and said, "Those match the pitcher."

Noel nodded and clinked ice into the glasses. Then he dashed in liquor at the same time that Aqua poured the freshly made lemonade.

Offering her a glass, he took the other. With his raised, Noel nodded. "Cheers." He also kissed Aqua mid the mouth, a loud succulent smack.

Gaily, she laughed, sipped, and smaacked him right back.

What a buzz! Before Noel knew it, his hand was behind Aqua, pressing her close. His lips possessed hers as he pried away her glass. She tasted similar to her scent—fresh, zesty, and with a hint of heat.

Moments later, Noel let Aqua go, while he still could. Raising his glass, he gulped. "I'd better show you the house."

"Yes." She eyed him over the rim of her glass, "Because that makes *twice* that you've shown me more than you *say* you intended."

Noel took the woman's hand, gesturing at her drink. "Bring that."

He walked a little ahead of her, and he almost smiled. Berserk that it was, he would just bet...he was a goner, already. She had him sprung.

Noel escorted Aqua around his Mislaid Mountain home. It had honey-hued glossy wood floors and maize colored walls. These seemingly brought the sunshine in, and Aqua noticed comfortable but lovely furniture. Throughout the house, there was artwork and earthenware vases in various shapes and sizes. Some were squat and round, while others were long-necked and regal, exhibiting bittersweet branches.

Aqua realized she and Noel had similar eclectic tastes.

While showing her around, he comprehended that he *wanted* her approval... since she *would be* the lady of the house. *That* he had also just realized. Although the notion made him nervous, Noel did not want to think about being without Aqua, as he had been before.

Unaware, Aqua was awed by the multi-functional gym and running track and by Noel's bedroom. Its cocoa-colored accent wall appeared surprisingly neutral. Aqua glanced at the massive bed perched mid the room. On a plush hand-knotted rug, it sat. Aqua admitted to liking the cream-colored linens. She touched the comforter with its raised feather pattern.

Noel had seen her yawn. Thus, he advised Aqua to sit or lie on the inviting bed upon which a neckroll and other pillows were artfully tossed.

Tearing her gaze from Noel's handprint in the comforter and from all that was luxe and sophisticated, she eyed him. She wondered whether he was trying to seduce her. Lord knew he wouldn't need to try hard. She had been all but man-less for three months, so if Noel simply breathed on her... However, Aqua didn't think he took that route, so gingerly she sat.

Before she knew it, she exclaimed, "I love this house! You've done such a wonderful job decorating it –and those front doors!"

Noel was so pleased he could burst. Reaching for Aqua's hand, he told her something no one else knew. He had not known *why* he'd bought the property or why he'd had the house built because previously, his condominium apartment had been sufficient for him.

While speaking and looking at his and Aqua's intertwined fingers, Noel recalled other women. They always tried to hold his hand, something he dissuaded. Now though, as he brought Aqua's elegant fingers to his lips, he understood. Handholding was part of the closeness equation. "You have beautiful *dedos*—fingers," he told her, eyeing them.

"You too," Aqua softly returned. She watched as slowly Noel leaned in for a kiss. He started at her cheek. His soft full lips met her neck and ear. Then they feathered across her luscious pout.

Sucking on Aqua's bottom lip, Noel wanted to do the same elsewhere. Knowing it wasn't time, he settled for cradling her head and taking her lips captive. Plunging his tongue into the fragrant depths, he managed to ignite an indescribable yearning within them both.

Still, Aqua fought her way up for air. With a hand at her heart, she suggested they see the rest of Noel's home.

He chuckled, knowing she meant to distract him. However, many times, with other women, he had been unbelievably bored. With this woman, though, he didn't think it possible. Amused, he noticed Aqua's breathing and that her large breasts heaved slightly, as her nipples pearled against her blouse, and he had one thought.

If he could just get her naked.

Noting where Noel's eyes lingered, Aqua used a finger to raise his head. "The house," she softly reiterated. "May I see the rest?"

Noel grinned and groaned. "Come on, nosey."

Aqua snagged both their glasses, grateful that Noel could not know how wet she'd become. "I'm nosey," she stated, "but only because you've piqued my curiosity."

Embracing her from behind, Noel huskily murmured, "Have I now?"

Aqua enjoyed the feel of the man curved around her. "Oh, please," she quipped. "Nobody's interested in *you*; I'm curious about this house."

Noel turned Aqua. "I know *la verdad*—the truth, when I hear it."

"And I'm lying," she laughed. "Come," Aqua ordered because they really had to leave Noel's plush, inviting bedroom. "Show me around."

Holding Aqua at her waist, Noel walked behind her, his legs outside hers. "Turn right. Now down these stairs." Freeing Aqua, Noel realized he was captivated. Therefore, he would tell her of his plans.

"*Lirio*, I want you to hear me out," he began as they turned in and out of his elegantly dressed dining room. "I also want you to go with me."

Noel reminded Aqua that she'd said she was off for a few weeks, so that was perfect. He did not admit that he had not known he would feel this way earlier when they'd met at the restaurant. At that time, he'd only wanted to spend time with Aqua; but while driving, the idea struck. Thus, the current tour of his home.

"*Aqua Mira*, I'd like you to remain my guest this evening. If you agree, then tomorrow, *mañana*, I'll take you back to get your car. However, as I said, I *want* you to accompany me. Two days from now, I have plans to visit the barrier island where I have another home." Other homes, plural, Noel did not yet divulge. Truthfully, however, he informed Aqua. He was going to the island because there were things to check on and work to do while there.

As he and Aqua stood in his sumptuous sunken living room, Noel turned Aqua to face him. Lowered, his voice became sensual. *"Aqua Mira*, I ask you to go, not to bed you—though the saints know I want to—but more because you need to see that house too." Noel gazed into the woman's amber eyes. "Since you'll be the lady there too."

Noel wondered why he said such things, with conviction, seemingly on a whim. At the same time, Aqua's heart nearly rocketed from her chest. She forced her gaze past Noel. The sun slipped from the horizon?

Following her gaze, Noel said they should eat. "Got fresh steaks—"

"And we could make a salad," Aqua absently offered, while her mind attempted to wrap itself around Noel's prior pronouncement.

"You know," he stated, aware that she needed a moment. "Your second name is much like the Latin word for *look. Mirar.*" Although Noel did not say it, he suspected that Aqua did just that as a spiritual woman. She most likely looked, and could probably see, on many levels.

Aqua took a seat on the sofa, her and Noel's glasses forgotten. "I'm stuck on what you said," she admitted. "About your other home, and me, concerning it."

"I'm serious, *lirio*." Noel turned Aqua's face toward his. Sure, he longed to kiss her, but he refused, unwilling to cloud her judgment. He would not have her believe his only need was sexual. "I want you with me. I enjoy your conversation and your company, but further, that, I cannot explain. I don't know *exactly* why I *need* you to go. However, I do. So think about it while I make dinner. Then let me know. Heck, tell me tomorrow, in the evening, after you're back in your own surroundings. Call, or let me come up to you." And please, *let me love you*, he silently pled. "You will pay for nothing," Noel vowed. "Just accompany me."

Aqua nodded. Her gaze flitted about as she realized she could not seem to pull herself together now. She wondered if it was the pussy willows in the earthenware vase. She hated that she had seen them. They suddenly reminded her of *Dyson*. He had the same in vases at the club.

Lord, what was she doing? Aqua wondered. Shouldn't she be someplace working things out with him? Nearly ten years had to mean something. Right? Although they had been virtually done since autumn.

Noel intruded on Aqua's thoughts, intuitively inquiring, "What about *you?*" Seated beside Aqua on the comfy sofa, he took her bare foot in his hand. Massaging it, Noel said, "You're thinking, about him." It was why *he* would not sleep with her this evening. Noel had just decided. It seemed that for some reason, Noel needed Aqua to want *him* exclusively.

"Ask yourself, *lirio.*" Noel gently kneaded Aqua's foot. "If *he* was what you needed, would you have agreed to come here, with *me?*"

Aqua stared. "How do you *do* that?"

Noel shook her foot. He also managed to keep his eyes from straying to her ta-tas when sighing, she leaned back. "This is just reflexology."

"Not that. It *is* magic though; I'm calmer, but you read my mind."

"I'm in tune with you. I'm attuned *to* you." Noel spoke slowly. "It is crazy, but I feel I have known you…forever —*por siempre.*"

Aqua caught Noel's face in her hands. Forgetting Dyson, she kissed the man with whom she sat. Afterward, she announced, "I am not gonna sleep with you tonight, Ocaña. But if the offer stands tomorrow, Sunday, I may take this trip with you. Oh, and since my *appetite* ratchets up, just being with you," Aqua suddenly grinned, "maybe now we can do something about it."

With his eyes gleaming, Noel inched his hand up, from Aqua's foot to her calf, and higher, along her thigh. "Speaking of appetites…"

Aqua tapped his head. "Not tonight, Ocaña."

Noel exacted a stunned look. "You *said* you're hungry."

Aqua stood. As she sashayed toward the kitchen, her voice carried. "Don't confuse my appetites. Still," she winked. "If you play your cards right, maybe I'll need an 'appetizer' later."

Alone on the sofa Noel guffawed, remembering in the car. Meanwhile, in the kitchen, his houseguest hummed and opened cupboards. He liked that she was present and felt comfortable enough to make herself at home—when she wasn't brooding over that other cat.

With closed eyes, Noel's mind drifted back to appetizers. Maybe he would munch on cookie in the kitchen, later. She would be nude, and he would be down before her, her supplicant. Her bulbous breasts and rounded belly would be exposed and inviting. Her shapely legs would be over his shoulders, and she would be open. He would lick, kiss, and caress her. Right now, though, he remembered and stood, they had to do dinner *junto,* together.

Chapter 22

SHE would go. Sunday morning, she'd kissed Noel stupid—because she had fallen asleep on him the night before. Then she'd rolled from the restaurant parking lot, leaving him staring because she had things to do.

One of those things had been to call Dyson. Aqua knew he was up. Sundays, Dyson got to the club early. He checked things and just plain annoyed his staff until opening time. While she brewed coffee and vacuumed, she recalled. Sunday mornings Dyson and the twins, Stanton, and Zion, attended a makeshift male coffee clutch.

Aqua remembered that Dyson had taken her call. He'd acted stank, though, as if it didn't matter whether or not he saw her. That had been all she needed. Aqua was sick of the man and his indifference. She had tried to give him, and them, one last chance, when the truth was, she no longer gave a damn. Big, swaggering, self-centered Dyson was the past.

Now it seemed Aqua had been offered more elsewhere. True, she did not know if what Noel said was gospel, but it was nice to hear. And she needed something other than her stupidity to ponder. Aqua felt like she had wasted nearly *ten years* on a man who had only wanted to sex her senseless! How had she thought she could make Dyson want her like she had once wanted him? And to think, Grandma Bayliss had said, 'Baybeh, you can't make someone love you.'

Aqua tossed items into her bag. She was moving on. Moreover, even if Noel wasn't *it*, at least she'd get in a bit of fun, for once. That was one reason she'd agreed to this trip. Aqua was curious too. She wanted to see this 'island' of Noel's and his other home. Right now, the man was interesting, so Aqua wanted to know more about him.

She also wanted to bed the gold-skinned thick-bodied man. Aqua held a nightie to her chest. Just thinking of that sexy scoundrel made her heart go pitter-pat. Therefore, even if Ocaña wasn't for always, she would hang tough now, and she would do so because it was what *she* wanted.

DYSON sat in *Apropos,* which wasn't yet open, although his staff was busy. The kitchen was fired up, and the house band fine-tuned for the Sunday Brunch. Dyson sat with his brothers. It was what the Eamon men did. They got together over Sunday breakfast to discuss things.

Dyson ran a finger around his orange juice glass. Although one of the twins drank a Bloody Mary, the older brother never drank early or at work. It wouldn't do to become impaired, not when he had to think.

Seated in the comfortable booth, glasses-clad Zion noticed Dyson's frown. "Yo Dys, man, you'd better do something, and soon, too."

Dyson lifted his glass. He and the twins had briefly spoken of third hostess Zenda, so he nodded. How, he wondered, had shit come to *this*?

Stanton with the twisted hair said he'd not wanted to mention it, "But the boys overheard A and her girlfriends talking, last time they were in here. The kids mentioned some man, some No—Noble, I think, Noble Steed. Seems this dude and A are getting pretty close."

Dyson slammed a fist onto the table, making china and cutlery clink and jump. Hadn't he known Aqua and Big Spender looked too cozy? The club owner had noticed the Sunday that Spender had his Mama's party.

"Dys, man," Zion voiced pushing up his glasses, "maybe marry her."

Stanton snickered, aware of Dyson's aversion, "Yep, put a ring on it."

Dyson growled that the twins were stupid. He said he didn't have to do anything that drastic. Dyson said he had seen how much Aqua liked playing hostess. "So," he stated, leaning forward so his staff wouldn't hear, and blab. "Since we're opening The Ta-Daa Café, I'll say I'm doing it for her. I may even give her a stake in it."

Stanton and Zion stared. Dyson drank more orange juice, and Gary, the bartender, refilled his glass. When Gary walked away, Dyson spoke. "Don't look like that, y'all. I'll let A come up with the money, like you two, like a real partner. We can even let her sit in on the showcases for the new band. I'll let her do the décor, too." Dyson waved. "Whatever. She'll feel needed." He made a face, "Then she can focus on that, not on me. Then maybe I'll get laid, and my kid can be happy again."

"Isi would be happy if you got some?" one of the twins asked.

They guffawed as Dyson scowled. "Shut up, Stan. You know what I mean. My kid adores A. If Aqua comes back—because I'll tell her this café shit—the kid'll stop sulking, and A can suck my dick."

Stanton and Zion exchanged glances. Their brother really did not know Aqua. She wouldn't trade marriage for a café opening. The woman wanted *a life* with someone who should have been her man.

Twisty-hair Stanton was disgusted, "Yo, don't talk vulgar about A."

Zion agreed, pushing at his glasses. He added, "I'm shocked."

When Dyson asked why, his younger brother did not admit it. However, after years of believing Dyson was the man, with women, it was crushing to discover he really wasn't. Dyson was a blooming idiot.

Stanton twisted his hair. "Yo, I thought we'd agreed to go with our sons' band." His two, and Zion's young man; "The Brothers' Three."

"We did," Dyson reminded his brother, who uncannily enough, was the father of twins. "I mentioned that Aqua shit to keep *her* happy."

"She'd be happy to be wifey'd," Zion retorted, wiping his glasses. "Dys, man, you've got a good woman, and you still running amok."

Dyson's retort was mean-spirited. "Least I do so with *sistas*," mostly.

"Go to the devil," Zion spat. "I love sistas, but I also take care of mine. Nadia got pregnant. So what, she's Columbian? She's cool, and I love her. I did, before Maxwell. Twenty years in, and we're still happy."

"Calm down." Stanton twisted his hair. He did it whenever things went wrong between his brothers. "Dys, just lose chickie who claims she's pregnant —if you're sure she's lying. Then work it out with Aqua."

"There'll be no working it out if A keeps up the marriage shit."

Yet twisting his hair, Stanton asked, "Why are you so against it?"

Dyson growled, "Mama didn't need a man."

Twisty-hair Stanton threw up his hands. "Mama—it's always Mama. She was married, fool—to our father!"

"Well, he died," Dyson mumbled. "Then she was no longer married."

Zion spoke. "Mama had a man, though. Who you think Rucker was?"

"Rucker, the plumber?"

Stanton and Zion guffawed. "He sure was," Stanton finally managed. "When Rucker wasn't fixing other people's pipes, he laid his *own*, right under Mama's roof."

"Yep, the roof that Dys paid for before he got sent up."

"Don't talk about that, Zi," Dyson grumbled, forgetting incarceration.

"Stan," Zion called, removing his glasses, "maybe Dys felt *he* was Mama's husband. He was the oldest and took over when Dad died."

"Maybe so," Stanton with the twisted hair agreed. "Dys, you feel like you've already been married and got nothing for your troubles?"

"Shut up with the psycho-babble." Dyson eyed his watch, "And get out. It's opening time."

"Think about it," Zion advised. "Then there might be hope for you."

Dyson sighed, watching as a staffer unlocked the door. "Showtime," he announced, elated that his brothers stood to let team members ready their table.

Unlike family, patrons would not try to analyze him.

WHY now? Why was she running 'round at darn near midnight because Rayfa couldn't handle her own business?

While driving, Aqua hit speed dial. "Ava."

"Hey Aqua—uh-oh….What's wrong?"

"How do you do that?" Aqua asked her slender, buxom sister. The one whose husband said she looked like a magazine centerfold. Saucy Ava often teased that she and 'smoov' Melvin would never have met if such were true. *She* would have beat Jada to Will.

"How do I do what?" Ava asked.

"How do you know when something's wrong?"

"I know *you*, A. I know too that this has to do with Rayfa."

Aqua hit her wheel. "Why'd she call me, two hours ago—"

"Begging, no doubt," Ava interjected.

"And why is she not where she said she'd be?"

Listening, Ava became disgruntled, as she often did. "That's grimy. Aqua, say you're not out, chasing her, at this time of night."

When her older sister remained silent, Ava guessed what happened. Rayfa called, probably near 10 p.m.—an ungodly hour as far as Ava was concerned. Rayfa had probably also begged for money. Aqua didn't want to oblige because Rayfa needed to go to the big mart for a job, but after getting fired months ago, Rayfa yet wanted time off, with pay.

"Oh, and Rayfa doesn't want you to deposit the money," Ava sarcastically drawled. "Ma Hag has an overdrawn account, and Western Union's fee will eat into her profits."

"Bingo. Now I'm out here combing the hood, looking for her."

"I'd roll home," the younger Ava revealed.

"Is my niece still awake?" Aqua inquired, attempting to re-focus.

"Yep." Ava, the bank manager, jiggled her nine-month-old. "Little Miss Tawny would rather play than sleep, but *she* can sleep all day tomorrow at GB's house." Ava sounded more amused than annoyed. "My Tawny," Ava cooed, "doesn't care that Momma's gotta be up at the crack of dawn. Judging by her father's snores, neither does he."

"Let Melvi-o alone; he gets up before you." Aqua spoke over her niece's chatter. "Tell sweet-pea Auntie loves her— Oh, hell no."

Ava spoke quickly. "You must have run up on Rayfa. Tell Ma Hag this is the last time! Quit allowing her to pimp you, A. Bye!"

Aqua jerked to a stop in the pot-holed parking lot of the Danceria. The run-down titty bar was the gathering place for those with whom Rayfa readily identified, saddle-bagged strippers, and men who could care less. Aqua jumped from her car. "Rayfa," she called, dodging a drugged-out man. "Ray-fa."

Leaning into an old car resembling the seventies Bat-mobile, only Rayfa's scrawny behind and spindly legs were visible. In a scrap of fabric she considered a skirt.

Striding through the littered lot, with her head pounding due to anger, Aqua grabbed her mother's skinny arm. "You working here now?" Sliding down some pole. "Is this why you weren't where you said?"

Rayfa looked dazed as she was pulled from the fat man's window. "Hey baby," she slurred. "You got a light?" With an unlit cigarette between her lips, Rayfa forgot the curious man. "You got *that* for me?"

Over the distant, angry wail of a police siren, Aqua could have yelled, because why hadn't her drunken mother gotten the money from Chubby in the car? Aqua could have yelled too because Rayfa didn't care that she had gone to a lonely ATM after dark and could have been accosted. Rayfa didn't care that on narrow mean streets, Aqua had been inconvenienced. Nor would it matter that Aqua should have been readying herself for a trip in a few hours. All Rayfa cared about were the crisp green bills in her daughter's pocket. This Aqua realized with startling clarity. Rayfa only wanted the means to get sloshed.

Shoving money into Rayfa's hand, without a word, Aqua turned. She, Ava, and Grandma Bayliss had said it all before. Suddenly Aqua knew. She could no longer be Rayfa's enabler. Therefore, as Rayfa called out, "Love you…" without responding, Aqua drove off, because as Ava had alluded, Aqua was no longer willing to be pimped, by anyone.

AQUA turned over when her phone rang. What time was it? Five forty a.m. Oh, Lord. They were supposed to leave at six a.m.—in twenty minutes! She snagged her cordless. "Hullo."

His voice was soft, soothing, and intimate. "Hey, *niña.*"

Aqua immediately felt like crying, although she didn't fully know why. "Ocaña." She sighed, recalling they were to be on the road by six.

April Alisa Marquette

The timbre of his voice remained soothing. "Talk to me."

"I should have been up," Aqua explained, "but I was sleeping."

He knew she had a lot going on, so he asked, "Hard night, bae?"

Again, Aqua sighed because the man was too sweet. "You don't know the half." With a headache hovering, she wanted to burrow back beneath the covers after mentally suggesting he go without her.

"Look," Noel softly began, sensing something was amiss. "I wanted to see if we were still on, but you need time. You know, we can always go later. So take a shower, maybe aspirin too. Then *llámame*, call me."

Aqua was torn. Noel wanted to get an early start. Now he'd have to wait, on her. It was the wrong way to begin. "Can I decide not to go?"

Noel told the truth. "I'd feel bad. I wanted to walk the beach holding your hand. I wanted to see your eyes in the moonlight and at dawn."

Aqua melted. Lord, did she hope this man was the one! She spoke, putting her pedicure-pretty feet on the floor. "I'll be ready in half an hour." She wondered if she had time to make java for a boost.

"No rush," Noel said. "I'll be waiting, with pastries and coffee."

Aqua had to ask, "Hot, *gourmet* coffee?"

Noel laughed. "There is another kind?"

"And you say some woman hasn't snatched you up yet?"

"Well, there *is* one who *might* make an offer."

Aqua chuckled. "I suppose you'll see her today, huh?"

Noel's smile was audible, "If she doesn't back out on me…"

IN the rear of a hired car, on the hours-long ride to the ferry, Noel told Aqua about Georgia's Barrier Islands. They were also called the Golden Isles. With his laptop open, Noel suggested a visit to the Marine Sanctuary for a dive. That way, he didn't say, he might get to see her in a bikini. Good googa-mooga!

Looking delectable in a white knit, sleeveless v-neck, and flowing peach pants, Aqua wrinkled her nose. "No fishing for me, thank you."

Darn. Oh well. Noel asked if Aqua knew that black sea bass and snapper inhabited Georgia and Florida's shallow coastal waters.

"I knew. I also know those waters are the calving grounds for the endangered Northern Right Whale." Aqua digressed, "Now let me get this. You have an office on St Simons, and you've visited Blackbeard Island. I've always wanted to do that, and you have a home on Sapelo."

"I've a home on little-known *Miraunga* Isle, too," Noel divulged. He wondered, again, why'd he tell *her* things he'd previously kept close?

"You mentioned that." Aqua's eyes narrowed because something about *Miraunga* sounded familiar. Suddenly she wondered, why was the morning sun so bright? It became blinding, although Noel didn't seem to notice. Calmly, he read the *Brunswick News* online.

Aqua tried to ponder the unspoiled beaches that she and Noel might explore. They were only accessible by boat in the early morning. Wow. This whole trip would be a welcome step back in time, Aqua thought. She would visit the Gullah community that Noel had become part of since he'd become an island property owner. It was the community that Grandma Bayliss had been part of, before getting married, years ago.

Aqua also wanted some of what was said to be the best Sturgeon caviar in the world, yet she had to close her eyes because the sun was brutal. Aqua wanted to stop breathing heavily, too like she had been running, because contrary to what she suddenly felt, she had not been chased by –she knew not whom, or what.

MAN, was he getting carried away. This Noel thought as he and Aqua rode, but he couldn't help it. Aqua was *it*. For him, there would never be another. Noel didn't know how he knew, but he realized there had not been another, not before her. Sure, he'd laid and played with women. Still, his heart had been what? *Imprisoned.* He had never felt as others did when with someone. His soul had been locked away, until her.

In the past, Noel recalled, Aqua had indeed stirred something within him. He'd thought it was simple desire. Aqua *was* gorgeous, impeccably groomed, with her shapely ass and come-suck-me tits, but, Noel realized, there was more. That more had touched him, even when he hadn't had time to get to know Aqua as he now intended. Back in the day, he'd have gotten her naked. Noel would have slid all over her, but that would have been it.

Ugh! Noel now knew why he had been called callous, remote, and cold. He'd heard variations of that theme when women all over the world had done all they could, to make him feel, and he had not. Every so often, he had been slightly amused, but he had mostly felt old, as time itself. Therefore, for him, sex had become a pastime and not even an exciting one. Noel had indulged, to get through to the hours when he could work, like a demon. To keep his mind off...what? He couldn't figure it out. Even though now his heart and emotions were unfurling. Noel no longer felt so *caged.*

The man wondered about one thing, though. Why the weird dream that had a few deviations? In it, he was always on an island, tromping through a swamp, or a copse of trees, cypress to be exact. He ran too, like he was being chased or like he searched for someone. Other times he felt euphoric as brilliant sunlight flooded a clearing. Often powerfully bright, the sunlight from his dream blinded him, but he could always feel. Someone waited for him, and he often felt overjoyed to be nearing that person. The one that he could never see.

Noel forgot all that. He told himself that he had to stop wondering. Would Aqua like the island? Noel reminded himself that he couldn't order a particular reaction. He had to let things be. Whatever would be, would be.

Now *that*—had someone said that eons ago?

But really, what if Aqua didn't like the island? Moreover, what if she moved from him back to that other cat? Noel tried to forget it. But he couldn't. If Aqua gravitated back to Mr. Selfish, Noel would kill him.

Now, where had *that* come from? Noel wondered because he was laid-back. With all he had going on—his business ventures, the women chasing him, and his renovation projects—he had no cause to hate. Noel didn't have the time. *And* killing was extreme, *but* he *would* protect what was his.

SUNDAY Brunch progressed, but Dyson could only think of Zenda. Feeling moody, he closeted himself in his office—the scene of the crime.

Why had he been so stupid? When she'd come to his office after most everyone had vacated the premises, Dyson should have sent her home.

It was Aqua's fault. If she hadn't been off somewhere, trying to make a point, he would not be in trouble. And she'd called this morning. Aqua had probably wanted him to say he missed her. Heck, since she needed time, he did too, now, and quite a bit, to fix the situation.

If he hadn't looked at Zenda after realizing she had been naked under that coat, Dyson could have gotten away unscathed. What kind of nut was Zenda anyway, removing her clothes before coming to his office?

Dyson scrubbed his hands over his face. Now he nearly hated to remember. Yet when it happened, Dyson hadn't felt bad. His pulse had quickened as he'd risen. The club owner had walked around his desk, and Zenda's eyes had glimmered. He should have registered then that she was wicked. Instead, he had inhaled, and she'd smelled like pineapple and pure sin. Now he felt stupid because kissing was personal, and who had Zenda kissed before him? Who had the skank let bend her into pretzel shapes? Now she hounded him, calling his workplace, his home, *and* she had gotten into it with his kid. Then he'd had to go 'round with Edna. *She* had jumped to her daughter's defense, and to Aqua's.

Edna didn't know he felt terrible. He'd had to go to the doctor, and Dyson hated doctors. They were the people who had not saved Lena, his mama. However, Dyson's privates had been on furious fire!

Now he had to slather some greasy, Ben Gay-smelling cream on himself, to kill all the little bugs. He now had to use a baby doll comb, on his wiry private hair. That hurt, but it had to be done, twice daily.

Now Dyson only wanted to *off* Zenda, third and ex-hostess, who claimed she was so sick. She was hinting, but he would not get taken. That little stunt wanted money. And Zenda really could turn out to be pregnant. But she needed to go see the dude who'd given her the crabs— the ones that were now eating Dyson alive. Zenda kept talking baby, but it wasn't his. That, Dyson had told her.

Then the trick had threatened a paternity test. Well, young Zenda could pay for it, whenever, but that stunt would wind up with a surprise. Dyson shot blanks. He was no longer making damn expensive babies.

Dyson Eamon had had a vasectomy, years ago.

He had done so when Isis had been three, not long after he'd met Aqua. With the way he'd been cruising up in Aqua's plush pussy, he had known it would only be a matter of time before she turned up pregnant, birth control or not. Dyson hadn't wanted any of that. He wasn't that crazy about kids, and another one would have cramped his style and ruined what he and Aqua had. She'd have turned mean, and unsexy. The kid would have been crying and in the way. Two kids would have made him feel old, so although scared, Dyson made the appointment.

He got snipped.

Still, with Zenda sweating him, now, his secret was nearly blabbed. Dyson wondered, what would Aqua think? She wanted a kid, his kid. Oh, well. Dyson sadistically scratched his burning balls.

He forgot Aqua because she would get over it, like he would one day get over this fire ball crap. Aqua would have to, if she wanted to be with *him*. Heck, in this little topsy-turvy triangle that he had gotten himself into, Dyson thought, *he* was the only one that mattered.

Chapter 23

SHE looked up. "So this is Cricket Hill," she murmured as warm winds waved her hair. Aqua saw crepe myrtle and dogwood. Pink and white oleander hugged the large old house with the wraparound porch.

With the sun warm on her back, Aqua looked about her and remembered. Yesterday, off the ferry, she had been led to a beachfront condo. Handing her the key, Noel had explained that she should settle in, then see St. Simons Island, quite the place. He'd pressed his credit card into her hand, telling her to shop if she wanted. A driver would take her.

Noel had gone to his office after suggesting they play tennis when he returned. Or, he'd said, he and Aqua could miniature golf or go to the lighthouse while soft breezes blew in from the sea. The choice was hers.

However, the couple had gone to dinner. She'd gotten her caviar. Afterward hand-in-hand, Aqua and Noel walked the moonlit beach. Carrying her sandals and trekking along in racing and receding water, Aqua recalled. Never had she and the other man gone to the beach. Forgetting that, Aqua and Noel chuckled as her long skirt became drenched. Clinging to her legs, it impeded movement. So, swinging her up into his arms, Noel suggested heading back. At the condo, they'd rested, spooned together, before getting an early start to Sapelo Island.

Now there, Aqua eyed the moss-draped oaks that shaded the lane on which she and Noel stood. She smelled fragrant island flora. And she felt... like she had come *home*. Blinking away inexplicable tears, Aqua was pulled up the wooden steps of the antebellum house. Well cared for, its shutters were pristine, and its glass gleamed. When Aqua stepped into the cool of the grand foyer, the place seemed to whisper, *welcome...back*.

"Genieee!" Noel near whistled, startling Aqua. Passing the large curved staircase, he strode toward sunlight. It streamed through a doorway at the long hall's end. "Genie, love," he called, "Papa's home."

Was Genie Ocaña's *child*—one that he had not mentioned?

Noel stopped walking because silhouetted in the sun was a small person who screamed and hurtled forward. Noel crouched and whirled, causing a denim skirt to billow. "Meet someone special," he whispered.

Aqua watched as with a wizened little face and wrinkled hands, the tiny brown woman extracted her loving gaze. The small woman wore a milk-white bandana and cap-sleeved blouse. When set down, she smoothed her apron and inquired, "Now what have we heeyah?"

"Genie, this is *Aqua Mira*. Aqua, love, meet my Genie."

Aqua stepped forward as Genie proudly spoke. "I am *Eugenia*. Like the famous author who wrote books about these Golden Isles."

Aqua said she'd heard of Eugenia Price, who had indeed written plenty. Ms. Price created *Unshackled*, "My Grandmother loved it," the dramatized radio broadcast. "And it's nice to meet you, ma'am."

"I'm ret pleased too," pint-sized Genie stated, reaching for Aqua's hand. "Call me Genie. I takes care of this big fine boy." She gave Noel a grin. "Well, I did before *you* got heeyah." Genie's eyes twinkled. "But honeh, that's yo' job now. I'll jest keep cooking if yuh don't mind."

Genie turned, pulling Aqua toward the sunlight. In a beautiful, old-fashioned kitchen, they passed windows, a square wooden table, and chairs mid the floor. Retrieving a spoon, Genie spoke. "I was cooking for my love there. Knew he was coming and bringing a surprise—and heeyah yuh are! Such a beautiful gurl you are. Set." Genie gestured. "Yuh hongreh?"

With a shoulder against the doorframe, Noel grinned. "Genie, love, my *lirio* can't get a word in edgewise."

"Shush now." Genie waved. "Disappear. Come on back for her in a while. Ret now, we getting to know one another."

Aqua smiled, and Noel said, "*Lirio*, I'll soon show you around."

Aqua had never seen him so happy, so relaxed. Remembering what happened when he meant to show her anything, she blushed.

Noel blew a kiss and turned. "Holler, bae, if you need me—"

"He'll be in that office," Genie finished. "All he do is work...but maybe, with you heeyah, we get some fun! Maybe some *babies* too, eh?"

At the table, Aqua heartily laughed. "Genie, are you being bad?"

With hands clasped as if in prayer, Genie spoke. "I am, baby."

A man appeared at the kitchen door. He was the lean one who had taken Aqua and Noel's bags and pointing, Aqua informed Genie.

"Oh." Wearing terrycloth slippers, Genie turned from the stove. "Want yuh to meet someone." Pulling the multi-paned door open, the small woman turned from Long 'n Lean. "Ms. Aqua, this here's Jethro Tulle [Tool]." Genie turned to the gaunt-cheeked sinewy man whose tee shirt sleeves had been hacked off, probably with the machete he'd set beside the door. "Jet, meet Ms. Aqua, Massa's sweetie."

Aqua nodded, and the man's dark eyes flickered over her as he inched a bony hand out for the glass that Genie offered. Guess he was thirsty, Aqua thought, from hacking at that palmetto out back.

"Jethro's people, the Tulle family's been here at Cricket Hill near 'bout a century, or more," Genie stated. "Ain't that right, Jet?"

The man gulped, handed the glass back, wiped condensation onto his worn jeans, and never said a word. With a nod for Genie and a seemingly disdainful eye flick for Aqua, away he strode.

Noticing Aqua's look, Genie cackled. "Don't mind him. He don't say much, but he works 'round heeyah from sun-up to sundown."

Oh-kay, Aqua thought. She would remember to stay out of that weapon-wielding man's way. Aqua forgot the dour-faced man-Friday to say, "Genie, something smells really great. What is it?"

"Got my oven going since ol' Massa loves my cookies."

Aqua appeared puzzled as she asked, "Why do you call him that?"

Genie whistled with laughter. "Yuh worried? Gurl, don't be. That young fella up them stairs is so high-handed—when he's working—which is always, until I talks to him and he waves me off. I threaten to set this place afire, and still he waves me off. *But* when he ain't working, he's sweeter than sugar in the cane. So one day I teased him about his ways, called him Massa, on account of how he owns this place and others. The name stuck. Jet calls him Massa too, but we mean no harm."

"I didn't think so," Aqua admitted, semi-stunned that long 'n tall could even speak, much less use a term of endearment.

"Taste," Genie ordered and slid browned cookies onto wax paper.

Aqua did. "Mmm. Different, delicious. What's flavor is that?"

Puffing her small self up with pride, Genie grinned, and the sun shone right out of her. "Come wit' me," she said, inspired. As she ambled to the back door, Aqua hoped they would not run into Mr. Tool Shed.

Out in the sunshine among fragrant flora, Genie pointed to a vast funny-looking plant. "Is that a cactus?" Aqua inquired.

"Sho is. It's a prickly pear cacti." Genie handled the fruit. "Can eat it. With it, I make jams, teas, remedies, and so many thangs."

"This flavored the cookies," Aqua surmised. "I'm impressed."

"Good," Genie headed back toward the house, "because I'll show yuh how to make 'em. But first, take this here tray on up to Massa—I mean Mr. Noel." She winked. "Then later, you take some sweets out to Jet, and we'll tell him you made them. He be yuh friend for life."

April Alisa Marquette
99

Aqua frowned. As she listened to Genie tell her that Sapelo had once been a haven for slaves, Aqua began to think...

"Some folk even have the nerve to say this place paradise," Genie stated. "But I say paradise nowhere on earth." Genie folded a napkin. Pouring lemonade, she spoke of people she'd known. "Lot of them gone now. Some took to the ghost walk." Genie shrugged. "Others just up and moved 'way. But me and my friend Jet, we's heeyah until. And you and he," she nodded at Aqua, "will become ret good friends. You'll see."

Aqua continued to think. Indeed, she had heard of Sapelo Island. However, she did not know if she wanted a friend who appeared that much like...a seasoned killer.

Just before sunset, Noel found Aqua. Grasping her about the waist, he said he was stealing her away. He took her on a tour of the well-appointed old house, the workout gym he'd installed, and the meticulously cared-for grounds. Outside, walking beneath moss-draped ancient oaks, Noel explained about the coastal salt marshes. He pointed out flora indigenous to the region and explained how Sapelo Island was a veritable reservoir of African-American culture, customs, and songs.

Then knowing Aqua had to be hungry, he suggested they head back.

FOLLOWING the lovely but straightforward meal that Genie prepared, Aqua only wanted to lie down. She hadn't realized she was so tired, not until she again got in her beautiful room. The one that Noel had shown her earlier. Eyeing the mahogany four-poster bed, the drapes, and the delicate rose-dotted wallpaper in the bath, the houseguest sighed.

After a relaxing soak, Aqua padded across the plush rose-colored carpet. She thought about her host. Grabbing her flowing mint-green robe that matched her gown, she exited to find Noel.

As it was, he was coming to meet her. "So you're all ready for bed, I see." His eyes traveled over her. Wow, did she look and smell tempting. With her girlz barely concealed beneath that thin fabric, he could see stiff peaks, and he wondered. What would she do if he bent to suckle one through her soft green silk?

Noel recalled, he hadn't ever been a breast man, not before. Legs and bootay had been his thing; the bigger, the better. However, he forgot that and that somehow he had known that even when Aqua went to bed, she looked alluring. Noel had to, so his eyes could meet hers as he reached for her hand. He tried not to inhale Aqua's intoxicating scent. The one she'd used to cream herself. She was unaware, but for a few moments, he'd watched her do so before he made himself turn away. However, not before he had seen more than he needed. Now, the scent reminded him...

Aqua had been gloriously nude and bent, with a leg up on the side of the tub. She'd massaged fragrant cream into her calf. With his freaky self, Noel had imagined standing behind Aqua while rubbing big boy between her slicked butt cheeks. When she'd gotten to her breasts, Noel had left. He couldn't take watching Aqua's beautiful hands travel over her bronze skin. That had aroused him as much as the goosebumps that appeared as Aqua's nipples had stood in stiff little teasing peaks.

Noel could not have known that while buttering herself, Aqua had thought of him, of how it would be to have his hands traipsing over her, his and her mouth fused, as his member pushed into her. Therefore, he'd turned, while he had yet been able. He left as soundlessly as he'd come.

Noel almost wished he hadn't gone to make sure Aqua was okay. Then he'd not have that wickedly arousing picture etched in his mind. Noel had knocked, but he'd received no answer. He should have turned, instead of entering Aqua's private quarters. Then he would not have seen her, silhouetted in soft light, with her hair atop her head.

"So you need nothing," Noel queried as Aqua stood before him, the flare of her hips beckoning. "No bedtime story? No warm milk, no me?"

Aqua chuckled and leaned to place her arms around Noel. With her lips and curvaceous body pressed to his, she spoke. "If I wasn't so tired, I'd let *you* be my nightcap." She kissed him, "But I need rest, tonight."

With his male member pressed to her, and his large arms encircling Aqua, Noel placed one hand on her back. With the other, he squeezed her derriere. Then his large hand moved to Aqua's thigh. He gently brought her leg up as he bent her backward. With his lips pressed to her neck, Noel murmured, "You're playing with *fuego, lirio*... with fire."

He backed her against the wall. With her leg yet raised, Noel stood between Aqua's thighs. Grinding himself against her, he wanted her to feel just what she would be missing, and with longing, Aqua moaned. Although challenging, she eased away. Yet Noel reached for her, held to her.

She spoke of desire. Still, Aqua pushed off the man's attractive physique while allowing her palms to linger on his expanse of chest. "I hate to leave, but you'd be too much for me tonight, and I wouldn't be enough for you. So I'm saying goodnight now because if I pull this gown up—"

"It'll be on," Noel finished as his male member strained within his pants. "I'll put this in you." He massaged his bulge. "I'll give it to you good," he promised, catching at her robe and inching it upward. Pressing himself to her, he said, "You will *mendigar*, beg me."

"For more, or for you to stop," Aqua asked, seeing them intertwined.

Noel shrugged. "It will be your choice." He visualized himself hovering above her, right there, on the hallway floor. He could see himself driving into her lush, warm body, drowning in her. He would cover her with his hands, his mouth, his tongue; he would slather her.

Aqua didn't miss the heavy-lidded look as deftly Noel's fingers curved around the back of her thigh. Quickly though, she stepped away. Softly she said, "Goodnight, sweet man."

Noel caught Aqua's hand as she turned away. He kissed it but let her go. The thickset gold-skinned man thought about having put Aqua in the most feminine room. He had done so and had not insisted that she sleep in his room. He was trying not to push up on her, even though he wanted her, mightily. Still, she needed time…because when they finally came together, she had to be free.

Therefore, for now, Noel reminded himself as his nether region throbbed, he would allow his lily to adjust. He did not want her to ever regret being with him, in his home, one of the many homes that would be *hers* also, because he simply wanted her –for *life*.

HER bedroom was lovely, the bed comfortable, and after removing her robe, Aqua drifted quickly.

With the window open, the filmy sheers fluttered in the breeze. As they rose and fell, moonlight, pale and milky, pooled on the floor. The luminescence spilled over the furniture, and waking, Aqua noticed. Her bed was also swathed in moonglow. Aqua heard something then, other than the rustle of trees, bushes, and the night.

There it was again, the sound, and it was inside her room, she realized. Despite her frightened fluttering heart, Aqua again heard the barely discernable rustle. Fearful, she allowed her gaze to slowly wander beyond the window to the wall beside it. Afraid to turn her head because whoever was there might see, Aqua silently prayed they'd not realize she was awake.

For a moment, Aqua wondered if it could be Noel checking up on her. Instinctively she dismissed that idea. It was *his* house—for crying out loud—he didn't have to sneak anywhere. Moreover, *his* presence was warm. With the chemistry and the heat they generated, he'd *want* her to know he was there. He would never pretend otherwise. Right?

Wanting to bolt, but knowing she might be caught before she reached the door, Aqua attempted to breathe as though she yet slept. She also strove for calm, so she could think. Feeling terrified, her eyes passed over the wall beyond the window to the closet's closed door. Her gaze slid beyond to the enormous armoire.

Aqua sighed because sometimes she could be such a jittery chicken. However, that was when she glimpsed something—or someone! With her heart racing again, she realized there *was* a three-dimensional shadowy form in her peripheral. What if it was Mr. Tulle?

The form stealthily moved to stand beside the armoire. As Aqua watched, the figure stepped back and braced itself against the wall.

Before Aqua was aware, she screamed. Her eyes widened in terror as quickly the figure loped over to stand above her.

Leaning toward her, a knee was placed on the bed beside her, and she attempted to scream again. She had to draw the attention of the house's inhabitants. Yet to her horror, all she could manage was guttural gagging.

"Shhh," the shadowy form prompted, and Aqua's mind reeled because something about it was familiar! It should *not* have been because she was Lord only knew how many miles from her home.

Truly terrified, Aqua realized if she did not get someone's attention, she would perhaps be raped or killed. So gearing up to scream, with the shadowy figure kneeling on the bed, she thrashed about, fighting.

The figure turned as the door was thrown open.

Half dazed with terror, Aqua's eyes flew to the door, to the person who entered, as simultaneously he called, "*Aqua Mira.*"

Ocaña! Aqua's heart frantically beat, like the wings of a captive creature, because he walked into the equivalent of a trap!

Unaware, again Noel called out, as quickly he covered the distance between Aqua's bed and the door. With one last long-legged stride, he bent to take Aqua in his arms; but as relieved as she was to see him, yet she was panicked. Inside, something screamed, because *where* was the other man? Hiding, he could re-appear and hurt Noel.

Struggling up, Aqua frantically whispered. "He's still here!"

"Who?" Noel asked, not comprehending the danger.

Aqua turned Noel, who insisted on holding her. "Around!" she hissed. At least if the man hurtled back, Noel would have a fighting chance.

Reaching a shaky hand out to the lamp with the rose voile shade, Aqua felt deflated. Yet she hung on. "He's gotta be caught."

With the light now on, Noel dashed around the room. He threw open doors, looked in the bathroom, the closet, and even in the armoire. The homeowner checked under the bed and peered into the large fireplace. Then at the window, he scanned the sill and the floor. He raised the window high enough to look down and out. "There's nobody here, bae." He returned to Aqua, who stood beside the bed, an obelisk clutched to her chest.

"And good for him too," Noel smiled. He helped the rapidly breathing Aqua to sit, "Because you'd bludgeon him to death with this."

Noel pried her fingers from the heavy decorative object. When it was back on the nightstand, Aqua shook her head, because that man— whoever he was—had to be nearby. Now, she would never sleep.

"He's here still," she whispered with eyes on the door. "I know it."

"Baby, had anyone been in here when I tossed that door open, I would've seen him, and I'd have *romper,* smashed his trespassing ass."

Immediately, Aqua needed to know. "Why'd you come for me?"

"I heard you." Noel crossed the carpet. "You sounded warbled. Like when somebody sleeps and tries to scream because of a bad dream." Noel sat down and put his arm around Aqua. "I knew you needed me."

His weight on the mattress was comforting, especially when Noel pulled her close. With lips on her forehead, he mentioned the new carpet. As Noel spoke, Aqua realized he was right; it was so thick. There *would* have been footprints, other than those of his bare feet. "Had there been someone at your bed, I'd have seen him, but I only saw you, thrashing and wrapped up. These bedclothes had you mummified."

Perhaps Noel was right. Clinging to him, his warmth seeped into Aqua. Maybe she'd *dreamed* the shadowy figure that seemed so real.

Noel spoke quietly to allay Aqua's fears. "There'd have been some sign at the window too. It would have been higher had someone escaped. Below, the rhododendron bush would be mangled, as would anybody falling from this height. And I'll tell you something else…"

Noel stood, because being so close, on the bed, with only a thin layer of silk between them, conjured thoughts for which now was not the time. "Maybe we should get some tea downstairs. Then I'll tell you."

Aqua nodded. Tea would be good because although the evening was warm, she was freezing. A hot toddy would chase the chill. Pulling her robe, Aqua eased her arms in and stepped into her slippers. Yet apprehensive, she asked if Noel would turn on lots of lights.

The man squeezed her hand. "Sure, bae. Those up here are already on." He winked. "I wanted you to easily find me if you'd wanted."

Downstairs, in the bright old-fashioned kitchen, Aqua sat while Noel prepared tea. "Is Darjeeling okay?"

She nodded, rubbing her cold hands. When Noel poured from the steaming kettle with the wooden handle, Aqua said, "Now tell me."

"What do you want to know?"

"Upstairs, you said there was more, after the window."

"Ah, yes. I wanted to say that while you slept, it rained, hard. We had raging winds that snatched leaves and branches off trees. Jethro Tulle's got his work cut out tomorrow."

"Why tell me that?"

"Because," Noel set a mug and a teaspoon before Aqua. "It means anyone entering this house would've made a mess. There would have been puddled water, mud, tracked-in leaves, something. I'd have noticed, on my nightly check, just before I was drawn to your room."

With both hands around her mug for warmth, Aqua sipped. Softly, she admitted, "That makes me feel better."

Noel stirred. "Got something else to make you feel better."

Aqua's lips curved in amusement.

"See, nasty girl? I was going to offer you my bed—with me in it, of course—but only for the feel better. Before your mind went to the gutter, I was gonna say that in my bed, I wouldn't touch you, unless you need holding, *or* you can hold me. You can even get on me, or under me, whatever will make you feel better because I'm that kind of man. I'm willing to help any way I can." Noel nodded. "I'd do that and more."

Aqua laughed, then soberly stated, "I'd like that Ocaña."

"*My* bed? Then that it is." His voice remained neutral, although he wanted to crow. "I'm telling you girl, no funny stuff, or taking advantage, because this," he lifted his cup, "is all the 'appetizer' I'm offering."

Aqua chuckled, no longer feeling ill at ease. Actually, she felt warmth and a naughty tingle. She looked askance, "What if I want more than an hors d'oeuvre?"

Noel kissed Aqua, lasting and sweet, and pulled her onto his lap. Seated on him, she felt him swell beneath her bottom.

"Well *lirio*," Noel sighed as though all was tribulation. "I guess I could offer something a bit more substantial than a… cocktail weenie."

Aqua grinned as Noel's hand slid up to cup her neck. As she enjoyed his kiss and ardent caress, the houseguest knew. She was a goner.

WEARING a short-sleeved v-neck, a lengthy khaki skirt, and sandals, Aqua entered the sunny kitchen where Genie smiled.

"Mo'ning Ms. Aqua. Don't you look fresh 'n darling?"

"Hello, Genie. Thank you ma'am, you look nice too." Aqua's eyes darted to Noel, who stood barefoot at the stove. He looked scrumptious in well-worn jeans and a Braves tee. "Hey Ocaña," Aqua breathed.

Turning from the cutting board lined with mini squares of ham, diced peppers, onions, and slivers of soft potato, he extended a large arm.

Aqua walked into Noel's embrace, and he took his time kissing her.

"Hey to you too, *linda*." Aqua heard it through the lustful haze that Noel's kiss caused. "You have finally appeared." Noel's eyes twinkled, and because he held her tighter, Aqua suspected he knew he had weakened her knees. "Genie said I might have to rouse you."

Wearing sandals and a floral sheath, the older woman chuckled.

"Wow, Genie," Aqua said, "something smells delicious."

"Not me cooking this mo'ning. That's all him," Genie pointed. "Massa told me to move it. He ain't ever done that befo'e, but I did make the bread. The rest is on 'sweetie' there, who done give *me* the day off."

"Genie, love," Noel called, adding tomatoes and shredded cheese to the omelet in the iron fry pan. "Tell my baby the whole truth. I gave you *and* Jethro today, and tonight, off—with extra pay."

"I'm grateful. Jet is too." The older woman's uncovered hair was all gray waves. "You take care'a my boy now." She squeezed Aqua's arm.

Realizing Genie was hinting, Aqua caught at the small hand. She missed, however, because Genie shuffled to the door. Turning from the streaming sun, the wizened little woman smiled. "Gurl, ol' Eugenia's got no doubt you'll do fine." With a wink, small fry popped out of doors while calling, "Y'all be sweet now," and with that, she was gone.

Aqua stood in the middle of the floor, not knowing what to think or do, with everything hushed all of a sudden.

"Sit," Noel commanded, as expertly he flipped golden fluffy egg onto a plate. "Drink your juice."

Aqua did; while placing steaming food before her, Noel leaned close, resting one large hand on the table, the other on her chair. "Why do I get the feeling you're nervous, *lirio*, now that those two are gone?"

With a laugh, Aqua told the truth, "Because you're gonna try to have your way with me."

Before she could breathe, Noel gathered her close. Her breasts flattened against the hard wall of his chest, and he took her mouth. He kissed Aqua with urgency and pounding need. Then Noel let her go. Catching her face in his two big hands, he again took her soaring. Easing her back down, he turned toward the stove. Pivoting, Noel leaned so close until Aqua could again smell his skin, soap fresh with a hint of cologne. "I never try *nada*," he whispered. "I *do* it, well."

"Ohhh-kay—" Silenced by an additional kiss that left no doubt, Aqua realized. Noel had already seduced her. As her heart seemingly slammed into her ribs, he spoke. "Eat, before your food gets cold."

Conversationally then, he said, "I've got maybe two hours of work this morning. After that, my time is yours."

With a shiver, Aqua obediently picked up her fork, but she already knew. With the way she felt, and with her swirling thoughts, she couldn't eat. Nevertheless, she attempted, and she moaned. "Ohhh, seduce me with food, will you, tricky man."

Noel shrugged, as holding his own plate, he slid beside the woman who made even eating a sensuous pleasure. Between bites, he watched her linger over what he'd prepared. "If I had no work this morning," he told her, "I'd let you teach me to eat like that."

Aqua eyed Noel's toned physique. "You look like you do fine."

He caught her wrist, and staring into her eyes, he lowered his head. He placed his lips on her jumping pulse. "I meant: I'd want to learn to enjoy *you* like you're enjoying my efforts."

"Why don't I just undress," Aqua wondered aloud. "And dispense with the suspense?"

Noel guffawed. "Girl, you *want* all this. You need me to put the moves on you. Heck, *I* want to, now, just to see what will make you cum...undone. Since you wouldn't let me touch you last night while I kept you safe."

Aqua smiled. "You did put your arms around me."

Noel's plea was hoarse, "*Niña*, I want so much more..."

"You know I want you," Aqua whispered, her hand rising to Noel's nape. Cupping his neck, she slowly guided his head to her breast. "You know," she seductively whispered, "I want to feel you inside me. I want to ride you. And when your two hours are up, I just might."

Hungrily, Noel opened his mouth, and Aqua flipped the script, lifting his head. Placing her mouth on his, she sought his tongue while her hand sought his shaft. Within his jeans, she squeezed his elongated member.

Nearly moaning aloud, Noel realized, she too had measures. Inching his fingers upward, to cup the fullness that he hadn't gotten to suckle, he revealed, "You bewitch me, *lirio*."

"Oh, I'm going to do more than that," she promised and arched into his hand. "Now," she said, just as he bent to place his lips on her. "Are you gonna eat that piece of ham, or am I?"

Against her breast, Noel's laughter was like a clap of thunder. "I do believe I am going to love your appetite, *lirio*."

NOEL wound up working later than he planned, and Aqua did not bother him. She simply neatened up and put things in the lavender-scented drawers, Genie's doing, no doubt. Then Aqua passed Noel's office, not disturbing his conference call. Downstairs, she cut through the lovely old kitchen, passing glass-fronted cabinets.

Out of doors, the air was warm, the sun bright, and Aqua descended wide wooden steps to stand on an old grassy path. Looking back at the house, she thought it a beaut, just like an elderly woman. Both would have been privy to a plethora of secrets, laughter, and tears, yet both would bear all with grace.

Suddenly the dappled sunlight became too bright, and Aqua raised a hand to shield her eyes. She also staggered, feeling stabbing pains in her abdomen. She placed a trembling hand at the ache. Open-mouthed, she attempted to breathe as she wondered, what was happening?

Then Aqua noticed the wooden bench; her back was pressed against its slats. Somehow, she knew lots of time had elapsed. She could tell by the not so bright sunlight. It peered through the canopy of leaves overhead. On the grass, a squirrel chattered before scampering upwards.

It had been morning when she'd come out. Although she wasn't wearing a watch, she hadn't done so since taking up with Noel, she knew. It was now afternoon. Therefore, that meant she had passed out?

No. Aqua shook away the disturbing thought as slowly she rose. Climbing the back stairs, she pulled open the wooden screen door. In the cooler, dim kitchen, she realized Noel was probably still working. So Aqua drank a glass of ice water. When she climbed the stairs and passed Noel's office, he called out to her.

Entering his private domain, Aqua saw there was nothing ancient about it. The large suite had been transformed into a state-of-the-art work center, and Aqua had to chuckle.

Seated on his desk edge, Noel pulled her between powerful thighs. "What's so funny, *lirio?*" he asked, his muscular arms encircling her.

"You are," Aqua replied. "You're just so full of surprises."

Feathering kisses over Aqua's neck Noel spoke. "By that, you mean?"

"This room, it belongs in a New York skyscraper."

"Ah, and not here, in back of beyond, gotcha. Where you headed?"

"I was thinking about a nap, then a nice soak."

"So you've got the next few hours planned," Noel surmised, placing his lips on Aqua's. He also said, "I'm sorry, *lirio.*"

"For?"

"Well, although I've got work, I wanted you here. And I promised to spend time with you. I truly meant to, but I'm tied up. Can I make it up to you this evening?"

"Ocaña, I understand." Aqua left the comfort of his arms. "Making up sounds promising, though..." She blew him a kiss.

"Then I'll have something for you." As Aqua exited, Noel told himself to concentrate. He had to stop his mind from drifting to getting between Aqua's shapely legs. However, toward that end, hadn't he given his staff the evening off?

The homeowner sighed. If he was going to put the evening to good use, he had to get a move on. He had calls to make and email to send, right away.

WHEN Aqua woke, she could tell, the sun would soon set. She also smelled muget as she walked toward the bathroom.

Inside, Aqua was stunned because candles surrounded the old clawfoot tub and flickered from everywhere. Bending to trail a hand through warm fragrant bubbles, she turned at the light rap. "How'd you know?"

"What?" Her look of awe made Noel's effort worth it.

"How'd you know I like the scent of lily of the valley?"

"You told me, one evening as you seduced me, over the phone."

Aqua slowly repeated, "I seduced you..." She recalled the night she had spoken with Noel just as she'd been about to bathe.

Softly he revealed, "I never forgot, because I heard you, in the water. I pictured you, looking as you do now. So, today when you said I'm full of surprises, I thought of this." From behind Aqua, Noel placed both hands on her waist. In her ear, he whispered, "Let me help you."

With her back to him, in the flickering flame light, Aqua peeled down one shoulder of her thin chemise. "Only if you don't look."

Noel's accent became more pronounced, "But *lirio* I must." He turned her to face him. His eyes were on her exposed breast. "Understand." Expertly, he ran fingertips around her nipple, barely touching her darker areola. "You beg for notice, like a rose, or fine artwork."

Then in the flame-light, Noel silently aided Aqua to undress, and feeling pulsating in his loins, he pressed his lips to hers. "I can tell that with you," he began, "sometimes I'll just have to have you." He gazed into her amber eyes. "I'll want you fast, minus finesse. Shhh, shhh, my baby, because *other* times, I will make slow sweet love to you. Tonight," Noel advised, unable to wait any longer, "we will experience both."

With her chemise pooled at her feet, Aqua felt speechless. So clasping Noel's hand, gingerly, she stepped into the tub.

Watching, he could only think, what a bronze goddess. Aqua No longer felt self-conscious or heavy. She only felt beautiful, as she slid down into scented bubbles and warmth.

Noel bent to run a gentle hand along her jaw. "I'll check on you." Planting a kiss on her forehead, he mustered every ounce of willpower. Turning, he left, although everything in him longed to join Aqua.

In his bedroom suite, Noel showered. Erotically massaging himself, he deduced that he, too, should clean up before dinner. As Noel exited, he heard the phone. With his thick body glistening, hurriedly, he stepped into navy silk. Not drawing the string, the lounge pants hung loose, thereby exposing part of his pelvis. Snagging the cordless, Noel pulled on a long-sleeved gauze shirt, just as his doorbell also rang.

"Hey." He spoke into the phone, as again the doorbell chimed. Cradling the phone, he strode barefoot down the stairs, his white shirt streaming out behind. Opening his front door, he spoke into the phone and nodded at his flirtatious neighbor, Lorna or Luna.

Wearing short shorts, high-heeled flip-flops, and a blouse tied beneath her breasts, the redhead slyly spoke of jumper cables. Then her eyes fell to Noel's golden, hair-spattered chest. They traveled slowly downward.

Saying he'd return the call, Noel turned. With the phone at his ear, he began buttoning, from his shirt bottom up. Again, his phone rang, while behind him, his neighbor trod too close. He pressed talk. "Yeah. Hey!"

Was that the doorbell *again*?! Noel wondered, turning quickly and causing his neighbor to bump face-first into his chest.

Noel eyed the unidentified man who stood in the drawing dusk. Peering from behind Noel, his neighbor sighed.

"Yes?" Noel addressed the thin, balding man whose face pinked up when he glanced from Noel's chest to the near-hidden woman.

"Lance." Noel's neighbor sounded countrified exasperated. "Noel here was gonna get me some cables. I drove your car over for them."

"I know." Hypersensitive, Lance whined as angry perspiration dotted his nose. "*I* called Mr. Wheatley." Therefore, Lucy had no business with this—Gigolo! Good thing he'd arrived, Lance thought, or Gigolo would probably have tried to seduce Lucy. Puffing up with indignation, Lance announced, "I rode Sugar," the mare "over, to tell you."

Lucy became annoyed. "Lance, the auto body shop closes at five."

"I called Dan Wheatley's home," Lance stated, wanting to attack the big man who'd probably crumple him with one punch. With his woman's honor at stake, though, Lance became authoritative. "Home, Lucy."

Into his phone, Noel said, "Hang on, *Mami*."

Lucy appeared disappointed as Noel held the door wide, allowing her and Lance to exit. Suggestively licking her lips, Lucy winked up at Noel before flouncing down the porch steps. She would return.

Glad his troublesome neighbors lived miles away, Noel resumed his call and barked with laughter. "You're right, Mama. I *am* entertaining. Surprise. So I know you won't mind me calling you tomorrow." Noel cajoled, "Aw, come on, you know you're my one true love. *Mañana...*"

Upstairs and unaware, Aqua blissfully relaxed. However, Noel's tread on the stairs roused her. Blinking, she realized. She had dozed, and dream Noel had done deliciously enticing things to her.

When flesh and blood Noel entered the candle-lit bathroom, Aqua's dreamy gaze bespoke her thoughts. Taking her outstretched hand, Noel's heart raced as shiny-wet she stepped from the tub.

As though in a trance, she walked into his arms. Pressing herself flush against him, she breathed. "I'm wetting your clothes, aren't I?"

Wryly, he admitted, "I'd rather you wet *me*," as smoothly his arms sailed around her, crushing her to him. Noel also wondered if the candle heat had him feeling warm in the area surrounding his heart? Or was it something that he dared not name, yet?

With a hand, Noel cradled Aqua's plump bottom. With the other, he pressed her to his erection while whispering, "Give me you..."

Seductively, Aqua smiled. "First, let me undo these buttons." With her lower body pressed to Noel's, through the silk of his pants, she could feel the hardness that made her crave. Running hands over his broad chest, she wanted to eat him up. She flicked his shirt from his shoulders.

That caused a full-fledged fire to flare within Noel. He enveloped Aqua's mouth with his. Tonight, he knew, there would be no going back. Not after he entered her. He would always do so, exclusively, and raising his head, he told her. "I don't want you with other people."

In the flame light, Aqua's eyes narrowed. "That's presumptuous."

Noel held her hips while grinding himself against her. "Well, if you feel any better, I don't want me with others either. I want us, for us."

Saying it shocked Noel because never before had he felt so, but it was true. On the day of his mother's party, the need for sampling dissipated.

Aqua's heart gave a little leap, as she simply said, "So be it." Freely then, she ran her hands over Noel's golden skin. She toyed with the silken hair on his chest. She ran a finger down a dark skein of hair. Somehow, she had known it would lead from his navel to his nether region. These things she had only dreamed of; however, kissing him, she knew. Dreams did not compare with reality. With a leg raised, she murmured, "I want you...*now* Ocaña."

Her words brought the annoying, blinding sunlight from his dream back, when Noel only wanted to see Aqua. It also seemed that before Aqua had spoken, Noel had known what she would say. Like she had said that very thing to him before, perhaps in another lifetime, if such could be.

Nude, in candlelight Aqua turned, pulling Noel's arms around her. From behind her, he lifted his hands, to the breasts he wanted to devour.

With a sexy booty dance, she teased his groin, and amid, Aqua wondered. Why did she feel she had known Noel far longer than she had? Why did she also feel she had waited, perhaps centuries for him, and for this? "I know you meant to give me time," she said, her voice sounding far away. "However, I think it *is* time."

Abruptly turning Aqua to hold her close, Noel's eyes traced the smooth planes of her face as he agreed.

"Then let's get you out of these," she suggested. To her immense relief, Aqua sounded more like herself. Pulling at the drawstring of Noel's navy garment, she blinked and was back in the bayou, among a copse of cypress...

The low evening sun glinted off a much browner Noel as he lay gloriously nude at the base of a tree. His head rested on one large hand as the other held his formidable man piece. Penetratingly, he gazed at Aqua while overwhelming power emanated from him.

Aqua blinked, and back in the flame-lit bath, her heart beat loudly as beneath Noel's navy silk, she found him well-endowed. As his impressive male member strained toward her, Aqua licked her lips. She could almost taste the pink tip. Wrapping a hand around his thick shaft, she said, "Now I can finally have you."

She drew Noel to her. Standing on her toes, Aqua parted her legs. She slid Noel into her wet, and light, like too-bright sunshine nearly blinded her. Aqua felt Noel within as he caught her, kept her upright. This time, however, she saw herself, not him, in the forest. She lay at the base of a huge tree, and he—she believed it was Noel who hovered over her— kissed her. Aqua saw the white of the man's cotton shirt as it strained to encapsulate his muscular shoulders and torso.

"Love me, now," Aqua urged, in the bathroom flickering with sputtering candlelight, while she was somehow also in the sun-dappled forest.

Noel eased Aqua down to the floor with the tiny tiles *and* down to the forest floor. Between her bronze thighs, a thick male member entered her, and Aqua felt two worlds collide. Her limbs surrounded the motionless man, who allowed her to adjust to his circumference and his length. Cradled within the sweet cavern of Aqua's body, he whispered, too lowly for her to hear. *He loved her*. He always had.

Moving within Aqua, Noel kissed the column of her neck and the sensual slide of her shoulders. He squeezed her and savored every moan, each shiver, every caress...until desire became a beast that drove him. Pulsating within Aqua, but marshaling all his strength, Noel...pulled *out*. Swiftly he stood. Lifting Aqua, he strode from the room.

Chapter 24

In his darkened man suite, decorated in ebony and gray shades, nude, Noel laid Aqua on his leather chaise. "This, unlike my bed, isn't wide," he explained. "So you'll have nowhere to hide," he teased before his eyes and lips dropped to devour her.

With gentle but knowing hands, he parted Aqua's thighs; and because his moves were so smooth, she had to wonder. How many had there been? Had countless women lost their hearts to him, as indeed as she was losing hers? Add to that, she now lay before him, body bare.

With hands beneath Aqua, Noel raised her. He parted her curtain. Then with lowered head, his lips met her lower lips. Languidly, his tongue slid across the stamen of her flower. With slow, unerring strokes, he took her up, kissing her, there, like he had often kissed her mouth. Noel deliberately aroused a desire so fiery within Aqua, until she thrashed about, begging. As he had said she would.

The man kept at it. For a moment, he drew back, but torturously began again. He did so several times until Aqua nearly wept for release. She pled for Noel to collapse on her and still the need.

Then, as though he would, he rose above her but did not enter her. Lowering his head, he kissed her breasts. He also used his teeth and his wicked tongue. "Real tits," he murmured, cupping them together. Burying his face in the fullness, he laved her nipples.

Aqua guided his head upward as she lay writhing beneath him, and when his mouth neared hers, she kissed him until he believed himself silly. Then with a sly smile, she ordered him to "Stay."

He laughed and asked, "What am I now, your *cachorro*?"

"No puppy, shush," she said. On her back, beneath Noel, she slid downward, while he remained with a knee on the chaise. His other foot was on the floor. Aqua slid low enough to take him into her mouth.

Noel moaned as warm jaws surrounded him. He pushed deeper as Aqua worked him. Purposefully, she sent him spiraling. Until he pulled free.

Amid suck, Aqua's glistening mouth slightly popped, and with desire-glazed eyes, Noel slid his scathingly hot body downward over her. He allowed his rod to linger in the valley between her breasts. Again Noel gathered the fleshy mounds together around himself. Then he slid further downward. Down her belly, to the apex between her thighs.

Wantonly Aqua raised herself, as her breath emitted in spurts. Anxious to feel him, to have Noel fill her, she placed both hands on his buttocks, intent to guide him forward.

Noel shook his head, although he nearly relented. "Not so fast, *lirio*." Yet she fit herself to him. Watching him draw back, she braced herself.

Masterfully, he surged into her, and her body welcomed him. It cushioned him, as Aqua sighed with relief. Her fingernails pricked Noel's flesh as his chest hit her breasts. He barely noticed drawn blood as he drew back, to smoothly sail within again. Then as he stirred and stroked, both people experienced a flurry of need and greed. She scratched as he bit. He nipped as she gripped, and both extracted all.

"Ohhh," Aqua moaned, as Noel voiced that he had waited too long.

Although she desperately tried to cling, to prolong the ecstasy, Aqua climaxed. Her legs trembled as her whole body became nerve central. Bathing in her juices, Noel was not yet ready. Therefore, he aided her to turn. With his lips on Aqua's cheek, and his rod at the cleft of her behind, the thick-bodied man straddled her. Softly he asked, "*Quieres esto*? Do you want this?"

Aqua wanted all Noel had to give, so she nodded. She shivered when he used her wet to lubricate her. Then with infinite tenderness, he entered. Noel kissed the side of her face. He sucked at her puckered mouth as she lay facing the window. With unseeing eyes, as night steadily approached, Aqua clutched the sides of the chaise. She clawed its nail-head base as exquisite painful pleasure radiated.

Clamping her in place, Noel rode her, before his seed seeped into her.

When he regained a modicum of strength, he disengaged and turned her. Involuntarily, Aqua trembled, but Noel cradled her and repeatedly kissed her, the woman he had once believed he would never find.

Sated, they stretched out together, as in the other room, the last of the candles flickered and hissed out.

Then both people heard it. Out of doors and off in the distance, something howled. In the deep dark heart of the bayou, it did so, angrily.

WHEN Aqua could stand without bonelessly slipping to the floor, the couple showered. Noel's placid sudsy hands lingered lightly at each now tender place on Aqua's bronze body. Rinsing her, he gently attempted to kiss every place his hands had been. And they hungered again...

In the kitchen, wearing the navy silk pants they'd earlier removed, Noel spread a faded red cloth on the table, saying, "We'll have a cold picnic." While pulling items from the huge refrigerator, he turned.

"*Lirio,*" Noel spoke as he opened chilled wine. "It seems you are air to me. Now. I do not think I will ever get enough of you." He poured and set the bottle on the woodblock countertop.

Leaning against it, Aqua drank as Noel scooped up potato salad.

"You know what I love about you, girl?"

"What?" Aqua took an offered fried chicken wing.

"You're uninhibited. You want as much as I do, and you show it."

"I haven't always," Aqua admitted, "but for some reason, with you, I feel I can get what I want, what I need. You know?"

Fully aware, Noel nodded because he felt the same way. As they ate wedges of soft smoked gouda, he had another thought. Before Aqua, he had slowly grown tired of women who relentlessly pursued him. First, because Noel preferred to chase. Secondly, because he was not attracted to hairless, boyish bodies that sported bought breasts.

As he halved an apple, Noel's mind drifted back to voluptuous Aqua and the triangle of trimmed hair beneath her satin robe. To him, she was woman epitomized. Aqua was witty, wise, challenging, and so gol-dang sexy it was insane! Looking over, Noel suddenly rasped. "I must have you again."

Downing the last of her wine, Aqua threw her head back. She exposed her inviting neck and frontal nudity. "If you must," she mock groaned. As Noel's hands explored, she felt wood behind her as she and he sensuously slid to the kitchen floor. Good thing the staff had off.

HE awakened her, and squinting, she noticed it was morning. She was in Noel's bed. Aqua did not remember getting there. She only remembered the kitchen, the woodblock cabinet, and the floor. Then she felt the sore, the sweet swollen. Despite it, she wanted again.

Noel pushed past all, this time slowly and gently. As he did, aloud Aqua surmised that he too must have been a glutton for punishment.

Noel grinned, mid-pump. "I'm a glutton for you."

With her hands fisted, Aqua murmured. "Mmm. I love you."

She stiffened because she hadn't meant to say it, not out loud. However, gathering her close while pouring into her, Noel whispered.

April Alisa Marquette
117

"You're mine." It seemed she had always been, even though only recently had he found her again. Nonetheless, the man could not shake the feeling that he had always known Aqua, had loved her, and had always resided within her body.

When Noel rolled aside to hold Aqua, reality surfaced. As it eased back, she felt chilled because she would have to face that *other* man at some point. Aqua needed to close that chapter, to free herself. Although she and Dyson were over, she needed to *say it*, to him.

So to garner the necessary strength, Aqua decided. Since she and Noel had been working up to...*this* for months, why not hear it?

"Ocaña, no pressure," she began, rising on an elbow. "But if you think we can really make a go of this, as you said in the beginning, I'd like to hear it, again." Aqua pulled up the sheet. "I'm too old to blindly play games. If we're just hittin' it, or if it's more, I want to know."

Noel crushed Aqua to him. Accented, his voice became emotion-filled. "How can you wonder?" Did she really not know? When it was written all over him? "In the car," he reminded her, "You asked about Ms. Cole's song, *el dia que me quieres*. That means *the day you love me*. I said I would tell you when it happened to us..."

Aqua stared. *The day you love me*. That was today.

"*Lirio*, I asked you to marry me," Noel continued, looking into Aqua's eyes, "when you called me that first time. I was not playing. I have no time for games. I am a man most busy. I know my heart; thus, I know what I want and need. Also, I'd never have brought you here, or to any home of mine, had I simply wanted to lie with you."

Noel looked deep into amber eyes. "I have no time for games. But, then," Noel rationalized, "You could not know." Aqua could only know what he told her. "So I am telling you, *lirio,* and I will show you that there is no need for worry. And though you think you've not known me long, I've known *you*, somehow, *Aqua Mira*, and I love you."

Then Noel's words warbled and crashed into Aqua like the waves that dashed against the jetty. The bronze woman knew she was losing it because she *thought* he said he'd loved her since the *eighteen hundreds*.

WHEN Aqua entered the sunny kitchen, aromatic with the scent of coffee; Genie was there. Humming, the small woman sat at the woodblock table. Wearing her white bandana and white cap-sleeved blouse, she snapped beans. "Well, hello, Ms. Aqua. Yuh want breakfast?"

"Hi, Genie. No ma'am, since it's late, I'll just pour a bowl of cereal."

Genie glanced up at the shapely woman. Aqua looked quite lovely in a lengthy, lemon-yellow halter dress. "Get a cup, honeh. Coffee's fresh." Genie stopped speaking. "Why, child, you glowing..."

Aqua put her mug down. While arranging breakfast items, she kept her eyes averted. "It's a wonder what a dusting of powder will do."

Genie gazed speculatively. "No. *Thet* glow come from something else." Genie cackled, "I should go 'way again! What you think?"

"You're naughty," Aqua smirked. "That's what I think."

"You too! Ol' Eugenia knows. She smells your purty perfume. Hope yuh wore thet last night when you were naughty, with sweetie pie. Hope yuh did real good because Lord knows before you come, thet man never brought a soul to this house—save for his mama and daddy. Gurl, I started to feel ret badly for him. Started thinking if I was many years younger, *I* would give him a tumble. Yuh know?"

Aqua burst out laughing.

"It's funny." Genie innocently inspected her bowl of beans. "But I was a beauty, and a big fine man like that should not be alone."

Aqua agreed, just as the thickset, sexy, golden Noel, wearing a tee and faded jeans, entered the sunlit kitchen.

"Coffeee..." Genie sang out.

Noel did not respond. With blazing eyes, he grabbed Aqua's wrist.

Seated across from Eugenia, Aqua appeared startled. "Ocaña, I thought you were working."

"Upstairs," Noel barked because he had been unable to think.

Aqua rose, as confused, she inquired, "What's the matter?"

Noel spoke softly. "I need you. I haven't gotten any work done."

In the hallway, Aqua stopped for clarity. "How am I gonna help?"

"*Yas a ayudarme.*" It was said simply. "You'll get at me."

Aqua noticed Noel's smoldering eyes. Instinctively, she knew he would never hurt her, just before he jerked her to him. Ravenously, he kissed her, licked her, and very nearly lapped her up, before giving her backside a torrid slap. Then with a slight push, he ordered her to move, "In my office, *lirio*. Lean over my desk." He could barely wait to see her curvy buttocks. "Better yet, take off that dress, *el vestido.*"

Knowing it was about to become fast and furious, Aqua hurried up the sweeping front staircase. All her senses were on alert, while close on her heels; Noel pulled the strap at her neck. As her halter top slid down, Aqua swore she heard a loud amused cackle. It floated from the kitchen.

AQUA checked her messages and found out she had quite a few. Cadence called to say she missed her friend. The petite powerhouse with the corkscrew curls also said she'd made the most interesting discovery. Aqua wondered if it had anything to do with Cae's husband, Yael. Aqua deleted the message, and the next was Edna and Isis, checking on her. Isis dramatically bemoaned not seeing Aqua. She said, "I'm worried." Aqua grinned, even as the youngster said her dad was messing up, "But don't make me and Mom pay, okay? Let us girls stick together." Isis sagely suggested, "Dad can stay miserable; it's what he wants, anyway."

"Okay, Isi," Edna said, obviously talking to her daughter. "We'll let Aqua go." Back into the phone, Edna said, "We'll talk A," just before Isis yelled. "We bought you a present!"

Aqua laughed. Next message. Gray-eyed Phédra was excited because she'd found the woman—*Priestess Odyssey*! The one from the *Newsweek* article. Phé said she'd spoken with the Priestess's son. "Listen A, the Priestess can't possibly come to me, her son said, because thousands of people want her, but he said *I* could visit *her*. His name is Kijana."

Aqua wondered why that name sounded familiar, as the expectant mother continued. "The High Priestess lives on an island called Karina Cay. Sounds lovely, right? Well, it's not far from where you are now or where you're going. I'll look it up. Hey, if the baby wasn't due next week, I would pass you 'n your hunk on the ferry. Gotta go! Love you."

Next message. Rayfa, whining, "Where you? My car note is due."

Aqua sighed and pressed for the next message. Rayfa again. "You 'posed to help me. Dammit!" Rayfa yelled, "Call me! I'on't like this hide-'n-go seek shit. I need money, A. You know I'm laid off."

Rayfa called back after an interruption. "You *want* these people to take my car? Pick up the phone! This ain't no joke. What if they shet my shit off with that GPS mess while I'm driving? Um scared. If my car gets taken, or if I get hit, on the highway when it shuts off," Rayfa threatened, "*you* gon drive me to the hospil-la!"

Aqua deleted her mother's worrisome tirade because Rayfa should have job-hunted instead of lollygagging after rightfully being sacked.

Aqua pressed for the second to the last message. She smiled upon hearing her sister and her small niece. "Hey A," Ava sang out. "It's me and lil' Tawny. Say hi to Auntie. Girrrl, Rayfa's fighting mad, but *do not* give in. Ma Hag has to get another job. Live your life A—and ride big sexy like he's a thoroughbred!" Aqua laughed at the same time that her sister did. "Call me. Melvi-o says hey."

"Hi Melvin," Aqua absently breathed, pressing for the final message.

Dyson. He bellowed, "Yo A, what's up?" He hemmed and hawed before he threw in, "Guess I miss you."

Aqua's lips twisted. She knew what he missed. She laughed loudly. Well, Mr. Eamon was going to miss *it* a whole lot more, because she was no longer his jellyfish. She'd gotten a spine. Now she was *out*, done, *caput, finito*! Aqua continued to laugh while realizing. That was the first time, in a while, that Dyson aided her to feel good, not guilty.

LATER, at Genie's urging, Aqua carried a plate of cookies out to sullen Jethro Tulle. In the side yard, he stopped yanking weeds. Not taking the plate, his long fingers grasped one cookie. While munching, he eyed Aqua. Leather-faced, he scowled while reaching for another.

Aqua turned to set the plate down because heck if she would stand in the sun holding it for the grimy gardener. She bumped into something.

Genie. The little woman spoke, handing over a glass of ice water. "Miss Aqua baked that batch. Pretty good, huh Jet?"

The long, lean man grunted, as unable to abide him a moment longer, Aqua headed for the house. She recalled Noel saying they would go out. She knew he would make good on the promise, most likely later. She really didn't mind hanging around Cricket Hill. There was much to see and do, and Aqua actually wanted to get into the extensive library. First, however, she went upstairs to remind Noel of their drive.

Just as she reached the top of the stairs, he swore, and she saw him. On the phone, he paced his office and fumed about unexpected project costs. Therefore, while headed away, Aqua decided she would wait.

As she entered the hushed two-story library with the Aubusson carpet and the comfortable leather chairs, Aqua was not disappointed. In the room that smelled of polishing oil and fresh flowers, Aqua realized. She did not want to be out and about. It was funny, but she actually felt so at peace at Cricket Hill, until it nearly felt like *home*. Besides, she and

Genie would go to an outdoor market soon. Therefore, in the beautifully appointed burgundy library, Aqua selected Edgar Allen Poe's *The Cask of Amontillado*. She had long wanted to read it. Now, Aqua thought, passing a hand over Genie who stirred something, Aqua would.

"Need to eat, gurl," Genie advised. "All you had today was a cup of coffee and a few spoons of soggy cereal. Got soup here, or a sandwich. "

Yeah, the caveman upstairs had dragged her off, Aqua fondly thought. "I'm fine," she replied, realizing she really wasn't hungry. Strange, for her. Aqua descended the back porch's wooden steps. Carrying her book, she took a grassy path, headed for the old magnolia some fifteen feet from the house. Settling beneath it, Aqua glimpsed squirrels scampering around an oak. In the dappled sunlight, bees buzzed at Jethro's flowers. In addition, she heard the scratching of chipmunks and other small fauna beneath a hedge. Yet, in time, Aqua became so lost in Mr. Poe's world until it was a few moments before she felt the presence.

Raising her eyes, she saw Jethro. He stood a yard off, scowling.

What the devil, Aqua wondered, annoyed at being disturbed. Trying to ignore the lean brown man who towered over her, she allowed her eyes to drop back to the page before her. She also vowed to talk with Noel about Mister, who was starting to make her skin crawl.

Aqua again raised her eyes. Jethro stood before her, shiny with sweat, and ever so slowly, at his side, his machete rose. Aqua felt the scream as it gathered in her throat—because the man was mad!

Before she could blink, Jethro hurled his weapon.

Singing ominously, quickly it turned, over and over in the air.

Aqua knew she was dead, that the gleam of the blade would be the last thing she saw ...but she heard a thud. Wide-eyed, she realized. The hatchet had sunk into the tree trunk behind her.

Not wanting to take her eyes from Jethro, who tromped forward, perhaps to finish what he'd started, Aqua saw that his crazy behind did not see her, at all. Then she heard it, the slithering overhead, and the *thunk*. From her peripheral, she saw something fall from among the magnolia branches. Aqua glanced down, and air backed up in her lungs.

Scrambling up, she found her hand on Jethro's calloused work-worn palm. The sinewy man gently pulled Aqua away. Swiftly retrieving her book, Jethro handed it over, and grasping it, Aqua wanted to run.

She turned back, though, her mind whirring. Before the man who easily jerked his machete free from the tree trunk, there on the ground was the head, and at least four feet, of a snake. The ugly thing had been unfurling from the big glossy leaves under which she'd sat, unaware.

Aqua's breath hitched as with wide eyes, she clutched her book. Jethro Tulle had saved her life! Here, she had thought the man despised her, for whatever reason. Furthermore, she'd believed he was around the side of the house, or somewhere else, doing Lord only knew what. But there Jethro stood. He had appeared, without warning, to see about her.

"Why?" Aqua asked, feeling the man wouldn't deign to speak to her. "Why'd you come, Mr. Tulle? How'd you even know to come?"

Jethro used the back of his hand to swipe sweat from his brow. As he bent to pick up the spoils, his voice was rusty, perhaps from disuse. "Name's Jet, and I come becuh yuh needed me. I could feel danger. My job is to tek cyare the flora, Massa said. Now git. Gotta clean this mess."

Aqua near-hysterically laughed because these island men sure liked to order her about. She pivoted but hesitantly turned back. "Jet?"

He nodded. "Ma'am."

Aqua forgot all she had once believed. "Thank you."

She hurried away, and Jethro called out, "Mek some mo' sweets."

With a laugh, Aqua realized the man wanted Genie's prickly pear cacti cookies. "We will," Aqua called back, hurrying to the house. Breathing heavily, she slammed through the back door.

"Gurl!" Genie squealed, eyeing Aqua. "Look like yuh seen the devil."

The younger woman dropped her book and placed a shaking hand at her heart. Then she tumbled into small open motherly arms. Against Genie's sweet-smelling neck, Aqua murmured, "Maybe I have."

AS she drove from the outdoor market; Aqua could not wait to get back to Cricket Hill. There, she and Genie—who had so quickly become like a loving mother—would pore over their purchases. While driving, Aqua thought about their shopping trip.

It had been postponed because early the day before, she and Noel had taken a picturesque jaunt. The couple visited a serene, mostly unpopulated beach. Nude and buoyant, in the water, they fervently sexed; he, filling his hands with her, and she, filling her body with him.

Half-dressed, on the sand, they kissed, caressed, and hunted for large shells. They ate a tasty cold lunch, as warm salt wind and waves tangoed.

Then later while wheat-hued sea oats swayed, again they delectably indulged, riding waves of ecstasy.

Aqua remembered Genie, who rode beside her. Aqua and small fry had risen early this morning. In a quaint shopping area, crammed with charming shops, theatres, museums, and art galleries, they'd browsed. In the heat, they'd walked the historic district where people sat amongst flowers on second-story black iron balconies. Amid stately architecture and those hawking wares such as yucca, potatoes, grouper, and snapper, the women nosed about. They made purchases at a colorful stand of traditional Gullah basket weavers. Then down an aged street and through a crumbling passageway, they found a treat. There Aqua splurged for lunch at an elegant restaurant, its back overlooking an estuary. While watching the partially enclosed body of water, Genie shared information.

Jethro Tulle had a wife, Jacinda, and a fine boy-man of nineteen. The youngster, called Jet Tu, was a first-year college student, courtesy of Noel Ocaña. Aqua had actually met Jethro's wife that morning. The slender, attractive woman had arrived to clean or do laundry. Jacinda did so twice a week because Noel said Genie was not to do those things. Driving along, Aqua heard the older woman's voice and was pulled from remembrances. "What was that, Genie?"

"Said I don't like thet place." The cook grumbled, "Shouldn't go."

"Where are we going?"

"Not me, no." Genie shook her bandana-sporting head. "I stay heeyah. That is why Desdemona is there, cooking. She's a little strange that one, but living in a place that progress forgot... Well, you go on, make friends wit' her— becuh yuh jest may need huh."

Aqua glanced aside from the sun-dappled road. "Where are Noel and I going, Genie, and *who is* Desdemona?"

"Y'all going to the isle. *Miraunga* Isle," the little woman ominously spat, as though it were distasteful. "I told Massa I *neva* go back dere!"

Genie sounded so vehement until Aqua glanced over again. Small fry sat with her arms folded, when before she had been so happy. Although Aqua did not want to cause more gloom, she inquired, "What don't you like about it?" Steeple Chase, Aqua thought the house was called.

Genie patted Aqua's arm. "Don't let me fret yuh, baby."

Aqua pulled beneath the shade of the ancient oaks lining the drive at Cricket Hill. Putting Noel's old jeep in park, she faced Genie." Talk to me. You're obviously upset, so I want to know why."

"You should *not* go dere!" Genie yelled, startling Aqua. "Is spring break and Jet Tu going wit'cha. Big Jet too, but still, thet place is among the *dead*—ain't no place for the living!" Genie hissed, "I tole Massa. Tole him do not take my gurl dere, *you*. He says yuh don't have to go, but yuh weeell. Yuh *must* go. You go where he goes." Genie slumped, as though she were spent. "It is written. Even your two names say so, the 'water' and the 'look.' Yuh must travel the water, to look…"

Aqua frowned and remained quiet.

Suddenly Genie appeared quite angry. "Sundy mo'ning, rise up, gurl. You get pretty-up. Yuh go to church, and yuh *pray*—real hard." Genie grabbed Aqua's hand. Holding it to her rapidly beating heart, Genie's eyes filled. "I'll be dere, 'fore day, lying before the Lord, becuh you my daughter, now. The one I never have. So I tell yuh: pray hard, baby. For the storm that's a'coming. Then, mebbe…" Genie moaned loudly, "God brang yuh back to me, to Sapelo Island …I pray; not in a *box* though, wit' a shroud on yuh face!" Then in the jeep, Genie sat and silently wept.

AQUA heard Noel and Genie on the back porch that evening.

In the dark, a creature took flight. In the dense night that had not a smidgen of moon glow, wings flapped.

Out of the night, Noel spoke. "Genie, you with them cards again?"

"No Massa." The woman in the rocker sounded sullen. "Yuh said the tarot is evil. Yuh said to get rid of my cards, so I put them away."

Noel's voice was gentle. "Then why you all worked up, love?"

Aqua stood quietly in the kitchen, at the screen door, her perfume a whisper about her. She knew she should have been upstairs, packing, but she planned to do it tomorrow, after morning service.

Catching her scent, those outside knew she was there. Yet Genie spoke. "Ain't nobody het up. I just don't want yuh takin' huh wit' you."

"Eugenia, if *lirio* wants to go, I'll not dissuade her. The purpose of us coming here was to be *junto*. She needs to see what will be hers."

In the distance, something howled, and Genie sounded bitter, "Hoon-toe—together—bah! Take her home."

"She is home."

"No!" Genie spat as the howling started again. "Take her stateside, 'way from these isles, where she be safe. Yuh made me lose my cards, but other things got stories to tell, like trees, leaves, and the *sun*… And though you're no *believer*, them things already whispering *to her*."

The eerie loneliness and the underlying anger in the new howl chilled Aqua as Noel sighed. "I want you to rest, Genie. No work tomorrow, Sunday—*Domingo*. We can manage without you."

"Yuh telling me too late! Yuh know I start my Sunday dinner on Sat'day evening. And I enjoy her company—you'll do without me," Genie harrumphed. She stopped rocking, and the floorboards creaked when firmly she planted her feet. "One day, it be true. You'll manage without me, but without *her*? Keep scoffing and not believing. I told you, for one like you, the fates conspire…to *make* them believe."

Noel's voice was like thunder in the night. "Enough!" For a moment, the night creatures' song stopped. Then outside the screen, a mosquito whined as Noel continued. "You are too superstitious, Eugenia. I know you see things. I know you get signs—"

"Then yuh know my heart aches," Genie interrupted, sounding tearful. "Jest found her." She bitterly spat, "Now yuh might lose her, from both of us." Genie pled, "Do – not – take her, Noel. *Please*. Lemme keep her heeyah, while yuh go. Then she be safe. She be heeyah when yuh return. Okay?"

Again the howling came, closer this time, and Aqua had to wonder. What was it that made that anguished cry? Aqua also marveled because she had just heard Genie call Ocaña by his given name.

As though he had not heard, the man sighed. "Genie, I was going to mention these dreams I've been having."

Aqua heard him walk toward the steps. When he spoke, he was seated on them and facing away. "I wanted you to tell me what they mean, but all you want to do is harp on this other stuff."

Genie was rocking again, "Ain't harping hard-headed boy."

Noel's voice was soft, tender. "Ain't a boy anymore, Eugenia."

"I know, precious, but you'll always be *my* sweet boy. Even though you're a man. A man who must set things right with the fates that have conspired to take what is his."

Noel clapped, once, sharply, and sent night creatures scurrying and flying. "No more, Eugenia." He stood. At the screen door, he said, "Church *manaña*. Be ready, no scurrying back and forth like always."

"Shush." Genie waved. "I'll be gone 'fore you. Now leave me. And take thet listening gal jest inside the door. Keep her upstairs. Get her naked—you know what to do because the beast is out tonight."

SUNDAY morning Aqua descended the sweeping front staircase. She wore peach silk. Floating on peau de soie heels, her dress cascaded around her.

At the foot of the stairs, Noel gawked. He took in Aqua's haute couture, her wide-brimmed hat, jewelry, and expertly applied makeup. Shaking his head, all he could say was, "Oooh baby!"

That was enough for Aqua. With a smile, she noticed Noel's beautiful summer suit. He wore a French cuffed shirt, a lavender tie, and neutral leather shoes. "You look extra yourself," she stated. Glancing around, she asked, "Where is Genie?"

From a tray on the foyer bureau, Noel lifted a mimosa flute. "Gone, already. She left this and said I had to make sure you eat something." Noel pressed a linen napkin into Aqua's hand. "Bring your drink. I had the car brought around."

Aqua followed, peering at the napkin. "What's in here?"

"A pastry." When the woman protested, Noel silenced her. Holding wide the door, he reminded her, "Since you got here, you have eaten like a bird. I know that's not you, *lirio*. Force it down, or you'll be sick."

With Noel holding her elbow, Aqua knew eating would make her feel worse. Indeed she had been miserable since the prior evening, hearing all that talk about needing to stay put.

During the moments when she and Noel had joined bronze and golden bodies, Aqua had been able to forget. When she'd knelt over him, open and moist; when he'd been below her, splaying and licking, she'd been mindless. When he'd flipped her, then squeezed, fondled, and glided inward, she had enjoyed. But afterward, Aqua wondered.

Why had Genie said things had spoken to her?

Aqua *almost* felt like something was being shown her, but she could not decipher it. Grandma Bayliss always did say Aqua had 'the sight' and that Aqua could sense things. Still, Aqua felt she wasn't truly seeing. GB would say that was because she wasn't ready.

Allowing Noel to help her into the rear of a gleaming black sedan, Aqua's mind went back to Genie. Maybe Eugenia just wanted company.

Somehow, Aqua knew there was more. Due to that, wildly, Aqua's stomach lurched and roiled as they bumped down the tree-lined drive. Oh

Lord, her hands were clammy too. Suddenly, Aqua felt just like she did whenever she was about to board a roller coaster.

Chapter 25

AQUA had been told about the inhabitants of Steeple Chase Place. Therefore, when the driver pulled up, and Aqua saw people queued on the front steps, she mentally assigned names.

On the top step, there was a bright-skinned, slender young woman. That had to be Sonsa. The girl-Friday wore a triangle bandana. Still, her wavy hair spilled down her back in a long, thick, sandy brown braid. In the sparse sunlight, some of Sonsa's hair appeared blond.

Why did Aqua feel like she'd seen the young woman before? Aqua knew it was unlikely as she noticed the average woman on the step below. That would be Katherine. Her husband was the houseman, Eldon. The pair served and did a host of unsung oddities.

Approximately five-eight, with close-cut graying hair, Eldon wore dark trousers. In his crisp white shirt, he stood ramrod straight.

The round older woman on the ground had to be Desdemona—the one with whom Genie had said make friends. Wearing a white kerchief, the woman smiled, and the sun glinted off a gold-wrapped tooth. Her gold wasn't showy brash or ghetto, but the buttery smooth metal that had once been a dentistry staple. Like GB's late husband, grandpa Bayliss, Aqua suspected Desdemona's gold was more a corrective measure.

Aqua glanced at yet others as she placed her hand in Noel's to exit the touring sedan. Ms. Gold Band stepped forward. Knowing a moment of inexplicable joy, Aqua walked into the outstretched chubby arms adorned with silver bangles. In the embrace, Aqua chuckled when she smelled the spices.

Feeling as though she already knew Aqua, Ms. Gold Band gleefully rasped. "Welcome to Miraunga." She nodded, "Been waitin' on yuh."

"Thank you; Desdemona—right?"

"Thass right." The round cook squeezed Aqua's hand.

So *this* was Steeple Chase Place, Aqua thought, walking with the woman who cooked. Beneath the graying sky, Aqua hardly noticed flurries of activity. However, she saw the house and grounds. Both appeared spooky. Aqua suddenly remembered a morbidly mysterious movie classic. *The Spiral Staircase.* The place reminded her of it.

Jethro and Jet Tu whisked baggage around the side of the house while Noel spoke with Eldon. As Aqua passed, the trusted houseman offered a regal nod. To meet Aqua, slender Sonsa gracefully descended the wooden stairs. Then formally, Noel introduced Eldon. Aqua met Aaron, the property-keep, and his wife. Aqua met others she would not remember

After moments of inane pleasantries, Noel placed a hand on her elbow. As if on cue, those who served filed silently into the old house.

It was massive, Aqua thought. The place also appeared nearly overgrown. Dotted by centuries-old oaks and brushwood, the land felt wild. Involuntarily, Aqua shivered before turning to Noel. "How long did you say you've lived here?"

"I've never lived here," he divulged. "I've been out a few times, trying to create order, because I recently came into possession of it. The property was passed down through my father's family. The staff came with."

Aqua opened her mouth, "But Genie said—"

Noel cut her off. "Genie, Jethro, and I came out last year for the first time. That's when I found out the place needed a complete electrical overhaul. However, we got nothing done. Genie made our stay miserable. Then at night, she walked the floors. I'm sure she told you."

Glancing at the overcast sky, Aqua wondered if they should get inside. The wind angrily blew leaves, and branches bowed and creaked.

Startling her, but not Noel, Jethro appeared, seemingly on silent cat feet. His voice squawked like a rusty hinge. "Look like a mighty spring rain's a' coming, suh."

Noel nodded, grasping Aqua's hand as thunder cracked and made her jump. "It sure does. Go relax, Jet—and save me some sweets!" Beginning to jog, Noel pulled Aqua. "Come! Quick tour," he called over the whir of leaves and the whistle of the wind.

Hurriedly, Aqua tromped with him around the side of the house, on a broken brick path. Beneath an arthritic swaying branch, she noticed a black iron pole. Attached to it by rusted links of chain was a small black metal sign. Covered with the detritus of years, it could not be read. Forgetting it, Aqua trotted after Noel, who held her hand. He gestured at the back yard that appeared somewhat better, like the two Jethro's and Aaron the property-keep had gone at it. Aqua scanned the large expanse of land pricked with unkempt shrubbery. As the wind furiously whipped, she saw various flowerbeds, swaying trees, and a leaning gazebo. In the distance, she saw a fence. It surrounded a primeval graveyard. Further beyond, towering pines swayed, and Noel yelled over the wind. 'Back there' was a swamp and authentic Negro slave quarters.

Nice, Aqua sardonically thought. Suddenly, her mind drifted to the young woman with hazel eyes. Bright faced Sonsa. There was something about her. Aqua could not figure it out, but perhaps it also called to Noel. Therefore, Aqua stopped. "You ever slept with her?"

With warm wind whipping his pant legs, Noel turned. "Who?"

Aqua's amber eyes held Noel's darker brown ones, "Sonsa."

Puzzled, the homeowner frowned. "Why would you ask that?"

Aqua's gaze remained steady. "Why don't you answer?"

In the wind, Noel walked toward Aqua, "I've not had Sonsa."

"Why not?"

"Why would I? Simply because she's here? You think so little of me that you believe I'd have any woman present if she'd let me?"

"I believe there's something...*intriguing* about her."

"To *you*," Noel countered, his eyes on Aqua's. "However, to *me*, Sonsa is my employee. Secondly, she's twenty-something, too young. I need a fully blossomed woman, one who knows her own mind. Thirdly," Noel was on a roll, "for me, a woman needs to be built like...*you*. Not *flacca*, like a reed-thin *niña*, a skinny baby. Ah, and lastly, *Aqua Mira*," Noel's Latin accent became more pronounced. "I believe in *fidelidad*."

"But you're not married."

"Sonsa is, and thereby, off-limits to me."

Despite the wind, Aqua began walking, but Noel remained. So gracefully, she turned, peeling strands of hair from her brow. "Thank you for answering." Aqua's voice warbled on the wind that plastered her long skirt to her and outlined her shape. "Now, we were going this way?"

Noel's smile was slow. It also lit up his eyes, because man, was Aqua something! "We were," he acknowledged, wanting her. "I think we've got to change course, though." With the wind at their backs, tetchily pushing, Noel sprinted forward. Grasping Aqua's hand, he steered her to the house. There, with heads lowered against the first fat drops, they took the back steps. The couple dashed inside, just as furious rain pelted, and loudly, Noel kissed Aqua before they collapsed in gales of laughter.

April Alisa Marquette

Afterward, Aqua gazed around. This kitchen was nothing like the inviting one on Sapelo, at Cricket Hill with Genie. There were dull black and white tiles, and the white-washed cabinets did not brighten the space, perhaps because of the dark curtains. Well, there was the good smell of food, Aqua thought as she and Noel entered a darkly paneled hallway. The dining room was another drab affair, but at least the windows were clean, displaying the havoc wrought outside. Aqua wondered about the funky wallpaper. Velvet pineapples dotted a faded shimmering background. Aqua eyed a long table and giant wooden chairs. The carved arms ended in animal paws with talons. The only thing that kept the room from being a dragon's lair, Aqua mused, was the massive chandelier. Glass double doors leading out to a stone terrace and a curved balustrade were redeeming qualities.

Aqua was led into a parlor, then a library, not nearly as extensive or as inviting as the one at Cricket Hill. She was led into a room with lead-paned windows instead of walls. This, the most modern of all, was clearly Noel's office. In his receiving room, the sad, red, velvet settee had seen better days. Over the mantel, a painting caught Aqua's attention.

A woman in white sat on a carpet of grass. While gazing, Aqua spoke. "How strange... her *back* is toward us."

"That is going." Noel said there were several throughout. "All destined for the fire," when the property-keep burned leaves and refuse.

Upstairs, the second level was better, a bit more lived in. Among others, Noel's room, and his sitting room, were there. A room for Aqua, if she wanted, housed her belongings. It had a connected dressing room.

"You know I want you with me, though, right?" Noel inquired.

Down the corridor, was a small water closet. Beneath a window, it housed a white commode. There was also a small sink. At the hall's end, Noel turned into another door. It was a huge bath with a two-sink vanity and a large cushioned window seat. It had been newly done in tiny aquamarine colored glass tiles. There was no commode, but an open shower and a massive tub, so Aqua figured the room was for bathing, alone. There were fluffy new bamboo towels, rugs, and candles. Chuckling, Aqua said it was the first luxurious thing so far.

Noel said, "Despite the work done, it's mildewy. Water damage."

During their short speak, Desdemona had indeed mentioned a fire. Perhaps that was to what Noel referred, Aqua surmised. They passed a narrow, darkly paneled stairwell. "That leads to the third level." Noel waved. "I've yet to get to that. The *electridad* is my main concern."

Passing that close, dark staircase, Aqua felt inexplicably chilled. Although she did not altogether dislike the house, Aqua could see why Genie had—especially if she'd stayed in its vast underbelly. It did not matter that a gym had been installed. Down there was most creepy. *Lord*, Aqua thought, one couldn't aptly call that nether region a basement because the water table was too high. She shivered. Those lower windowless cement rooms probably sat in the water surrounding the island—this Miraunga Isle, whose name even sounded wrong.

Suddenly, Aqua wanted to grab Noel's hand and run away. However, she steeled herself. She rationalized silently; she could just wish for the comfort of her ever-praying Grandmother, or for sweet Genie.

AQUA sat at the kidney-shaped vanity, readying herself for dinner. She thought she heard Noel silently enter the dressing room behind her. In a moment, he would probably hug her or trail his fingers over her exposed shoulders and make her tingle, as he often did.

However, when he did not touch her or say anything, Aqua turned. Noel was not there. Therefore, in the light of the fringed lampshade, Aqua again leaned toward the oval mirror. Moments later, something moved in her peripheral. Now *that* had to be Noel. Aqua had seen his large frame. She'd heard what, too, whispering? Yet when she again faced the moldy-smelling beige and green room, no one was present. Therefore, Aqua turned, busying herself. However, while applying fragrance, she glimpsed someone behind her. The fine hairs on her nape stood, and she jerked around, not liking this cat and mouse mess, and especially not in an old house the size of this one.

Attempting to shrug the creepy, barely-there feeling away, Aqua's eyes roamed the empty room. She tried to soothe herself by reasoning. The house probably felt strange to her because it was huge, and she was not used to it. That old *graveyard* out back didn't help matters, either. Come to think of it, the way Genie had acted, before what she called 'the family' had left for Miraunga was enough to—

Aqua stopped thinking. She forgot things that might make her jump. She wouldn't make something out of nothing, so she called, "Ocaña…"

He did not answer, but she could have sworn she'd seen him a moment ago. Done with her ministrations, Aqua rose. About to walk to the closet at the far end, she glimpsed a *man*—swiftly entering it.

April Alisa Marquette
133

Aqua blinked because that could not have been! Why would Noel, or any man, need to go into what was now *her* closet?

"Ocaña." Loudly Aqua called out, palming the dressing room's brass doorknob because indeed she was beginning to feel skittish.

"*Liro*?" Noel's voice and muffled footsteps floated from the hallway.

Now that was strange, Aqua thought. Why was he in the *hall*? Why would he have slipped out? Why had he said nothing before exiting?

Aqua shook her head because she only wanted her wrap from the closet, but heck, if she would go in that dark space alone. Therefore, she needed Noel physically present. Now that he was not in the room.

He entered, looking his usual, sexy and relaxed, and Aqua immediately wanted to hop his bones. Instead, she concentrated on his clothing. He wore eggshell-colored slacks and a short-sleeved shirt.

"You called me, *chica*?" He admired Aqua's filmy dress, the color of a midnight sky. Against the backdrop of her beautiful bronze skin, her jewelry winked like stars. "You look amazing." His kiss caused her head to buzz, as though she'd drank too much.

"Thank you," Aqua smiled before her voice lowered with need. "And don't *you* look scrumptious?"

"Good enough to eat?" Noel winked. Cupping her bottom, he growled. "Girl, I want you right now."

"Later," she promised as he kissed her cleavage, "I'll drop this dress. Then you can be the stallion, and I'll be the maiden, riding bareback."

"Why torment me *lirio*?" Noel groaned. "*Diciendome que tengo que esperar* –telling me I have to wait."

Aqua smiled, remembering why she had initially called him. "O, I saw something." She gestured. "I thought you walked into this closet."

"Why would I? I was on the phone with Italy," he apprised her. "But you saw what?" Noel grasped the chain-pull. "A *lagartija*, a lizard, or a palmetto bug?" In the light, he peered in, pushing clothing aside.

"No bugs." Aqua made herself reach in beside Noel. With her breasts pressed to his back, she hurriedly grasped her wrap. "Guess it was nothing," she murmured. Maybe being in a strange place had her mind playing tricks. She probably needed rest too. Thanks to Mr. Good Stuff, Aqua remembered, she really hadn't slept much the past few nights.

"Well, *lirio*, Noel pulled the light. "*Vamos*. Let's go downstairs."

DINNER was an elegant semi-formal affair, with Noel and Aqua seated in the large old dining room. The damask drapes were drawn, and candles threw shadows on the velvet-patterned walls. It seemed Jethro and Jet Tu had eaten earlier, in the kitchen with Katherine, Eldon, and Desdemona, who'd cooked.

"I'm thinking about throwing a party," Noel said. He placed his napkin on his plate. "I'd like to invite a friend—and his wife, from Karina Cay," a neighboring island. "I'd like my doctor friend from here to come too. The three of us went to Tulane together; Doc went on to Emory, while I went to Spain. *Lirio*, you and I should decide on other guests."

"Sounds like it could be fun."

"I wondered," Noel began, "if you might like to host?"

Aqua smiled because a while back, she had been asked something similar. It was how she had again met Noel. "What would I have to do?"

"Just be your effervescent self," Noel advised. He, too, remembered seeing Aqua again at *Apropos*. And since she would one day—hopefully soon—become the lady of the manor, Noel told her, "Just let Katherine, Eldon, and Desdemona know what you'd like; they'll make it happen."

"Well," Aqua began. "Fresh flowers for a start...and we could spill from this room out onto the terrace since it is springtime," Aqua said if the double doors were open, and if the balustrade were alight, things might appear inviting. Ideas lit up her eyes. "We'll need music, too."

Noel's heart nearly stuttered then because Aqua's amber eyes, aglow in the soft light, took him back to a different time and place. Attempting to grasp the memory, Noel sighed as the threads fragmented. When Katherine appeared to mention dessert, he nodded.

Aqua spoke to Katherine, and the accommodating woman nodded. "Very well, Ma'am."

IN his near-dark room, Aqua watched as Noel unzipped his slacks. Her eyes widened when she noticed. He wore nothing beneath. She grinned as his thick male member jutted forward, seeking her. Noel's muscular thighs whispered of power and thrusting, and Aqua felt liquid desire. With her breath quickening, she watched the gold-skinned man point the head of his shaft at her. Several times, he pumped himself. After that invitation, boy did Aqua want! She raised the hem of her dress as her whole body resonated with desire. Seeing that she too wore nothing beneath, Noel told himself he should not have been surprised.

April Alisa Marquette

Snagging Aqua's wrist, Noel pulled her close, pressing her nude lower body to his. Ohhh, she moaned, and her heart hammered as Noel's lips demanded, while his seeking tongue, like his pushing shaft, promised pleasures to come. Breaking free, Aqua gave Noel a little shove. He plunked onto a ladder back chair. Reaching up, Noel's fingertips skittered over Aqua's plump twin orbs. Greedily raising her dress, he dipped his head and sucked. Then, using his teeth on a nipple, he drew a cry. Satisfied that indeed Aqua felt, as he did, Noel held the bottom curve to tip Aqua's breast up, where it might meet his lips.

Aqua moaned, and within seconds, she and Noel were ravenous. As Aqua removed her dress, Noel watched. Midnight blue pooled at her feet. Noel blinked when Aqua stepped from it and dropped to her knees before him. Reaching to unbutton and push his shirt from his shoulders, she flicked fingertips over his chest. Seated with legs wide and his testes and cock beckoning, the man moaned. With anticipation, he spoke.

"*Lirio, poseer*, let me have you."

"Not yet." Aqua worked Noel's shaft, as conversationally, she spoke. "I agreed earlier that you looked good enough to eat. So," using her mouth, she encircled him. With warm jaws, she laved him until he glistened. Covering his small silken head, Aqua did the delectable. They were things of which Noel had only dreamed. When he could no longer stand it, Noel jerked Aqua up. With her straddling him, he murmured. "Lemme suck these big sexy *tetas*."

She thrust them forward as his body tried to breach hers. Feeling his hands vise at her hips, she said, "Make you a deal. You suck *and* fu—"

Feverishly, he covered her naughty mouth with his. With large hands cradling Aqua's backside, he pried her apart, as slowly she lowered herself, until he filled her. She sighed, and Noel jiggled her bottom. "No, *lirio*, you cannot just sit here."

Aqua moaned and savored the feel of him, despite knowing why he whined. "Oh, so you need me to *move*." Ravenously, she kissed Noel as she did. "And you want me to take you… deeper."

When she did, it was with torturous and slow precision, and Noel felt he would lose his mind. Slowly building momentum, Aqua felt him push back, higher and higher. Experiencing unbridled ecstasy, she arched her back.

Watching, Noel thought her glorious. The very sight of her, nude, with her head back and one arm raised, while her teeth clenched her lip… That picture he wanted to always remember.

When Aqua sank downward, Noel met her. He strained to get more into her. As he did, Noel became cognizant that never before had he felt so primal. Sure, there had been others. He had screwed the hell out of them, but this was different. It was ferocious, but it was also tender. As he angled himself to drive deeper, Noel felt Aqua's body clamp around him. With a near scream, she shuddered. Then he plunged.

Moments later, feeling mellow and such gentleness toward her, Noel gathered Aqua close. Rubbing her back, he noticed. Perspiration thinly veiled her. Forgetting it, he kissed her face, her eyelids, and her lips.

Noel also whispered. "I can't lose you, *lirio*…ever."

Draped loosely around him, Aqua was too drained to speak.

Unaware, Noel only knew that never before had he felt this way, and it hit him. He *loved* Aqua! He felt in some way, he always had.

Noel pondered loving Aqua. But how did he *know*? He had never loved another. However, before, with others, it had just been sex. With her, sex was excellent, but there was more. Noel felt admiration and amusement. With Aqua, there was crazy need, wrapped up in adoration. When he looked in her eyes, he saw the future, the one he now wanted. When Noel saw Aqua's naked body, he saw the home of his unborn children. Now when he thought of her, he felt protectiveness, and fear…

Though he was not fully aware of it, Noel sensed he could lose Aqua. To what, or to whom, he did not know. However, Noel felt the lurking. Therefore, with lips at her temple, he whispered. "Stay with me, *lirio*, forever. Marry me."

Speechless, Aqua's heart beat double time. And though she remained silent, her heart had no such qualms. It sang yes!

Aware that she'd said nothing, Noel held Aqua tightly. When she rose to go lie on his bed, he followed and curved around her. As she drifted off, against her bottom, Aqua felt Noel enlarge, again. Sleepily, she murmured, "Ocaña, never again talk about *my* appetite." With him wrapped around her, she snuggled closer. "My big stallion, I'm ready."

He liked that she was as greedy as he, yet Noel said, "Later. Now *silencio*. Just sleep," he advised, because, wanting intensely, he would not.

FITFULLY, Aqua slept, drifting in and out of dreams. Then floating silently down the long hall outside Noel's room, she found herself climbing a carpeted staircase. Directed by indecipherable whispers, she found herself on a small landing. She climbed higher still.

Did she actually hear young children's idyllic laughter? It floated to her. Drawn to the half-open door that sunlight streamed through, Aqua tiptoed. Wanting to peer inside, she hoped to glimpse the children and the reason they laughed. Hurrying forward, Aqua ached to see the children, carelessly splashing about, because they sounded darling.

The sun's rays pouring from the bathroom suddenly became too bright. Blinding, the light caused Aqua to stand a moment, to get her bearings. When she could again see, perhaps because a cloud passed over the sun, she felt so different... With purpose, she strode forward. Her feet felt heavy, and sweaty, as though she wore boots when she had been barefoot. Now she felt inexplicable anger. Bursting through the doorway, she heard the laughter dissolve. Now there were frightened whimpers.

Aqua did not see the babies, but she felt their fear, fed on it. She felt their small bodies, too, beneath her hands—*man* hands! Aqua felt silken curls as angrily she pushed on little heads. Ignoring strangled struggles, her clothes became wet. She forgot the frantic thrashing because all she cared about was her own deadly exertion. Aqua felt the grunts. Beginning in her chest, they emitted through her parted lips. Anger was expelled from her body. It gave her a burst of energy. This she used to submerge and hold the two small bodies down, beneath the warm water. Then somehow...she felt anger seep away. She felt smug and satisfied. There. She nodded, as just that quickly, the flailing and the bubbles ceased. With heavy footsteps, she backed up –and wildly ran.

"*Lirio*," Noel called. "*Aqua Mira*, wake up."

Opening her eyes, she saw that it was morning, and not afternoon, as it had been, upstairs. Aqua's eyes hurt as she peered at Noel, who rubbed her shoulder. "What did you dream?" He took her elegant hand.

Aqua blinked. So *that's* what that was? She'd *dreamed* that? Not entirely sure and dreading what she'd feel, she touched at her torso. Above the sheet tangled at her waist, she felt no wet! Oh, thank God!

"Ocaña," Aqua finally managed, her heart aching along with her pounding head. "It was *awful*."

Seated on the bed, shower-fresh and sexy in a tee and nylon b-ball shorts, Noel handed Aqua a glass of apple juice. "Want to talk about it?"

She sipped. "What time is it?"

"Eleven-thirty. I let you sleep because...well, you know."

Aqua remembered last night. *That* had been real; with his body, Noel had covered her and taken her from the rear. The stallion and the maiden, not a dream. But the other? Following a cold sip, she tried not to shudder. "O, there were babies, here—upstairs, on the third floor, in the bathroom. Things were different than I suspect they are now. The bath had a rag rug, a basin, and a pitcher on a stand—just old-timey stuff, along with a big washtub, but the place seemed so lived in..."

Noel remained silent, willing Aqua to continue.

She sipped and spoke. "In the—*dream* I up—and killed...them." Aqua whispered that last because the very notion sickened her. "I drowned them, Ocaña!" Aqua's eyes widened with horror. Attempting to calm herself, Aqua admitted what she had experienced had been so unlike anything she had ever before dreamed. "It was *real*. I could *feel* those small children's *hair* under my hands...as I held them down in their own bathwater." Aqua swiped at a tear. "I feel nauseous." She gagged, and cried. "I feel like the biggest *monster*."

Suddenly Aqua appeared frightened. "What rational person dreams that?" She needed to know. Aqua did not care that not having known her long, Noel might wonder about her sensibilities.

However, only believing Aqua had had a rough night, Noel offered comfort while using a thumb on a tear. "That's awful, bae, but dreams come, and sometimes they're strange." He well knew.

Aqua grasped Noel's wrist. "In my family," she stated, her amber eyes capturing his, "dreams *mean* something. Either they're a *foretelling*, or they scream of things that have *already been*."

Suddenly, Aqua realized why her mother drank. Rayfa most likely could not deal with what GB called the 'sight.' It caused one to see, in dreams and visions, and Rayfa was said to have it, like her daughter.

Unaware of Aqua's musings, Noel attempted to be accommodating by saying he would get Katherine to bring hot tea. "I should not have offered that cold drink. Your insides need warming. I'll get Sonsa to run you a hot bath," he offered. "She can lay out your clothes too if you want." Kissing Aqua's forehead and encircling her, Noel rocked. "My *niña*, I should not have fed you so late last night, and plied you with drink, all before I took advantage of you, several times."

Aqua smiled and relaxed within the protective cocoon of Noel's large arms. She knew different, although she remained silent. What she'd dreamed had nothing to do with gorging herself on man, food, or drink.

Chapter 26

SHE felt tired, drained, really. It was the only reason Aqua allowed bright-faced Sonsa to run her bath, that and the fact that a shower seemed like work. At least in the tub, Aqua could sit and become restored.

Done straightening and dusting Aqua's room, Sonsa returned to see about the mistress of the house. Lightly the young mother rapped. Entering and eyeing aquamarine tiles, Sonsa laid huge fluffy towels aside as she also insisted on washing Aqua's back.

Aqua finally agreed. With eyes closed, she asked, "How long have you worked here?"

"Since Mister Noel first come out," Sonsa's voice was surprisingly deep. "But my family's been in and 'round this ol' house for centuries."

Aqua sighed because, expertly, Sonsa kneaded the kinks from her back. Previously, Aqua hadn't been aware that they were there.

"You like it here, buttercup—" Aqua caught herself and explained. "I mean no harm; it's just that your face reminds me of sunshine."

Sonsa chuckled. "It's butter-colored, I know, and I don't mind. Name's cute, especially since I've been called worse, on occasion."

"Good. Do you like it here?" Aqua asked again.

"I like to feed that growing boy baby of mine," Sonsa chuckled. "And it's not bad working for Mr. Noel." She quickly explained. "He's fair, and I get the time I need to finish my second degree." Sonsa murmured, "If one can forget all that's happened in this house…"

Aqua thought it best to get out of the tub before falling asleep under Sonsa's gentle hands. Rising, Aqua admitted, "I've heard that a couple of times. Now, I'm curious. What happened here?"

"Ain't Desdemona hinted at the telling already?" Hazel-eyed Sonsa held out a large warm towel, shielding Aqua's nudity.

"She said a few things," Aqua revealed, knotting the warm fibers at her chest. "I know there was a fire. Was anyone hurt?"

"Des told you…" Sonsa ran water. "Lotta folk been hurt 'round here."

"At that swamp out back?" Aqua inquired. "Are there alligators?"

"Maybe a few dead men's bones too," deep-voiced Sonsa murmured.

"Really? Why would those be there? Is it easy to get sucked in?"

Sonsa did not reply. Running water, she unnecessarily scrubbed.

"Talk to me," Aqua requested. "I'd really like to know."

When the younger woman benignly smiled and continued to work, Aqua knew she would get no more, not then, so she thanked Sonsa.

"No need to thank me." The slender one stood. "It's my job."

"Yes, but you went the extra mile, you know?"

Beatifically, Sonsa smiled, and Aqua mused aloud. "I'll bet your son is a handsome lil' thing, right—does he look like you?"

Sonsa beamed, "My Hiram says baby boy favors the ancestors."

Aqua nodded. "I'd like to meet your boy, shake his little hand."

The very thought tickled Sonsa. "Yes, ma'am, I'd like that."

Headed to her dressing room, Aqua pondered Sonsa's words and those she'd garnered from the gold-toothed raspy-voiced Desdemona. Aqua realized she'd believed Desdemona to be a disgruntled older employee. Now Aqua wasn't so sure. Desdemona had intimated that Steeple Chase Place had many secrets. The cook said the house had caught afire but had been restored, just before Desdemona mumbled. By right, it should have burned clean away or been razed to the ground. Then the older woman had vehemently muttered 'wicked, wicked.' She shook her covered head. At that moment, Desdemona had reminded Aqua of Genie. Wonder what *she* was doing, back at the beautiful, inviting Cricket Hill? Aqua vowed to call Genie.

Dressed, Aqua did so, and though tired afterward, she itched to explore the upper floor. She and Noel had not toured the third level. He hadn't said not to go up, so Aqua intended to, before she took an exploratory walk outside, to familiarize herself with the grounds.

Aqua left her room. In the second floor hallway that possessed one window to let in light, Aqua walked to the narrow stairwell. As the fine hairs on her nape began to stand, Aqua heard nearly inaudible, indecipherable whispers. Then she also felt as though a louder voice admonished her to 'go back.' Heedless, she allowed herself to be drawn up the stairs, sliding her hand along the dark, wide-plank wood paneling as she went. At the top, Aqua glanced into the room directly across the hall. She felt a chill when it was warm out, and ceiling fans whirred in the majority of the house. Aqua sure hoped she wasn't getting sick.

She stepped onto the worn brown carpet, also on the stairs. It covered the second-floor hallway too. Why the dirt color? Aqua wondered. Whoever had selected it, she thought, had very little decorating sense.

Up here, Aqua noticed, the hallway was wide, like the one below. There was no hall window, but on the gloomy third floor, there were more rooms. It also had the distinct feeling of a prison. It felt like a place where a woman and her dreams could wind up on lockdown, forever.

Forgetting that, Aqua noticed. Some rooms weren't large, but all were dusty and unused. To her, this part of the house seemed forgotten. Most of the furniture had been, or appeared about to be, thrown out.

The room that fronted the house was sun-filled. That light spilled into the hallway. Entering the room, Aqua found it stifling hot, and the windows were stuck shut. Above lousy linoleum, cracked and yellowed with age, dust motes danced. Aside stood a small chest of drawers. There was a drab, upholstered chair and a lumpy twin bed. Scattered on it were a profusion of dolls. The sad lot were old and naked. Most were missing limbs or eyes, and what hair remained was matted.

"Why these ugly babies could scare The Bride of Chucky," Aqua said into the quiet. She dropped one dusty creature back to the uncovered, stained mattress. Turning to leave, she saw Jethro Tulle. Out of doors, sweating, he marched around with his hatchet. Aqua smiled and entered another room, then another, the one across from the staircase. That eerie-feeling room she did not like. Its windows were also immovable. Turning, Aqua realized on that side of the house, the sun wasn't visible. Seen only was a thicket of gnarled trees, quite a dismal view.

Aqua quickly exited and found the small water closet, just above the one below. However, the brown ring inside the commode, and no water, suggested it was non-working. Dry, the small sink faucet sputtered.

When she got to the bath, Aqua pushed, but the door seemed jammed. She used her shoulder, but it would not yield. That piqued Aqua's interest. She would ask Noel about it or one of the others who worked the property. Surely, somebody would open it for a harmless peek.

Forgetting the bath, Aqua headed back to the stairwell. In route, she passed a linen closet and another small room with no door. Peering into the dimness that seemed to be a catch-all, Aqua saw an old metal bedpan. The two ends of a wooden crib were against the back wall. In the tiny dim space was a dilapidated rocker, a walking stick, and other items, including a soft, graying baby shoe.

With a shiver, Aqua hurried to the staircase and nearly tripped down it because it was all too creepy. Though there were no more than twelve steps, she could not seem to move fast enough. Racing, Aqua actually felt like she fled someone—or something. Dashing onto the second floor, out of breath, she nearly collided with Sonsa. Serenely the young woman carried a laundry basket on her hip but seeing Aqua, Sonsa's eyes immediately rounded. Noting the bright-skinned woman's alarm, Aqua asked what was wrong. "Buttercup," Aqua called out.

Sonsa shook her head as steadily she backed away. She stammered as she did, "It's n-n-nothing." Yet Aqua tried to catch up.

However, Sonsa hastened away, her deep voice floating back, "Ain't good to go up there, Missy; and *never* by your lonesome."

Staring after slender Sonsa, Aqua felt chilled, to the bone.

IN the black and white tiled kitchen, with pen and pad before her, Aqua discussed party arrangements. Also, with suggestions, short round Desdemona bustled about while preparing the evening meal.

"Ain't ever been a party here," the older woman rasped.

Aqua appeared shocked, "Why not?"

With a white kerchief on her head, round Desdemona shrugged. "Ain't ever been a thing to celebrate."

That was strange, Aqua thought, and all the more reason to party.

Passing the woman of the manor, Desdemona took a good look. She inquired of the younger woman. "Missus, you been sleeping alright?"

With a sigh, Aqua told the truth. "Not since we arrived." She knew why she hadn't slept at Cricket Hill; Noel was partially to blame, as was her greed for him. Just thinking about him could cause her to grow wet with want. However, since arriving on Miraunga Isle, Aqua could not say why she had not slept. Perhaps it was because Steeple Chase was big, old, and musty; for her, the house conjured up ugly images, none of which was conducive to peaceful sleep.

Desdemona appeared concerned. "Yuh been dreamin' and tossing?"

"I have," Aqua admitted, penciling something, "but I'll be alright."

Desdemona said nothing, although she genuinely did not like the darkness beneath Aqua's eyes. And the purty thang had not eaten much of anything—that Desdemona had seen. Not a good sign.

Perhaps, Desdemona mused while cooking, she could talk Mister Noel into taking his bride away. Wasn't that what he'd called Mistress Aqua? At least Desdemona thought he had.

THAT evening following a wonderful dinner, which she barely touched, Aqua left Noel. As he lingered in conversation with Aaron, the property-keep, she climbed the stairs. She had a relaxing soak in mind.

Aqua found a surprise in her dressing room, the most exquisite gown, spread on her bed. The style was from another era. It was ecru silk, and perhaps it had once been pure white. Beautiful seed pearls graced the neck and sleeves, and Aqua surmised. The nightgown had probably belonged to Noel's mother. Maybe it had been part of a peignoir set. So how special, Aqua thought, that Noel wanted her to have it.

Feeling honored, Aqua told herself she really had to ponder Noel Cristián Ocaña's proposal. Although he'd been patient and hadn't pressed, she knew he wanted an answer, if possible, by Saturday, the day of the party. Perhaps, he wanted to announce their engagement.

After she bathed and slipped into the oh-so-delicate gown, Aqua looked at herself in the mirror. How perfect. The garment fit as though it was made expressly for *her*. The neck revealed the graceful turn of her shoulders and the soft swell of her breasts. As in the mirror she preened, Aqua blinked. She wondered. Was it the dim light? Did it make her look ethereal and so unlike herself? Unnerved, Aqua turned away because never before had she looked so unlike herself. However, she glanced back. She wondered. Why did it seem she wasn't looking at herself in the mirror but at another woman? Aqua shivered. With hammering heart, she marveled at the eyes, sorrowful and darker than her own amber eyes. Then Aqua recalled a dream... Forgetting it, and what she deduced to be the tricks of dim light and a mirror, Aqua headed toward Noel's room. Scented candles burned as he too entered, from his adjacent sitting room.

"There you are, love," he said, "I thought I might have to fetch you." Noel's eyes traveled admiringly over Aqua as the timbre of his voice lowered. "You look exceptionally beautiful tonight, *lirio*."

She had *him* to thank for that, and walking forward to take Noel's outstretched hand, Aqua noticed his other.

In it, Noel held a small, felt jeweler's box. Not releasing it, he pulled Aqua toward the bench at the foot of the bed. "Sit down. *Siéntate*."

She did, and he knelt before her in the candlelight. "I know you probably didn't take me seriously when I asked before. So..." Noel flipped up the lid. "I'll ask you again. Marry me, *Aqua Mira*. Take this ring," Noel admonished, "and let me prove I will love you—with my body and my mind. Let me cherish you, forever."

When he slipped the dazzling fiery stone on her finger, Aqua grasped Noel's hand. With fingers intertwined, she kissed him. Then when she took his face in both her hands, Noel experienced déjà vu. It was as though he and she had done this very thing *before*.

Aqua kept her lips pressed to Noel's as softly she spoke. "I will marry you." She kissed him again, "And thank you."

His large elegant hands slid to her waist. "For?"

"For being you." He was everything she had ever dreamed of and more. He was real; he was into her; Noel did not care who knew it, *and* he wanted her, not just to lie with, but to commit to, to build a life with. "O, I'm thankful for everything," Aqua acknowledged. "For this time together, for this beautiful ring, and for this gown."

Noel appeared puzzled. He'd had nothing to do with the gown, and so he said. "This is the first time I've seen it. And no, I did not have someone purchase it," he admitted. "Although I'd like to accept the points, I cannot—even though it is exquisite."

Aqua blinked. "Then who...would have?"

Noel shrugged. He had no idea. He only knew that the women employed in both this home and at Cricket Hill seemingly doted on Aqua. Perhaps one of them had secretly presented it. The men knew better; he would take it as a personal affront. "It does not matter," Noel softly stated, his mind returning to the goddess before him. "The gift came from someone here. So," he told Aqua, using a thumb to smooth her frown. "*Mañana*, I will ask, solve our little mystery. Now, did I say you look beautiful?"

Aqua chuckled, admitting he had. She tried not to feel icky and strange, now. To combat the feelings, she focused on Noel's ministrations, his lips on the curve of her breast, but she recalled the gown. Again, questions rose. Whose gown, or whose gift? Perhaps it had been hazel-eyed Sonsa, Aqua thought, because it had been said Desdemona rarely braved the stairs. The cook had arthritic knees. *But*, Aqua thought as Noel kissed and laid her down, Sonsa had been gone *before* dinner. Aqua had bid the younger woman adieu, before Aqua had changed for dinner, so, who? Finally, she stopped wondering, and drifted away, on the erotic wave created by the man she had agreed to marry.

Chapter 27

THAT night, Aqua left Noel's bed. Amid incessant whispers urging her on, she floated up the small narrow staircase to the third-floor bath. This time the door was not stuck. Partially open, familiar children's laughter floated out. It seemed Aqua had heard the airy giggles many times before. But hadn't...she—or someone—killed the children?

As she glided forward, her feet never seeming to touch the floor, Aqua's heartbeat quickened. With her hand on the brass knob, she peered inside and saw two golden-haired babes. Perhaps they were three-year-olds, but they could have been four. They had halos of spiral curls. Splashing and laughing, their little faces beamed like sunshine. Their butter-colored skin was smooth, stretched taught over curvy small arms, legs, and unblemished backs.

When they turned their heads, still giggling, Aqua saw their little button noses and lush lips. Aqua wondered, where the children bi-racial?

Then one child pivoted to look at her. Slowly, the other child faced her too. Aqua squinted as she wondered what color their eyes were.

They were...amber, like hers. No, green. Wait, were they gray? Unable to tell, Aqua moved forward. Suddenly she screamed and backed up because the children's eyes were actually hollowed-out sooty *sockets*!

Tickled at her distress, the little ones turned to face away.

Horrified, Aqua watched their hair begin to droop as though it were wet. The spiral curls straightened, right before her eyes. Covering the children's necks, their growing hair hid their backs before covering their bodies, and slowly the children slid downward in the water.

Aghast, Aqua ran forward. Slipping in a puddle outside the tub, she did not care. All she cared about was saving her babies. Reaching into the tub, she grasped an arm, but boneless, it slid from her grip. Desperate, Aqua tried again, and again, to save the children as they slid around in the tub like eels, covered with sleek wet hair.

Where were their faces? She frantically wondered while fighting to part the tresses that had so rapidly sprung from the little heads. In horror, Aqua realized, the little ones had no faces, not anymore!

Then she woke, to Noel's distressed call. He appeared strained, as holding her tightly, he asked, "Another bad dream, *lirio*?"

SHE was so sick. Aqua could hardly get out of bed. She didn't even try, although there were many things she and Noel had planned to do. However, Aqua barely had the strength for a shower.

Even that, she found a struggle. In the sizeable sunlit bathroom with water pelting, Aqua leaned against shimmering tiles. Attempting to catch her breath, she wondered why she felt like she was coming down with something. Was malaria like this? Raising her face to the warm spray, Aqua prayed that whatever this was would pass before the party.

Finally able to exit the shower, she sat on the vanity bench. Wrapped in a bath sheet, the bronze woman stared out of the window. With a hand on herself, she attempted to still her rapidly beating heart.

Outside, the sun was bright, and the verdant green vista slowly took shape. Jethro, Jet Tu, Aaron, and others had beaten and hacked the wild growth into submission. She gazed out at colorful island flora. Aqua felt the out of doors was almost ready for Saturday. Indoors, with its dreariness, was another story.

Narrowing her eyes, Aqua suddenly wondered. Why did it feel like she had been outside, recently—like this morning? Why was the knowledge strange...and ticklish to the edges of her consciousness? It almost seemed as though she should not have been out, like when she was young, and GB had said stay in, but Aqua had snuck out anyway.

Aqua shook uneasiness away. She was grown, and feeling chided was ridiculous. Especially when the truth was she had been in bed. She remembered. She and Noel had gone to bed after he'd removed that lovely gown from her. Hey, she would ask Desdemona if she knew who'd presented it. Exiting the bath, Aqua wanted to thank whoever had offered it. Actually, she mused, it had probably been Eldon's wife. Unlike Desdemona, Katherine climbed stairs. And unlike Sonsa, Kat had been around at dusk the prior evening. So Aqua would find the thoughtful woman before Kat started to believe Aqua was an ingrate.

Back in her room, Aqua laid down. With bent knees and her feet hanging off the side of the bed, she stared up at the ceiling. When Noel appeared, offering to swing her legs up onto the mattress, Aqua waved. Listless, she let her hand drop wearily to the bed. She could only hope big sexy understood because she just did not have the energy to move, not even if he aided her.

Vaguely, Aqua noticed Sonsa. Slender, she bustled about. Aqua thought the younger bright-skinned woman brought soup, but it had seemed dark outside when she'd carried in the tray. That was strange. First, because Aqua could have sworn she had just laid down, after her shower, in the daytime. Besides, Sonsa always went home before dark; Sonsa said she liked spending daylight hours with her small son.

Again, Aqua drifted off. When she woke, she wondered about Noel. With all the companies he had his hands in, she knew he was busy. He had the company that acquired marble from the quarry in Carrera, Italy, and the factory that used timber from Honduras. There were others too, so why, Aqua mused, did it seem he rarely left her side? It was as though Noel stood guard. And what fell off her forehead? A cool compress. Had she been feverish?

Aqua felt herself drift once more. Lord, she sure hoped she wouldn't see her babies again. She didn't like knowing what she had done to them.

Suddenly with alarming clarity, her eyes fluttered open. Why, Aqua wondered, did she feel like the bathwater babies were *hers*? Why did it feel as though she had seen them outside her dreams? The overwhelming feeling that she knew them and loved them was real. She felt as though she had longed to see them while she'd carried them in her womb. As ridiculous as it seemed, Aqua even remembered the song she'd sang to them when it had become evident they were growing inside her…

Oh, God. Aqua struggled up to further analyze disturbing thoughts. The ones that somehow seemed like her own. These feelings were not fleeting, she realized, not like those after a dream. Neither was the anguish she suddenly felt. As unbearable grief washed over her, Aqua fought not to moan aloud. As tears rolled from her eyes, she silently cried and felt as though her heart would break, all over *again*.

Noel's voice drifted to her. This time he seemed so close, with a hand beneath her head. Aqua realized her eyes were closed. She heard how weary Noel sounded as he pled, "Come on, *lirio*, please…Des said eat."

Again, Aqua felt sleep claim her. Then when she woke, Aqua noticed Sonsa. The bright face did not appear so sunny. Sonsa seemed sad and silent, as near soundlessly she moved about, like a ghost in the night.

Aqua tried to turn her head, to let Noel know that he could take the spoon from her lips, and she heard Sonsa speak. Aqua felt warm liquid, too, as it dribbled down her chin. She wondered, why did it seem like Noel had tried to feed her okra soup before?

What was going on? Aqua wanted to know as she attempted to sit up. She was tired of feeling this way! She was weary from crying, and she was sick of this house! Even as a kid, she had hated being cooped up indoors. She wanted to get dressed and go outside. Aqua wanted to go down to the kitchen. She wanted some of Desdemona's jollof rice or homemade lemon meringue pie, but… then again…

Aqua realized she was too tired. So she closed her eyes. She figured she would sleep for just a few minutes more. Aqua was unaware that Noel glanced up at the young woman who said she would take over.

When they changed places, Sonsa pressed a soft cloth to the wet at Aqua's neck. Gently Sonsa spoke. "Come on, baby, we need you to eat."

Aqua felt Sonsa hold the spoon to her lips. Why was someone always at her with that spoon? Aqua was tired of it. For crying out loud, she could feed herself! Why, she could sit at the table, down in that drab-assed pineapple dining room, and she opened her mouth to say so.

"That's right, baby." Sonsa massaged Aqua's throat. "Swallow." Sonsa's deep voice was so soothing it caused Aqua to forget what she had been about to say. Aqua wondered if Sonsa was speaking to her the way Sonsa talked to her small son. Thinking about the little boy, Aqua recalled she had never seen him; but she *had* seen those other children, *her* children.

Aqua felt tears and immense grief. She bawled her heart out, then drifted, once more. She had a lucid moment, however, when she saw Sonsa, who sat bedside. Looking up, Sonsa spoke to Noel. Entering the room, the *prison*, Aqua wondered why he said the doctor was on his way.

Though Noel appeared worried, Sonsa nodded and sighed. "That makes me feel a little better, becuh Doc Dear is the best."

Noel pressed a kiss to Aqua's forehead. Currently, it was cool, a good sign. He hoped. "I'll be back in a bit, *lirio*," Noel said, then he was gone.

Chapter 28

DOWNSTAIRS, in his lead-paned glass office, Noel dialed his college chum. Kijana Kyree lived on the neighboring isle of Karina Cay.

"Oh, hi Noel," Kijana's wife cooed. "How you today?"

Reluctantly, Noel said he was fine, all things considered. He did not fail to add that he sure needed his friend.

Sangria revealed that her husband was at a Chamber of Commerce meeting. "He most likely has his cell phone on vibrate, but I'll ask him to call you the moment I speak with him."

"Would you please?" Noel inquired. Then before he knew it, he tumbled headlong into telling Sangria about Aqua's sleepwalking. He said he was sure Aqua was unaware of it...

One night when Aqua re-entered Noel's bedroom, he'd slowly come awake. He felt her weight on the mattress. Then he woke, when by rote, she sat to slide beneath the sheet. He'd thought she'd come from the water closet. However, the morning after, he noticed small cuts and that the soles of Aqua's feet were dirty. He'd seen a bevy of scratches on her legs too as exhaustedly she'd slept, mostly uncovered. Noel knew those small inflictions came from brambles, low hanging twigs, and rocks. On the floor, he had also noticed bits of leaves and other earthy debris. Noel had gotten the women to clean up and administer a *linimento* that would take the sting from Aqua's nicks and bruises. To Sangria, Noel admitted, "Knowing my Aqua walked while she slept scares the daylights out of me." Noel said it scared the women of the house as well.

"And she's not aware? My Lord," Kijana's wife murmured. "Now I'm scared. Why, at that swamp, Noel, she could become gator bait!"

He well knew. Noel also revealed his fear that Aqua didn't even know she had lost two whole days—with the *current* day being the second.

And instead of returning to his bed, Noel did not say, he'd heard the whine of Aqua's bedroom door when she returned to a bed in which she had never slept. Although he didn't reveal it, Noel knew he would not sleep *at all* when night fell. Noel would need to keep his lovely lily safe. Hadn't he promised to do so, to protect and cherish her, when he'd proposed? That was another thing Noel did not mention. It was personal, although he'd wanted to announce it at the party. However, Noel recalled, still on the phone, since proposal night, Aqua had changed.

To his friend's wife, Noel didn't mention another something he did not like. No one at Steeple Chase had any idea where that gol-dang *gown* had come from! The following morning Noel inquired. When no one knew, although it was very unlike him, Noel had gone on a tirade. He called everyone into the foyer. He had then demanded to know who had neatly placed the garment on Aqua's bed.

"And where the devil is the thing this morning?"

Noel had barked at Sonsa, who did laundry. With tears in her hazel eyes, she'd truthfully said, again, that she had no earthly idea.

Then as Eldon and others stood in Steeple Chase Place's foyer, eyeing the old wood floor, Noel had turned away. Then swiftly, he'd turned back to those who had not moved. "I must apologize." Noel's voice became heavily accented as he took Desdemona's dimpled hand. He said he felt like such a cad. "You all know I would never hurt you. Never before have I berated or attempted to cause anyone to feel small.

"*Lo siento.*" Noel repeated it, "I am *sorry.*" He swallowed hurt. "I loathe my behavior. I will not blame my actions on the fact that so much has happened these past few days. Sonsa..." Noel touched the reed-thin young woman's arm. "Look at me. Please. Will you?"

When she raised brimming hazel eyes, Noel's heart lurched. "I apologize, Sonsa. Please understand, and forgive me."

Loudly then Eldon cleared his throat, as Jethro and Jet Tu looked awkward. "Master Noel, no one blames you." Regally, Eldon stepped forward, gesturing. "I believe I speak for all in saying that within this short time, each of us has become fond of Mistress Aqua. Therefore, if I may say so, sir, perhaps, you should take her *away*...from *this* house. Although we're all aware that you're not particularly a *believer*, this house does seem to have an uh—*unnatural* hold upon the lady." Eldon solemnly nodded and stepped back. "It is merely a suggestion, sir."

None of this did Noel tell his friend's wife, who'd had her own share of hell. Noel did admit one thing, though. He was beginning to believe his and Aqua's arrival on Miraunga Isle had *not* been a good idea.

Chapter 29

SONSA informed Aqua that she had a thing or two to do downstairs. "I'll look in on you, though, before Doc gets here."

When Sonsa was gone, Aqua managed to struggle up. Pulling on a short wrap, she tied the sash. With alacrity, Aqua *knew* she had to get to that murky narrow stairwell, again. She needed to, because when she had run from those sightless children, her hand had slid along the staircase's dark-paneled wall, and one panel had revealed a hidden door.

Slightly unsteady on her feet, Aqua listened before quietly, she opened her bedroom door. She poked her head into the hallway. Again, she listened and heard the usual house noises, but nothing to suggest anyone was near or approaching. Therefore, mustering her strength, Aqua stealthily crept to the staircase. Careful to avoid the creaky places beneath the brown carpet, she hurried. With her heart hammering, Aqua tiptoed upward, feeling the paneled wall as she went.

Nothing. When she felt zilch beneath her fingertips, Aqua's breathing quickened. Feeling around, she knew she would soon become frantic. Someone would come poking about, or the doctor would show up and ruin her plan, and Aqua had to find that door! It was there, she knew, so anxiously, she scratched at grooves and indentations. Aqua damaged her natural, neat-length nails, but she didn't care. This was for her babies!

Aqua shook away the thought that maybe she'd dreamed the door. She had *not!* However, feeling slightly imbalanced, she turned away. She vowed to try again later when everyone was otherwise occupied. Tremendously wearied for no apparent reason, Aqua placed her hand on the wall. She would return to her room. Feeling let-down, she leaned against the dark wood as she put a bare foot out for the lower step.

Pop. She heard it, a little sound. Then the small door opened! Like magic, like she had known. Suddenly feeling buoyed, she slipped inside.

Ick! It was stuffy, dusty, and dark. Despite her attempt to muffle it, Aqua coughed; and nearly shrieked before realizing she'd walked into a spider web. OMG. She heard scurrying noises. Ugh, most likely mice. Suddenly, a thought struck, and Aqua ascended, pushing her way out.

She was nearly blinded by late afternoon light, after the pitch dark. Squinting, Aqua made sure the panel slightly protruded. She needed to again find it. Knowing it was risky, she tiptoed back to her room. Avoiding floor creaks, she hoped Sonsa wouldn't reappear because Aqua would howl.

Through her nightstand, Aqua quickly rummaged. She had seen it. Oh where was it? There! She snatched up the half-gone candle. Good thing she kept a lighter in her purse, just for Rayfa. That Aqua pocketed.

Back at her room door, Aqua listened. Then in the hallway, avoiding floorboards, Aqua realized. She did not feel sick at all. However, she was aware that beneath her bare feet, the horrid brown carpet felt awful. She wondered. How many people had walked on it? Whose dead skin cells and hair was embedded in it? Oh, it didn't bear thinking about.

Tiptoeing quickly to the stairwell, Aqua didn't know *why* she had to do this. Nevertheless, standing on the step next to her invisible door, she listened. She peered downward. Nothing. She cradled her lighter as the candlewick caught. Dipping her head, she entered. Seeing the small handle, she pulled the little door to, but not all the way. She would need out. She couldn't die within those close walls. She'd much rather expire of malaria or whatever island flu the doctor would say she had.

In the flickering candlelight, Aqua turned about, looking. She stood in a wood-paneled staircase, narrower than the one opposite her little door. This was how *slaves* had once moved about the house, unseen, she realized. Aqua walked up. She felt years of dust coat the undersides of her feet as she mused, that was the third floor. Aqua walked down, slightly past her entrance. Was that raspy singing and clanging Desdemona? So, Aqua was near the kitchen. Mental note, next time she went to eat, Aqua would see exactly where the entry was. Before she went further down, perhaps to a cellar, Aqua found herself on a small landing. Stumping her toe, she realized it. Ahhch! That hurt. Well, no wonder; there was a plank of wood, about an inch wide, sticking up. Gently, with her foot, Aqua pressed. Then up stuck the other end.

Immediately, near her ear, it seemed as though someone whispered. *Kneel.* Without question, Aqua did, setting her fat stumpy candle on the step above. Gingerly, Aqua pressed on the plank so as not to break it, old that it was. Again the other end rose. Well, why not? Aqua put two fingers beneath the up end and hoped not to get splinters.

To her surprise, another piece of wood stuck up too. The flickering allowed Aqua to see a small square. Reaching for it, she angled her candle. Not a square, but a box, shoe sized, and made of...wood?

Aqua planted the candle and struggled to remove the box from its dusty burial place. How long had it been there? Who had placed it there? She wondered as she felt the tickle. Oh no! Remembering that Des might hear, Aqua pressed her face to her sleeve. She nearly blew her brains out, muffling the sneeze. The gown she had worn when Noel proposed crossed Aqua's mind. She really needed to know who had given it.

Careful not to fall face-first down the remaining steps, Aqua reached for her candle. With it in hand and the box securely under an arm, unsteadily, she rose, her fingers pressing the wall.

At her little door, she listened. How awkward it would be to smack face-first into Sonsa if slender bounded up the regular stairway. When Aqua heard only distant everyday noises, she slipped out. Was anyone in the house even aware that those stairs existed? Hurriedly entering her own domain, Aqua did not exhale until safely ensconced in her dressing room. Locking the door, she forgot anyone who might look for her.

Aqua told herself she would only take a few minutes. She devised a reason to give if anyone appeared. She would mention her monthly. *On the other hand,* she could say nothing too, because she despised lying.

Seated at her vanity, with sunlight filtering through the old curtains, Aqua eyed the dusty box. It was sealed. Using her fingertips, she picked at, and pried it. It did not open. Grasping her tweezers, then scissors, she leveraged them like a small crowbar.

Finally! With the box open, Aqua saw a wax seal, similar to those GB used when she made preserves in mason jars. Why had someone gone to so much trouble? Aqua wondered. Puncturing the thin wax, Aqua reached past a square of yellowing gauze. Beneath it, she found—what? Reverently, she removed a tiny *gown.* She could see that it had once been white. Gently laying it on her lap, between her stomach and the box, she lifted out another. Both had miniature rosettes made of satin ribbon. All had faded to nearly no color. The garments were doll-sized— or *new baby-sized*! Examining the satin, Aqua could just make out a hint of pink on one and a bit of blue on the other. *Two babies* was the whisper.

Suddenly Aqua's breath hitched, and her heart began to ache in earnest. Grasping the sides of her kidney-shaped vanity, she lowered her head. She felt *all* the anguish again. It slammed into her, bolted through her, just like when Grandpa Cyril Bayliss had died, but worse.

Oh, God! Aqua agonized, nearly torn asunder. Unable to stop the tears, she gasped for breath through the heartache.

When she could finally think despite the onslaught, Aqua realized. She held the christening gowns for both a boy baby and a girl. Someone must have dearly loved those babies, *her* babies. Why else would they go to the trouble of preserving the now nearly dry-rotted garments?

Aqua heard someone coming. Gingerly handling the gowns so that they would not merely disintegrate in her hands, she tried to move quickly. She had her menses story ready. Putting the box top back on, Aqua vowed to return, to go through the remainder, even if the sorrow killed her.

As she slid the box beneath her vanity's faded fabric skirt, Aqua could only wonder.

What *happened* in this house?

The children that she kept seeing, had they worn the gowns now in her possession? Aqua needed to know. She had to ask someone, but the question was, ...*whom*? Noel probably didn't know, and out of all the others, who could she really trust?

Chapter 30

DELL Wynne Dear rang the bell. Standing just outside the old oak and glass doors, he heard the ominous chimes. That dreary racket, the physician thought, Noel really should have it changed.

"Doc-*tor*." Opening double doors, Eldon gestured the slightly tanned physician into the darkly paneled foyer.

As he was escorted upstairs, it was not lost on the tall, raven-haired physician that most of the staff hovered in the hallway or just beyond. In his estimation, that often meant the patient was well-liked. Following Eldon, the doctor realized he would soon know.

Well aware of the doctor's routine, Eldon led the way to the upstairs bath. In the shimmering tiled room, Dr. Dear opened his bag to obtain absorbent paper sheets, his own hand solvent, and surgical gloves. After washing up, the forty-something shouldered his way through the half-open door. Sure to touch nothing, he waited for Eldon, who retrieved his bag. Then Dr. Dear followed the houseman to his patient.

In the faintly mildewy beige and green room that also smelled of expensive lingering fragrance, Dr. Dear noticed the woman. Generously endowed, she pushed herself up in bed. Although her hair was matted, and there was darkness beneath her eyes, she was lovely.

Noel stepped from the shadows beside the door. Knowing the doctor as he did, Noel dared not shake Dell Dear's hand. Instead, Noel nodded. "Glad you're here, Doc."

His drawl southern, Dr. Dear replied. "Ready to be an aid." He took the chair that Noel quickly placed beside the bed. Eyeing the woman through glasses that had slipped down his nose, the slender, forty-ish physician congenially spoke. "Most people call me Doc Dear, and I was told that you are Aqua—a lovely name, I must say."

"Thank you, and for coming to see me," Aqua said, hoping the Patrick Dempsey look-alike would not tell her she only had days to live.

"Now, Ms. Aqua, let's find out what's happening with you…"

Throughout the examination, Noel remained. And often, before Aqua could respond, he replied to the doctor's inquiries.

Stripped of his gloves, Dr. Dear said he would write a prescription to better help Aqua sleep. He also said he would see her again.

Aqua thought that was strange because she hadn't mentioned not sleeping well. However, she had mentioned feeling groggy and like she had lost time. Deftly, the nice-smelling doctor had evaded her questions, but he hadn't said she would immediately expire. Oh well, Aqua sighed. Country island doctors, it seemed they were a strange lot. She would ask Noel what was really the case, since it seemed he and the doctor had a rapport.

Before he left, thickset golden Noel blew Aqua a kiss. Then escorting the doctor out, Noel and the physician remained curiously silent.

Meeting both at the stairs, Eldon led them downward. "Doc-*tor*," Eldon's cultured voice was level, "I am to inquire if you have eaten."

"God love Ms. Desdemona," Dr. Dear chuckled. "Eldon, do tell her that, unfortunately, I had an early suppa with Judge Griswald. However, if I had not, to eat Ms. Des' cooking would have been mah pleasure."

A pity, Dr. Dear thought, that the brown kitchen wiz wasn't many years younger. If she were, he would woo her. Since she wasn't, he would continue to see women who only knew how to microwave. Forgetting others he'd bedded while wearing a surgical mask, the doctor spoke of Desdemona. "In the near future, I will have one of her meals."

Eldon nodded. "Very well, sir."

As the front double doors were opened, Dr. Dear spoke. "By the by, how is your Katherine?"

Eldon's smile was unexpected. "She is…dazzling, sir."

Dr. Dear patted the houseman's arm. "Indeed." Never would the doctor disagree with a thunderstruck husband. "Good evening, Eldon."

"To you too, sir." Eldon clicked the doors closed.

Outside, with crickets chirping and dusk pursued by darkness, Noel spoke. "Okay. Give it to me straight, Dell. What's the deal here?"

Dr. Dear sighed, noticing that Noel looked like he hadn't slept well lately. Also, judging by the shadow on Noel's jaw, he hadn't shaved, either. Well, given what *he* knew of the situation, the handsome physician figured, he too would be bereft of sleep and a shave.

In the gathering dark, Noel rocked on his heels. "Come on, Doc."

As he did with friends and family, the lowcountry doctor slipped into an easy drawl. "Dammit, Noel." Then Dr. Dear exploded, "Ah felt like an effin' fool up there! I haven't felt that way since—my residency. You saw how that woman wanted to know what was going on with huh. All

Ah could do was dance around the issue, so as not to scare huh half to death."

As the two men stood in the gloom, warm winds blew, and an owl hooted. Dragging a hand through raven hair, the lowcountry doctor sighed. "Damn it, Noel," he repeated. "Ah hate when I cain't fix shit."

Something rustled in the underbrush, but in the near dark, Noel ignored it. "No more pins' n needles, Dell. Spit it out, whatever it is."

The physician put his bag down and patted his pockets. When he found it, in the dark, the end of his cigarette glowed. Following a greedy pull, he exhaled. "Yuh know what I'm gonna say."

Light spilled through the front door glass. In the shafts, Noel appeared stricken as he used Dell's nickname. "Vanilla, gol-dang, is it that bad?"

The physician nodded. "Bad enough fuh me to say call Priestess."

Noel's eyes rounded, "But, what *is* it?"

Again, Dr. Dear dragged a hand through thick, raven hair. "Ah honestly don't know. So as your friend, I've said what Ah would do." Again, the physician inhaled, causing cigarette embers to glow.

Noel coughed and waved. "You, of all people, should know better."

Dr. Dear shrugged, "Hey, Ah could be a drunk." The doctor forgot his unhealthy vice. "Ah am aware that many in my field do not believe in alliances between the medicinal and the spiritual. I happen to be different." The physician admitted, "I am also your *friend*, Noel. I know you. You love this woman. It's all over yuh. I know the history of this house too, this land...and it's all spiritual." The doctor gestured. "I've heard the stories, as have you, some firsthand, from Doc Senior..."

Noel knew his friend spoke of his father, the elder, blue-eyed physician from whom the lowcountry practice had been handed down.

"Thangs that old guy experienced *here* were no joke," Dell Wynne Dear voiced as again an owl hooted. "So take my best advice, buddy. Send somebody for a ride. Get that prescription filled, and hope to God it knocks that pretty lady clean out until daylight. Then you get Priestess here as quick as is humanly possible. And for Lord's sake, say somethin' to that doll up there. Explain to huh—"

"*What*, Nill?" Noel angrily interrupted. "What to say, *forzado* shit?"

In the dark, Dr. Dear's eyebrow rose. "Some forced far-fetched shit. Hmm, looks like someone's becoming a believuh..."

"Kill that noise," Noel scoffed.

"Nope." Dr. Dear shook his head. "Living here, all except for when I was in training, Ah know the signs. You're believin' man, so explain it, as far as yuh know." The physician sounded exasperated. "I'd say yuh owe doll that much *—if* you love huh." He shrugged. "If yuh don't, make her go away. Hopefully, this shit won't follow..."

"How am I gonna sound, Dell, repeating all those irrational stories?"

Dr. Dear appeared wry. "Noel, I'm sure she has already heard. As you are well aware, the help is notorious for carryin' tales."

"But what if—"

"She don't believe yuh? Is that it?" Dr. Dear sounded cynical. "Or is your real question what if she'll think *you're* a kook, lak the rest of us? Well, if she thinks it, shouldn't yuh know, now? Shouldn't you find out what mettle she's made of? But—on the other hand, what if you find she's stronger and wiser than yuh think? What then, man?"

Noel rubbed his aching temples. He turned away as his friend lit another cigarette. Walking beyond the realm of light, Noel wondered about Aqua. It seemed he had searched so long to find her. He hadn't even known he was searching until she'd stepped into his life. It had then settled so neatly around her. Could he risk losing that and her?

Walking further, Noel wondered. Why did people always say he wasn't a believer? The bi-racial man knew about spirits, Voodoo, white magic, *and* Santeria. For crying out loud, he was half Latinx! How many African-American-Latino men had no faith, no belief in things beyond themselves?

Not many that Noel knew. But just because he was *aware* of the paranormal didn't mean it had to affect him. Right? Indeed, he didn't have to be like superstitious little Genie, afraid of everything.

Meandering back toward the doctor, Noel recalled his beautiful brown mother. She often said *some things* defied rational explanation. So maybe Noel needed to preface his talk with Aqua by saying that.

"I guess it's bad, Dell." Noel spoke as the physician crushed his waning cigarette underfoot. "If you are advising me to tell my *niña*, and call the High Priestess."

"Ah am *ordering* it, buddy." The doctor, one of a handful on the island allowed to have a car, walked toward his vehicle. "Get your lady some spiritual help, bro. Do – it *—now*."

Chapter 31

IMMEDIATELY after Noel and Dr. Dear exited her room, Aqua drifted off to sleep. Although she'd desperately wanted to get up, to further poke around in her newly acquired box, she hadn't the energy. Amid sleep, Aqua registered that she was freezing. So, not waking, but with fleeting thoughts of curling herself into a warm fetal ball, she pulled the covers up. That was when she heard it, the creak of the wooden chair beside her bed. Hazily, she wondered if Noel was back. Or perhaps someone else was at her, with that soup spoon again.

Rousing herself, she squinted over. Not recognizing the man who sat bedside, Aqua felt a scream gather in her throat; the man wasn't one of those who worked in or around the house, one whose name she could not recall. All were people of color too, and this man was white, wrinkled, age-spotted, and leaning toward her, as though he would speak.

In the darkened room, warily Aqua watched. Oh why, she wondered, hadn't she, Noel, or Eldon thought to turn a light on at dusk, when Dr. Dear had been leaving? Aqua saw the unknown man heave a sigh. Who *was* he? And where had he come from? Ever so slowly, she stretched a trembling hand to reach for her soup spoon; it would become a weapon, if necessary, because what could this man possibly want?

Aqua knew what she wanted. She desperately wanted *out* of this god-awful nightmare. And she wanted the bedside lamp on!

Funny—her eyes narrowed—but she really wasn't afraid. Darn it, she was really sick, perhaps unto death, she mused. Maybe that was why the doctor had circumvented her questions. Perhaps upcoming death was why she was so cold, too. She had heard, from old people mostly, that cold crept upon one when they were dying. Or when ghosts were present.

Surprisingly though, the man in the chair wasn't menacing. He simply leaned, with hands clasped between his knees, as though he wanted to…talk. Crazy question, what could he possibly want to talk about?

Beyond her bedroom door, across the hallway, the top step creaked. Beside Aqua's bed, the white-haired man shifted. Guess he'd also heard. Facing the door, beyond which muffled footsteps sounded, the older man wearily got to his feet.

Watching, Aqua wondered, what would he do, where would the age-spotted man go*?* The doorknob was turned. Hearing the click, Aqua did not have the wherewithal to alert whoever was entering.

Something was definitely wrong, with her, Aqua opined. Perhaps she was being drugged. She knew that peyote, a hallucinogen, was used in transcendental meditation and such. Hey, wasn't peyote a type of cacti? Weren't these islands full of the prickly flowering vegetation? But *why* would someone want to drug *her*? Aqua drowsily wondered as the man left her bed –dematerializing as he went.

"Baby...baby," Noel crooned, gathering Aqua into his muscular arms. Also, pulling the cover higher, he tucked it all tightly around her.

Noel had turned on the bedside lamp, and to Aqua, he felt so warm and comforting as his body heat penetrated her frigidity.

"You're *frio, lirio*, ice-cold," Noel murmured, soothing and rocking. "What's that?" He bent to better hear. He could not, however, because Aqua's teeth chattered. Therefore, he kissed her forehead and thought about all he needed to say to her after she warmed up. *Lord*, it was as though everything around them was going to hell in a handbasket. And he did not know the first place to begin, to make sense of things.

At the knock on the bedroom door, Noel called, "*Venir*, come."

Eldon's 'dazzling' Katherine appeared.

Noel sighed as quickly she walked over, unfurling a pair of thick socks. "Kat, you are the best." The landowner said so because it couldn't have been more than two minutes ago that he'd called, upon entering and finding Aqua asleep and curled in a shivering ball. Immediately, Noel's heart had gone out because his lovely lily was so precious; and now she suffered because he had been stupid enough to bring her *here*, to this house, on this land.

Noel saw Katherine nod as she bent. Finding Aqua's feet beneath the cocoon of bedclothes, Katherine socked and re-wrapped both. Then the middle-aged woman pivoted while promising to return.

Within minutes, she was back, offering a hot water bottle. Following his wife, Eldon carried a tray. "This," Katherine murmured of the heated water, "should go against Missus' back."

"Sir." Eldon sardonically raised an eyebrow. "Desdemona says that a bit of her uh 'tonic' should quickly warm Mistress Aqua."

Despite the dread, and other unintelligible emotions swirling within, Noel nearly chuckled. He knew about Desdemona's 'tonic.' White

Lightning it was, nothing more, or less. Homemade distilled liquor. In these parts, it had once been outlawed. Where Des got it, though, Noel didn't care to know. All he knew was that it worked. His mother, also a lowcountry girl, had dispensed it when her children had been ill. She, too, thought it cured all.

Disapproving, with his back ramrod straight, Eldon left the room.

"Mister Noel," Katherine began, her voice soft, "shall I help get Miss Aqua back in bed?"

With Aqua on his lap, Noel continued to rock. "No, Kat, but thanks. I'll just give her the uh 'tonic' and then—"

"You'll sit a spell," Katherine finished. "Good, sir." She backed out. "You have only to call if you need."

"Thank you." Scooting over with Aqua on his lap, Noel grasped the glass left by Eldon. "*Lirio*, this—"

"Is moonshine," Aqua interjected, reaching for it.

Noel smirked. "You did say your gran is from these parts. So you would know;" a great many things, he suddenly realized.

Aqua frowned at the familiar tangy smell. She geared herself for the blue streak the corn liquor would burn, going down. Yep, she'd get warm. Then she'd be knocked out—later for Dr. Dear's prescription.

As Aqua sipped, Noel's mind whirred with how to tell a tale that even he didn't fully understand. "*Lirio*, I—I know you've probably heard things since we've been here." Noel did not know how to continue.

Aqua giggled. "You're cute when you're flustered."

Noel kissed her nose. "You're getting tipsy, and I am trying here."

Having totally forgotten the man who'd sat, not long ago, on the very chair upon which she and Noel rocked, Aqua gasped at the heat that was new with every sip.

"*Chica*, I am trying to tell you—things you need to know. I learned them about this house and the land. You do know this house, and these grounds have been in my family, in one way or another, for a good while, right? My paternal ancestor, a Spaniard, married a female descendant of those who had once been enslaved here."

Following another fired-up foul sip, Aqua nodded. She leaned a shoulder into Noel's chest, and with the hot water bottle at her back, she nearly felt right as rain. "So the story goes. Now what else, O?"

Holding her, Noel wondered if he should mention his dreams. Or rather, the one dream that he'd had since he'd again met her. It was somehow connected to whatever it was they were experiencing. Noel had no earthly idea how or why, but bravely he said, "*Lirio*, I think I should start by telling you about my dream. I've had it since we met again. It's always the same, but then it's a little different each time. I'm usually running—come to think of it," Noel mused aloud. "I'm on my own land, I know that much."

"But why are you running," Aqua inquired, toasty warm.

"I don't know," Noel admitted. "I only know that sometimes it seems I'm desperate, searching for something, or someone. Then other times, I'm euphoric, running *toward* something or someone. It's strange. Then when I wake, I'm out of breath and sweating."

Noel sighed, wondering how to tell the woman in his arms the rest, without sounding psycho. "*Aqua Mira*, there is more. This part," Noel whispered, "is about the house. Some think it's *embrujado*, inhabited."

"Ah, haunted," Aqua succinctly supplied. "I believe that."

Stunned, Noel shifted to look into her amber eyes. Aqua appeared lucid, save for the darkness beneath her eyes and the now gaunt, unfed look. But that was because for too long, no one had been able to get her to eat. However, not dwelling on that, Noel asked, "Why do you believe this place is inhabited?" Later for that *other* word, "Because of Genie?"

"No." Aqua palmed her empty glass. "I *feel* it," she divulged.

Comfortable on Noel's lap, Aqua wondered if she should mention the box she'd found. Perhaps if she did, she could start to get answers. However, suddenly she felt catty and shrewish because the box was hers, alone, and she did not want to share it. Through the haze of cloying selfish feelings, Aqua wondered at not wanting to mention the box or its little-known contents. Then she heard a whisper, *not yet*. And that fast, Aqua rationalized. She needed more time. She needed to pore over the contents, perhaps revisit the stairwell, and that ghastly third floor.

"Genie has nothing to do with me knowing this place is haunted," Aqua began. "There are things I've felt and seen." Like the woman in the mirror, and the woman in several paintings, whose back was always shown, but never her face, in profile or otherwise. Then there were the children, upstairs, the hidden stairwell, and now the box.

"Ocaña," Aqua ventured, "some awful things happened here..."

Noel was semi-stunned at her conclusion, but then again, Aqua was a spiritual woman. She got up each morning to pray. Faithful, Aqua had something far more knowing within than woman's intuition. Therefore,

Noel should have known that *she*, of all people, would sense what he had not because *she* was a true *believer*. When he was what?

"Tell me, *Lirio*," Noel began, "why you feel bad things occurred."

"Well, I have dreams, like you, but mine are rarely the same. Like yours, though, mine also seem real. Now that I've thought about it, I believe I've gone into fugue states and have become another person..."

Noel felt incredulity as he asked, "And you're fine with that?"

"Fine or not, Ocaña, I've actually become *several* other people, who must have lived here. Anyway, now I need to know the history of this house, these people's stories, and someone real around here can tell me.

"Ocaña, I *need* the puzzle pieces; because I've begun to live portions of these peoples' lives; it's scary, and I've seen things."

Noel's heart hammered.

"Things like what?"

Aqua sighed. "You'll think I'm crazy."

His sweet baby, Noel hugged her tightly. With his chin atop her head, he divulged, "*Aqua Mira*, you don't want *me* to think *you* are nuts, and I was worried you'd think that of *me*. My *niña*," he murmured, and kissed her forehead. "I know you are not cray." Noel sighed and felt like an albatross had been removed from about his neck. "Tell me, *lirio*, about the things you have seen."

Noel prayed that some of the genuinely mystifying things Aqua had *not* seen, things upon which many long-standing tales were predicated.

"*Lirio*?" Noel gently shook the woman whose head rested against him, the woman he would marry, come hell or high water. "Bae, talk to me," he coaxed, hoping she hadn't gotten the proverbial cold feet.

When Aqua remained silent, gently Noel again shook her. The glass fell from her hand. *Thunk.* It rolled, and liquor pearled on the rug.

Noel sighed, guessing she had dropped off to sleep. Well, Des' 'tonic' had done its job. *Wait*, why did he feel that had been too fast? Hadn't Aqua been speaking only a moment ago? With awareness singing through his veins, Noel heaved Aqua up, looking into her face. He gasped as apathetically, her head fell back over his arm.

"Eldon!" Noel yelled. "Kat!" he called, transferring Aqua to the bed with the cover yet wrapped around her. "El-*don*!" Noel thundered, as gently he slapped at Aqua's face.

Lifeless, her head lolled. Terrified, Noel's heart hammered as Aqua's eyes walled up into her head while her jaw went slack.

"Come on, baby, come on," Noel urged, his voice thickly accented. "Talk to me, *mami*. Oh shit!" He shook Aqua, "Baybeee..."

At a run, Katherine flew into the room, followed by Eldon. "Oh, Lawd," she murmured, seeing Aqua cocooned. Aqua's open eyes were unseeing and rolled upward. "Get the cover off her," Katherine ordered. "El-don," normally soft-spoken Katherine barked, suddenly in charge, "Send for the healer, *now*! Doc Dear, too!"

Hurriedly, Noel peeled bedclothes from Aqua. He and Katherine gasped when they saw the slashes.

On Aqua's pastel nightgown, there were crosswise slits. From her belly beneath, the nasty gashes oozed blood that puddled at her crotch.

"Jeeesus!" Katherine moaned before ordering Noel to run tell Desdemona they needed the flow-stop.

"The *what*?" Noel asked, sprinting to the door. "*De que?*"

"Just say what I say. The flow-stop, you need it."

At the door, Eldon heard and turned, saying he would relay it. "You tend to Mistress," Eldon admonished, hastening down the stairs.

Dios mío! Noel thought. My God, what the devil was going on, now? "Kat, *Aqua Mira* was fine, a minute ago. I swear."

"Towels," Katherine directed, gingerly raising Aqua's gown from her bronze knees. "Wet some!"

Noel dashed down the hall. He soaked washcloths and hand towels in cold water. Then with them dripping and bath sheets over a shoulder, he raced back. Katherine was down on her knees beside Aqua. She had one brown hand fanned over Aqua's face, her fingers over Aqua's unseeing eyes. Katherine's other hand was splayed but not touching Aqua's bronze, bleeding, and slashed abdomen. With her face upturned and her eyes closed, Katherine mumbled unintelligibly.

Loath to disturb her, yet Noel needed to know what was going on, especially since puddled blood was coagulating. In the apex between Aqua's thighs, it made her bikini panties invisible. "Kathereen!" Noel thundered. "What ees this?"

The woman did not open her eyes as in monotone she spoke. "I'm calling her back. Hush now. Wait. She wasn't here."

"What do you mean?" Noel was aghast, "She wasn't here?"

"Her body was, but *she* was gone. Her eyes said so. Her spirit was being stolen away." Katherine opened her own eyes, just as Aqua coughed, and slowly raised both her knees.

Closing eyes that felt dry and scratchy, slowly, Aqua opened them. Then she cried out as shakily, her hands hovered over her midsection. How it *hurt*, Aqua moaned as tears leaked from the corners of her eyes.

"I know, Missy," Katherine soothed, reaching for Noel's dripping towels. "So we gon get you fixed right up."

Noel was transfixed as he stood watching Aqua with her knees drawn up in what had to be searing pain. She lay on her back. Wincing, she half rolled from side to side, causing blood to run onto the white sheet.

"Hold still, Missy," Katherine softly advised. "Kat's got yuh."

Noel could not believe this—*whatever* it was—was happening and to Aqua! What had *she* ever done to anybody, for someone to want to hurt *her*? For Lord's sake, she was an innocent bystander! A beautiful flower that he had simply brought to Miraunga because... Damn it! Now Noel could not remember why the devil he had ever brought Aqua to the isle. Why, oh, why hadn't he listened to little wizened Genie?

Perhaps, Noel hurriedly thought, he should take *lirio* away as soon as she was fit to travel. He would take her back to the mainland, or even back to Sapelo Island, to Cricket Hill. Genie would know what to do.

Cripes! *Genie*! All her words came dashing back. They pummeled Noel because he – had – not – listened. He saw himself, as he must have appeared, to Genie and to the fates, and to whatever had an unnatural hold on Aqua, as Eldon had previously stated. Noel must have looked like a big, ignoble, smug ass! All while little Eugenia had been right. She had begged him to not take Aqua to Miraunga. Genie had spat as though the idea was distasteful. And when Genie had visited, she'd hated every moment of her time spent there. She had not slept. She'd walked the floors, wringing small hands while praying and moaning. Afterward, Genie had commanded Noel to get rid of Steeple Chase Place. He had nearly laughed. Now Noel wondered if he would ever laugh again.

Steeple Chase, Genie had hissed. Noel remembered all as Katherine sopped up Aqua's blood. "This place needs to chase a church, a steeple, or even the saints," Genie had grumbled. She had insisted that with all the evil at Steeple Chase, it was no wonder the place stank. Genie had insisted it reeked of demonic despicable things. She had said the earth cried out. It begged for a cleansing. Later, Genie moaned that if Aqua stayed at Cricket Hill, she'd be safe. Noel wondered if little superstitious Eugenia had seen *this* when she laid out the same tarot cards that he'd made her toss. She had also said that although she didn't want Aqua to leave Cricket Hill, Aqua had to make her peace. What did that mean? Noel wondered, through the stunned ice that ran through his veins, as absently he handed Katherine another wet cloth.

Eldon banged, very unlike him, and his voice was garbled coming from beyond the door. "I can't look, Mister Noel, but take this."

A dish?! Noel wondered if Eldon had gone crazy, along with everything else, because why in blazes would he bring food, now?

With a shove, Eldon kept most of himself beyond the door. Yet, he managed to get the covered dish into his employer's hands.

Seeing all, Katherine spoke. "I need you to take off that lid."

Noel did, smelling the familiar, as steam wafted up from the…rags? White, they lined the inside of the stoneware.

"Lift that out," Katherine instructed, as with *her* knees raised and her hands fluttering over her torso, Aqua writhed and moaned. "Two hands sir," Katherine ordered, "fingers under. Lift it out, in one piece."

Noel set the dish on the edge of the bed and did as bid.

Tobacco! There were whole leaves of it between the folded towels.

Katherine spoke before laying the heated square on Aqua's stomach. She warned it would be hot, "But the pain will end, and," Katherine glanced at Noel. "The blood flow will stop. It will cease, and Miss Aqua will live… For now."

Chapter 32

NOEL sat beside the sleeping Aqua. Doc Dear and Katherine had fixed her up; thus, when Aqua's breathing had become rhythmic, Noel beckoned Katherine. "Kat, please sit with my love for a while."
Doing so, Katherine prayed and wove a protecting spell.

Downstairs, Noel called his friend who lived on the neighboring island of Karina Cay. "Kijana, all hell is breaking loose here," Noel divulged, sounding worn. "I need Priestess, right now." Noel promised he would send a boat to fetch Priestess Odyssey. So now, Noel thought, as he sat watching over Aqua, far into the night, perhaps the Priestess would arrive in two days. That is if the storm that was sweeping the coast allowed for travel.

At Aqua's bedside, Noel ran a hand over the stubble on his face. Got-durn, it was already tomorrow, daylight, and he could hear the wind. Gathering speed, the gale-force raced around the old house, making it wearily creak. Hopefully, Noel mused, Priestess Odyssey would arrive the next day because no one wanted her, or anyone, riding the water in this weather. Noel realized; whenever the Priestess appeared, it would not be soon enough. He just prayed his lily had that much time left.

Leaning forward and assuring himself she yet breathed, Noel began to recount many things because he could not lose Aqua. Trying to make sense, he pieced together the chaos that surrounded him and Aqua.

First, Noel thought, after a few years, he had again met Aqua, at his mother's party, at the supper club. Then he and she conversed, hung out, and had gotten frightfully close in what could be deemed a short time. It was during this period that Noel had begun to have a recurring dream.

Then he'd met Aqua at the restaurant they had not entered because he had upped and decided to show her his home. He had also felt if she was amenable, all his homes could become hers. Wild, right? Then Noel and Aqua made the trip to St. Simons Island. They'd gone to dinner and walked the moonlit beach. From his island condo, they'd traveled to Sapelo Island. At Cricket Hill, Genie had fallen in love with Aqua, as had Noel and most everyone else who met Aqua. Genie had begged for Aqua to stay; Genie said going to Miraunga Isle would be a mistake...

AS Aqua slept; she, too, subconsciously chronicled the recent past. She attempted to examine and understand.

Again, she had met Noel. With him, she'd traveled to three islands, and during that passage of time, she'd fallen hopelessly in love with him. All while experiencing things out of the ordinary.

Often the sun became too bright, rendering Aqua helpless. Then she found herself re-living reels of other people's lives. She'd had that shadowy figure in her room at Cricket Hill. Aqua remembered the snake that had ominously slithered overhead while she sat outside, reading.

Oh Lord—Genie! Little Eugenia had told Ocaña that the *sun* and the *leaves* had spoken; and, they had! Each time the sun 'spoke' to Aqua, it had been blinding. It had thereby clued Aqua into another sensory episode or memory of someone else. These people had once lived, Aqua suspected. Perhaps they were even alive at present, in a parallel universe. Therefore, indeed the sun *had* spoken to her on numerous occasions. Then the *leaves* had rustled everywhere she had gone, sometimes even when there had been no wind. They had spoken too. Hadn't Jethro's killed snake hidden among the magnolia tree leaves? If not for Jethro, Aqua would have become snake bait. Therefore, it made sense that as Genie had said, the leaves *had* alerted her that death lurked.

Then Aqua had seen people—those children, and the sad woman in the mirror, and the man who had disappeared into her dressing room closet. She had also become one with someone else when they—not she—had murdered the bathtub babies. Then there had been the old man on her bedside chair. He'd seemed to want to tell her something. And though she hadn't mentioned it to anyone, why in blazes had she been about to ascend the stairs one morning after leaving the kitchen when she'd seen an older white man? The same silver-haired man from the chair! But the first time, he'd worn a dark cape. Stunned, she'd watched him float down the front staircase before he disappeared. Then as Aqua shook away the vision, the same older man *flew* down the steps as though he had been tossed. He had rolled, repeatedly downward as horrified, Aqua could only watch. She hadn't heard him bumping along though; that was strange. But she had seen him in a crumpled heap at her feet. Then when she'd raised her voice for help, he had disappeared.

Also, why had Aqua often seen a darker, browner Noel in the eye of her mind? In the bayou, he always laid in wait for her. He had done so even before Aqua and Noel had become physical. Oh, and where on earth had her gown gone? The one she'd worn the night Noel proposed. From where too, were the incessant whispers coming? Why now was something lurking, with the intent to kill *her*?

Amid sleep and subconscious probing, Aqua knew there were things she needed to know. Her very *life* depended on it.

She woke and saw Noel. Slumped, his chin was on his chest as he rested on the bedside chair. Aqua tore her eyes from him to lightly touch at her stomach. She looked from her sparkling ring to her clean gown. Aqua moved, noticing. Her wounded torso no longer hurt like all-get-out. Sure, she was sore, but amazingly the screaming pain had dissipated. Thanks to Kat and Dr. Dear's ministrations. Kat had even said that in a few days, Aqua might forget she had lacerations.

Who had slashed her, Aqua wondered, re-living the incident, and why? That knowledge might be the key to all the unholy goings-on.

Therefore, while Noel slept, Aqua eased up. Wincing in minor pain, she prayed not to re-open her wounds. Bent, like the elderly, Aqua paused. Careful not to wake Noel, who really should have been lying down, she blew a kiss. Avoiding creaky floorboards, bronze Aqua entered her dressing room. Quietly, she closed the door.

Easing onto the vanity bench, Aqua slid her box from beneath the skirted table. Uh-oh. Aqua noticed. The gauze taped to her abdomen felt sticky. Forgetting it, she opened her box. Reverently, again she placed the tiny baby gowns aside. Picking up a square of paper, she noticed its thickness, the curled edges, and that the top layer had come slightly apart from the cardboard backing. Wiping away layers of dust, Aqua saw a woman's eyes peering at her from the lightly glossed sepia paper.

The eyes! They were startlingly like hers! The only difference was the irises appeared slightly darker. Aqua stared at the cut off photo, so wanting to see the rest of the woman's face. Finally, she placed the eyes aside to retrieve another image. This one, uncut, depicted a woman walking away from the camera, before…*this* house!

Aqua's eyes widened. Sure, the picture had been taken in a different time, what appeared to be a prior century actually, but there was no mistaking. The house in the background was Steeple Chase Place! The sign in the yard, hanging from the un-rusted chain, had not been bent or mangled.

"Oh my God," Aqua breathed aloud. Then she caught herself, hoping she hadn't startled Noel, just outside; but heck if the woman was not wearing her nightgown! Blinking, Aqua corrected herself. The Daguerreotype—that's what the picture was, Aqua knew, due to her friend Phédra's incessant photography lessons—had to have been taken eons ago. Gray-eyed Phédra had also explained that this photo process had reached the public in the *1800s...*

Therefore, Aqua realized, the gown was *not* hers. Aqua closed her eyes. The gown belonged to the photo woman, the one whose back was turned. With unsteady hands, again Aqua reached into the box. Shakily, she removed parchment from its matching envelope.

dear est, the note read, *meet me. I can not wait to be joyn wif you. if I not come evr agin you no HE did it, but no wor ree. look for me in all my lifes to come. then we be one at last -- for evr.*

It was simply signed, *Des ree.*

Ohhh...with tears blurring her vision, Aqua touched the nearly faded words. So this woman and her man had been star-crossed lovers. But who was *he* that Des Ree mentioned? Why had *he* wanted to keep her and her beloved apart? Aqua wondered. Now she really wanted to see the woman in the picture. Could she be the woman in all the paintings, always with her back turned? Had she been the babies' mother? Was Dearest their father?

Aqua pondered all as she took a small square of cotton from the box. Unfolded, it revealed a thick lock of curly golden hair. It very nearly disintegrated, as staring at it, Aqua wondered. Just how long had it lain in its dusty burial place beneath the stairs? And whose hair had it been?

The last item in the box was a button. It had been folded into its own cache, a piece of parchment like the note. Aqua frowned because the button looked like it had perhaps been on —Oh Savior, she knew! Aqua had seen it in one of her trance-like states. She just had to concentrate.

Aqua closed her eyes, allowing her mind to take her back. She had seen the garment, with the button attached. She had seen the *person* who had worn it...The memory hovered, then like dust in the wind, it dissipated. Aqua felt deflated as she looked down. She noticed blood seeping through her clean nightie. It must have soaked the gauze beneath. Carefully, Aqua returned the contents to her box. With a foot, she again pushed the box beneath her dressing table's fabric skirt.

Back in the bedroom, feeling worn and sad, Aqua managed to lie down, as a knock on the door caused Noel to stir.

Katherine called out and entered to change the dressing on Aqua's wounds.

Noel rubbed an eye with his fist. "How are you doing, *lirio*?"

Aqua reached for his hand. Tightly, each held on; Aqua had so much to tell Noel, but then again, she probably should remain mum. Thinking it, she managed two words. They were the truth. "I'm drained."

Feeling similar, Noel pressed his lips to Aqua's elegant hand.

"But Ocaña," Aqua managed as silently Katherine cleaned and re-dressed wounds. "I need answers," more than ever, now.

Eying her multi-faceted engagement ring, Noel thought he and Aqua needed the same thing.

Chapter 33

THE house was abuzz. Aqua could feel it the moment she woke. Turning her head, not her wounded body, she glanced out the window. The day was gray, ominously so, and leaves rippled, nearly trembling in the wind, as a storm approached, literally and figuratively.

Katherine knocked. Entering, she asked how Aqua felt. Bustling about, Katherine said she would change the dressing on Aqua's wounds. She also announced Sonsa would bring up breakfast when she arrived.

Wasn't it the young mother's day off? Aqua inquired before she knew she would. "Why's Sonsa coming out in all this rain?"

"It's not raining right now," Katherine replied, replacing gauze. "Anyway, hear tell, she's bringing the baby. That girl'a be here, and gone 'fo the first drop falls." Katherine also informed Aqua that Mister Noel was seeing to a few things. "What, with the storm a' coming? But he said to tell you he won't be long." Katherine then marveled at how Aqua was healing, and Aqua was amazed the gashes weren't causing her more pain. She mentioned that she might attempt to wash her hair.

"Oh no," dissuading, Katherine reminded Aqua that she had been ill. "With this weather, you don't want to take cold, now do you?"

Aqua guessed she could wait.

"Careful now," Katherine said, watching the younger woman slowly rise. "You keep that gauze dry."

After Aqua showered, something she felt she hadn't done in a while, she pulled on a billowing caftan. On her bed, she found a breakfast tray. Nibbling bacon and sipping hot tea, Aqua deduced that Sonsa must have arrived. Perhaps that was why Aqua had felt a buzz upon waking. She bit into marmalade toast as someone knocked. "Come in," Aqua called.

Bright-faced Sonsa entered. On this dreary day, her thick, wavy mane was free. Cascading over a shoulder and down her back, the glorious sandy brown and gold appeared to house the missing sun. To the little boy on her denim-clad hip, Sonsa spoke. "Say hello to Ms. Aqua. This here," Sonsa beamed, "is Hiram, Jr. We call him Hi. Say hello, Hi."

Tentatively, Aqua made herself say, "How are you, Hiram?"

Both Aqua and the child stared curiously at each other as Sonsa approached the bed on which Aqua sat.

Stunned, Aqua watched the child who wriggled and thereby managed to slide down his mother's side. Flummoxed, Aqua could not speak as the small boy raced from the room. She could only think that he looked...just like *the bathwater babies*!

Aqua's mind spun as his mother dashed after him. It could not be! Sonsa was too young! But somehow, was she the woman in the pictures? And if so, *how*? The daguerreotypes had to be a century and a half old. Oh, Savior. Aqua felt light-headed with questions.

Reappearing, Sonsa announced her busy boy was in the kitchen. "I see you're eating," she mentioned, just as Aqua grabbed her wrist. Appearing bewildered, Sonsa's hazel eyes darted between her captor and the door. "Ms. Aqua, something wrong?"

Aqua narrowed amber eyes. "Who are you?"

Confusion reigned, "You know. I'm Hiram Sr.'s wife, Hi Jr.'s mom."

"No," Aqua insisted. "Who *are* you?" Holding tighter as the younger woman struggled, Aqua spoke. "You once told me your family's been in and around this house for centuries. What does that mean?"

All light left Sonsa's face. Her eyes and her deep voice became devoid of emotion. "My family's worked here for many lifetimes."

Aqua would not so easily be put off. "Sonsa," she hissed, fighting to grip the younger woman tighter. "Why does that sound like a line that you're reciting? Don't shut down. Please," Aqua insisted, feeling as though Sonsa might be the key. "I know it. You can tell me things."

Sonsa remained stoic, her voice monotone. "I can't tell you nothing you don't already know, nothing you ain't already heard."

"You can," Aqua hissed. "I saw your boy. He looks just like...*other* children here."

Sonsa's eyes flared with recognition, before quickly she banked it, retreating to blank.

Aqua had seen the knowing. So she fought to grab Sonsa's other arm and shook Sonsa, hard. "You know about the children," Aqua hissed, unwilling to play cat and mouse, not at this late stage. "Talk to me!"

Despite herself, Sonsa warily asked, "Where you seen them?"

Aqua wanted to slap or shake the truth loose. "Does it matter?"

Yet, Sonsa tried to wrench free. "I gotta go, Ms. Aqua! I shouldn'a even come, on my day off, but I was *pulled* here, prob'ly by you."

"Sonsa *please*," Aqua pled, nearly crying. "I *need* your help!"

"You need what I ain't got, Ms. Aqua, that's the God's honest." The slender woman tried to turn away. "I ain't being mean, but the one you need is the Priestess, the healer. Yuh need to save yo' strength, too."

Aqua flung Sonsa away and turned petulantly aside, her gashes again oozing. "No wonder you're not really living," Aqua disgustedly spat. "You're a shell of a woman, floating miserably through here—like the woman in the other realm. You're stuck here too because you're closed. You just don't know it. Why *she's* stuck, I don't know."

Feeling like she had been slapped, Sonsa wanted to cry as she righted herself. The truth hurt. Through tears, she watched Aqua slowly get off the bed. "Don't say them thangs," Sonsa moaned, compelled to follow Aqua into her dressing room. "Why would you say that to me?"

With a shrug, Aqua thumped onto her vanity bench. "I speak the truth, and you know it. You also know," Aqua sounded worn, "I'll be dead soon. And when I go Sonsa," Aqua predicted, "I will remain here, in this house, on this land, un-free. Then…*my only mission*, I promise you, will be to haint your ass! I will visit you, your mama, your child—"

"Don't you curse me like that!" Sonsa screeched. "Don't you dare!"

Aqua no longer heard. In her own world, with her box, she opened it. She hummed the before birth song, the one for the babies. Reverently, Aqua arranged the box contents on her vanity.

Sonsa peered curiously, "What's all dat?" Sonsa's widened eyes were riveted to each item laid out as she asked, "Where you get them thangs?"

Aqua sounded far away and so unlike the woman Sonsa had grown to know. "You got questions, Sonsa. I've got questions too, but nobody got answers, according to you." Busy, Aqua hissed, "Get – *out!*"

Without a word, Sonsa stumbled and ran—as if for her very life.

Chapter 34

THE approaching storm meant there was no way Priestess Odyssey would get to them today, either. This Noel thought, knowing it was even doubtful—that Priestess would travel the next day due to the hurricane. What *else* could go wrong? Seated in his office, Noel thought of all that he and the men had done to batten down and ride this thing out.

With the wind rattling and banging out of doors, Noel got up to check on Aqua. He saw her floating down the stairs.

"*Aqua Mira?*" he called, as barefoot and unseeing, she glided past. Standing on the miniature black and white tiles at the front door, she opened the two outer wood and glass doors.

"*Lirio,*" Noel called, standing between the doors Aqua had left open. With his voice snatched by the wind, he yelled. "Where are you going?"

Out of doors, Aqua floated down the broad front steps as trees swayed and the wind picked up. For one moment, the sun burst forth.

Shit! Noel thought as he pulled the first door and then the second set closed. How was he supposed to get any work done on this crazy island when stupid stuff kept happening? In the wind, he ran down the steps of the great house that groaned like an old man. Nearly skidding, Noel turned because he'd glimpsed Aqua floating around the side of the house. Was she sleepwalking again? He wondered, sprinting after her.

Noel halted, pondering what Aqua could be doing at the sign in the side yard. Aqua appeared to blindly run her fingers over the metal, like someone reading Braille. Cautiously, Noel approached. Gently, he placed his hands atop hers. Touching her beautiful fingers, he saw that the pads were red and scratched from the sign's rust and caked-on debris.

Above the airstream, Noel suggested, "Let's go home, love."

"I have no house," Aqua said, sounding strange. "I have no home." Turning, as her caftan billowed like a sail about her, she stated the name she'd felt on the sign, "El Diario." With her hair wildly waving about her head, and strands entering her mouth, she repeated it, "*El Diario.*"

What was she saying about—a *diary*? Noel wondered, following her.

"*El Diario,*" Aqua repeated, walking on. "That's it, *not* Steeple Chase."

For Noel, something suddenly clicked! All the stories, all the mystical tales about the house and grounds, now made sense! –If it was true that things that had taken place there were re-enacted every so often, as legend stated, then the site *was* a diary! And it had taken *Aqua*, an outsider, to pinpoint it for him.

Then again, was she really an outsider? Noel wondered, running through thigh-high grass and pushing wind. Vaguely, he realized. The wind chimes behind him sounded faint, yet he strove to keep up with barefoot Aqua. It seemed she was now being *carried* on the whipping wind. Strange too, Noel could not smell oncoming rain, as was usually possible in these parts. However, he forgot that to redouble his efforts. He needed to catch the woman who appeared ghostly in the waning light.

Aqua neared a copse of trees, and Noel's insides twisted. Was she headed for the swamp, and *why*? Noel only knew he had to stop Aqua before she got sucked to her death in boggy earth, the equivalent of quicksand. Noel had to get to Aqua before she was whirled under murky water—another possibility—by ravenous alligators because as it was, the glowing orbs that were their eyes hungrily tracked him.

With reed and rushes growing to shoulder height in the murky bayou world that was eerily quiet, save for the belching of frogs, and the swamp song of insects, Noel began to know real terror.

Where *was* Aqua? Running, he glanced from side to side. Lengthening his strides, he tried to peer through the thicket that he hacked his way through with his bare hands. Noel did not want to think about the sucking noises he heard. He tried to forget that his feet nearly stuck in the mud, as continuously he put forth the effort to pull free and run. With his lungs beginning to burn, Noel had one terrifying thought. He was awake, but *this* was his dream! Noel was running and seeking someone. Now he knew. That someone was *Aqua Mira*.

As he ran, through the murky swamp world, with vines snatching at his ankles and briars tearing his clothing, Noel thought it was all so crazy because this was some shit! Moreover, where was his baby? With his heart hammering, Noel burst into a clearing. Hazy with dark clouds low-hanging overhead, Noel noticed a carpet of wildflowers. Angrily, the wind whipped the colorful field from side to side. Then in his peripheral, Noel glimpsed a ghostly figure.

Through the rusted cemetery gates this apparition floated.

Skirting a gnarled ancient oak, the limbs of which creaked in the ferocious wind, Noel ran. His heart viciously pumped, while his lungs felt filled with fire. Yet somehow, he managed to yell, "*Lirio!*" The moment the sound left his lips, Noel's voice died on the menacing wind. Therefore, he tried again, putting more into the emission. Yet, the effort was wasted. Tripping over a boulder that proved to be a broken-down headstone upon closer inspection, Noel swore. Then he asked forgiveness because a centuries-old cemetery was no place for cuss words.

Frantically searching, as leaves and dust swirled in the air and burned his eyes, Noel could never have described his distress. *Where* was Aqua?

Gathering his wits, as practiced in Zen meditation, Noel forced himself to stand still. He willed his heart to slow its frenetic pace. Then in moments, despite the wind, Noel heard...*crying*, so near, but below him. Crouching, he dared to peer around a lichen-covered headstone.

Aqua knelt, hugging a different marker, a cold, stone cross.

"Oh *niña*," Noel moaned, somehow feeling moved to tears himself. He felt mixed up with relief, but also with agony. The landowner felt distress and self-loathing because none of this would be happening had he forgotten the 'bright' idea to bring Aqua here. Why hadn't he left her alone? Now, because of him, because of his lust and greed for her, the woman was slowly being tormented out of her mind.

Amid whipping wind and the fat raindrops that began to fall, Noel again crooned at the only woman who could claim his heart.

"*Chica amante*," lover girl, "I've come to take you home." He would, Noel realized. Some way, he would get Aqua away from this God-forsaken island. Noel would get her to safety and to the best care. He owed her that and so much more. Suddenly, amid reaching for Aqua, Noel stiffened. What was *that*? The growl sounded again, closer this time, and unearthly. Some type of predator was way too near...

Having also heard, still Aqua clung to the moss-covered cross.

Knowing he had to hurry, as rain fell faster, Noel bent to lift Aqua in muscle-corded arms. He spoke, not knowing if she could hear him above the wind's wail. "Let's go, baby."

Aqua's face glistened with rain and tears. "He told *her* that."

"He who?" Noel asked. "Told her what?"

"Dearest told Des Ree."

In the howling wind and rain, Noel stiffened as though he had been struck. Standing stock-still, he realized. He *knew* those names. "They lived here…" Noel marveled aloud. "At *El Diario*," he murmured, using the original name as he tromped through flotsam.

Brushing his head on Aqua's shoulder to remove rain from his eyes, Noel recalled that he had heard, and had dismissed, the legend of *Desiree*…the desired.

"My stuff belonged to *her*," Aqua stated, turning her face into Noel's neck, as up in his arms, he finally got a firm hold on her.

"And that man killed her," Noel murmured. In the dark that appeared nearly like night, hard rain pelted him and Aqua, yet Noel held her tightly. Rain ran down Noel's face too and obscured his view. Despite it, he steadily moved, getting farther away from Aqua's cross.

Noel was unable to analyze or recall any of what he had theretofore known. At the moment, he could only do one thing. Noel remained homeward bound. Trudging along in the wind and rain and stumbling every so often, Noel securely held to his woman.

Puffing and blowing, he promised himself one thing. He chanted it to himself. They would make it. They had to make it. He would get Aqua to shelter before the raging storm consumed them both.

Chapter 35

WIND raged and howled out of doors. Angrily, it shook the old house to its very foundation; yet Aqua slept. Seeing this, Noel decided that perhaps, if he could, he too should rest.

While showering, he recalled having finally made it back to *El Diario* from the cemetery. He and Aqua were both sodden and shivering by the time he stumbled into the backyard. Noel had seen Jet Tu walking toward him. Still, Noel had not believed the young man was actually there. However, Jet Tu had been standing guard, wearing a rain slicker and carrying a hurricane lamp. He had been a welcome sight. Rushing forward, the young man had pressed the lamp into Noel's hand. The youngster had taken Aqua into his sinewy capable arms.

At first, feeling most protective, Noel had not wanted to let go, but he realized. His own arms had cramped from being bent for so long. Therefore, with the lamp swinging stiffly at his side, he had turned. Noel followed Jet Tu, and Jethro had appeared. Aaron, the property-keep was there as well. Silently, both other men pulled Noel's arms over their shoulders. They all but dragged him the half-mile back to the house.

In the old, cozily-glowing, drab kitchen, Katherine had had warm towels ready, and so many. Then, in turn, in the small powder room, she and Eldon had patiently peeled plastered wet clothing from Aqua and Noel, respectively, to vigorously dry them. While out of doors, the storm raged and did its best to tear the roof, shingles, and shutters clean away.

Back in the warm kitchen, Desdemona's silver bangles musically clanged as she clucked about like a mother hen. She plied Noel and Aqua with corn liquor tea. That got their blood moving. Then the cook set hot, soft, buttered bread before the pair and a savory steaming stew.

While Noel enjoyed the cooked-to-perfection tender beef, potatoes, and vegetables, Desdemona slapped at Jet Tu, who cut her peach pie. "Get outta here, boy." She tried to frown. However, when the young man leaned to kiss her, Desdemona grinned. "Don't get sweet on me now. Here I done fed y'all," she merrily rasped, "And how yuh repay me? Yo' young sef done ruint my pie!"

Forgetting the ministrations and the antics of those who had become family, Noel stepped from the shower. He pulled on a pair of cotton drawstring pants. Barefoot and bare-chested, he lay down beside Aqua.

Before he knew it, Noel slept, and he dreamed, as did Aqua. However, Noel's dream was the same; Aqua's was different...

She saw herself walking through the house. As she passed, the door of each room ominously slammed shut. Therefore, Aqua began to run while noticing the door hinges. They were no longer *in* each room but in the hallway. Fleeing, Aqua also heard all the air being sucked from each now closed room. Hastening, she knew she had to get to some chamber that she could get out of, a space that had no door, so she would not suffocate when it closed.

Tearing out from the first floor, Aqua ran. Up the carpeted stairs, she raced, while doors slammed throughout the darkly paneled, grossly papered house. Bewildered, she reached a dim landing, and Noel's bedroom door slammed, as did his sitting-room door. Then slammed the doors to the bath and the little privy.

Aqua lurched up another flight of stairs to gain the third floor. She wondered where to go? She was too high up, she thought, as Aqua ran toward the little room she disliked. It was across the hall from the top step. That room had no door, so quite possibly, she might get out.

The disliked room faced the side of the house; its view of old gnarled trees in the side yard was always dreary. Frantic; however, Aqua rushed forward to heave up the window—but found, again, that it would not budge! Lord Jesus! She had forgotten. It was painted shut!

Turning in a semi-circle, Aqua heard all the third-floor doors slamming, one after the other. Then she saw the old walking stick, and the wooden ends of that crib—the detritus of past lives—fly past. Those things, she thought, were from that other small room. The one that had no door. A metal bedpan flew past, along with a soft graying baby shoe. Ducking other junk from the windowless room, Aqua realized. A whirlwind of some sort had been created! In the hallway, many things, including the ugly dolls, were mystically being sucked into this angry vortex. Balding and sightless, some of the dolls appeared to reach for Aqua, and somewhere, someone screamed.

Severely panicked, because she could not go back into the swirling hallway miasma, Aqua stiffened. What was that *tearing* noise?

Aqua saw the curtain. It had been snatched free from the window behind her. It flew past, sucked into the hallway mass. Aqua watched with widened eyes as, beside her, the bedspread and the top sheet were next to pass. Oh no! She realized, even as the wallpaper in the room began to peel away, the plan was for everything to go—including *her*!

Again, Aqua faced the window. She hit it with the heel of her hand because she had to get out!

Asleep, Noel heard breaking glass and a crash. He woke with a start. Sitting up, he looked over, hoping Aqua had not been disturbed. She was gone! Lunging off the bed, shirtless and barefoot, Noel allowed instinct to carry him upward. On reaching the top step, he saw Aqua, silhouetted, in the moonlight. Noel noticed. The window was not broken yet. However, with her back to him, Aqua rammed the heel of one hand into the windowpane. Then as though in slow motion, she used the other.

With startling clarity, Noel realized. He'd heard the crash *before* it happened! How strange. He watched as again, Aqua slammed the window with both her hands. Noel heard the glass shatter. He saw it break and fall, scattering into pieces at Aqua's bare feet. He saw her blindly shove her hands through the jagged shards that were still stuck like stalagmites in the frame.

Galvanized, he leaped forward and wondered at the old rocking chair that suddenly blocked his way. Hefting it aside, Noel somehow knew. Aqua was asleep. In her slumberous world, she was attempting to get out, to get away from *something*. Noel knew not what. He only knew if he did not stop Aqua, she would never get out. Of course, she would be out of this house. She would roll, tumble or plunge to her death, three stories below. Then she would become part of the tales and the mystery that surrounded *El Diario*. Then his lovely lily would be stuck, never again to be free. She would then be caught between two worlds, the here and the after, just like...*Desiree*, the desired.

Grabbing Aqua, just as she made to surge through the opening created by the shattered glass, Noel fell backward. He took Aqua with him.

Aqua woke. She moaned because her hand-heels and wrists hurt. Disoriented, she watched as blood dripped from her onto Noel beneath her. Pressing his face to Aqua's back, Noel sighed. The man also felt as he had on so many occasions since this awful ordeal had begun. He just wanted to know *why*? Why *her*? Why him, why them, and why now?

Slowly, Aqua pulled herself up by clutching at the fitted sheet left on the bed. Blood seeped into the sheet. It spread beneath her hands, as on her knees, Aqua pressed her face into the mattress and wept. Bitterly, she cried. She sobbed for all the evil that had been done in this house. It had happened to many people on this land. Mostly, however, Aqua wept for *her*. Des Ree.

Getting to his feet, Noel laid a gentle hand on Aqua's back. Soothingly he rubbed and said, "*Lirio*, I will take you away from here."

"Too late …now," a raspy voice stated.

Desdemona? Noel whirled. What was *she* doing up here, on the *third* floor? With her arthritic knees, the cook did not climb stairs.

With downcast eyes, she offered cloth strips, as unaware, yet Aqua wept. Noel looked askance, and in front, Desdemona pulled her housedress closed. Softly she rasped, "They's old curtains. I tore 'em, *before...*" Days before, knowing what was coming.

Noel turned the strips in his hands, as his mind would not accept what plump Desdemona knew. "Hurr' up," she ordered and felt shame at urging her employer to bind his love.

Appearing visibly sickened, Noel knew he could do nothing less.

"Ain't another way," Desdemona rasped, looking away from her employer's muscular bare chest. "She bleeding, maybe unto death."

Noel reached for weeping Aqua's hand. Quickly he applied pressure and made a tourniquet. As he worked on the second, he thought about getting her downstairs where there was water. He would wash the wounds and have Doc Dear called. Noel would then do whatever was needed—including tying Aqua, hand, and foot, to the bed—if necessary. Noel could not allow her to injure herself anymore, not before they left.

"Know what yuh thinking," Desdemona rasped, as on her knees, Aqua stared vacantly through the shattered window.

Knotting Aqua's wrist, Noel recalled *the tale of a woman who had once lived at Steeple Chase*—well, at *El Diario*. Legend said *the woman had lost her mind. She'd had to be restrained, tied down.* It was *after her children drowned.* Noel's heart stopped. Dare he believe it? He could hardly breathe as he lifted the vapid Aqua. Noel's mind refused to accept the notion as he rubbed her back. But hadn't Aqua told him she'd seen children in this house, those that had drowned?

As he plodded heavily toward the stairs, he noticed a shimmer. Glancing over, he saw a bedpan and a cane. As he eased down the stairs, carrying precious cargo, Noel frowned because had that been a crib end lying askew at the other end of the hallway? Shaking the unexplained from his mind, Noel only knew one thing. He had to get Aqua away. As Aqua's man, it was his job to protect her.

Following her husband, Katherine met Noel on the second floor. In matching plaid robes with pastel pj's showing beneath, somehow, the duo still appeared formal. "Master Noel," Eldon spoke. "The doc-*tor* has been called."

Entering Aqua's room, carrying a washcloth and a blue and white speckled metal pan filled with water, Katherine did not speak.

"Thank you, Eldon," Noel was beyond weary as he deposited Aqua on the bed. With his pants and his shoulder bloodstained, Noel turned. He spoke more to himself than to the couple or the plump woman who clutched the blood-soaked sheet from the third floor. "I'm getting her out of here."

All solemnly spoke in unison, "Too late."

Noel exploded. "I *can* take her out of this hell, I brought her in!"

A deep voice countered, "You didn't."

Sonsa. Noel whirled. "What are *you* doing here, before dawn?"

"I come, Mister Noel," Sonsa's deep voice rang out, "becuh I couldn't sleep. I paced, trying to wait out the storm, but Hi Sr. got up. He brought me 'n the baby. Mama come too."

Noel blinked. "Ms. Azalea is here?" He was almost afraid to ask Sonsa why. All was surreal, and so like a pre-dawn vigil, for the *dead*.

Sonsa walked around the bed, attempting to dry her sweating palms on her jeans. Watching Katherine bathe Aqua's cut wrists, Sonsa revealed, "Granny Hy and Granmama Blossom done come too."

Noel noted the metallic taste of fear as Sonsa divulged, "Miss Aqua and I spoke yestidy, in the mo'ning. She asked me questions 'n showed me things."

Noel realized he needed to know this, despite not wanting to know.

"Ms. Aqua asked me questions, you see." The slender girl woman rubbed her palms on denim before she bent to touch Aqua's shoulder.

The bronze woman did not move, nor did she appear to have heard.

Still, whispering, as everyone watched, Sonsa said, "Ms. Aqua, I done come back, to tell you the truth. Yuh got a right to know. Mama, Gran, and Great Gran made me see. You had questions; now I got just one, too. Are you …you yet willing to listen?"

Chapter 36

2008~ Three hazel-eyed women silently entered Aqua's space to flank Sonsa.

Aqua was weak and disoriented from her ordeal and from the loss of blood. Still, she discerned crackling electricity in the room. Glancing at Noel, she guessed that all he, a non-believer, could feel was tension. However, with her strength waning and aware that she hadn't much time left, Aqua shakily reached for Sonsa. Aqua knew she had been right to believe there was something about Sonsa, a connection. Now all Aqua wanted was the truth.

Sonsa introduced those with her. "This is my mama, Azalea."

The sandy-haired woman with the short natural, the sides of which were white, solemnly nodded. "How do."

"This here," Sonsa gestured, "is my Gran. Her name's Hy—"

Aqua did not precisely know why, but she asked. "Ma'am, if you don't mind, is that short for something?"

The elder version of Sonsa's mother graciously replied. "Yes, my full name's *Hyacinth*." Then the woman patted long brown braids spiked with gray and artfully wrapped like a crown around her head.

"Nice to meet you, Ms. Hy-acinth." To herself, Aqua repeated the vaguely familiar-sounding name as Sonsa introduced an elderly woman.

"This is my great granmama Blossom. She's ninety-seven."

Although Noel knew the women, he had never before cogitated that they all had flower names.

"Ninety-seven—God bless; and nice to meet you, Ms. Blossom," Aqua managed, wondering at the underlying reason for the introductions.

"We make four generations," Sonsa shakily announced. "But *I* am the *eighth* generation removed from *Desiree*, *The Desired*, of legend..."

Noel did not understand, but immediately, Aqua did. "That's why—"

"I said we been in 'n 'round this house for centuries," Sonsa replied.

"She was your *ancestor*," Aqua surmised.

"Yours too," the younger woman stated and shocked Aqua.

"Must have been," ninety-seven-year-old Blossom advised.

Aqua felt her strength gradually decreasing, as though something sucked the marrow from her bones, yet she was curious, "But how?"

"That we don't rightly know, yet," Sonsa stated, "but when you spoke of Desiree and the babies, I knew. When you said my little Hi Jr. looks like them babies, it liked to scare me out of my ever-lovin' mind. I ran right home and told Mama and Gran."

"Sho did," Sonsa's mother and grandmother chorused.

"I told the family, we got more kin," Sonsa admitted. "I told them you, Ms. Aqua. I said 'she done seen Desiree.'"

"Ain't no way you'd have seen huh," Sonsa's grandmother Hyacinth reproved, patting her braided crown. "Unless you're kin, in some way..."

Aqua stared as Sonsa took a seat beside her on the bed. "Yuh see," Sonsa began, "Desiree can't or does not appear to anyone but family."

"Tell her the story, chile," Sonsa's great grandmother prompted. The tiny wrinkled woman's skin appeared to once have been the same color as Sonsa's. "It's only proper," Blossom said, seated on the plush chair that Noel had pulled in from his sitting room.

Aqua looked at the nonagenarian's milky eyes. Perhaps she had cataracts. Aqua guessed Ms. Blossom's eyes had once been hazel, like those of the other women. Nearly the same, Aqua thought, as hers.

"Well," Sonsa sighed. "What I'm going to tell you, Ms. Aqua is what I know from my studies, as well as from legend. Desiree, the woman you 'saw' was a slave, born around 1808, 'bout two hundred years ago. However, I've found no record yet—perhaps because back then, slaves were viewed much like cattle—by those who 'owned' them. I'm still hoping to come upon some type of record, though.

"Anyway," Sonsa murmured, "I know that our ancestor Desiree was a beautiful brown girl—a curse for any slave girl or woman. Anyway, Desiree grew up here, at Steeple Chase, with a friend. He's only known as Jeremiah, the smith. Now old My," Sonsa dragged the name out, "is said to have loved Desiree. Ever' body thought they would hop the broom together.

"At one time, My was apprenticed to the blacksmith. So working with all that iron, fire, and shoeing horses is why it's said he was bronze, broad of back and shoulder, and had might, even in his legs and thighs.

"Now, as Desiree grew, so did her beauty. Many whites remarked and wanted to purchase her' way, but the Master of Steeple Chase said no. *Then* in time, his son, blond, green-eyed fella, started sniffing 'round.

"Most of the time, the story goes, that son was out, carousing, drinkin' and getting into devilment. But he brought his wicked self home, sometimes, to mess with Desiree."

Aqua knew what was coming as Sonsa continued.

"Hear tell, this fella—we never speak his name because it would give him too much power—often chased Desiree. She would hide when she could, but one day he caught her and *forced* her. Tore her up real bad. Fella hit her too. He did that mess a time or two, and she became frightened because who could really protect her from him? Not the aging Master; the overseer couldn't, becuh in essence, that overseer worked for fella, the young Master.

"Anyway, that fella got Desiree with the child that she named Mara. I've found in the bible where it says that name means bitter. And bitter Mara was. It's said she was sullen as an old mule. But her being conceived in fear wasn't the only reason. Hear tell, Mara watched fella knock her mama around whenever the mood struck him. Mara saw ol' My the smith whupped too, to keep him away from Desiree.

"Whupping didn't do any good, though, because them two still snuck to the swamp and beyond to be together. Cook and others warned Desiree, but she said fella needed to go on and kill huh. Then she'd be free... to love My.

"The Missus, fella's mama, fancied herself a painter. She suffered mighty headaches, though, that laid her low for days. Legend says Missus felt Desiree's presence was soothing, and her voice had a lovely cadence. So Missus secretly taught Desiree to read, maybe so Desiree's voice could help the spasms. However, we don't know how true that reading bit is."

Aqua spoke up. "I think I can prove it's true..."

Each woman's rapt gaze swiveled to Aqua. With her eyes on Noel, who appeared stunned too, Aqua spoke. Her breathing was ragged. "When Sonsa's done, I'd like to show you all something."

"Well, hurr' up Sonsa," her crowned grandmother, Hyacinth, prompted.

"Okay. So when these spasms passed, Missus tried to paint Desiree, but all Missus managed was Desiree's back. We know why, though, because even to this day, my granmama believes the same way." Sonsa looked lovingly at the woman with the braided crown. "Granmama Hy and Great Gran," tiny Ms. Blossom, "both believe that letting one take your picture, or capture you on canvas, means they've captured your soul."

Aqua's grandmother, Gloria Bayliss, believed the same thing.

Continuing, Sonsa said, "The story goes: ol' drunken fella ran 'round after Desiree and My for years, instead of just selling My off. Truth was, fella couldn't. Old Master wouldn't allow it ...because bronze Jeremiah was Master's son. My was fella's half-*brother*. Old Master also did something nobody understands. Master had ol' My and all his little mulatto brothers schooled, a bit." Sonsa then admitted, "For the life of me, I still cain't figure out why he'd do such a thing."

"I tole you why," tiny Ms. Blossom offered, her small hands on the upholstered chair arms. "That old slave master knew his slavery stuff couldn't last. He knowed them boys would one day be free."

"How, Great Gran?" Sonsa asked, like she had, umpteen times prior.

Aqua didn't hear the gentle bickering. Instead, she pondered what had been bronze Jeremiah and his white brother's twisted *sibling* rivalry.

"So 'round and 'round them two went. It got so bad," Sonsa revealed, "till My near 'bout went mad, longing to see Desiree. She kept hid. My didn't know it was because fella had got Desiree wit' child, again. Anyway, the story goes: fella took an interest in a white woman. Some figured he would marry, then Desiree be sold off, or not. Still, fella came on back here, looking for Desiree. One night, in particular, he was drunk and enraged. He saw Desiree's round belly and went mad. The telling is that fella grabbed a fireplace poker, struck Desiree, then got the idea to cut My's whelp out of her. Fella made cross-wise slashes down her belly.

Aqua's eyes widened, as did Noel's. He and she both knew it was *not* a coincidence that the same had recently happened to Aqua.

Continuing, Sonsa said, "It was not My's seed that fella would have destroyed; it would have been fella's own. Well, 'nuff folk got him off Desiree. When fella left, old Master went to Desiree. Missus said to keep her upstairs." Sonsa gestured, "And Master set in the chair by her bed. He told Desiree he would sell her away. The old man thought he was doing a good thing. He said people wanted her. For whatever they reasons."

Astonished, Aqua figured *he* had been the elderly white man she had nearly forgotten, on the chair by her bed! The elderly man who had seemed to want to talk.

"Desiree cried and pled," Sonsa continued. "Said she wanted to stay. Said she'd stay 'way from fella; because here was the only place she knew. And Desiree didn't want to be torn from her sullen blond girl. Desiree also wanted—once in a while—to glance out the window to maybe see My, sweating down yonder. Well now," Sonsa sighed. "Desiree baby was born. During the birthing, Desiree screamed to wake the dead because she jest finish pushing 'n what? A boy baby followed the girl. It's said Missus give Desiree beautiful baby gowns, kept from her own babies, years back."

So the two precious gowns she'd found, Aqua thought, awed, had most likely been worn by Desiree's twins! And the whispers that led her to the box housing the gowns –had that been *Desiree*?

"The twins grew to be high-yella thangs, not coffee-with-milk color like Mara," Sonsa continued. "But it was clear all three looked alike. All had the same noses and Desiree's mouth. Their *hair* was the giveaway, though, blond like fella's, their hair curled, a cross between Desiree's and his. What them babies had, that nearly *all of us* have, is the eyes."

The *hazel* eyes. Vaguely, Aqua remembered something. Hadn't Grandma Bayliss often said her own hazel eyes were *that* white man's mark? She had also said that Rayfa's drinking was the same, a curse.

Aqua forgot GB to tune back in. Twenty-eight, Sonsa said, "Desiree nursed them twins and kept them 'way from fella, after he inspected them for 'turning darker.' If they turn, he said, they be not his. However, Desiree knew they wouldn't, but fella was scared all the same. He believed My, the smith, had sired them babies.

"Now, fella's drunk and fighting all the time; got the big house filled with strife. Old Master was up in age and couldn't do a thing. Everybody knew fella was gon run this place in the ground, soon as his daddy died. Fella was already selling thangs to pay his gambling debts. So it was common knowledge, he would practically give 'way Missus cameo brooch, slaves, and livestock alike, soon as old Master gave up the ghost.

"Well, sho 'nuff, the old man took sick, and fella didn't care. When old Master went tumbling down the front steps, hear tell, wearing his riding cape, it wasn't suicide. Most believed fella give him a shove."

It was too much! Aqua thought. She had *seen* the white-haired man take a spill, as she'd stood at the bottom of the stairs one day.

Unaware, Sonsa spoke on. "When fella's daddy was buried, all fella worr'ed about was tormenting Desiree, who sickened him with them babies. So he killed them. Folk said Mara, who was hidden, watched him drown them. She whimpered that he had fire in his eyes and animal sounds in his chest."

Aqua was astonished because had she not felt the feral anger, when—obviously now—she had re-lived that portion of fella's life? Oh! Aqua wanted to weep with the knowledge and the renewed anguish of knowing that fella— not she—had killed those children, Desiree's children! However, striving for calm, Aqua made herself listen.

"Fella left them lifeless babies for Desiree to find, and his coat button on the floor gave him away."

Suddenly, Aqua relieved it all again, vividly. She'd felt sweaty, heavy boots when before, her feet had been bare. *That* was why Sonsa had said it wasn't good to go up there alone. Perhaps that was why the bath was barred from inside. Now Aqua understood why the button in her box!

Yet Aqua could not grasp why *she* had seen it. Even if by some remote chance, she *was* related to the women seated about her. The women whose eyes were just like those in the picture in her box.

Sonsa continued. "Folk tried to keep Desiree from finding her babies. However, she overcame them with sheer mother-strength. Then she darn near lost her mind. Desiree had to be restrained. Afterward, no one could keep her from racing through the swamp after the children were buried. You know, yuh gotta pass through it to get to the graveyard...

"Desiree was never the same again, out there all the time, looking for them babies. Old Missus thought Desiree might come 'round. Missus said she too had evil visited upon her. She lost a girl baby, an older boy, and had gotten stuck with fella. Some say fella killed his older brother, a pure white boy, while out riding, so his brother wouldn't inherit. Say fella goaded brother into taking a jump too steep. Brother's horse stopped shy of a gully. Brother flew headfirst over. Broken neck. There were other 'unexplained deaths' and mutilations of cattle and slaves. Missus claimed she'd mostly recovered, though her heart remained sore; said Desiree might, too, so Missus had Desiree stuck up on the third floor.

"Unable to bear being locked away, with only grief over her twins, one night Desiree crashed through the window, to die on the ground beside this house. Legend says the sadness from her blood gnarled the trees. It still stunts anything that attempts to grow on that tract of land, to this day."

April Alisa Marquette
191

No doubt, Noel thought, Desiree's window was the very same one Aqua would have crashed through had he not been awakened beforehand. Noel shivered, aware that something had aided both him and Aqua. This he now knew, without a doubt. So, did that mean... he *believed*?

Sonsa spoke on, saying that Jeremiah the smith became crazed. Lovelorn, at all hours, he was found defiantly prowling about. "The overseer darn near whupped the hide off My, and nobody could stop it because My kept raising up, almost like he wished to be flayed alive.

"Then the day came, when 'fore dawn, fella stumbled into the stable, his horse gone. Maybe he give it to pay a debt. Anyway, fella was pitch drunk, and My was in a beastly rage, prowling for just such a chance.

"Fella and My got to fighting, two brothers, like the bible's Cain rose up against Able. Everybody knew My most likely killed fella, because My was big and strong, working with all that metal, iron, and fire. Fella was soft and pampered, a drunk who'd spent all his hours just waiting to inherit. Therefore, the fact that Jeremiah bloodied fella beyond recognition and snapped fella's neck gave everybody pause *and* the fact that there was an unearthly howl. Some say it was fella, 'bout to meet his maker and realizing he'd been bested by his enslaved black brother.

"We're told Jeremiah was meaner and faster than drunken fella. However...a ball from fella's pistol was lodged in Jeremiah's gut. My should *not* have been found with his sightless eyes open or his essence gone. So folk deduced *he* turned the gun on himself, to find his way to Desiree...

"My didn't realize that Desiree was caught, between this world and the next, because she took her own life. Now his fate was the same. Neither had thought they'd need freeing in the afterlife. They lived here and needed freeing. Then they got caught, between here 'n after, and to this day, still need freeing.

"But ol' My was smart, I must say, because that brutal overseer would have loved to break My and kill him, on Jeremiah's white daddy's land. As it was, his body was strung up, after being desecrated..."

Sonsa sat back, spent from her tale. "That howling? We hear it now and again. We believe it's fella who still cain't have Desiree.

"She still cain't have Jeremiah either, though he most likely would love to wait beside Jordan for her, but now they both need freeing. Again."

"That's where *you* come in, Ms. Aqua," Sonsa's mother, Azalea, with the short sandy and white natural, nodded. Azalea turned to Noel, "*You* too."

Chapter 37

With a new dawn approaching, the women wracked their brains. Down in the kitchen, Desdemona cooked enough to feed an army. Katherine and Sonsa carried coffee, then victuals. In the slightly mildew-smelling beige and green room, five generations of women sat. They sincerely prayed and wondered what to do *before* they lost Aqua because no one had ever been this close before.

Sure, old stories said that Desiree's granddaughter Lily had cast a spell. This spell made it so that the family member able to aid Desiree would see her. However, in nearly two hundred years, never had it been that *Desiree herself* had helped. And indeed, it seemed she had. Who else would have led Aqua to the hidden narrow stairwell? Who would have known the small box was buried beneath the landing? The question was why, though, had Aqua *alone* been made privy to things that theretofore had only been speculation? Why, too, was something or some*one* desperately trying to kill Aqua?

All these things led Sonsa and her family to believe. Aqua could free Desiree. The only deterrent was that neither Aqua nor the family knew *how*; yet, but there was a way. It had to be found, fast.

Sonsa deduced that Aqua had to be closer than anyone knew. Yet, the women of differing ages could see Aqua waning. They could hear her labored breathing. Noel did not like the darkness beneath her eyes. He despised that Aqua's collarbone was now highly visible because she'd barely eaten since leaving the mainland.

Quietly, Noel asked the women to excuse him and Aqua for a moment. Then when the hazel-eyed were otherwise occupied, Noel asked Aqua if she wanted time alone. Seated beside her, with an arm around her and his lips lingering on her forehead, Noel whispered he would do anything she wanted.

Aqua pressed closer as she said, "I don't need quiet time. Look at how things are going." Softly she stated, "If I don't get a miracle, soon, I'll get quite a bit of quiet—in the hereafter." Aqua then called for the hazel-eyed women with whom she was kin. All believed Noel was quite a distant relative due to an ancestor of his. That man had married a woman whose ancestors had once been slaves at Steeple Chase.

When Noel released Aqua, he stepped over Sonsa, seated cross-legged on the floor. He heard short-haired Azalea, Sonsa's mother, insist on kinship. Her mother Hyacinth agreed. To Sonsa, her grandmother Hyacinth said, "It's the only reason both Aqua *and* Noel are involved."

Sonsa took the monogrammed notepad Noel offered. She drew a family tree, starting with Desiree, born enslaved in America in 1808.

Although Desiree had two children prior, they had been sold. Therefore, Sonsa only listed Desiree's daughter Mara. Absently, Sonsa reported that all accounts pointed to Mara's birth in about 1828.

"But," grandmother Hyacinth interjected, "was no real record."

Sonsa nodded, divulging that Mara had later stepped over the broom, to the surprise of all, with a man whose name was forgotten. However, through this union, Mara had children. At seventeen, she bore a son, Zedekiah, then in 1849, she bore a daughter named Lily.

Mara's son Zed was outrageously handsome, like his grandmother, Desiree. He was purported to have been quite virile. However, Mara did not live to see it. Mara's daughter Lily, a slave, and a born healer, grieved over her mother's death. Lily wanted to right the wrongs done in and to her family. Lily believed that only then would her deceased mother Mara, and her grandmother Desiree find peace. So Lily wove a healing spell to bring Desiree and her lost love, Jeremiah, together, through their descendants. Despite most people thinking Lily's herbs and potions had addled her brain, Lily was sure this would happen, but she did not know when.

Then Lily, Desiree's granddaughter, stepped over the broom. Lily cried because her mother, Mara, was not there. However, like her brother, handsome Zedekiah, Lily too parented a heap of sons. At twenty, Lily, the healer, finally gave birth to a daughter in 1869.

Jonquil was born technically free.

Free Jonquil bore Rose in 1886. A free woman too, beautiful Rose later married a Spaniard. Rose bore him sons, then two daughters. Rose's first girl was born in 1908; her second, Blossom, was born in 1911.

"Blossom is *my* great grandmother," Sonsa announced. Lovingly, she gazed at the elderly woman with the rheumy eyes and softly folded skin.

No one had noticed when Ms. Blossom left her plush chair to climb upon Aqua's bed. In her stocking-feet, with her small white head on a pillow, Blossom had stretched out. Her little wrinkled hands were folded. Slowly she spoke. "My *father* was the Spaniard. Papi bought this place

April Alisa Marquette
195

and renamed it *El Diario*, for many reasons. Beautiful Rose was *my* mother. Mama was a descendant of Desiree. Yuh know," Ms. Blossom, seemingly digressed, "in the 1700's the British and the Spanish fought over these Golden Isles."

"Those battles caused Fort Frederica to be established," Sonsa recited. "Now the national monument is on St. Simons Island."

"Well, *I*," Blossom announced, forgetting battles and tours, "am the descendant of a free woman and a Spaniard. *I* am Hyacinth's mama. My older sister," Blossom announced, "was Ursaleen. Lord rest her soul."

"Oh!" Aqua yelped. Despite her wounded torso, she strove to sit up.

Startled, everyone wondered if she was about to transition.

"That's it!" Aqua hoarsely called. "Ursa—*Ursaleen* was *my* great grandmother! My sister and I called her Great Ur."

"What chile?" No one knew what to make of Aqua's ramblings about Great Ur and GB; Noel weaved among the women toward her. He had a good mind to stop the family-tree shaking if it would further upset her.

"Don't you see?" Aqua asked, grasping his large arm. "Okay," She gulped, slowing down. "My grandmother's name is *Gloria*, she's—"

"Ursa's *daughter!*" Sonsa's grandmother Hyacinth interjected.

Sonsa's eyes widened. *"That's* the connection. We *are* kin..."

Stunned, Sonsa turned to her grandmother, Hyacinth, with the braided crown. "Gran, do you *know* Aqua's grandmother?"

The room became quiet as Hyacinth's eyes shimmered with unshed tears. "I sho do. *Gloria was my first cousin.*" Hyacinth turned to the tiny Ms. Blossom. "Mama, we're talking about your sister Ursa, and her daughter Gloria."

With closed eyes, Ms. Blossom, now beneath the cover, laid beside Aqua. "That's nice," she sang out and caused all to laugh, all but Noel.

Leaning to peer closely at Aqua, Sonsa's grandmother Hyacinth patted her crown, nearly afraid to ask. "Chile, yo' granmama..."

Aqua understood. "Gloria Bayliss is alive. And wait till I tell her!"

"Bayliss –that's it!" the crowned Hyacinth whooped. "Ol' Glori marr'ed up with the *Bayliss* boy. Cyril. He took Glo 'way from here."

"No, mama," Sonsa's mother, short curly-haired Azalea dared. "Mr. Bayliss didn't take your cousin Gloria from *here*. The family was on *Sapelo* then. Glori got married and left *Sapelo* Island."

Where Genie was now, both Noel and Aqua thought.

Sonsa's mother, Azalea, continued. "We came back *here* Mama, to the family seat, when I was ten, near 'bout forty years ago."

"You are right," Sonsa's grandmother Hyacinth nodded, as with her fingers, she worried the back of her braided crown.

"My grandmother, GB," Aqua put forth, suddenly tickled, "searched for you, Ms. Hy." Though it hurt to laugh, Aqua did because she felt *joy* again when she'd believed it was a thing of the past. "My grandmother told stories about *you,* the girl, Ms. Hyacinth. *You are* the first cousin who was a sister to her," Aqua marveled. "My grandmother called you Hy. GB was devastated when she lost track of you years ago."

"We lost touch when we moved back *here*," eighty-year-old Hyacinth admitted. Her eyes twinkled, "Glori was older than me…"

"I know," Aqua smiled. "She's eighty-two."

Tickled to her toes, Hyacinth beamed. "I'd sho love to see ol' Glori."

On her haunches, Sonsa touched Aqua's bandaged wrist. "Now we know where *you* come in."

"Yes," Aqua managed, understanding why she had felt a connection of sorts with Sonsa since the first. "Now we know."

"Well, Ms. Aqua…" slender Sonsa offered. "Welcome to the family."

Noel's eyes widened when Sonsa's mother, Azalea, turned to him. He also wondered if he really *was* becoming a believer when her words didn't surprise him one bit. "Now the pieces fit, Mr. Noel. *Your* ancestor was the Spaniard. He married into our family."

"Yes, I'd heard of the beautiful Rose that my father's ancestor married," Noel acknowledged.

"Well…when Priestess gets here," the rheumy-eyed small Ms. Blossom sweetly sang from the bed, "we can wrap up this thang."

Chapter 38

NOEL excused himself, to follow his regal houseman downstairs.

Eldon spoke as they walked. "Doc-*tor* Dear has called upon us."

Noel felt relieved. Although Dell had said he could not really help, it wouldn't hurt to have his friend present. Having another man about, one that the ladies liked, would also take some of the female focus off Noel.

At the double front doors, Noel slapped hands with Dr. Dear. "Dell, man, I'm glad to see you."

"Ah hear you called the Priestess," the doctor revealed.

"You said I should." Noel entered his office, where it seemed Eldon had read his mind. On a polished silver tray, the ever-efficient houseman had placed linen napkins, cut crystal, an ice bucket, and brown liquor. God love that man, Noel thought as he poured ice water for the doctor.

"Thanks. So you've got a house full of women," Dr. Dear drawled, after a refreshing swallow. "Lucky man."

Noel tossed back his drink. "Lucky for *you*, they're being herded out of Aqua's room as we speak. Try doing your work with several pairs of eyes—including mine—piercing you."

Dr. Dear shook his head. "Ah told you, Noel, there's nothing Ah can do. I'll check doll's vital signs." And pray there's no further lousy news the physician thought; "But I'm here because Priestess is coming."

Noel turned from the lead-paned window and the gray beyond. "You still stuck on our friend's mother? She's old enough to be *your* mother."

"Ahhh," the tanned physician drawled, raising his glass. "But she's *not* my mutha, and I ain't 'stuck' as you so ungraciously put it. Ah am *awed* by her. Priestess is a true healer, and I find it purely amazing to watch huh work, especially since—I hear—she's had no formal training. She's not hard on the eyes, either."

"As I said," Noel scowled. "Stuck. And yes, Mr. whom the ladies think isn't hard on the eyes, Priestess didn't get her clinical experience at Emory like you. Still, what she says you can look up, and it'll be so."

"Yuh don't have to convince me," Dr. Dear stated, setting his glass down. "It's why I've come to watch a master at work."

"Careful, Vanilla." Noel's brow rose, "Using that word around here."

Dr. Dear was not offended. "Ah shan't forget. So yuh sent a boat?"

Half-seated on the desk edge, Noel nodded. With folded arms, he spoke as Dr. Dear walked to the door. "I sent the Mariner."

Whistling low, the doctor turned back. "Not playing, are yuh? You really love that doll upstairs, don't yuh?"

"Sure as the sun rises, I do; I'm curious, though. How do you know?"

"Yuh pulling out all the stops. You didn't send a mere boat for our Priestess. Yuh sent a motor yacht," aptly named Thunder. "That baby's got a 5.7 GXI engine. She's luxe and fast—like I like my women."

"Well, I wasn't thinking about her flybridge," hydraulic steering, dripless shaft logs, or her cherry wood bulkheads. Noel nodded. "I sent Thunder due to her high-speed ability. Vanilla, man," frustrated, Noel ran a hand through hair that had garnered more silver in just a few days. "I don't know how much time we've got. According to Sonsa's family— Aqua's family, now—no one's ever gotten this far."

The doctor nodded. "Ah heard." It was one reason why the physician did not want to be the one to give his friend terrible news.

"Dell, the women have even figured out how *I* fit into all of this."

Dr. Dear stared, shifting his bag. "You're okay with that."

"I am. That's my wife up there." Realizing what he'd said, Noel closed his eyes. "Well, if I had my way, she *would* be, right now."

Dr. Dear turned to follow Eldon into the darkly paneled hallway. Standing beneath the illuminated wrought iron chandelier, he said, "Buddy, someone's become a believer."

AFTER Dr. Dear had seen her; Aqua was worn but glad to see Noel. "Where are the ladies?" she asked as quietly he closed her door.

"Little Ms. Blossom is in my bed, re-made for her because she refuses to leave." Noel pulled the curtains. "Her daughter Ms. Hyacinth is with her, watching the evening news. I believe Sonsa's out back with Hiram Sr." Noel sat aside. "Ms. Azalea," Sonsa's mother, "is *en la cocina*, in the kitchen. No doubt getting in Desdemona's way, and you know how Des is about her kitchen."

With closed eyes, Aqua smiled. "Yes, she's like Genie." Before knowing she would, Aqua mused aloud. "Wonder if I'll ever see her again…or GB, or Ava and my niece. I wonder if Cae will work things out with Yael, and I keep wondering if I'll ever get to hold Phé's baby." Aqua's voice got smaller as tears slipped down her cheeks because she wanted to live. "I wonder too if I'll ever see sweet young Isis again…"

Noel's heart broke as he sat in the upholstered chair. Stroking Aqua's hand, tears filled his eyes. "*Aqua Mira*, I don't know what to do. I wish," Noel admitted as a tear splashed onto his cheek, "the flower ladies could tell us what to do."

Aqua choked on a chuckle. "You did not just call them that."

Emotional, Noel's Latin accent became more pronounced. "Ees that not what they are? There is Rose, Lily—" he stopped. "Don't you find it amazing that I call you *lirio*, which means Lily, like your *ancestro*?"

Aqua smiled and nodded because, indeed, she had thought about it.

"*Lirio*, you must know," Noel was earnest, "I *will* save you." He bent closer, his warm breath feathering across Aqua's lips. If not, he would have to kill himself, like Jeremiah, because there would be no living without Aqua, not now. *Dios mío!* Noel thought, feeling powerless. "I hate that I brought you into this lion's pit. *Lirio*, I will die for you, like Jeremiah for Desiree."

Aqua squeezed Noel's hand. "Shush. Don't talk like that." With tears assailing, she whispered. "Just find a way to help me, or go on ...after."

In the lamp's warm glow, Noel grasped Aqua's shoulder. "*Lirio*, my magnificent *love*, I cannot lose you..."

Using the sheet, Aqua dabbed her eyes. "Kiss me, Ocaña. Tell me that whatever happens, we will meet again. Tell me," Aqua choked out, "that should I fail Desiree, you'll forgive me. And tell me, sweet man, that you'll come for me, in as many lifetimes as it'll take for you to find me."

"Just like Jeremiah, love," Noel murmured, his face beet red, no longer beautifully golden. "I will never stop looking for you. Actually, I believe that's what I was doing before we met. I searched endlessly for you. My dream proves this, does it not?"

"Oh, Ocaña, I wish I knew. However, I need you to do one thing."

"Anything, my *wife*..."

Aqua nearly sobbed, upon hearing Noel call her the very thing she'd longed for, for almost as long as she had known him.

"Make me laugh," she managed. "Then when I'm gone, don't forget that this time—my short time with you—has been my life's best. I really do love you, Ocaña...I will, forever."

Aqua could not continue because she cried so. All Noel could do was hold her. His throat ached at the thought of never holding her again, never again hearing her laughter, or seeing her radiant smile.

With a sigh, however, he attempted to compose himself. "So," he said, breaking the dismal spell, "To make you laugh. How will I do that?" Noel could hardly think, watching the life being leeched out of Aqua. Instead of focusing on that, he forced himself to remember how she loved to laugh. Actually, it might do them both some good, he thought, because if they didn't get help soon, there would be time for tears.

Aching with thoughts of loss, Noel could only think one thing. He was losing Aqua *all over again.* That was odd. Why did he feel that way, he wondered, because to lose again, there had to have been a prior loss.

Forgetting melancholia, Noel asked, "What should I tell you, *lirio?*"

Aqua whispered, "Tell me about…a weird date you had."

Noel swallowed past anguish because how could he speak—much less think about other women—when not one compared to her.

"Come on," Aqua coaxed. "Something funny happened."

Though Noel could not think of laughing at a time like this, he managed. "The only thing I can think of would be slightly sexual."

Aqua vowed not to be upset over something that had happened before she and Noel met. So she said, "Go for it."

Noel sighed. "Well," his eyes nearly twinkled, as they had before this ordeal. "I attended a conference. An attendee gave me her room key."

Aqua smirked, knowing this was uncomfortable for big sexy. However, her interest was piqued. "And…"

"Muffie, we'll call her, opened her room door when I appeared."

"But she gave you a key."

"Guess she couldn't wait, for all of this," Noel gestured.

Aqua grinned, wanting to know. "What was she wearing?"

"She was naked, and she walked toward the bathroom, and did not close the door, so I saw her get down on the floor."

Aqua smirked. "Why?"

"*Niña,* let me tell my story."

"You ain't got to get all huffy."

Aqua had sounded like her sassy self, and it pleased Noel. So maybe the story-telling business wasn't such a bad idea after all.

"Wait," Aqua interrupted. "I've got a question."

Making his voice high, Noel mocked Aqua. "What did she look like?"

Aqua shook with the laughter that it hurt to emit.

"Women!" Noel shook his head. "She was *flacca*, skinny, not *appetizing*." Noel licked his lips, and Aqua grinned. "But I went up because she'd have been something to do, and she got on the floor, grunting and pushing a tube-like thingy up her butt."

Aqua gasped. "No!"

"Yes. No joking," Noel smirked. "Then from the floor 'Muffie,' propped her feet up on the counter's edge."

Aqua's eyes were round. "Why?"

"I asked, and she grunted that she was administering an…enema."

Aqua laughed, despite the pain. "No more," She waved. "Stop."

"No *chica*, listen." Noel grinned, "I asked why she needed that, and she said…you ready for this?"

"Ocaña, I am not."

"Well anyway, she had a British accent. And she said she wanted me to mmph her –in the arse."

Trying to contain mirth, Aqua balled the sheet in her fists. "Stop it."

"Listen," Noel called. "Muffie jumped up then, with liquid streaming down her leg—as she ran screaming to the commode."

Aqua laid her head back and *guffawed*, despite the pain.

Noel chuckled, too, although he hadn't thought it funny at the time.

"You better not have done her," Aqua ordered. "Say you didn't."

Noel kissed Aqua's nose. "Indeed. I left."

Aqua hugged Noel tight. "That's my man."

Chapter 39

THERE was a commotion downstairs. In his sleep, Noel heard it. Waking, he was careful not to disturb Aqua, who slept in his arms. He hated to leave her. Since they had been on Miraunga Isle, this seemed like the first time that she had peacefully slept, if only for a few hours.

Barefoot, in badly wrinkled linen pants and a tee, Noel crept to the door. He knew what the noise in the foyer was. Houseguests. This new set had finally arrived. Noel felt excitement. Pulling Aqua's bedroom door to, he only hoped his new houseguests wouldn't wake the others.

Noel crept across the hall carpet—the *icky* brown carpet as Aqua called it; she was right. He wanted it yanked up and burned. Forgetting it, Noel descended the stairs. If he didn't, those currently looking up at him would wake itty bitty white-haired Ms. Blossom and Sonsa's grandmother, Hyacinth, with the beautiful braids.

Noel could imagine those two elderly dolls—bless their hearts—as sleepily they would sit up in his big bed. They'd gaze about and wonder at all the fuss. Noel smiled. His new guests thought he was happy to see them. He was, but thinking of small Ms. Blossom and Ms. Hy, he'd been reminded of his mother. *Mami* would love those two, and vice versa. *If* he and Aqua could get extricated from this nightmare. Noel nearly chuckled because *Papi* would love all the female attention.

Noel grasped the hand of his college chum. "Kik, man," the homeowner spoke within an embrace. "I am so glad to see you."

Noel felt a weight lift off his shoulders when the tall, stocky male said, "We'd have been here sooner, if we could have." Fawn-colored, big, bald, Kijana Kyree stepped back. "How is she?" He asked of Aqua while gesturing for his mother.

She stepped forward, a tall, surprisingly younger-looking woman than one would expect. Like Aqua, the Priestess was lushly built, but older, with, knowing, coal-black, beautiful eyes, in a smooth, unblemished face. Her skin, too, was fawn-brown, like her son's. Her naturally curly hair—kinky hair, she lovingly called it—was covered by a regal wrap, her body sheathed in a matching loose-fitting shift. She wore sensible-heeled sandals; no doubt, her daughter-in-law's doing, because rarely did the Priestess wear shoes. Her manicured toenails were scarlet. They had been for as long as Noel could remember. Priestess Odyssey's fingernails were neat and natural.

As the woman who was grace personified moved closer, Kijana lovingly passed her into Noel's arms. Then Kijana extended a hand to his curvaceous wife, redbone Sangria, with the auburn mane.

Noel's arms were around Kijana's mother, who though tall, was shorter than he. In her timeless motherly embrace, Noel allowed himself to relax, to just let go. As the woman held him, he felt her pillowy bosom pressed to him; he felt her sturdy warm body surround. He smelled the muget, the lily of the valley, that she always wore—like Aqua. With his massive arms about her, Noel turned his face into the woman's neck. He did not realize tears streamed from his eyes.

Somehow, all felt right, there in the Priestess' arms. Later, Noel might think it embarrassing, but right then, he didn't care. Noel only knew that in Priestess Odyssey's embrace, he felt like he was being restored. He felt like she was giving him back part of himself. The part that had been stolen by the distress brought on by his and Aqua's ordeal.

Dios mío! What if he *lost* Aqua, after having just found her? That particular fear assailed Noel more than any other. In the Priestess' arms, Noel realized more. Before that moment, he had not known how deeply he'd felt. Noel had not recognized how isolated he'd deemed himself and Aqua. Now, he sighed because they were no longer alone.

When Noel loosened his hold, he did not let the Priestess go. Looking into her eyes, he advised, "I'll never be able to thank you enough."

"Hush," Priestess scoffed. Her honeyed voice was smooth and sweet, like the *Tia Maria* Spanish Coffee his father favored. Gazing at Noel, the Priestess realized something. The man who stood before her was now the fulfillment of the promise. She had seen it resting on him years ago. Tenderly, she placed a hand at Noel's face. Her dark eyes searched his.

It seemed the Priestess attempted to ascertain something, but what? Noel wondered, content to say nothing, as the Priestess stared.

Noel forgot his college chum Kijana and Sangria, his wife; both were only feet away. Vaguely, Noel smelled coffee. He was aware that Eldon, Katherine, Aaron, the property-keep, Jethro, and Jet Tu, bustled about. Noel had seen sleepy-looking, slender Sonsa slip into the kitchen. In some far off corner of his mind, Noel processed hearing Desdemona clack about. Yet, his attention remained on the woman who sighed.

With coal-black eyes holding his, she softly proclaimed, "You love this woman, and your love is strong. Good," the Priestess nodded. "Strength is needed." Turning then, Priestess Odyssey faced her son and his wife, yet she spoke to Noel. "When your lady wakes, I will see her."

Dismissed, Noel hugged Kijana's wife.

"We've got everyone back home praying," Sangria whispered.

Noel could not believe how relieved he was to hear it, even as from the shadows, the ever-efficient Katherine stepped forward. She offered a little bow as she said, "Ma'am, I will lead you to your quarters."

When the Priestess and Sangria acquiesced, Noel's eye fell on someone he had not seen. With a smirk, he shook his head. "Dell. I thought you left. What the devil are you doing here, at this hour?"

"Ah belong here," Dr. Dear drawled, pushing off the paneled wall upon which he'd insouciantly leaned. He straightened to his full height.

His voice contained reverence, "Priestess…" Chivalrously, the doctor bowed, as following Katherine, the women began to pass.

Priestess Odyssey laid a hand against his cheek. "Vanilla Bean."

Laughter burst out of the doctor as he clasped her unlined brown hand. If she hadn't just used his pet name! Back when he'd been a long, lean, motherless, besotted boy, the Priestess had nicknamed him. That was many moons ago, back when Doc Sr. had been in love with her. "Priestess," Dell smiled, feeling warm all over. "Yuh remembered."

The woman's lilting voice floated back to the handsome, tall, tan physician. "There's not much I don't remember, Bean."

Dr. Dear stared after the small female procession and winced.

"Dell, I'ma tell you the same thing I said when we were kids." Kijana, the Priestess' tall, stocky, forty-something son, growled. "*Forget* my Mama. As a matter of fact," Kijana grinned at having jabbed the wind from his friend. "How 'bout you just forget *all* sistas? *Bruh.*"

The physician's mind veered to honey-hued Tula. Often she danced for him, sensuously bobbing her apple-round behind. He thought about the adored, mocha-skinned, brooding, and mysterious Violet. He recalled the swags of sheer mosquito netting that surrounded Violet's bed. He remembered Vi, of whom he never tired, in candlelight. Therefore, Dell refuted Kijana's forget sistas statement. "In yuh dreams, pal."

Noel nearly smiled, because with his friends going at it, like when they'd been at Tulane University, it almost seemed like old times.

April Alisa Marquette

Then again, Noel mused, sobering up. Nothing was really like old times. None of this was anything he had ever before experienced.

THE Priestess took over the little hut, shed, lean-to? Noel didn't know what to call it. He only knew that during the American enslavement of Africans, the small structures had been their quarters.

However, to Noel, the small wooden structures were so much more. When he'd first laid eyes on them, windowless and sad, with one room and a fireplace, something within him had tripped. As he'd walked around, touching things, he'd felt a mix of melancholy, fear, and elation.

The sorrow and the fear had been for the slaves—the *people*— who'd resided there, for that is what they had been; not cattle, and not property. The slaves had been living, breathing, *human beings*. They'd had hopes, dreams, and too many realized fears. The *elación* Noel had also felt was because finally, some had gotten out. Many had given life and limb for freedom. Therefore, Noel was elated that there were people today, himself included, who would never forget. Sure, some believed African-Americans needed to simply 'get over slavery' and 'let it rest.' However, Noel wondered, did those same people tell the Jewish Diaspora's descendants to 'get over the Holocaust?' That would have been profane, as well as inhumane. Therefore, in the same vein, Noel figured, remembering was the only way to never revisit either heinous period.

Again, these things crossed his mind as he strode through grass wet with dew. He headed for one cabin in particular. He'd had a few restored. In the one he walked toward, he'd had a rustic wooden floor installed. It replaced the hard-packed dirt. Noel did not know why he had done so, but it had seemed significant at the time. It was his offering, his gift.

Gaining the windowless structure, he noticed. Off behind distant towering pines, the sun raised her rosy head. Noel saw smoke billowing from the repaired brick chimney. Knocking and entering, he saw a fire blazing in the blackened hearth. The property owner noticed a small steaming cauldron. He smelled the spices and the Priestess' herbs. He saw her paraphernalia lying about; in so short a time, she had willingly made the place her own.

Noel remembered requesting her presence. The Priestess had sent word. She would not stay in that big house, the main house. Now Noel noticed the rocker and the woman who sat in it, and wearily he smiled.

The Priestess nodded. Her shawl was pulled tightly about her, although the room was swelteringly hot.

If Noel had not known before why he'd had this particular cabin refurbished, he did now. Somewhere deep inside, he had known that one day he would require it. Yet, he struggled, internally, because that was *all* he knew. Going forward, he had no idea what to do. Therefore, he lowered himself to sit at Priestess Odyssey's feet. There, he divulged his dilemma while barefoot and seated, the Priestess listened.

Then quietly, she explained. Noel had had promise etched on him since he'd been young; "No doubt since you were born." It was the promise of more, things that only *he* could accomplish. The Priestess' voice was musical as she divulged, "In a place deep within, son, you have always known this. I gather though," she nodded, "that you've passed the feeling off as fanciful. Thus, you have not believed."

"Now, baby boy," the Priestess sighed. "There has come a shaking, in the nether world. It has reverberated back to *our* world because the time has come...for recompense, for a cleansing." The Priestess looked beyond Noel, out of the open wooden door. "In the past, only a few people knew of this. Today, all that are involved know ...all but one."

Nearly holding his breath, Noel dared to ask, "Am *I* that one?"

Quietly, the healer offered, "Only you have the answer."

Noel inquired, "Are we—Aqua and I—the ancestors reincarnated?"

Priestess Odyssey remained silent a moment. Then she answered, "Not necessarily. I will say, the two people who began this had longings so strong until those longings became part of those in their lineage."

"Aqua and I," Noel breathed from his place on the floor.

"Yes. I do not doubt," the Priestess candidly revealed, "that other descendants of theirs felt as you and your lady have. Yet, it took you two, strong, mature people, to accept the task—the reverberations of your ancestors' desires. *Now*, my darling, greater strength will bring all to fruition."

"So," Noel mused aloud, "I *had* to love Aqua. I had no choice."

The Priestess rocked. "There is always a choice."

"Do you think," Noel dared to ask, "that my *lirio* knows this?"

The Priestess' hands were clasped in her lap. "Your lady is aware of many things. She *feels* deeply. She connects. She *sees*. She is led."

Noel thought about Aqua's first name, which meant water, or the color, a greenish-blue. Had not they traveled by water to get here?

Wasn't Miraunga Isle surrounded by water? Noel was reminded of Aqua's middle name, Mira. In Spanish, it was *mirar*, which meant look.

How apropos, he thought. Then appearing much like a child at mother's knee, he inquired. "Did my baby know she could lose her life?"

"She has proved she is willing. Has she not?"

Noel exploded then because he knew there was a technologically modern world beyond this stupid island. Stock was being sold. His companies, and others, were thriving. In space, satellites spun. Scientists and students studied. People cruised the world, while others sat typing. New York tourists rode the subway. In the Midwest, a dedicated doctor, one like Dell, tended the sick. Kids played baseball; someone ate apple pie, while another checked their blood sugar. The military embarked on unsung heroics, so that little girls could ride bikes and talk shows could be aired. That was Noel's world. He wanted that, with Aqua! He didn't want this obscure, endlessly scary, movie-of-the-week mess!

Attempting to calm his racing heart, he asked, "But *why*? Why would my lady risk what we have? *What* could be a reason to do *this*?"

The Priestess' answer was simple. "She is a *believer*. Perhaps she risks all—as you put it—*because* of what you and she have. Mayhap she does it for love."

"What does that *mean*?" Noel asked, sincerely wanting to know. He got up on his knees. On the Priestess' lap, his hands grasped hers. With his face tilted upward, he bared his soul. "Help me understand. Please. People always mention belief. I do believe—now. Still, it seems my baby knows things I don't. What am I missing? I'm *tired* of being in the dark. Priestess, please help me," Noel pled. "I am normally fearless, yet now I fear... losing *her*."

The Priestess sighed, allowing her hands to remain in Noel's. "Your lady understands that without struggle, without the ancestors, none of this would be possible, not even you and her. So, valiantly the beauty soldiers on, *alone*. She wars—what *you* deem risk—to save that for which others fought and died."

Though he struggled against the very notion, perspiring in the heat, Noel had to ask. "And if my Aqua dies?"

With her coal-black eyes glittering, the Priestess grasped Noel's face. She jerked it closer to hers. Sounding ancient, she hissed, as her cinnamon breath feathered across his lips, "*What* if she succeeds?!"

Noel's eyes flew open. He felt...*recognition*. He guessed it had always been there, like a low-banked fire. He scrambled to his feet. "I can help. She—*we* can win," he marveled aloud, the new knowledge suffusing him with hope.

Priestess Odyssey solemnly nodded. Within, her heart leaped, and she felt pride. Reaching for Noel's strong hand, she whispered, "My son." Her eyes were shining. "The mantle has fallen on you. In this hour, you have cloaked yourself. Yours is the strength of Jeremiah, the smith. You are the pride of your Latin warrior ancestors. You are wholly you, at last. Go." She pointed, "as part of all that was, all that is, and all that will ever be."

"Priestess!" Nearly down the path, Noel turned, calling out. "You would say if you needed anything, right?"

Barefoot, the woman crept out and nodded. Standing just beyond the door of the hovel that Noel had not known he would one day need, thoughtfully, the Priestess watched. The gold-skinned man's long strides took him away.

Quickly, he loped toward the life that he had chosen to save.

Chapter 40

UPSTAIRS, in the house, Aqua showered. Remembering Isis, she got the idea to wet and slick her hair back into a ponytail. There, Aqua thought, a bit worn from her exertions, she appeared presentable.

Noel was on his way up, in the now-stirring colossal house. He had checking on Aqua foremost in his mind, so he was surprised to see her.

"*Lirio*." On the steps, he surmised that she had more strength today. Placing his hands on her hips, he asked, "Where you going, sweet *mami*?"

"She's here," Aqua replied.

Noel stood two steps below her, looking up. "Who?"

"The High Priestess, Ms. Odyssey, I can feel her. I need to see her."

Before Noel knew it, Aqua fell backward! However, quickly, instinctively, he stepped up. At the same time, his hands slid up Aqua's back to enfold her. Had he not, Noel realized with his heart hammering, she would have fallen and hit her head on the floor, or worse.

Hurriedly, Noel gathered Aqua in his arms. Dull with fright, he wondered. What happened, and what to do?

Aqua appeared dazed. She held to Noel as he asked, "You alright?"

She blinked because she did not know. Aqua glanced aside and wondered. Why was she on the hallway floor? Ick. Why did Noel appear worried? What had they been doing?

Oh. Aqua had been —Jeeezis! She thought as her air supply quickly diminished. Her throat hurt like hell, and her head was erupting!

Noel watched Aqua's face contort. He braced his knees as she flailed, almost as though…she could not breathe! Quickly bending, he lowered her to the nasty hall carpet. He tried to sit her up, but Aqua fell back and downward, furiously kicking and clawing at her throat.

Damn him for not taking CPR! Noel's mind thundered it when Aqua arched up and off the floor. She gasped and wheezed for air. As he watched, not knowing what to do, Aqua dug the skin from her neck; but her hands remained locked in one spot. Strange. Her nails did not rake downward, and it hit Noel—she was being *choked* to death! He knew it. He could not see anyone, but now he had a good idea of who it was. Hurriedly, Noel reached out but felt no body.

Jesús María y José; Aqua was being strangled! However, not with corporeal hands. Therefore, quickly, with his hands at Aqua's throat, Noel frantically fought to aid her, knowing she hadn't much time. A vein in her head bulged, as did one in her throat. Her face had turned a burnt sienna, and Aqua's watering eyes were beginning to protrude. Still, she kicked, less forcefully now, and with his heart in his throat, Noel heard the whisper.

Use yuh mind. Fight back wit' yuh mind...

Noel closed his eyes, keeping his hands on Aqua's throat. He summoned all his fighting skills. What would he do, Noel quickly wondered, were the person flesh and blood? Hastily, he created a scenario. Noel envisioned *fella* attempting to strangle *Desiree*. Noel envisioned himself as Jeremiah, fighting fella, pulling him off Desiree.

Noel felt it then, his own hands prying those evil hands away! Scared, he kept at it. He pictured himself dragging fella, saw himself draw back his huge hand and send it sailing into fella's face. In his mind, Noel felt the blow connect. Noel hit fella again! He then saw and felt himself pummel the low-down coward who had terrorized women, killed children, mutilated and murdered others, and tormented animals.

Aqua no longer struggled. Her hands fell limply to the floor. Lying on her back, she raggedly coughed and gasped for air.

Noel had done it! He realized it as he crawled up to cradle his woman. Then he became aware, as Aqua coughed and hugely wheezed, that together, they'd bested that bastard. Noel dragged himself onto the hallway floor beside Aqua. He pulled her, coughing, against him. While they lay there, with pounding hearts, Noel slowly became cognizant of Ms. Hyacinth.

With her braids not yet forming her crown, but swinging on either side of her face, monotonously, she chanted. Opening hazel eyes, she continued in prayer. Noel saw, too, through the balusters that his bedroom door was open across the hallway. Small, white-haired Ms. Blossom stood silhouetted in the morning light. Slowly, she rocked from side to side. With little hands clasped together, she too prayed, with rheumy eyes fixed on the couple who lay spent. Both Noel and Aqua's knees were bent, and their feet rested on the steps below.

Aqua attempted to raise herself somewhat. She gave up, though, because her throat was raw, and she had very little strength left. Her lungs stung, and suddenly she wanted to give up because it had become too much. She no longer had the fortitude for *this*. Had she been well before the attack, and had she not been so insidiously attacked for a while, perhaps she could have fought on. However, now all she wanted was rest. She wanted to sleep away, and with her throat aching, she whispered that to the man she loved.

Hey! Aqua realized *she* did not want to leave. Those were someone else's thoughts and words. Aqua and Noel had a lifetime of loving before them...if they could get through *this*.

Suddenly, with more strength than she should have had, and as venomous anger welled inside her, Aqua watched her hand grasp the tee that Noel had worn since last evening. Forcefully, she pulled him to her.

Noel's eyes narrowed, because wait... Something was wrong, again. Noel was sure of it, hearing the voice emit from Aqua's lips. He saw the red-hot rage blazing in her eyes. "She's leaving," a mean-spirited voice announced. "Ain't a thing you can do about it—*boy*."

Oh, hell no! was all Noel could think through the fury and the haze, even as he heard Ms. Hyacinth gasp. Bolting up from the waist, his feet were on the steps. Noel was unsure of what to do. Even as Aqua, looking more like herself, and worn from the possession, hesitantly reached out.

Noel knew it was she. Aqua had a specific look, all her own. She had her own signature sweet movements. So Noel tried not to stiffen when gently she caressed him, but he couldn't stop the tears. They welled in both his and Aqua's eyes. She swallowed, against pain, and the heartache of defeat, because she could not go on. Not this way. Aqua was simply too worn. Thus, she tearfully whispered, while she still could, "He's gonna kill me, Ocaña. I'm scared because I know it, but *I love you*. I did from the beginning, even when I didn't call. Now I need you. Do something...for me."

Noel pressed his face to Aqua's neck before he remembered the torn flesh there. Moving his head, he gazed into Aqua's beautiful, but now so troubled amber eyes, "Anything, my love."

A tear rolled from the outer corner of Aqua's eye. "Call GB..."

"Oh!" Ms. Hyacinth cried out at hearing her first cousin's moniker.

"Tell my GB," Aqua moaned. "You know. Tell Genie, too."

Noel's fading lily closed her eyes. *Nooo!* he hollered, grabbing her.

From everywhere, the house's inhabitants gathered as though they had been summoned. At the foot of the stairs, they watched, as carrying limp Aqua, Noel trundled wild-eyed and heavy-footed downward.

Aqua's arm loosely swung over the arm that Noel had beneath her. Out he raced, to the healing place, the place of pain too, from which he had so recently come. Those who loved both him and Aqua trailed them. Somber-faced, they followed, mirroring a sad procession of mourners.

With Aqua clutched tightly, Noel raced beneath a cloud-filled sky.

In the near-dark windowless little hovel, the High Priestess waited.

She saw the tormented couple.

She felt what arrived with them.

Slowly rising, as Noel strode toward her carrying his precious bundle, the Priestess shook off her shawl. "Lay baby doll down."

Doing as bid, Noel got to his knees. He was concerned that Aqua was cool to the touch. Lovingly, he caressed her face and kissed her eyelids.

"Move," the Priestess instructed.

Noel looked up because Priestess Odyssey did not understand. He wanted to be with Aqua, especially now.

"Move, son." The woman glanced at her offspring, standing just inside the dark room. "No-el," she called, "move, or—"

Stocky, forty-something Kijana leaned to lift his friend away.

Angrily, Aqua began to buck, thrash and kick. Noel then understood.

The Priestess whispered, "It - is - war." Slowly, as though time were eternity, she bent. Leaning forward, she spoke in an ancient voice. "In the name that is above all names. In the name of the One to whom *all* must bow, I command you… take – your – leave."

Aqua thrashed and angrily flailed. To Noel, it looked like she was being ripped apart from the inside out; yet the Priestess crouched beside her. Calm, the Priestess appeared to gaze down into nothing more than a lovely flowerbed.

"Stop," the Priestess said. "Stop." Above Aqua's torso, brown fingers trembled. No. Noel realized Priestess's fingers wiggled because she willed it. "Sweet girl," the Priestess's voice became syrupy. "Come up now. Rise above, sweetness, rise over this storm." The Priestess's voice became that of the ancient as she began an incantation. "Rrrise sweet one," she commanded, "above all that has brewed for centuries."

Noel watched with reddened eyes, in awe, as outside the cabin, the wind picked up. He could hear it loudly and eerily blow.

Closing her eyes, the Priestess spoke, as Aqua's body stilled. "There is a gathering." Suddenly the Priestess shouted, tossing up her hands. "What say you?"

The hut was still, save for smoldering embers in the fireplace. Again, the Priestess inquired. "What is it yuh want? Not that it will be granted."

Outside the door, redbone, curvy, Sangria hissed at those attempting to peer into the cabin. "Go!"

Only Dr. Dear escaped her, to slip into the dimness.

"Back!" the Priestess absently ordered. Obeying, Noel and the doctor's eyes were on Aqua. She lay prone on the floor. Watching, the men nearly flattened themselves against the wood of the cabin walls.

"What say you?" the Priestess whispered. Then she began to speak as though in conversation, but in a mother tongue. Those present could only make out the words, "What desire yuh?"

Aqua moved. Slowly, she turned her head. With mean eyes, she heaved herself up, and spat on the Priestess' leg.

As though unaware of the glob of saliva dripping onto her foot, the Priestess sounded resigned. "Yuh still must go. There is no other way." She began an invocation, marching round and round.

Aqua turned her head, watching with another's eyes, as the Priestess trod back and forth. Suddenly, Aqua's hand, used by another, shot out. It was an evil attempt to grab the legs of the Priestess, to thwart her.

"Nooo!" It was the man's voice from the house. The one from the upstairs hallway. Noel remembered it from when he and Aqua had lain spent on the floor. Noel's blood boiled hearing that voice and knowing it wasn't Aqua's. "No!" The voice thundered. "Give me what's mine!"

Softly then, a melodious woman's voice called, "My?"

Noel nor the doctor knew if the voice had come from Odyssey, Aqua, or someone otherworldly. As though she had not heard, the Priestess worked, fighting to place and bind banana tree leaves over Aqua's eyes. The woman did it so that the entity that possessed Aqua would no longer see.

"Mine!" There was no mistaking *that* voice, Noel thought, as Aqua violently tossed her head. When the Priestess stepped back, an unearthly howl rent the air.

Moving quickly, the Priestess slid what looked like substantial oily leaves beneath Aqua's caftan onto her bare chest. The woman chanted as she bound Aqua's hands so that Aqua could not strike or hit anymore. Again, the Priestess spoke in the mother tongue, a holy language. Every so often, Noel understood a word or two. The Priestess hissed as she worked, immobilizing that one who had to be bound.

"You who shall remain nameless..." the Priestess patted Aqua's tied hands, "take your leave." Over the banana tree leaves, she anointed Aqua's head. "Not beggin' yuh," the Priestess spat while grasping Aqua to her bosom. "I command you, in the name of the One who is, and all else that is Holy..." The Priestess rocked as blood-curdling angry screams rose from Aqua's throat. Undaunted, the Priestess chanted, while Aqua's whole body wrathfully shook. "Oh-ho," the Priestess mirthlessly cackled. "You're an old one, an ancient from the pit! You possessed the boy and drove him as a man. And you have remained, down through the ages, wreaking havoc. Now it will cease.

"To the pit," the Priestess continued. "Back there, you must go. You can no longer possess another—not any other! Thus saith the Holy."

Aqua continued to scream and flail, becoming hoarse. To Noel, it sounded like she was being torn asunder. He wanted it—all of it—to end.

The Priestess jerked her head up while closely holding the bound but fighting Aqua. The older woman felt all, aware that Aqua, the body owner, needed the human connection.

The Priestess called out, "Noel, this is no place for indecision. There is no turning back, now." With accusing eyes, she glared at him, backed against the wall. "Yuh drainin' me...and her, son. Each time I grab her from the nether region, *you* pull me baaack. Hindrance! Either believe— now, or go, alone! If I lose hold, you will go," she hissed, "but know this, alone will be *forever*."

Seeing and knowing beyond knowing what was happening, Dr. Dear quickly took Noel's arm. "This is it, pal," the physician whispered. "It's boys or men. Ride or die." In the dim light, the doctor's blue eyes pled, while Odyssey and Aqua continued to engage in spiritual warfare.

"Man, it's yuh mind." The doctor told Noel this because he could see. The golden thickset man truly did not understand.

Noel's eyes darted from screaming Aqua and the Priestess back to his friend.

"Noel, *you* are the one creating a barrier." Dr. Dear shook the man he had known since they were college-age at Tulane. "Ah heard what happened upstairs. Open yourself, again –believe!" The doctor was insistent and laid all on the line. "Yuh got one course of action, buddy because your doll's life is at stake. Look how limp she is! *Believe* man!"

Mentally, for Noel, the refrain of Rod Temperton's song played.

...Can't go back to living without –Aqua.

April Alisa Marquette

Noel strained then, with all that was within him, to summon the whispers from upstairs.

Use yuh mind. Fight back wit' yuh mind...

He conjured calm, as practiced in meditation. Noel recalled sitting beside Aqua during quieter moments. His promises floated back.

I will save you; I will die for you, like Jeremiah for Desiree...

Noel's body suddenly went rigid. The doctor noticed Noel's vacant eyes. Dell Dear knew then that although his friend's body remained, Noel had essentially crossed a border –from which he would not return, unless he won this fight, to the death. "Give 'em hell, bro," the lowcountry doctor whispered, wishing his friend Godspeed. Like never before, he too joined those huddled outside. Beneath the glowering sky, they writhed and moaned in prayer.

HE did not know who he was anymore, was he was Noel or Jeremiah? An amalgamation of the two, *they* only knew they had immense power, and that despite it, the son-of-a-situation still would not turn loose. Sloshing through the cold-water creek, The Joined did not care because they would kill. It was the only way.

Howling, the tenacious character angrily dashed at them.

Furiously, The Joined head-butted; yet going down, tenacious swiftly raised a booted foot. It landed in the stomach of The Joined, inches from their groin. Winded, but not bested, The Joined grabbed hold of tenacious' neck. Mightily they squeezed, but tenacious kneed and swung. Winded by a kidney shot, The Joined forgot the pain. They slammed their fist into the jaw that went slack. It swung open, the angle unnatural. Seeing this, The Joined again rammed their fist into the bloodied face. They also felt a burst of unearthly energy. It suffused their whole being with power. Using that power, The Joined grabbed the scrambling character's shoulders and loose locks. They wound the hair around their large hand.

Then The Joined saw the large stone. It was clutched in tenacious' fist. With malicious intent, tenacious slowly raised it.

Breathing hard, The Joined knew. It was now or never. Therefore, they used their big hands and the immense strength coursing through their powerful arms. They jerked both head and shoulders in opposite directions.

Slowly then, the fight seeped out of tenacious...

Seeing and sensing this, The Joined allowed fight-less—now—to slip to the stony creek bed. The body weight, falling backward, caused the head to slam onto a large, worn-smooth stone. It was one of many that lined the watery creek bottom. A bulky stone, similar to the others, rolled from the lifeless hand.

The Joined knew, that character was no more.

The Joined felt it then, the separating... No longer one powerful entity, the amalgamation again became two. Centuries apart.

Flexing his large, bruised and bloodied hands, the bronze smith looked up. He smelled nature, loam, and flora. The sweet smell of honeysuckle overrode all, when for centuries he had smelled nothing.

The smith squinted at brilliant shafts of glorious, golden, late-summer sunlight. He saw color! He *heard* birds chirping and the trickling of the creek's cool, clear water. He also heard the drone of a fat busy bee, when before, he had only known the pounding of his own heart. He also noticed. Someone stood in the calm near-evening light.

She...wore layers of filmy white. Beckoning him forward, this beauty stood on the opposite shore. Like a lovely garment, behind Desiree, a carpet of wildflowers flourished, swaying in the gentlest breeze.

Jeremiah, the smith, smiled because he was free...finally *free*. Unencumbered, he knew too; it was the loveliest evening upon which to go for a walk. He would do so, unhurried, with his love, his life. At last.

BACK in the little lean-to, Noel fell to his knees. Exhausted, he heard the Priestess whimper. He saw her head-wrap. Askew, it had come undone. The woman appeared smaller and worn. She allowed the now limp but yet bound Aqua to slip downward and away.

And he had fought so hard, Noel dismally thought. Guess his efforts had not been enough.

Noel let himself crumple. His face hit the floor. Feeling the dull ache, he no longer cared because he knew one thing.

Without Aqua, he essentially had nothing. He was not living, again.

Chapter 41

THE High Priestess, her son, and daughter-in-law left just as they had come, before the sun.

"One thing about our Priestess," Dr. Dear drawled when he stopped by to check on his friend, "is that she's not one for fanfare."

Noel grimaced as the doctor examined and re-bandaged his ribs. "Yeah, Priestess moves like a shadow. She comes and goes quietly."

Dr. Dear stared at his friend's bruised face. "But unlike a shadow," he adjudicated, "Priestess has power. Ah am truly honored to know her."

Noel pondered it. "You know, Dell, for someone to be that knowledgeable and powerful, yet so humble, she's had to have gone through a *lot*."

Dr. Dear nodded. "Kind of sad *and* wonderful, don't yuh think?"

"I do. I also think," Noel smirked. "That if my *lirio's* new family could do any more for her, they'd fight each other to do it."

Dr. Dear checked Noel's scraped hands. "Them ladies are ret cute."

"Dell, to you, anyone female is cute."

The physician looked up from applying salve. "Ah beg to differ."

"Oh. I forgot, the female must be of color."

"Look who's talking," Dr. Dear scoffed, packing his bag. "Seems lak you too have a thing for color."

"Rightfully so," Noel pointed out. "My *mother*, remember? *Papi* too."

Dr. Dear turned. "Then you got it honest, from your old man."

Noel spoke, as slowly, painfully, he eased himself up. "What about *your* old man? I heard Doc Senior had a thing for Priestess, way back."

"That's right." Dr. Dear winked. "So, guess I got it honest too, huh?"

In the foyer, Noel laughed and winced. Taking the front steps, gingerly, so as not to upset his bruised ribs, he limped out into the sunshine. "Everything looks so normal, like nothing ever happened."

"Yeah, but *we* know," the doctor reminded him. "We actually *lived* the stuff of which legend is created. Can yuh believe it?"

"I can. I can do without a repeat, too," Noel admitted. He watched as the doctor strode to his car. Ducking a bumblebee headed for honeysuckle, Noel called out, "You will be there, right?"

Beneath a canopy of trees, the doctor threw up a hand. "Wouldn't miss it, my friend." His ancient luxury buggy zoomed back and away.

UPSTAIRS, Aqua got out of bed, despite protests. "I refuse to let y'all," she told her hazel-eyed family members, "make an invalid of me."

They watched the woman who wore the pastel nightgown that they'd gifted her. "Be right back," she advised, bent from her ordeal.

At the creaking of her bedroom door, the women pivoted. From the hallway, Sonsa poked her head in. "What's she want?"

Grandmother Hyacinth patted her braided crown. "Come see."

Aqua emerged from her dressing room as Sonsa moaned, "I gotta work, y'all. Mama, take them home, please. Ms. Aqua needs to rest."

"I told you, Sonsa, quit calling me that. I'm just Aqua, your cousin."

"I know," bright-face admitted, her hands on her apron. "But it's gonna take some getting used to, having no handle on yo' name."

Aqua waved and carefully sat at the foot of her bed. She faced the comfortable chairs that the male help had dragged in for her family.

Small Ms. Blossom mirrored a curious child. "What yuh got there?"

Sonsa peered over, and Aqua glanced up. "Come, buttercup."

Sonsa did not move, and Azalea chided her. "Your cuzin spoke. Git."

As Sonsa moved forward, rubbing damp palms on her apron, Aqua began. "Buttercup, you've learned our family history, *and* you're compiling volumes about us, and others—yes, I know about your book deal."

"Granmama, you told!" Sonsa shrieked, embarrassed.

"Watch yourself," Hyacinth advised. "And wasn't me, this time."

"Then who?" Sonsa asked, her eyes caressing the box on Aqua's lap.

"Matter of fact," the small white-haired Ms. Blossom chirped, "*I* told. We proud of you, gal. Yuh got a fine mind and a good education."

Aqua beamed, lifting the box top. "It's why you should have this."

Nervously, Sonsa touched at the white kerchief tied in a triangle over her thick sandy brown hair. "But Desiree gave that to *you*..."

"She *led* me to it," Aqua admitted, "but with all her whispering, she never said *keep* it. So it's yours. Write her story, so others will know."

Sonsa's face lit up. Tears sparkled in her hazel eyes.

Peeking into Aqua's room, Noel saw her, swamped in a group hug. Sheesh. He really had to get Aqua out of here, off this island, and back where he could have her all to himself.

Chapter 42

THAT night Aqua heard crackling. As she slept, in her man's muscular arms, she heard an electronic beep. Aqua roused herself, hazily wondering if anyone else heard. Perhaps her ears were just ringing, an after effect of all she had been through. Maybe she was simply exhausted. She knew that earlier, at barely seven p.m., after a shower with Noel, neither of them could keep their eyes open. But wait…there was that crackling again, and a *pop*! A *hissss*…and then nothing.

Easing up in the dark, Aqua heard the sheets rustle. Noel was repositioning himself. Aqua remembered. She was in *his* room. After presenting Desiree's box to Sonsa, who studied for her Master's Degree in anthropology, the younger woman re-did Noel's linens. She had done so after the small white-haired Ms. Blossom and her daughter, the crowned Ms. Hyacinth, had announced they had to go.

Ninety-seven, Ms. Blossom had crowed about a *boyfriend* that she had to see. The women had shuffled off, unwilling to wear out their welcome. Outside, Sonsa's mother, Azalea, an entrepreneur who ran a house cleaning service, awaited her mother and grandmother. Eagerly bouncing on the rear seat of his grandmother's golf cart had been Sonsa's small son, Hiram Jr.

Now, as Aqua's eyes acclimated to the dimness, she looked over at Noel. He was *so fine*, inside and out. Aqua thought it, as gorgeous lay there in the moonlight spilling in from the window. How she really loved him.

Currently lying on his stomach, Noel's arm hung off the bed. His fingers twitched while his other bruised hand rested beneath his face.

Feeling the urge to kiss his bare muscular back, Aqua wanted to make love with him because when had they last shared that? Forgetting the tangled sheet at his tapered waist, Aqua sniffed. Was that *smoke*?

It was –and a lot of it! Hurriedly, she shook Noel and tumbled from the bed. Sickening spirits and wretched wiring. She yelled. "Ocaña, don't lie back down! There's smoke—and fire!"

"*Fuego*?" He woke, kicking off the sheet. "What about smoke?"

"Something crackled, then popped." Aqua grabbed a few things.

"Damn faulty wiring," Noel swore. "Shit. Desdemona!" He jumped into pants.

Aqua yelped as Noel yanked her from the room. Bumping her with his knee, he wanted her to *move*, go downstairs, fast. With a grunt, he fought his way into the tee that he had earlier tossed aside. "Go, *niña*."

Aqua pounded downward, gasping, "But *Des*...and Jet Tu, and Kat..."

In the foyer, beneath the wrought iron chandelier, with her arms full, Aqua fought with the front door. In the dark, she glanced back. She saw Noel coughing, but racing toward the rear of the enormous house. "Ocaña!" she screamed.

"Go." He did not turn. "I must get Des. ¡*Siga*! —go on, *chica*!"

Suddenly it became too hot. From somewhere upstairs, there was a loud crash. With arms full, Aqua bolted through double doors and out into the humid wee morning dark. Aqua's breath hitched as she ran, because what if? What if Noel didn't find Desdemona? What if plump, arthritic Des was overcome, or... Aqua wouldn't think that, but what if Noel got trapped?

Aqua stood on the walk already littered with shattered glass and debris. She watched as the fire greedily gnawed at the old house, causing parts to crumble. As she took backward steps, Aqua's eyes were drawn upward. She noticed that the foyer ceiling was now afire. With eyes glued to the blaze that angrily billowed from the front doors, Aqua's heart began to ache. Vaguely also, she became aware of the sound of running. She did not register that she had dropped the few belongings that she'd managed to gather.

Jet Tu bounded up, his lean young face streaked with soot and sweat. Barefoot, he wore a wife-beater tank and lengthy denim shorts. Aqua's eyes darted past him because she heard a mighty clanging. Coupled with the fire, the noise caused her to feel frantic beyond belief.

Dazedly, she gazed about. The whole third floor was now fully ablaze. Flames lit up the night sky. Even some of the second-floor windows were aglow. What further disturbed Aqua was a new pulsing strobe-like light. Aqua wondered about Noel as Jet Tu pulled her farther from crackling and fast-falling debris. No doubt, the young man also pulled her from the path of men arriving in fire gear and boots.

Dully, Aqua realized, the strobe light was that of the fire truck. Her eyes stayed glued to the house, *El Diario*. With her heart hammering, from some faraway place, Aqua heard Jet Tu loudly speak. She could not respond. She could only worry for Noel and Desdemona's safety.

Over the roar of the fire, Jet Tu tried to make himself heard. He was drowned out by shouting, running, breaking glass, and spraying water.

Through it all, Aqua could only think of Ocaña. He'd had to be noble. That was the kind of man he was. He'd had to try to save Desdemona, but what if neither he nor the cook made it? With her stomach as sick as it had ever been, Aqua felt dazed, and she had to wonder. What if, after all she and Noel had been through, they wound up separated, in death? Was this it? Could this *be* it—all there was, for them, now?

Aqua simply could not wait a few more lifetimes to be with Noel Cristián Ocaña. She tore out running, around the side of the house.

Stunned, Jet Tu stared after her.

Aqua barely heard him or others who called after her. She didn't register unfamiliar voices barking commands. Running smack into a rescue worker, with wild eyes Aqua blinked. Quickly, she skirted him and continued to sprint. She did not care that her breasts and belly were mostly visible beneath the thin cotton of her nightshirt. So what, her shapely legs and feet were bare? She only cared about one thing. She ran around the back of the enormous house. There, chaos reigned as Katherine huddled with Eldon. Good, Aqua distractedly thought, the invaluable couple were alive, and not in a corner or a closet, burned to a crisp.

Still darting around, Aqua saw Aaron the property-keep. He and a firefighter gestured. Aaron shouted orders to Jethro. Appearing sinewy, sullen, and sooty, carrying his ax, Jethro strode alongside a rescue worker. Aqua tried not to cry. With her chest heaving magnanimously, she fought to contain the sobs welling within. She didn't see Katherine, who left Eldon's embrace. Katherine grasped the blanket that had been about her and Eldon's shoulders.

With her head wrapped, Katherine approached to cover Aqua.

As she clutched the blanket between her breasts, Aqua wanted to know one thing. "Have you seen..." my *husband*?

Pain and fire danced in the older woman's eyes as she watched the ferocious blaze. Without a word, she shook her head. No.

A man shouted the women needed to move. Aqua did. Grasping the blanket so as not to display the body that Noel wouldn't want others ogling, she left Katherine. Aqua made her way back to the front of the house. To do so, she took the side path, weaving through the gnarled stand of trees. The perimeter of the house was now off-limits. In front, all was confusion, with two-way radios beeping, disjointed voices commanding, and the complete house front blurred and tremendously ablaze.

Sinking to her knees in an out of the way spot, Aqua could only hug herself. As frightened as she had ever been, she began to rock and pray. She forgot time and place. She forgot people, fire, and her strewn and missing belongings. Mentally, she shut out all noise. Like she had seen GB do many times, and like she'd seen Genie do too, Aqua called on God. She prayed until every light and disturbance in the dark receded.

Then feeling suspended and no longer in time, it became only Aqua and her savior.

When at last the sun began to rise, there were only pockets of fire here and there to be doused and squashed. Shouts and orders died. Amid the stench and the ugliness of all that was charred or hacked away, Aqua raised stinging eyes. Like the house, she felt reduced to rubble. She could not fathom what she would do now because, in just a few short weeks, her life had become irrevocably intertwined with Noel Ocaña's, so much so that now she could hardly bear to breathe.

Someone with gentle hands squeezed Aqua's shoulder, but she could not raise her head. Although she heard a familiar tinny sound, Aqua dared not hope. Still, with widened eyes and her heart crashing against her ribs for sheer joy, Aqua looked up and clasped two hands. The huge gold one, and the smaller, older brown one, Noel's and Desdemona's.

Grabbing her head in his giant palm, Noel leaned toward the kneeling Aqua. God, he loved a woman who prayed! Firmly, he pressed his lips to her forehead, grateful she was okay and that she'd not gone back inside.

Holding one of Desdemona's culinary-skilled hands, Aqua rose. She allowed Noel's searching mouth to find hers. He kissed her as though he was dying of thirst and she was water. Aqua kissed Noel back with the same fervor, wanting only to be joined with him, now and forever.

"Everything's gone," she murmured, touching him, loving him; his computer, his office equipment, all the refurbishing he'd had done, gone.

Noel spoke into Aqua's mouth. *"Lirio,* I'd only be devastated if I lost *you.* The other things can be replaced."

Immensely grateful to be rejoined, again, the couple devoured each other. With Aqua's blanket falling away, Noel hefted her up and crushed her to him. He licked and lapped at her while with both hands he squeezed her bottom. He wanted to rock into her right then. He wanted to be joined with her, forever. Never before had he known a woman who always took him up so rapidly. Riding a passionate wave, Aqua clutched Noel tightly. Then sanity prevailed.

"I must go, *lirio*," Noel whispered. His lips were against hers. He fought to get his body to obey as he said, "I must tend a few things," really, a whole mess of things. Noel thought it as he allowed Aqua to stand. He placed the shorter round, Desdemona, in Aqua's arms. "I'll be back," he promised with a hand on Aqua's nape.

Watching him gallantly stride to confer with the fire chief, Aqua retrieved her blanket. Then beneath the morning sun, the women clung to each other, *laughing*, of all things.

Amid the charred ruins, shoeless and standing in what promised to be another day of scorching temperatures, Aqua, and the plump cook laughed. With mist from douse water and dew visibly rising, hysterically, they continued until they cried.

Even then, Aqua gasped. "Des, you told me, when I first got here, that this place had—" Aqua tried to collect herself, "burned before."

"Sho did." The culinary queen dabbed her eyes with some man's shirt. It was slung over her nightdress. "Thass why de place was musty."

"Years ago…" Aqua attempted to speak through the laughter. "My grandmother told me that *fire* can be a purgative. She said sometimes it cleanses…"

"Yes, chile." Desdemona grinned, her gold-banded tooth gleaming like the new day sun. "*Now* this place done been purified, for sho!"

Chapter 43

WHEN she arrived back in Georgia; Aqua had taken a few days to herself. Finally feeling right, she realized she had a lot of catching up to do; thus, she'd called her grandmother, Gloria Bayliss.

"GB," Aqua grinned through the phone, "Boy, do I have a surprise for you! Are you sitting down? If you're not, you need to…"

Aqua told GB that her first cousin had been found. After explaining, Aqua had to hold the phone away from her ear. Aqua even laughed, hearing all her grandmother's loud, joyful wailing and crowing.

AVA had been Aqua's next call. Her sister had vowed to stop by that evening, "I'll even bring your niece, when I pick her up from GB's house after work."

DYSON'S ex had been Aqua's next call. "Edna?"

"Aqua—hey! How *are* you?"

"Doing well." Aqua sighed. "However, I called because—"

Edna became alert. She genuinely liked the other woman, as did her daughter. Therefore, Edna interrupted. "Should I not mention that I've spoken to you—if Isi asks? You know she asks about you every day."

"Oh, tell her, and I'll text her." Aqua smiled, "But I wanted to speak with you." Again, Aqua sighed. "Edna, I love that girl like she is—"

"Your own, I know," Dyson's ex finished. "She feels the same about you."

"Well, that's why I need to sit down with you."

Edna felt a prickle of alarm. "Is something wrong?"

"No, but I have left Isis' father."

Edna sighed with relief before she felt alarmed. "Does Isi know?" It was an afterthought, "No. She'd have said so."

"You're right. I didn't tell Isis, but I don't know what he's said, since I haven't been around, and since she *is* inquisitive."

"Well…" Edna proposed, she and Aqua should meet, discuss things.

"I'm no longer at the publisher, Edna. I'm in the process of starting my own thing, so the time and place are up to you."

There was laughter in Edna's voice. "Why not meet at *Apropos*?"

Aqua's voice rose. "Have you lost your mind, lady? I just told you, I'm not *with* Dyson. Why would I want to converse at his club?"

Edna laughed. "Girl, *his* place is *apropos*—perfect for this."

Chuckling too, Aqua became pensive, "Well, the club is cozy..."

"It's private; if we go on Thursday," Edna piped, "*he* won't even be there."

"Edna, you devil!"

"Devil nothing," Edna's smile was audible. "You love me, girl."

"I do. Well, how about seven," Aqua suggested. "This Thursday."

"Cool, and Aqua? I really look forward to seeing you."

PHÉDRA had been the call after that. After catching up with the new mom, Aqua told her photographer friend, "I'd like to speak with Mycah. When he comes home tonight, would you mention it to him? Aqua divulged that she was thinking of turning her experience on the island into a book.

"And you'll need Mycah's help," Phédra excitedly added. She said the publicist could point Aqua in the right direction. "I know he has an author on his roster. Her name is April, and she's actually a friend of ours."

THE next day, Aqua spoke to April, the author. Come to find out, they had already met, at an award's ceremony they'd both attended for Phédra, the photographer, their mutual friend. Aqua was excited because, according to April, Aqua really had something.

After the call, as Aqua began typing up things that she did not want to forget, she realized. She really didn't mind allowing April in on nearly every aspect of her life. Perhaps, Aqua thought, once the book was published, it might even help someone going through a similar trial.

CADENCE with the corkscrew curls was excited about Aqua's proposed book. The petite makeup artist offered her services, should Aqua have a future need.

Cadence then mentioned her husband. She said she had things to share about Yael. "Maybe I need to write a book too," the curly-haired one mused aloud, "about what I've been through with him..."

AQUA arrived at Dyson's cozy club first. Inside, with jazz and conversation floating, she smiled at the staff. Artfully, she evaded prying inquiries. She thanked blond Gary, the bartender, for saying she was sexy in her sundress and sandals. "You look happy." He shooed a waitperson away to admit, "A, if I wanted classy, I'd choose a honey like you."

After saying Gary was sweet, Aqua marveled that no one could look at her and tell she'd been through one hell of an ordeal. Wow. Then before she could further muse, she saw Isis' shorter, hippy mother. The woman was so earthy and self-assured that they'd had to become friends. Putting her glass down, Aqua noted the patrician man who followed Edna.

On this evening, the shorter woman's wavy hair was sleek and back in her usual chignon. Her dangling gemstone earrings caught the light as she sashayed in dark leggings, spike heels, and a sparkly navy leotard.

Aqua smiled because only someone with a terrifically toned body could pull off that outfit with panache. "Hey sexy," Aqua grinned.

Edna air-kissed Aqua's cheeks, "Looking scrumptious yourself."

"And who do we have here?" Aqua's amber eyes twinkled.

Edna shook with laughter. Isis' mom placed a hand on the arm of the man whose white hair was scooped back into a ponytail. "Aqua, I swear you're nosy," Edna teased, "but since I was gonna introduce you anyway..." Edna turned to the slim, average-height male whose carriage suggested he was more than mortal. Edna very nearly purred, "Aqua, this is Rrree-no. Renault, meet my friend, Aqua Mira."

Aqua extended an elegant hand. "Nice to meet you."

Sexy in a subdued way, Renault bent to place his lips on Aqua's bronze hand. He smelled of something soft—whispering of secrets, and Aqua saw that female patrons had not failed to notice him. With a French accent, Renault admitted he was happy to make Aqua's acquaintance. He turned to Edna. "Quite true, my darling, this Aqua *MeeRAH* is luscious." To Aqua, Renault said, "Now when young *I-SEE* gushes about you I will have a mental picture."

As Aqua took her seat, Renault gazed at petite Edna. Curling both his hands around her upper arms, he bent, giving her a heartfelt kiss, French, no doubt. He also reminded Edna, who appeared dazed afterward, that he would pick her up later.

Seated, with fingertips pressed to their lips, both women waited until Renault sauntered out of earshot. Then raucously, they laughed. Aqua fanned herself. "Dang Edna, I ain't seen that much heat since...I can't remember. Whew! For a moment there, a sista felt like a voyeur."

Edna mirrored the cat that ate the canary. "On the heels of that statement, I'll only say one thing. Isi calls Renault 'gramps.'"

Aqua shook with laughter. "That girl..."

Edna curtailed a chuckle. "I know. He calls her insolent."

"She's irreverent," Aqua agreed, "but she's precious and exuberant."

"Thanks for saying that." Edna beamed, "And she loves that man."

"I know." Aqua nodded, "Everything is: Renault did this, and that."

Edna smiled. "He loves Isis too. He said she's the daughter he's never had because he has grown sons." Edna leaned forward. "I'll tell you another thing. That man is *no* 'gramps' in bed."

Aqua squealed. "Edna! Isis a spitfire because of her mama!"

Edna feigned innocence. "It's true. About Renault, I mean."

Aqua shook her head as Gary flicked a glance at the sophisticated ladies. It was funny seeing them reduced to girlish giggles. He nodded when Edna raised her glass bubble, letting him know she was pleased with the brandy. He refocused on pulling drafts for a large party, but amused, Gary thought, he would *hate* to be Dyson right now.

Edna set her purse aside. "So you're leaving Eamon. Can't say I blame you."

"I already have." Aqua nodded. "I was tired. It had been too long."

"You're a *saint*, A. Two years for me and that was an eternity."

"Saint schmaint," Aqua scoffed. "Sometimes I feel like a fool." But Aqua realized, Dyson had been a place-holder. He had aided her to mark time until both she and Noel were ready to begin their life's journey.

"Girl," Edna leaned forward, "it was right *at the time*. And not one of those years can be undone, so forget them, and him." And let's spotlight my child, Edna thought. "You know Isi will be devastated, right?"

Aqua whispered, "I know, but I don't want to lose her.*"*

"You don't *have to*; matter of fact," Edna became brisk. "You *must* stay in Isis Athena's life." The pint-sized powerhouse gentled and pled. "A, my baby has no God-parents. So, become her Godmother. You have been the most tremendous influence on her."

Aqua blinked. "I don't know what to say."

Edna reached for the bronze hand. "Say yes. My child wouldn't be the same without you. She—*we*—need you." Edna looked pained as she swallowed and sat back, her nose visibly reddening. "Aqua, when my sister Mia died—" Edna tried not to cry. "We were devastated. I still am sometimes, but *you* kept Isi from going into a shell."

"Edna, you told me." Aqua softly admitted, "I only did what I could."

"I'm grateful. You gave my baby back her shine. You and Ava gave Isis things to look forward to. By the way, how is your sister, and that big smoov Melvi-o of hers?"

"They're good. I'll mention you asked about them."

"Yes," Edna nodded. "Give my regards." Edna backtracked. "Listen A, I'd like to contact the parish, ask Father Jonah to officiate at Isis' christening—even though she's so big now; still, it'll be fun. We'll make a day of it. Then she and I will never lose you. You'll be our family."

Aqua was stunned. She had so many great things happening to her lately. Her family, it seemed, just kept expanding. "Edna," Aqua sincerely began. "I never expected all *this*." Then Aqua grinned. "You do know we're supposed to hate each other, don't you?"

Edna waved. "Let that shit go MaMa because it matters not how we met. All that matters is that even though *her father* is unwilling, you have provided guidance for Isis."

The words tumbled from Aqua's lips. "For him, she's not a priority."

"Neither were you or I. Big fat Eamon only cares about himself."

"I've faced that," Aqua divulged, "And it's okay, I'm happy now." Inadvertently, Aqua changed the subject. "Edna, you think you'll marry Renault? Y'all have been together a long time."

"No." Edna was sure. "He's done it before; she was a war correspondent who got killed. *I* no longer have the need. We like what we have. Marriage isn't in the cards, so we'll remain as we are." Edna's eyes sparkled, "But A…tell me about *your* him."

Aqua chuckled because golden, sexy, thickset Ocaña came to mind. "You know Edna, strange as it is, you and I really are friends."

"I know. It's part of why Eamon despises me." Edna triumphantly whooped, and people glanced her way. "Now, biggie will really hate me! Especially when these minions spill that you and I were here, together."

Aqua raised her glass. "Edna, I have *so* moved on."

Edna raised her brandy bubble. "Good. Now when is the wedding—because that immense shine on yo' finger shouts it will not be far off."

LATER, lying naked on Noel's slanted workout bench, Aqua watched him through the mirror.

Powerfully nude and sexy, he held one of her shapely legs up around his waist.

What a titillating sight, Aqua mused, sexy Noel between her thick thighs, his rock-hard hips pulsing, as within her, his rod ignited.

Aqua licked her lips, liking the way Noel worked it. She watched as perspiration gave a slight sheen to his golden skin, and the sparse hair on his chest curled. Aqua loved looking at Noel's pectoral muscles, and the others bunched in his massive arms. She loved touching him, kissing him, receiving him. She knew every vein, barely noticeable, back of his skilled hands. During this their latest romp, she enjoyed the racy noises they both made, and those created by the joining of their bodies.

Aqua liked the thin line of hair that meandered down Noel's rugged torso to his groin. There, at present, he appeared dewy. To Aqua, it meant her man was working overtime.

She loved every moment.

Aqua panted that she would turn over. Doing so, she slid back and onto Noel, knowing he would enjoy watching what he called her big fluffy *tetas*.

Through the mirror, as she had known he would, the man watched as her bazooms shimmied and bounced, every single time he bumped her with an erotic thrust.

Noel slapped Aqua's jiggling bottom. Then with big hands gripping tightly, he sped up the pace. "Let's go, *niña*…"

With Noel behind and within her, Aqua sensually moved. On his sturdy pole, she rode, quickly, up, and down, forward and back.

In the mirror, she took note of her man's perspiration, his concentration, *and* his camcorder's 'record' light.

A moment before she spiraled, Aqua managed to admit, "I can't wait…to watch the re-run."

Noel did her one better. Giving Aqua all, he panted that he could not wait to create another one.

Chapter 44

INSTEAD of a rehearsal dinner, Aqua told Noel she wanted a Burning Bowl Ceremony. The purpose was to rid both people of all that they were unwilling to take into their new life together.

When the day came, Aqua walked quickly through Noel's Mislaid Mountain home. Passing maize colored walls, she made sure everything was just so; she prayed too that all would go well.

Wearing tailored slacks and an untucked, billowing brilliant white shirt with cuffs and links, Noel caught Aqua around the waist. He eyed her emerald green caftan. He noticed her hair, a mass of curls, *and* that she reached to rearrange a ceramic vase, for the third time.

Therefore, Noel advised, "Deep breath, *niña*. Relax." Then he opened his mouth on hers before he slapped her behind. "Go get dressed."

Aqua laughed and stated as she ascended the stairs, "Most of the time, you tell me to get *undressed*."

At the mahogany double doors, hugs and kisses were plentiful, and Aqua appeared in time to greet their guests. She wore a long, form-fitting, sage green, alpaca knit dress. Her pretty feet were bare. She wore freshwater pearl and diamond earrings and her incomparable engagement ring. With her barely-there makeup and riotously curled hair, she appeared luminous.

Noel's friends from Karina Cay, Kijana, and his wife, auburn-haired Sangria, *and* Dr. Dell Dear, from Miraunga Isle, told Aqua she looked radiant. And so unlike the tormented woman they'd met months back.

Accompanied by a little brooding, mocha-skinned woman named Violet, the doctor appeared happy. The besotted physician couldn't coax Violet from her seat nearly in a corner, but rarely did he leave her side. When he did tear himself away, the doctor and Noel spoke.

"Vanilla!" Noel smacked the other man's hand. "Glad you made it."

"Ah told yuh, buddy, I wouldn't have missed this fuh the world."

Noel smirked, "Because you knew the Priestess would be here?"

"No, man," Dr. Dear smiled. "An old friend asked me to come. Since I value *him*, his new lady, and all we've been through, Ah showed up."

"Aiight," Noel raised his pilsner glass. "Yo, I see you brought Vi. "You get her some food? Plenty of stuff—paella, fried chicken, *sopa de lima,* enchiladas," mac 'n cheese, ribs, collard greens, salads, all of that and more, "in the dining room."

"Violet ate—something." Dr. Dear tore his eyes from the small-boned woman. "Hey, Ah am thinkin'a of following in *your* footsteps, man..."

Noel was taken aback, "Whuuut?" To be clear, he said, "I'm not just fuckin' Nill, I am committed. *Mañana,* I take that walk, hop the broom."

Dr. Dear nodded. "Ah know." Stroking his chin, the physician appeared pensive. "Scary, but as Ah said, I think I'm ready, too."

Surprised, Noel clapped his friend on the back. "Cool. So it's Vi?"

The evasive physician grinned, "Could be..."

Noel turned to a guest. "Good luck telling Tula. Or is she the one?"

Dr. Dear, with the midnight blue eyes guffawed. "Yuh had to throw that in there. I'll see, man. Go. We'll catch up. Kiss Doll fuh me."

Aqua's newfound Gullah family members, including Sonsa, her husband, and Sonsa's mother, Azalea, with the sandy and white natural, were all smiles. So was Azalea's husband, Sonsa's father, a broad brown man. He grabbed Aqua up in a huge hug. Spritely, Ms. Blossom had even made the trip with *her* boyfriend, a younger man of seventy-six.

Across the room, Gloria Bayliss, Aqua's grandmother, was in heaven. This Aqua's sister Ava pointed out. Just before Noel's large, close-knit family arrived in a multitude of vehicles.

With birdlike little hands, his spry, white-haired mother reached up to hug Aqua. Inhaling Mrs. Ocaña's preciously old-fashioned clean scent, Aqua was taken back. She mentally revisited the hazy, hot summer days of childhood. Aqua 'saw' linens on the line, popsicles, and a purple pinwheel, whirling in the breeze. The memory faded...

Unaware, Mrs. Elaine Ocaña's eyes danced. "I guess you found out, honey, that my son really *is* a gem."

"You told me that," Aqua recalled, "at your birthday luncheon."

Mrs. Ocaña reached for the hand of Aqua's soon to be father-in-law. "I did. And I *would* tell you that these Latin men make great lovers..." The older woman winked, "But I do suppose you know that –by now."

"*Mami!*" Noel exclaimed as his grinning parents ambled away.

Aqua chuckled. "Ocaña," she softly called, gazing up at him. "She's gotta know what we do. Look at how many children she has."

Noel closed his eyes. "I pray you are wrong, because what *I* do to you *niña...*" He recalled a few of their kinkier acts. "Heck, what *you* do to *me...*" Pulling Aqua close, he whispered into her curls. "*Chica,* you smell amazing. I know I was saying something about baby-making, but now all I can think is: maybe you and I need to disappear."

"From our own party? Don't tempt me, Ocaña," Aqua advised.

Noel forgot his and Aqua's sexy stunts to introduce a paternal aunt. "*Tia*, meet *Aqua Mira*." Noel called out, "Come, *lirio*, these are my brothers and sisters."

Laughing and with hugs for Aqua, Noel's siblings scoffed. Holding a wriggling chubby baby, his brother Alejandro teased.

"Maybe the old man's forgotten."

"He has, Alex," Aqua smiled, "because we all met—"

"At *Mami's* party, last fall," Alejandro interjected. "A full year ago."

Behind the massive stone house, tall sunny-faced Isis and her best friend Sherry sat on sweet grass. Nestled amongst hordes of small children, Isis read aloud. Engrossed, Ava's baby Tawny furiously sucked on a pacifier, while Sonsa's Hiram Jr. used dimpled hands to turn the pages, before time. When they became restless, the smaller children aimlessly ran in the grass. Absently watching, Isis informed Sherry that she'd pried some of Aqua's story out of her. Now more aware of what happened on Miraunga Isle, Isis was determined to become a writer.

Sherry shivered. "That sounds spooky...*Miraunga*."

Isis agreed. "Aqua said she started feeling like Miraunga meant *mirror* and *wrong*, because she kept seeing the wrong woman in the mirror. Aqua told me other scary stuff too, Cher." Revealing it, Isis felt proud to be included. "I can handle it, though."

"It sounds like a *movie*," Sherry grinned.

"I might make one!" Isis bellowed. "Thanks for the idea, Cher." Isis also spoke of college. She said that with her mom's permission, she and Aqua were looking online. "We're perusing schools with superb journalism and communications programs."

Sherry said she was jealous. She wanted someone like Aqua in her life too. "I want a fashion guru who cares about my grades."

"You've got your mom," Isis pointed out.

"You've got your mom *and* Aqua." Sherry shook back strawberry blond waves. "You know, as a dentist, I won't get to travel the world..."

"Not for your *work*," Isis agreed. "But *we* could take trips, like my godmother and my godfather, Noel."

Sherry hunched her shoulders. "*He's* dreamy..."

"Ew." Isis didn't think it was right to think of her godfather that way.

Up in the house, Aqua's sister squeezed her arm. Slightly shorter, buxom Ava spoke. "Silas gave you his tired excuse for not being here?"

"He did," Aqua said of their father, "but he's gotta please girlfriend."

Ava waved. "Ma Hag takes the cake. How dare Rayfa not attend?"

"She said she's not coming today or tomorrow," Aqua divulged, "because *I* let her car get repossessed. I was away! And I nearly died."

Ava sputtered. "Her car isn't your responsibility!"

Aqua grinned. "I know, but I'm glad Rayfa's upset because now she won't be around, barfing 'n pulling up her skirt." To her sister, Aqua admitted she hadn't really wanted their parents present; "They're embarrassing. Girl, I thank God they're not here. And I have moved on. Now I'm like Jill Scott," the songstress. "I'm living the golden life."

Ava hugged her older sister. "You're finally living for *you*, A, no longer letting people pimp you. I love it."

"I've finally learned to say no," Aqua stated. Then she pointed. "Look at GB…"

Ava smiled. "I can't remember ever seeing that white-haired lady so happy. Aqua, you gave GB back her Hy."

Damn near killed Aqua to have done it, but her new mantra was she would only focus on the good. Beaming with pride, Aqua nodded, "Didn't I? I gave *you* new cousins, new aunties, and uncles, too."

"Aqua," Gray-eyed Phédra glided up. The new mom spoke with her infant in her arms. "Don't you just love that woman?"

Both Aqua and Ava were curious. "What woman?"

"Priestess Odyssey." Phédra had had a feeling way back, when she'd read about the woman. "Isn't she extra, just a rose among thorns?"

Recalling the ordeal that the High Priestess had willingly stepped into, Aqua reverently stated, "She really is." The Priestess had even allowed Aqua to call her and ask all the questions that Aqua desired.

"Listen," Phédra, the new mom, began. She spoke to Cadence, who sashayed up. "The Priestess asked who told me there was something wrong with my gray eyes and my white skin. She said our people are all different, but no less a beautiful tapestry. She said I should surround myself with multi-racial people and those of different ethnic backgrounds to learn to appreciate differences. Aqua," the photographer called, gazing around. "*Your* family is full of those kinds of people. I never realized it before."

"Quit being coy," curly-haired Cadence waved. "Aqua's grandma just inducted you into their family, you shameless panderer."

Phédra laughed and jounced her baby. "I know you love me, Cae. That's why I'm not offended. And I'm definitely *not* passing my issues down to little Swan here."

Cadence stared at the gray-eyed woman who patted her tiny daughter. "You know Phé; I've listened to you whine for years about not feeling like you fit in anywhere. But hearing you today, girl, I'm proud of you."

Aqua was proud of the photographer too. Aqua even liked that Phédra had named her daughter Swan, so that the wee one would always know she was beautiful and unique.

Gray-eyed Phédra smiled at her friends.

The friend with the corkscrew curls admitted while glancing at Aqua, "My go-'round with Yael has made me re-think some things too." Cadence then ran her tongue over her lower lip while watching her tall, dark husband. She was amazed that she no longer cared that he wore panties. Actually, twisted that it was, she found it sexy, mainly when the big 'surprise' sprang forth. Maybe, Cadence thought, she'd drag Yael off to the bathroom right now...

Seeing her own Big Sexy approach, Aqua smiled. Standing aside, in leggings, Edna, Isis' mom, murmured. "A, will you look at that fine man? Y'all make such a beautiful couple."

Chuckling, Aqua inquired, "Don't we?"

"My love," Noel whispered with a hand at the small of Aqua's back. "Our ceremony is about to begin."

Softly she replied. "No, my sweet, it began the day I met you."

IN the large living room, all were quiet, amid the flicker of white candles for purity. Some people sat on the floor, as others graced furniture, while even others stood. All waited for the High Priestess to begin.

Kneeling at Noel's cocktail table, the woman raised a large clear bowl. She explained that Aqua and Noel, both on their knees opposite her, would embark on a new and wondrous journey. Sometimes it would be challenging, the Priestess advised, but they could triumph. Then she spoke to those gathered. "For the best chance to succeed, this glowing couple should not drag anything negative or unnecessary into their new union."

Thus, on squares of paper, in quieter moments, she'd had the two list things of which they wanted to live free. Now both people placed their squares of paper in the bowl where small charcoal rounds burned. The scent of frankincense, myrrh, and Jerusalem incense rose.

As all became ash, the Priestess asked the couple to affirm that theirs would be a fruitful marriage, one blessed with love, trust, lasting friendship, prosperity, laughter, posterity, "*And* a good dose of lust."

At that, many adults whooped, and an older, longtime couple nodded.

Following the dying comments and chuckles, the Priestess continued. She had Noel and Aqua affirm that to attain longevity, they would live peaceably with one another, and with others.

Then with bowed head, the Priestess whispered, "Let us pray..."

LATER, on the deck of the quiet house, because most of their guests were gone, Noel presented Aqua with her wedding gift.

Opening an envelope, she removed a sheet of paper. "It's a deed," Aqua gasped. Her bejeweled hand was at her heart.

Rocking on his heels, Noel gazed out into the starry night.

Holding the deed closer to the candle atop the teak wood table, again Aqua gasped. "Ocaña, is this for...*this* house?"

Noel did not turn from the lights glowing in the distant valley. "You loved it, *niña*," he reminded her, "from the first."

Aqua could not believe Noel. "So you're deeding it...to me?"

"As my *wife*, shouldn't it be yours? I told you, I bought it on a whim—I thought. Now I know. Providence had me purchase it *for you*. I only want to abide—*vivir* with you." Legalization would be easy.

Aqua's eyes shimmered, and she said her throat ached with joy.

In the night, Noel kept his back to her, his hands in his pockets. He very nearly chuckled. "It is yours, love. You did not see the check?"

Aqua grabbed the envelope. "This! No. Oh, Jeez!" she squealed. "What's it for?" Feeling shaky, she eased onto a plush seat cushion.

"Whatever you want, *niña.* The only thing is you can't give *any* of *that* to Rayfa. There will be more, but that is the deal. That, and no leaving."

Aqua hooted with laughter. "Deal, and no divorce."

"That is your house money," Noel stated, "for furniture, renovations, whatever." He smirked. "You might want a dancer's pole in our room."

"The house is perfect as it is, O. It only needs us." Aqua lowered her lashes. "How would you feel if I added this to what I've got and used it all to start my own business?"

Noel turned, taken aback. "I would be honored. I can be a business consultant for you, too. If you'd like."

"Ocaña." Rising, Aqua tossed herself at him. "You are so good to me!"

"You deserve it." Catching her, Noel palmed Aqua's nape while kissing her. Pressing his throbbing erection to her, he whispered. "I have stuff just stored up for you." When he began to fondle her breast, Aqua grasped and held Noel's big hand.

"You know I can't resist you, O," she whined, nearly liquefying with desire. "But we promised. Not before our vows."

Grinding himself against Aqua, Noel groaned. "You are killing me here. Just give me a taste *lirio*…I need to feel you, be inside you." He kissed her thoroughly, while seeing himself laying her down, right there on the chaise. Beneath the stars he would enter her. As his lips meandered down her neck, he could see himself gliding into her luxuriant bronze body, again and again. He kissed her collarbone and the swell of her breast while he envisioned Aqua's lovely arms and legs surrounding him. He loved her softness, her heart –just everything about her. "Let me have a little taste," Noel pled. "Please, my love."

"I'm coming apart too," Aqua admitted, squeezing Noel tightly, "but knowing our appetites, 'tasting' just won't work, for either of us. Hey…" Aqua squinted at the watch on the arm held out behind his back. "It's our *wedding* day!"

Chapter 45

THEY congregated in the beautiful old stone church, decorated and scented with flowers and candles. Seated on the bride's side, Genie and Desdemona were there, dressed to the nines in the second row.

While gazing at the groom, plump Desdemona rasped, "Look at our boy."

Genie considered Noel her son, even though she and Desdemona had chosen to be recognized as members of the *bride's* family. Genie smiled while gazing at the man in winter white.

He wore a pale gold satin cummerbund, and his neck was irreverently exposed.

With her wavy hair adorned with a rhinestone pin, Genie dismissed the fact that Noel had called both her and Desdemona turncoats just that morning. Loving him all the same, Genie asked, "Ain't he fine?"

"Inside 'n out," Desdemona rasped. "He is truly a fine human being."

Both women turned, prompted by the vibrant swell of the organ. Pulling themselves to their feet, the women heard Sonsa. Seated behind them, with Hiram Sr. and Hi Jr., slender, bright-faced Sonsa twittered with laughter.

Petite wizened Genie pivoted, and she too chuckled softly.

There was Jethro Tulle, looking lean, clean, and mean, in a tuxedo. Stiffly, he advanced, with Aqua floating dreamily along on his arm.

With a radiant smile, the bride, minus a veil, whispered, "Jet, despite your cussing, you're the perfect escort." And Jethro was, just as his wife Jacinda had promised.

"Oh!" Hyacinth exclaimed, "she is just beeyootiful."

"Why yes, she is." Grandma Bayliss agreed with her cousin, feeling so proud of her granddaughter.

Adorned in jewels, high heels, and the palest gold column, Aqua's daringly low neckline displayed lovely cleavage as well as her dangerous curves. Long and fitted, her sleeves ended in a flutter of fabric, just like the tail of her gown.

Noting the voluptuous beauty, Noel could not tear his eyes away.

Approaching the altar, lined with red and white roses, Aqua grasped the groom's outstretched hand. She also smiled at the High Priestess, who too was nothing short of magnificent, in a jewel-toned flowing frock.

There was a prayer, then the exchange of vows. The Priestess nodded, informing Noel Christián that he could 'salute' Aqua Mira.

Gathering the new Mrs. Ocaña in his arms, Noel touched his lips to hers. Then, as was his way, he palmed her head and became insatiable.

Unaware that those congregated were amused, Aqua held to him, kissing him back. When she could again breathe, the bride raised sparkling amber eyes. Demurely she whispered. "Ocaña... I am going to ride your ass to-*night*!"

The good-looking groom, with silver at his temples, appeared shocked. Then with a grin, he hauled Aqua to her toes to fervently kiss her again.

Friends and family alike cheered.

For the bride's ears alone, the groom whispered with his lips pressed to hers. "*Aqua Mira*, my love, I am going to let you." Turning to face those assembled, the groom whispered, "*Te amo* baby."

Squeezing his hand, Aqua replied, "Love *you*."

ON the steps outside the stone church with the steeple, the bride and groom greeted those who'd witnessed their nuptials.

Smiling, Aqua noticed almost everyone. She hugged Dr. Dear and spoke to Violet, who was actually more shy than brooding. Aqua also chuckled with the Priestess' son Kijana and his sexy Sangria.

Then Aqua again noticed her sister Ava, the sultry matron of honor. Windblown, Ava stood beside smooth, big black Melvin. On her handsome dad's arm, Tawny sat. For her Aunt Aqua, the child had been a perfect flower girl.

Then Aqua's eyes fell on her precious GB. Lovely in ice blue and a matching hat, her grandmother stood, clasping hands with her beloved cousin Hy with the braided crown.

Aqua saw the ever-stylish twosome, curly-haired Cadence and her husband, Yael. Both appeared happy, as did the gray-eyed Phédra, whose hand was held by Mycah, the publicist. Aqua waved at April, the author, with whom she had become fast friends.

With a dazzling smile, Aqua waved at the whole Ocaña clan, babies and all. Heartfelt, Aqua embraced the elder Mrs. Ocaña, her new in-law.

Even Gary, *Apropos'* blond bartender, was present.

For a moment, Aqua gazed at the now fourteen-year-old Isis, a bridesmaid. Then Aqua noticed Jet Tu. He watched Isis, and Aqua's eyes narrowed. No, no, Aqua thought, although the young college man was nice. Still, her goddaughter was too inexperienced for his attentions.

Very nearly, Aqua cried when Eldon approached with his wife. Ramrod straight, the Steeple Chase houseman bent, offering a graceful bow. "Mistress Ocaña."

"Katherine," Aqua called. Then to the most accommodating woman, Aqua revealed, "I will never forget all you did for me. I just want to thank you, and I want you to know, I think you are beautiful, just beautiful."

Katherine squeezed Aqua tightly, "I have never been called that before." Katherine giggled. "I think I like it. Oh, before I forget, Ms. Aqua, Eldon and I are so sorry that you and Mr. Noel's house burned – but then he turned right around and bought *us* one! *You* had something to do with that, Ms. Aqua. In my heart, I just know it, so please visit us when you can. Come and let me spoil you! I'd love that."

"Me too." Promising she would, Aqua then hugged Jethro Tulle, who pushed his way forward. He tugged his better half, Jacinda, with him.

"My protector," Aqua whispered within the man's sinewy embrace. With her face crumpling, Aqua cried right there. Dabbing her eyes, she tried not to boo-hoo and scare the strange, ax-wielding man who, surprisingly, did not seem uncomfortable. To Jacinda, Aqua whispered, "Your husband means more to me than my own father."

Jacinda patted Aqua's hand, just before Jethro tugged her away.

Then Aqua gazed about, and her amber eyes collided with brown ones all too familiar.

Across the street, *he* stood.

For barely an instant, Aqua knew a sliver of heartbreak. It was quickly replaced by free-wheeling joy and the knowledge that there were no more shadows. Therefore, Aqua offered a brief smile. Forever would she be grateful for Dyson. She would always believe that indirectly, *he* had led her to her life's love. Without Dyson, his club, or his hostess mess, she might never have again met Noel, now her husband.

In the park, devoid of its spring and summer glory, big Dyson Eamon leaned against a tree. He nodded at beautiful Aqua, aware that never could he have given her all she wanted. Dyson wished her no ill. She was a good woman; too good—his brothers, the twins, said—for him.

With hands in his pockets, on this, a day of joy for others, Dyson turned. Slowly, he walked past trees spearing up and into the overcast sky. Aqua's ex left his little family behind, his daughter, Isis, and Edna, her mom. Let them enjoy the wedding festivities, Dyson thought as he trod away. Alone.

Approaching the bride with a hug, the petite dancer Edna had not seen her daughter's father Dyson. Wearing dangling gemstone earrings, Edna whispered. "Aqua, my dear, it looks like you have finally gotten it all." Swirling her multi-colored wrap for warmth, Edna took patrician Renault's hand. Headed away she called out, "See you at the reception!"

Wearing the fabulous, faux fur-lined warm cape that matched her wedding gown, the bride carefully raised both hems. Escorted by her groom, she hastened down the stone steps of the old church.

She and Noel did so amid showers of rice.

Aided into their hired car, Aqua realized. She was delighted. With Noel beside her, she promised herself one thing. Never would she dwell on what was no more. However, she would always be grateful. She would never forget that for over a century, her ancestor Lily's spell had sought her *and* Noel.

At last, through them, love had brought two couples together, one past, and one present.

As the Priestess often said, Aqua and Noel were part of all that was, all that is, and all that will ever be.

EPILOGUE

FEAT of all feats, Aqua bore Noel a set of twins!

He could clearly remember the little scowling reddened faces, as one by one, the babes entered the world. Man, did they have strident yells!

The new papa thought the loud little identical beings were beyond beautiful; his *hermosas bebés*.

Noel remembered it so clearly, like it had been yesterday. He also recalled wondering, from *where* on earth had his daughters' blond-ish curls come? He'd thought that on birthing day, but he knew. Those curls were a reminder, for him and Aqua, of the legacy of which they were now a part.

Noel and Aqua owed the ancestors a debt that could never be repaid. Without them, how would Noel and Aqua have found each other?

Re-focusing, Noel bent to catch Neda [Needa], whose name meant Sunday's child. He caught Nyssa too, whose name meant starting point.

On the lush lawn of his wife's house, he folded both toddlers into his fatherly embrace. He kissed their now sandy-brown hair.

Noel laughed heartily as a silken, black, cocker spaniel bounded up. The creature pawed at his pants leg. Noel remembered giving Aqua the excited little pup not long after their wedding day.

Their fur-baby had made them pet parents. Now they were the parents of two little busy self-centered humans. To Noel it was amazing.

"Papa! Papa," the girls chorused, joined by the canine's yipping. Neda Christiana and Nyssa Noelle carried on a cacophony of two-year-old chatter, complete with fluttering hands and feet.

The wonder, the joy, and even the frustration of it all would never cease to amaze Noel Christián Ocaña. Forever would he be fascinated by the fact that he had made love to his love, and thereby produced those two. Nuzzling the girls whose hair now looked much like Sonsa's, a sandy-brown, he asked, "Do you two know how much you're loved?"

With her small nose scrunched, Neda Christiana threw her arms around her father's neck and grunted. "Papa is my love."

Aqua spoke softly, walking up. "He's my love, too." She also laughed because now in her arms, her dog wriggled while trying to lick her face.

"*Mami*," Nyssa Noelle held out small hands.

Unleashing the canine, Aqua allowed him to run free as she gathered her daughter close.

Noel watched as with the child on her arm, the momma slowly and carefully climbed the deck stairs. With his eyes momentarily glinting, he remembered. *He was Aqua's true love.* Sure, they had the kids and others, but Noel and Aqua had each other first. He would go to hell and back for her. As a matter of fact, she often reminded him, he already had.

On the teak wood deck, Aqua turned from the patio doors. She'd slid them shut behind her brown-haired girls. The mom was glad for quiet. Ahhh; now that the little ones were inside for the evening, they would receive a bath. Then it would be story time, read by the woman who'd tended them from birth, the displaced Desdemona.

Since only Aqua and her handsome husband remained out of doors, she sighed, able to speak without interruption. Before she did so, Aqua again gazed at the splendor of Mislaid Mountain. She never tired of it. She smiled at the man who had informed her that he desired just one more thing in life. Tearing her eyes away from his gorgeousness, Aqua noticed the sky. It was slashed with the peach and gold of a Georgia sunset. Placing elegant hands on her obviously swollen belly, Noel's wife spoke.

"You know I went to the doctor today, right, Ocaña."

He nodded as his heart began to gallop. "And?"

"They talked about my age, and risk –the usual stuff. Then, *Papa...*"

Noel knew Aqua attempted to sound nonchalant, but he had already seen the twinkle in her eyes, so why was she pausing? Unable to wait to hear her news, he yowled, "Talk, woman!"

"Well, Mr. Huffy," she chuckled, "I guess we'll have to soon call the Priestess. To make an appointment for your – *son's* – christening."

Noel did a double-take. Then jubilantly, he covered Aqua's grinning mouth with his own. Hugging her tightly, he inhaled the beautiful fragrance that ever surrounded her. He would get his dream!

The only other thing he'd wanted was a son!

As was his way whenever Aqua was near, Noel longed for her. Feeling the need to surround, enter and pour into her, he made a suggestion. "Why don't I follow you to our room—to 'celebrate?' I have oil, and stuff..."

April Alisa Marquette
243

"Why don't I meet you there, later?" Aqua winked. "We can play big round princess rides the pony, or I *could use* a massage... Right now, though, I want to finish your dinner."

"Deal." Suddenly, Noel groaned, "I suppose I should help you, huh? That way, we can get to the good stuff faster, right?"

Aqua laughed. With a hand on the door she asked, "By that, do you mean my icebox cake? I made one this morning, you know."

"You did?" Noel forgot sex, for just a moment, because indeed he liked sweets, which he seldom ate. He smiled too, because Aqua said her dessert, using GB's recipe, was a little thing, but she knew he enjoyed it. Therefore, she had taken time away from her growing business to make it, just for him. In a few minutes, she, a boss lady, would finish cooking, just for him. That she sometimes did, as well. Thoughtful, Aqua was that kind of woman. How blessed and enriched his life really was, Noel thought, for having her in it.

He took his wife in his arms. He nuzzled the neck of the beauty whose body nourished his seed. *Si Dios quiere*, God willing, within months, Aqua would give birth to his son; what a gift.

"You know, *lirio*," Noel stated as he often did, "I really wasn't living before *you*."

Aqua winked because she remembered wondering and praying. She remembered wanting a family, a real one, of her own. She had even wanted a bit of predictability. And, as Edna had said, it looked like she had truly gotten it all. Therefore, Aqua quickly acknowledged, "I wasn't living either, my sweetheart, not before you." Then with arms around Noel, she changed her mind. "Forget dinner. Let's get into a lil somethin'..."

"Really?" Noel grinned. "Then I'll bring the pie." He could see layering her with the cool, sweet cream and wafers.

Aqua laughed. Well, since her husband didn't talk about her 'appetite,' she didn't mention his. Aqua simply lead Noel into the house while admitting, "I'll just enjoy."

THE END

...

NEVER

If you've enjoyed Aqua's tale, why not meet her and Noel again?
in
The Sea Isles Series
Book II
Of four

A f f i n i t y

On the revisit,
get to know characters you only glimpsed
in

EXODUS

Take another insightful journey.
&
Hang on for the ride!

Photo: Tina Dennis©

As an author, editor, and freelance writer,
April Alisa Marquette
pens fiction as well as non-fiction.
A lover of art and literature, she is committed to creating beautifully
detailed works about people of color and others.
Ever working on something,
she is currently tweaking one of the exciting novels in her
Sea Isles Series.
Visit her at www.aprilalisamarquette.net

www.ingramcontent.com/pod-product-compliance
Lightning Source LLC
Chambersburg PA
CBHW020757250626
47155CB00003B/1112